THE GILDAR RIFT

'Brace for impact!'

The *Wolf of Fenris* was going to hit them. The two ships were going to annihilate one another.

But it did not.

The tiniest of mathematical calculations that had been input in the *Wolf's* helm several minutes earlier was enough to bring the ships agonisingly close. Yet in spatial terms, 'agonisingly close' was still an astonishing distance away.

'She's preparing to fire her port batteries.'

'Run out our own. They want to take a broadside swipe, then we will give them one of our own back.'

'Aye, my lord.'

Relentlessly pounding at each other, the two behemoth vessels ran parallel for a time. Void shields trembled and shrieked at the proximity, flooding the space between them with crackling, arcing discharge. The energy that each ship's shields generated sought to repel the other with equal ferocity.

A WARHAMMER 40,000 NOVEL

THE GILDAR RIFT

SARAH CAWKWELL

BLACK LIBRARY

*For my mum, who always told me I could, but never got to say
'I told you so', and to my dad – for everything.*

A Black Library Publication

First published in Great Britain in 2011 by
The Black Library,
Games Workshop Ltd.,
The Black Library,
Nottingham, NG7 2WS, UK.

10 9 8 7 6 5 4 3 2 1

Cover illustration by Jon Sullivan.
Maps by Rosie Edwards and Adrian Wood.

A CIP record for this book is available from the British Library.

UK ISBN 13: 978 1 84970 107 5
US ISBN 13: 978 1 84970 108 2

See the Black Library on the internet at

www.blacklibrary.com

Find out more about Games Workshop
and the world of Warhammer 40,000 at

www.games-workshop.com

Printed and bound in the UK.

It is the 41st millennium. For more than a hundred
centuries the Emperor has sat immobile on the Golden
Throne of Earth. He is the master of mankind by the
will of the gods, and master of a million worlds by the
might of his inexhaustible armies. He is a rotting carcass
writhing invisibly with power from the Dark Age of
Technology. He is the Carrion Lord of the Imperium for
whom a thousand souls are sacrificed every day, so that
he may never truly die.

Yet even in his deathless state, the Emperor continues
his eternal vigilance. Mighty battlefleets cross the
daemon-infested miasma of the warp, the only route
between distant stars, their way lit by the Astronomican,
the psychic manifestation of the Emperor's will. Vast
armies give battle in His name on uncounted worlds.
Greatest amongst his soldiers are the Adeptus Astartes,
the Space Marines, bio-engineered super-warriors. Their
comrades in arms are legion: the Imperial Guard and
countless planetary defence forces, the ever-vigilant
Inquisition and the tech-priests of the Adeptus
Mechanicus to name only a few. But for all their
multitudes, they are barely enough to hold off the ever-
present threat from aliens, heretics, mutants - and worse.

To be a man in such times is to be one amongst untold
billions. It is to live in the cruellest and most bloody
regime imaginable. These are the tales of those times.
Forget the power of technology and science, for so much
has been forgotten, never to be re-learned. Forget the
promise of progress and understanding, for in the grim
dark future there is only war. There is no peace amongst
the stars, only an eternity of carnage and slaughter, and
the laughter of thirsting gods.

ONE
INTO THE RIFT

THE EMPTINESS OF space buckled and bulged just for an instant as though it were being sucked into a vacuum. Stars wheeled and distorted and then the endless night shimmered, disgorging a single vessel back into realspace. Its engines burned white-hot for a few moments, the internally-generated field that had cocooned it on its journey through the warp flared briefly and flickered out. Then gradually, the thrusters began to cool, slowly making their way down through the spectrum to standard operating levels.

Space around the ship rippled as cycling shield generators doubled their output to compensate for the dense clouds of particulate debris, then the scene returned to normal as though the shipl had always been here.

The *Endless Horizon*, a lone trader vessel, decelerated dramatically as soon as it was able; a hot blast of plasma drives stalling its headlong flight from the empyrean to a crawl. Within the ship's interior, countless system checks and re-calibrations were taking place. Several of its crew murmured thanks to the God-Emperor and to the ship's machine spirit for a safe trip through the warp.

They had gotten this far intact, but whether they would survive their trip through this sector remained to be seen. They had translated into the fringe of the Gildar Rift.

'WE'RE DEFINITELY ALONE, sir.'

Silence followed this ominous pronouncement as the bridge crew of the *Endless Horizon* exchanged glances. There was concern in those looks; a deep anxiety that was almost palpable. Luka Abramov frowned, running a hand across his jaw as he considered the situation. His eyes passed over the unfortunate young man who had delivered this worrying report and his grey eyes steadily narrowed in obvious disapproval. It was not the news he had wanted to hear.

The youth shifted uncomfortably under the captain's gaze, aware instinctively that more was expected of him. A slow, creeping realisation that every pair of eyes on the bridge was riveted on him began to seep unpleasantly through his body and he cleared his throat, tapping at the data-slate in his hand. Before he could speak however, Abramov leaned forward.

'Let's try basics. Our coordinates are correct, yes?'

'Y… yes, sir. Captain.' The youth offered up the data-slate and Abramov took it without even bothering to look down at it. The lumen-strips on the bridge were still dimmed, not yet back to full power after their trip through the warp and in the dull half-light, Abramov's hawkish face was unreadable.

'Then the words "We're definitely alone" are, as I'm sure you appreciate Kaman, completely unacceptable.' Abramov rose from his control throne and stepped down from the dais so that he was on a level with the other man. 'Are we so very early? Or even late?' Abramov silently cursed the inconveniences of warp travel. Its time dilation effects were generally considered the very least of the problems a ship could encounter; but they were a frequently irritating side-effect nonetheless.

'Ship's chronometers put us approximately four hours ahead of schedule,' came the answer from somewhere over to Abramov's right. The captain glanced across and nodded curtly. When he spoke, it was with an outward confidence that he wasn't feeling inside.

'Then we keep going. We may as well continue onwards to our destination.'

'But, sir...' Kaman hesitated, biting back the words that rose to his lips. He used the honorific without even thinking. It was a sure sign he was nervous and Abramov noted it. He liked to encourage an element of informality amongst his crew. Some of them had come to him from spells in the Naval service. Sticklers for tradition and formality to a man. It seemed that some old habits died hard.

Kaman rubbed the bridge of his nose with a thoughtful finger. He did not wish to appear patronising or condescending, but every member of the bridge crew was thinking what he was rather clumsily attempting to put into words. 'But, sir. The dangers...'

'The dangers of the Gildar Rift are well known to me, Kaman. I would be most grateful if you did not presume to lecture me on that of which I am well aware.' A look of shame coloured the youth's features and Abramov softened his attitude slightly. 'For now, concentrate on assessing all available data so that our helmswoman can get us safely through the belt and to Gildar Secundus. I'm prepared to compromise. We'll wait a while for our escort. I'm sure that they will show up soon enough.' Or perhaps, he added mentally, not at all. 'You all know just as well as I do that we're on a tight schedule.'

This was not the first time he had commanded a vessel through the treacherous straits of the system and he sincerely hoped that it would not be the last. But without the safety net of their intended escort he could not help but feel an anxiety that would not settle. A knot of discomfort began to twist in his stomach, but he retained a stoic expression. There was little point in displaying uncertainty to his crew.

'Yes, sir, straight away.' Kaman crossed his hands over his chest and returned to his station. Abramov nodded. They were a good crew, reliable and trustworthy. There were a number whose experience was lacking but they would learn in time. Kaman was a case in point. But Abramov had very carefully cherry-picked his crew over the years. There was enough combined expertise on board to ensure that their journey to Gildar Secundus should have presented no major difficulties. He believed he had taken all the factors into consideration. Indeed, he was completely confident in that knowledge.

And yet...

Were he brutally honest with himself, he would have admitted the truth of the matter. Had he been allowed to have his own way, he would have preferred to navigate through the debris field with his crew alone. The *Endless Horizon* was a good ship; she handled well. His helmswoman was a skilled and seasoned veteran of many years and was without question one of the most extraordinarily gifted pilots he had ever known. They were a fine assembly and they had an excellent track record. So his ship may be old and, as he often joked, was held together with little more than wishful thinking. But she was certainly reliable. The old girl had many years of service left in her yet.

Abramov had not wanted an escort for this trip, but in the event he had not been given a choice. If there had been the option to refuse the vessel assigned to oversee their passage through the Rift, he would have taken it without question. However, he had not been given the chance to repudiate the suggestion. He had been *told* in no uncertain terms that he would receive the escort.

Luka Abramov was a shrewd man and an excellent captain – and he knew better than to refuse what was tantamount to a direct order from the Adeptus Astartes. They were, after all, entering the Silver Skulls patrol corridor and to have gone against that one instruction would have been a grave insult that would inevitably have courted disaster. On top of that, from what he knew of the Silver Skulls Chapter in general – and of Captain Daerys Arrun in particular – it would possibly be perceived as more than simple disobedience. The Silver Skulls were noted throughout this sector for their ferocity. To contravene an order was something that would be seen as a challenge, or something that would raise suspicion. It was the sort of activity that freebooters and smugglers engaged in. Abramov, whilst he may occasionally and almost always entirely accidentally have transported the odd microgram over his allowance, was no smuggler.

Not all ships were guided with an escort through the Rift. Most of the time, as long as their presence was made known, that was enough. But when the order had come through that the *Endless Horizon* was to rendezvous with another ship on arrival in the system, it wasn't something that could be lightly dismissed.

Abramov had enough problems to deal with – he neither wanted nor needed the displeasure of Captain Arrun adding to his load.

'Maintain regular augur sweeps,' he said to the operative at the scanner console. 'I want to know the very second they show up.' Unlike some other ships, the *Endless Horizon* had an almost entirely unaugmented human crew. Abramov had served in ships crewed largely by servitors and had never felt comfortable around them, at least not when he had employed them on his own bridge. As such, the moment he had taken command of the vessel, he had instigated his own rules. Lobotomised servitors still moved around the engineering section in their lifeless way, never needing their morale attending to and keeping the literal cogs of the ship turning. But all of Abramov's core crew were human. There was not a servitor in sight. He was proud of that fact.

'Of course, Luka,' the operative replied. She was more comfortable by far with the informality adopted on board the *Endless Horizon*. Like Abramov, she was dressed in dull grey overalls emblazoned with the ship's insignia, that of a sun setting on a horizon. Her dark blonde hair was pulled back from her face in a highly unflattering manner, emphasising the tired eyes and frown lines that marred her handsome profile. Abramov watched her with undisguised affection for a few moments as she expertly worked the buttons and dials on the archaic systems at her fingertips. The cogitators and systems groaned into semi-obedient life and she murmured soft thanks to the machine spirits that she had disturbed from their slumber.

After some time, activity on the bridge of the *Endless Horizon* resumed some sort of normality. Abramov allowed himself the opportunity to relax a little. The earlier tension had been uncomfortable, but had been inevitable. There was always a brief spasm in the bustle and flow of regular activity after re-entry from the warp. Those moments may have been laden with apprehension, but there was nonetheless a certain peace in the wake of re-entry; it represented a marked change from usual hubbub of life and animation that dictated his existence on board the freighter.

Information was passed to him both verbally and in the form of printed reports and as things resumed their normal pace, he took a great comfort in the perfect symphony of the workings of the bridge crew. It was a familiar, well-orchestrated pandemonium of sound that he could have conducted perfectly without even trying. The chimes on the quarter hour that reminded the machine operators to renew their litanies. The slow, steady growl of the engine's pulse far beneath them – and the occasional lull in that constant background noise as a slightly worn piston skipped a beat. There was the accompanying sound of the monotone responses of the few engine room servitors as they obeyed orders and relayed information across the ship-wide vox... Abramov leaned back in his command throne and closed his eyes, allowing it all to wash over him like a soothing balm. All was calm. All was well.

Abramov had taken ownership of the *Endless Horizon* several years ago and although his preference had always been for drawing up his own contracts and working for no master but himself, he had nonetheless served the Imperium well when called upon to do so. Particularly when the agreed contract was as lucrative as the one he had negotiated for this run to the promethium refineries. For all his strong and notable points, Luka Abramov's head was turned with promises of financial reward. It was not a trait that he ever allowed to display itself, though.

Known for his thoroughness and diligence and an honesty that was almost disarming, he was well respected and had often been entrusted with an assortment of precious cargo. He had spent the first ten years of his ship-board life working solely for the Imperium. It had been long enough to give him a strong urge to work for himself and so he had become freelance. Ironic really, that here he was, back under contract to them once again. He'd developed a taste for the life of a freelancer, however – and had already decided that once he had run a few more Imperial contracts, he would reclaim his independence. He had established that there were many opportunities for ships to make trade runs to the Gildar system. Blessed with a wealth of natural resources, there were always contracts available to this part of the Segmentum Obscurus. It didn't hurt to run a few more 'official' missions. Practice, he knew, made perfect.

There were certainly far more contracts than there were ships willing to travel there. Abramov had no compunction about such a journey. He knew the risks and welcomed them as part of what he considered his responsibility.

For countless centuries this part of space had always presented itself as a major hazard to all vessels entering its vast tracts. 'The Gildar Rift' was the name that had been bestowed upon the shipping channel cleaving its way through the area. Comprised of a number of scattered, largely uninhabited worlds, it was a potentially lethal zone to traverse.

Through the centre of the system, an asteroid belt orbited the densely populated planet of Gildar Secundus. The field's intrinsic dangers were made far more lethal by the vast quantities of space debris drifting eternally through the void. Remains of smashed vessels that had failed to heed warnings not to attempt transit were strewn throughout the Rift, an area that was too hazardous by far to salvage. Any opportunistic would-be looters who had tried to recover the wrecks often added their own ships to the mass.

Ruptured and broken, the ships slowly leached slow

trickles of plasma and other toxic wastes into the area. The lethal cocktail created a permanent chemical haze that constantly caused interference with auguries and communications signals.

So the asteroid belt was both a blessing and a curse; presenting difficulties for any who wished to descend to or leave Gildar Secundus, but also offering an excellent natural defence for a planet whose promethium reserves were a critical resource for the Imperium. The challenge faced by visitors to the system in the shape of the swirling band of rock and ship debris was only the beginning. Xenos ships were regular trespassers here and, so it was rumoured, pirate activity was increasing not just here in the Gildar Rift but in the whole of the furthest reaches of the Segmentum Obscurus.

Relishing the challenges that maintaining peace in the sector offered, the Silver Skulls had long ago set themselves to the task of patrolling the Gildar Rift. Other Chapters of the Adeptus Astartes would rarely volunteer themselves for such a plain, inglorious duty. But the Silver Skulls considered the sector as part of their territory. And the Silver Skulls were *proud*.

Their presence loaned an air of safety to what was otherwise a treacherous place. But it came at a cost. The Silver Skulls monitored and maintained control over passage through the system with a rule of iron. The more fortunate vessels, such as the *Endless Horizon*, followed protocol, alerting the Space Marines to their planned transit in advance. After the necessary approvals and verifications had been carried out, they were granted permission and provided with coordinates where they would be met by an escort. Those who simply translated into realspace on the fringes of the Gildar Rift were very swiftly met with a 'welcoming party'. A misnomer if ever there was one. The stoic Space Marines weren't known for their warm and embracing natures. They were, however, definitely well known for their adherence to and the enforcing of Imperial regulations and didn't take kindly to chancers. Woe betide any ship's captain who thought to argue the point with the Silver Skulls Chapter. No, there were protocols to be followed.

Yet for all he had followed the guidelines and adhered rigidly to instruction in this instance; for all he had dutifully waited a tedious length of time for Captain Arrun's grudging acknowledgement before he had arranged to travel here... for all he had ensured that the coordinates he had been given had been adhered to most rigidly, Abramov and his crew were completely alone.

The captain's hand ran over his jaw again. It was a nervous gesture and one that didn't even begin to hint at the sense of extreme caution that was beginning to eat away at him. They had been told that to traverse the Gildar Rift without an escort or without some sort of acknowledgement to a patrol vessel was a blatant admission of piracy. But there was no escort present and try though they might, no ships were answering their frequent hails. Abramov would be damned before he drifted idly in space, a sitting target for any *actual* pirates who might chance their arm.

He had always hungered for the autonomy of his own command and so when the opportunity to invest his dead father's money had come along, he had grasped it with both hands. The years of managing his own contracts and pulling together the best crew he could afford had given him a wealth of experience. Thus it was from this pool of worldliness upon which he now drew.

The choice as he saw it was reasonably straightforward, yet far from simple. He could either maintain his current position and wait for the Silver Skulls to arrive – or he could order engines to quarter speed and continue towards Gildar Secundus. It would not take them long to enter the planet's atmosphere and Abramov had every confidence in his crew's combined skill and ability to get them there in one piece. Exactly how the taciturn Captain Arrun would react to such a breach of verbal contract, he had no idea. He could hazard a reasonably well educated guess.

In the end, compromise won out.

'Very well,' he said. 'We will hold position for three hours.'

He dropped back down onto the command throne. 'If we have received no word from our escort by then, we continue onwards to Gildar Secundus. At the slowest speed we can manage.'

'Aye, captain.'

Abramov let out a rushing breath. With luck, he would not need to risk the wrath of the Emperor's Angels.

SLEEP HAD BEEN elusive during the journey to the Gildar system and Abramov had taken advantage of the grace period to retire to his quarters in an attempt to catch up on some much-needed rest. There had barely been opportunity for his eyes to close and for him to fall into a deep sleep before he was rudely dragged awake by the bellowing scream of the ship's alert system. Scant seconds later he felt the ship lurch beneath him. The suddenness of the movement tipped him ungraciously from the bunk, leaving him sprawled on the ground.

'Captain Abramov to the bridge,' an insistent female voice was saying across the ship-wide vox system. 'Proximity alert. Repeat, captain to the bridge.'

'I heard you the first time,' he grumbled. Roused into full wakefulness, Abramov hauled himself off the floor and rubbed sleep from his eyes. He caught a passing glimpse of himself in the tarnished mirror above his sink and immediately wished he hadn't. He was looking dishevelled and tired, many years past his Terran standard complement of fifty. He hardly cut the figure of authority he had always at least attempted to maintain.

He was still pulling his overalls on over his clothing as he strode through the door to the bridge.

'Report.' He stifled a yawn and glanced at the ship's chronometers. He regretted that almost as much as he had when he'd looked in the mirror. He had been asleep for barely any time at all. 'Is it the Silver Skulls? Have they arrived?'

'No, I'm afraid not.' Telyna, his pilot – and the most competent woman he had ever met in his life bar none – turned her head to study him with casual indifference. 'Debris field dead ahead. Mostly small asteroids, fortunately. I'm doing what I can to avoid the worst of it.'

Telyna's words made their way through his muzziness and snapped him back almost immediately to full alertness.

'Evasive manoeuvres? Yes. I could tell by the way you woke me up.'

Telyna tossed her long, blonde plait over one shoulder. It was a simple gesture, but there was a lot of suppressed aggression there. 'Well, *captain*,' she said, with heavy sarcasm, 'I could have just let the remnants of that ship hit us. Would you have preferred that?'

Their eyes locked for a moment and it was Abramov who looked away first, a slight smile on his lips. He considered for a moment. 'They never showed, then?'

'No. We've been travelling towards Gildar Secundus for the best part of an hour. Hence...' She gestured expansively, a means of indicating the debris field that lay ahead.

'Can we not simply go around?'

'Something's stirred up the field,' she reported, turning away from him and this time pointing out of the forward viewscreen. 'There's enough junk outside to ensure that no matter which direction we take, we're going to encounter obstacles of one form or another.' Telyna fell silent for a moment or two, concentrating on the matter at hand. 'Most of what's out there looks pretty old. But we've already seen at least one complete vessel. Recently disabled according to the preliminary scans.'

'Probably the last ship that didn't follow Arrun's orders,' Abramov muttered, then shook his head. Probably better not to let himself wander down that line of thought. 'Maintain course and heading. Be alert and prepared for anything. It's a deathtrap out there.'

'I am well aware of the dangers, captain.' Telyna's voice was so insulted that despite his weariness, Abramov's face split in a broad smile.

'I love you, Telyna, did I ever tell you that? Even if you do wake me up just to prove how damned clever you are.'

'You tell me constantly.' She returned the smile with one

of her own. 'I thought you would want to be awake in the event that I get things wrong and you can say "I told you so" as we're ripped apart.'

'Your concern for my ongoing welfare is noted.'

'Don't mention it.'

The brief, companionable exchange over, Telyna turned her attention back to the console. Someone, Abramov was too distracted to notice who, put a steaming cup of recaff in his hand and he muttered his thanks. He sipped the bitter liquid with a wrinkle of his nose. If he were brutally honest, he despised the taste of recaff, but its stimulating effects were certainly welcome at this time. He studied the printouts that had been placed on the arm of his command throne.

His feet settled firmly on the floor, unconsciously reaching out for the pulse of his ship's engine. Its ever-present hum was there, only just felt beneath the soles of his boots. It was a connection of the simplest kind, but it was a habit he'd never broken. Like most captains, Abramov had his own private superstitions. Like a warrior who would cup a handful of dirt before a battle, he stuck to them rigidly. As long as his ship still had a heartbeat, they would be fine.

Their speed now greatly reduced, Telyna concentrated on avoiding the debris outside the *Endless Horizon* as best she could. There was certainly a lot of it. Machine parts, chunks of metal, even several human corpses drifted by in an endless parade of the merciless nature of this part of space. Wide-eyed and rimed with a thin skein of ice, the corpses seemed to scream silent warnings to the crew of Abramov's ship. It was the stuff of nightmares and several of the crew were clearly unsettled and a little distressed by the sight.

For what seemed like an age, the freighter moved with excruciating slowness, its progress painstakingly measured. Telyna's eyes were watering with the effort of staring from the viewscreen to the console at her command and Abramov's headache was getting no better. There seemed to be no end to it at all and tempers were beginning to fray.

When the rear port thrusters began to fail, Abramov knew about it several moments before the message came up from the engineering deck. His unconscious connection with the ship's harmonies and rhythms whispered the news through the vibrations beneath him. Normally, the loss of one of the rear thrusters would have been something easily dealt with. In clear space, he would have sent service drones outside to deal with the problem. In this chaotic cluster though, he wouldn't risk losing one of his crew – soulless or not – to a glancing blow from the passing flotsam and jetsam. Not to mention that coming to a stop at this point was also no longer an option. If they maintained position, they'd likely be pulverised. He felt irritated more than concerned.

The dull monotone of the servitor's voice confirming the problem irritated him still further.

'We're almost through the field,' Telyna said between gritted teeth. Her jaw had been clenched so hard for so long that it ached terribly. 'If I can just use the remaining thrusters to stabilise our position... our shields should deflect the smaller stuff. I just have to avoid the rest of it.'

'Our shields *should* deflect, yes,' said Abramov grimly. 'They should – and I don't doubt that they will. But they won't do so indefinitely.'

'Do you have a better plan, captain?' Again, the rising sense of hostility on the bridge deck was detrimental to the situation and the captain bit back the harsh retort. He gripped the arms of his command throne until his knuckles turned white. All it would take would be a single big hit to their shields, enough to break through. Once that happened, they would be torn apart and join the unfortunate dead that they had observed already outside the ship.

'Anticipated time to exit this accursed junk pile?' His question came out as a bark. Before she could answer, Telyna let out a string of blasphemous expletives. At her outburst, several of the bridge crew hurriedly made the sign of the aquila, their faces horrified. When she spoke, Abramov merely nodded as though he had expected this to happen.

'New contact.' She looked round at him and her face was a picture of abject terror. 'Xenos raiders, sir.'

They were practically drifting, with very little in the way

of firepower to defend themselves. If they didn't collide violently with the debris and junk that threatened their path, then they would be blasted apart by the pirates, or worse, crippled and boarded.

All at once, the calmness of the bridge descended into a discordant babble, a far cry from the orchestrated glory of earlier. Voices spoke over one another, but with the ease of the years, Abramov filtered out what was important and added his own orders to the tumultuous noise.

'Front starboard thrusters are also starting to fail. Transferring power from port thrusters to compensate.'

'Shield generators still holding steady. Ninety-eight per cent.'

'Power to fore thrusters stabilising. Levelled at sixty per cent.'

'Time to exit?'

'Fifteen minutes.'

'Maintain current pattern. Telyna...'

A staccato of sound, a counterpoint of voices that rose to a crescendo of noise. Cutting across it all, the whispered, fervent litanies of each crew member as they prayed with due diligence to the distant God-Emperor of Mankind to get them through safely. The uproar continued.

'Incoming. Dead ahead.'

'Enemy ships are moving to intercept. There are two of them. No, not two. Three, sir! There are three of them! Holy Terra...'

'I'm trying to... damn it!'

'Impact in ten... nine...'

'All stations, this is Abramov. Brace for impact. Channel whatever power we have into the guns and fire on the xenos ships. If we're going to go down, we'll not go quietly.'

The three xenos vessels were manoeuvring their way with practiced ease through the field of destruction. The freighter captain had seen them before... eldar. In days past he had fought against them. 'Nightshade' was the human designation for the three vessels bearing down on them with silent menace. But they were now officially the least of their immediate worries. Let the eldar launch their torpedoes. It would be a violent, sudden death, but at least there was a chance of obliterating them outright. Better by far than what *could* happen.

The captain leaned forward, his hands clasped in silent prayer as he stared through the *Endless Horizon's* occulus. Their demise was spinning towards them: a twisted, unrecognisable hulk of girders, conduits and crushingly dense hull plating. Something so warped and broken had absolutely no right to be pirouetting with such majesty through the airless vacuum of space.

'Eight... seven...'

In seven seconds, it would strike their void shields. It was big enough to burst through the *Endless Horizon's* shields like its protective layer was nothing more than an ephemeral bubble. One good, solid hit and the freighter vessel would be ripped apart. Unlike the flare of pain and death of an explosion caused by a torpedo strike, they would be helpless as their ship was torn apart. They would be adding their corpses and destroyed ship to everything else that lay outside the hull.

'Six.'

We haven't got a hope. Abramov's confidence fled in the face of his imminent demise. For a fleeting moment, he despised everyone on the deck with him. Hated them for being here with him. Blamed himself for their deaths.

'Five.'

So this is how it ends, then.

'Fo– incoming vessel! Extreme proximity. It's... it's powering up its weapons, sir!'

Abramov should perhaps have been feeling terror, or at least a modicum of fear, but there was nothing. His heart was like stone. Instead of being atomised by a chunk from a long-destroyed ship, they were going to be vaporised by a hostile vessel. There wasn't time to ask why it was that nobody had picked this new threat up on sensors. Indeed, Abramov wouldn't even question that until much, much later. The moment was now, and he was irrevocably caught up in it.

The eldar raiders simultaneously turned; impossible angles that the bulky, practical transports of the Imperium could never hope to achieve and launched their torpedoes at the new arrival. There were three sudden blossoms of light as the projectiles detonated harmlessly against their target's shields.

A second later, light lanced from the ship that had apparently come out of nowhere, destroying the chunk of wreckage in a silent spray of molten metal. A second shaft of searing brightness incinerated one of the eldar ships immediately. The intense glare temporarily blinded the bridge crew of the *Endless Horizon* and Abramov turned his face away. Gradually, as the intense brightness dwindled away and vision returned to normal, the shape of their surprising saviour could be made out.

'Gladius-class frigate,' Abramov observed. An Adeptus Astartes escort vessel. Of course it was. Despite himself, a smile tugged at his lips. It seemed that their chaperone had arrived. Late, but perfectly timed nonetheless. The frigate banked slightly and moved away so that it was running alongside them.

Of the other two eldar ships, there was no sign. Abramov did not know if the Gladius had destroyed them or if they had fled. Either way, they had gone and that was a perfectly acceptable outcome. There was a crackle, a hiss and the ship-to-ship vox spat into life.

'*Endless Horizon*, hold your position. Slow your engines and wait for further instructions.' It was a clearly human voice; not desensitised and changed as one would expect from one of the Emperor's Angels. Doubtless it was one of the Silver Skulls Chapter serfs serving aboard the craft.

As quickly as the channel of communications was opened, it was silenced again. A reply was not invited, not that any of Abramov's crew could have found words anyway. The crew of the *Endless Horizon* drew a collective breath when the Gladius-class frigate veered sharply away allowing another vessel clear passage through.

It was an ugly thing on first glance; a closed-fist of a vessel with a prow bombardment cannon clenched menacingly at its fore. Uniformly painted in serviceable machine grey, it was possible at this proximity to pick out some of the painstakingly worked lettering on the ship's exterior. It was huge, a gargantuan monster of metal that filled the viewscreen completely as it placed itself between the ailing freighter and the punishing debris field.

The unseemly appearance of the front of the strike cruiser gradually tapered into a long, graceful neck and ultimately resolved into a veritable fortress astern. Abramov couldn't help but gaze at it with awe.

'They're forming a barrier!' Telyna leaned forward on the console as she stared up at the seemingly endless grey ship. 'They're shielding us from the onslaught.' Her voice was filled with astonished reverence, a far cry from her usual casual manner.

Abramov nodded, grimly. Ship-to-ship vox communication channels remained closed but he knew well who this monstrosity belonged to. The gold and silver worked insignias that could be made out on the grey ship's edge displayed quite clearly the Imperial aquila, the Chapter emblem of the Silver Skulls and the vessel's name.

The *Dread Argent*.

Abramov cleared his throat, which suddenly seemed to have become completely dry.

'Then we had better hail them,' he said. 'And we had better make it formal.'

CAPTAIN DAERYS ARRUN, Master of the Fleet and Commander of the Silver Skulls Fourth Battle Company loomed in front of Luka Abramov. His closely shaven head did nothing to hide the mass of scar tissue on his skull; something that on a human would be considered disfiguring, but which on a Space Marine could only be a mark of honour. His face was covered in swirling whorls of dark ink that all but obscured his flesh; the battle tattoos of the warriors that all commanding officers of the Chapter earned the right to. If his sheer breadth and height and forcible presence hadn't been fearsome enough, the tribal-like brandings would have done the job admirably.

Eyes that were ice-blue and just as cold pierced into Abramov for a while before Arrun spoke, his voice a deep and sonorous rumble.

'There are a thousand things I can think of that might have encouraged you to act against your very clear and very specific instructions, Captain Abramov.' Arrun held up a massive hand to forestall any protest. 'And yet for every one of those, I can think up another reason as to exactly why you should not have done it. I trust that you have something to tell me that will prove my thousand theories wrong?'

The *Dread Argent* had run alongside the *Endless Horizon* for some time, deflecting the worst of the debris field as though she had been flicking insects away. In time, the message had come that Captain Daerys Arrun would be boarding the freight vessel to speak to Abramov. An explanation, it was communicated, was in order. The *Endless Horizon* would also be subjected to the standard check for smuggling at the same time. Abramov was not worried by the latter. He had nothing to hide.

Talking to the Space Marines captain, on the other hand... that filled him with trepidation.

Abramov ran nervous fingers through his greying hair and looked up at the captain. He swallowed back the comments and self-assured responses that he had been so sure he would have been able to muster and shook his head. Arrun's sheer physical presence had quashed any attempts at being even remotely sarcastic. In the end, the best he could manage was a rather pitiful excuse that sounded plaintive and poor even as it left his mouth.

'You were late. We... are on a schedule and thought we would make progress until your arrival.' Arrun's brow arched, distorting the tribal markings on his face briefly.

'I am never late, Captain Abramov. In this instance, I was unavoidably detained. I deeply regret that our astropath's message did not reach you before you entered the warp. But you should have waited. You did not. Fortunately for you, the *Dread Argent* arrived before you were pulverised.' Those cold, emotionless eyes scoured Abramov once and in that penetrating glance, the *Endless Horizon's* captain was aware that he was being weighed and measured. He shifted uncomfortably. It was time to fall back on his only possible course of action.

'You have my sincerest apologies and deepest gratitude, of course, Captain Arrun...' Abramov hated how wheedling his voice sounded. He was guilty of no crime other than being in possession of an impetuous nature. If he told himself that enough times, perhaps he might start to believe it. He squared his shoulders and straightened his spine. With the very greatest of concentration, he injected energy and enthusiasm into his voice. 'Of course, now that you are here, we can resume our journey to Gildar Secundus.' He lifted his head and smiled brightly. He couldn't hold Arrun's gaze for longer than a few moments.

'Yes,' mused Arrun, turning his back on Abramov. 'Yes, I imagine you can.' He stared out of the view portal at the *Dread Argent*. As Master of the Fleet, he had a keen and abiding interest in all the vessels of the Imperium, particularly his own. With practiced confidence, he let his eyes roam across it, calculating its external condition. Despite his apparent distraction, he continued the conversation with Abramov. 'You have the report I requested, I take it?'

'Yes, my lord.' Abramov offered the cargo manifest in a hand that shook only slightly. One of the Silver Skulls serfs who had accompanied Arrun stepped forward to take it. It was duly handed to Arrun without words and the captain pulled his gaze from the *Dread Argent*.

'Confirm for me what your cargo consists of, if you please, Captain Abramov?'

'Of course, Captain Arrun.' Made more comfortable by the familiarity of this process, Abramov relaxed a little. 'We are taking replacement machine parts bound for the promethium refinery.' It was correct and the physical inspection of his ship would corroborate that statement.

From that point, the Silver Skulls captain was nothing but

solid business. No more was said about the transgression and when Arrun announced he would be returning to his own ship, Abramov allowed himself a moment to breathe.

'Be wary, Abramov. Something translated into the Gildar Rift several solar days ago and disturbed the peace. It appears to have gone again, but you never can tell. This debris field could well be the least of your worries.'

'Yes, my lord. Thank you, my lord.'

Offering Arrun a deep bow as he strode away, Abramov returned to his bridge and crew in contemplative silence. He knew he should count himself lucky that whatever it was that was distracting the Silver Skulls captain meant that he had escaped a sterner, more serious chastisement – but the sense of deep unease that Arrun's parting words had engendered in him negated any relief he may have felt.

The least of your worries.

TWO
RESURGENT

The Gildar Rift
In geostationary orbit above Gildar Secundus
++ One week later ++

GILDAR SECUNDUS WAS a harsh and cruel planet. Yet despite its inhospitable, almost suffocating environment, it was one of the wealthiest places in the segmentum. The promethium refineries sprawling across much of its surface like creeping mould were extensive, industrious, productive sites that churned out seemingly endless quantities of the much-coveted fuel.

Promethium, the life blood of the Imperium, not only sated thirsty machine spirits in vehicles and fuelled weaponry, but was the core ingredient in any other number of industrial products. Its value was incalculable and its appeal was a beacon to would-be raiders to take it for themselves.

Ever since the very first attempt at taking the spoils had been made, ever since piratical raiders had exploded into the Gildar system, the Silver Skulls had established their patrols across the Rift. From the moment they had responded to the first foray, any further such incursions that had been attempted had met with swift justice, delivered by a Chapter who were not known for their patience. Generally, the Silver Skulls delivered their judgement on transgressors with the minimum of preamble – and such judgement was invariably punctuated with a punishing and ultimately terminal salvo from a bombardment cannon.

The Chapter's home world of Varsavia hugged the outer rim of the Gildar Rift and in this far-flung, oft-neglected area of the Imperium they were the closest Adeptus Astartes response force. With the increasing, although still irregular raids threatening the region, Lord Commander Argentius had agreed the very real need for providing semi-permanent protection. Regular patrols were provided from the fleet, a rotating duty for those brothers who were not deployed on the field of battle elsewhere.

Captain Arrun had been Master of the Fleet for several decades and possessed a quicksilver mind and the forward thinking ability of a true tactical genius. At any time he knew the status of every functioning ship in the fleet. His eidetic memory allowed him to bring to mind every flaw, every weakness and, conversely, every strength. He knew in seconds which ship was the most appropriate to deploy to any given situation when the requests for assistance were received. He had overseen operations in the Gildar Rift from the very beginning. Now, in response to new orders received that morning from Varsavia, it looked as though the scale of patrols would be stepped down.

It was something of a puzzle to Arrun. The Chapter Master knew the dangers this system presented and yet still he had put out the order for them to return. The only explanation Arrun could consider was that Argentius must be recalling the fleet for deployment on a different operation. This would come as a relief to those patrolling the Rift. Space Marines needed purpose to their existence and whilst they may have been protecting the inhabitants of the Gildar system and overseeing the smooth operation of the Imperium at large – they were warriors first and foremost. They needed to be at war.

Arrun had consistently conveyed his personal concerns to the Chapter Master that the Gildar Rift possessed many hidden threats and had maintained his argument that the current numbers deployed in the system were necessary. Even if they had *not* been necessary, he had argued, maintaining a visible presence would be wise. Argentius, it seemed, did not agree. As such, the Master of the Fleet's mood was decidedly dark as he assembled his key advisors.

The strategium rested atop the pyramid-like interior of the strike cruiser. It was one of the few locations in the main structure that had something other than the functional steel mesh that ran everywhere else. In this instance, the floor itself was constructed from armaplas mesh. It afforded a dizzying view down to the bridge and with a little effort someone could see through the steel mesh even further still; to the deeper levels of the ship where the training cages and habitation areas were located. The interior of the *Dread Argent* had been constructed in tiers of concentric rings, each level getting smaller, ziggurat style, until it reached the top and this domed room at its pinnacle. The sounds of the everyday activity of the ship floated up to them in a muted murmur.

The only furniture within the strategium were the chairs and table that dominated the room's centre. All of these items had been specifically designed with the increased bulk and weight of the Space Marines in mind. On the extremely rare occasions when the regular crew members were brought up here, they looked ridiculously child-like in the immense seats. There was no décor on the walls other than Fourth Company's battle banner, unfurled and pinned out and the aquila that spread its wings imperiously across the wall behind Arrun's head. Seated at the top of the table, the wings of the Imperial symbol opened out behind him. It was not merely a design coincidence that situating the aquila in that location created an illusion that the captain himself bore the wings of the Imperium.

Captain Arrun looked from one face to the other, a slight tic under his right eye the only betrayal that he was struggling to keep his annoyance as well controlled as he could manage. Eventually, he spoke in a dark, gravelly tone. The discontent in his voice was evident.

'We received orders from Varsavia this morning. We scale down our patrols with immediate effect.'

The other Silver Skulls gathered at the table exchanged brief glances. It was unheard of for Arrun to begin such a meeting with anything other than requesting that the Prognosticator lead them all in the litanies. It certainly didn't bode well for the rest of this gathering. The battle brother seated to the captain's right reached out and laid a hand on Arrun's arm with easy familiarity. Irritated, Arrun was about to shrug off the touch, then glanced at the other warrior. The Prognosticator was dressed in a heavy, dark grey robe with a hood that obscured his features completely. All that could be seen of him was the glitter of two green eyes deep within the hood's depths.

Arrun felt the touch of his advisor's mind brush his own and gave a brief, terse nod. The unspoken chastisement was all that was needed. He adjusted his attitude with visible reluctance, but his face betrayed the fury bubbling just beneath the surface.

'My apologies, Prognosticator. Brothers, I beg your indulgence a while longer. Please forgive my mood, but as I am sure you can appreciate, this news concerns me deeply.' He ran a hand over his shaven head and leaned forward. 'I have communicated back to our Lord Commander my worries about activity in the system. Despite incursions into the Gildar locale being sporadic, the fact remains that they are still happening. The threat in this system is very real. And despite this...' Arrun scowled. 'Despite this, until our astropaths receive his response, we must make every move towards prosecuting his request to reduce the number of the patrols in the Gildar Rift.'

His words had an electrifying effect on his battle-brothers. The silence that descended was suddenly broken by the *crack* of a balled metal fist slamming down on the table. The suddenness of the noise reverberated around the strategium's dome and all eyes turned to the young Techmarine whose synthetic hand trembled with barely suppressed rage. Arrun's eyes swivelled to him, hardening like diamonds.

'Brother Correlan? Is there something you want to say?'

The Techmarine, never known for his subtlety, shook his head. His augmetic right eye whirred softly as he focused on the captain and the red lens flickered briefly. His voice shook with the irritation that Arrun was sure they all felt. 'After all our work, after all that we have achieved here, I hope the Chapter Master is not putting a stop to the project.' He kept the question out of his tone, keeping his voice moderate with obvious difficulty. The others seated at the table nodded slowly, each harbouring the same thought. They had been assembled as a team for a very specific reason and the project that was nearing its completion had taken each and every one of them firmly into its grip.

'You can consider yourself fortunate on that front, brother. To the best of my knowledge and until the Lord Commander decrees otherwise, the Resurgent Project will continue as planned.' There was a tone of something largely akin to disgust in the captain's voice. He had committed time and resources to an experiment that he had never wanted to truly be a part of. Events had overtaken him, though, and Vashiro's will was not something to be denied.

His words garnered no response. All present knew Daerys Arrun's thoughts on the Resurgent Project. It was something that he had inherited from his predecessor who had in turn, inherited it from the Master of the Fleet before him. A legacy of sorts; a plan that had been waiting to come to fruition for several centuries. It had waited on the orders of the Prognosticatum for the conditions to be right. Even with the Chapter Master's approval, even with the Chapter's wisest and most revered Prognosticators fully in support of the project, Daerys Arrun's open distrust and scepticism had remained. He had even tried to argue against it when he had been initiated into its deepest secrets.

It had been a tense, lengthy debate which had ultimately been swayed with the additional enthusiasm and backing of the Master of the Forge. Finally convinced that the idea had some small amount of merit and that to resist the will of Chapter command would be ultimately detrimental, Arrun had capitulated.

Correlan nodded and folded his arms before him, the servos and minute air compressors in his mechanised arm hissing softly as he made the gesture. 'Good,' he said. 'Because to be brutally honest, captain, we passed the point of no return several days ago. I very much doubt that the work Brother-Apothecary Ryarus and I have accomplished can be undone now.' His young face was open and honest, hiding nothing of his aggressive nature or underlying indignity and yet there was open challenge in his tone.

'Mind your attitude, Techmarine.' The hooded warrior seated next to Arrun folded his own arms, deliberately mimicking Correlan's body language. 'Captain Arrun must, as we *all* must, obey our Lord Commander's orders without question. Believe it or not, he has as much invested in this project as you do. More, in fact. You are not even an officer in this company, something which you would do well to remember. Remember your place and hold your tongue.'

Correlan scowled even more deeply and leaned back in his seat. In his life before his ascension to the ranks of the Adeptus Astartes, he had been one of the few Silver Skulls raised to adolescence amongst one of the semi-feral, aggressive tribes of the southern Varsavian steppes. Some habits and mannerisms took longer to overwrite than others and a tendency to fall prey to a hair trigger temper was one.

'My apologies, Prognosticator.'

The psyker threw his hood back and studied the young Space Marine with a cool, appraising look. 'Whilst your lack of sincerity in those words is duly noted, your enthusiasm is to be commended, brother. I ask you to not mistake my words for those of anger. Consider instead that I am offering you advice. You would do well to heed it.'

Correlan, out of a habit borne from months of working

alongside Prognosticator Brand let himself fall into sullen silence. He would never argue such a point. Fourth Company's principal advisor may have been ageing, his long hair threaded through with silver and his tattooed face lined and wise, but his acuity was as sharp as ever it had been. His not inconsiderable psychic abilities went a very long way towards ensuring that no secrets were ever kept from him.

'Thank you, Brand.' Arrun had used the natural pause offered by the brief exchange as an opportunity to cool his own temper and was already much calmer than he had been before. He had engaged Correlan's involvement in the project knowing that the younger warrior had occasionally been described as borderline reckless. It was a small price to pay because his particular skills had been perfect for this work. Varsavia was something of a technological backwater and as a consequence, those who demonstrated technical aptitude and who had undergone training at the hands of the Adeptus Mechanicus were afforded similar levels of respect as the Chaplain-Librarians of the Prognosticatum. Regardless of how bad-tempered they might have been.

Drumming his fingertips on the table, his chin held thoughtfully between his thumb and forefinger, Arrun considered his comrades for several moments. Then he nodded, his course of action determined.

'We will comply with Lord Commander Argentius's request, of course. I do not think that it is a secret that I am not happy about it. I am confident that by the time he receives the astropathic response, he will be more than aware of that himself.' Arrun let out an exasperated breath. 'As such, we must proceed to discussion of the fleet's redeployment.' He gestured towards Correlan who tapped out several digits on the control panel set into a recess before him.

A static hiss filled the strategium and a hololithic display flickered into life above the featureless surface of the table. Created almost lovingly after months of mapping the system, it was a perfect graphical representation of the Gildar Rift. Satellites orbiting the many planets in the system wheeled and spun in proper calculations of their trajectories. Even the asteroid field was recreated practically to the last piece of rock. Of course, it was constantly shifting. The recent transgression of the *Endless Horizon* had stirred up the asteroid belt in particular and it had taken time to settle back down.

'I updated the display mere hours ago,' Correlan, now unleashed from the constraints of obeisance and allowed free rein to do what he did best, was almost unrecognisable from the sullen, resistant Space Marine he had been bare moments before. His confrontational body language dissolved under a relentless assault of enthusiasm and energy. His hands moved rapidly and with great animation as he spoke. 'The Omnissiah be praised, I had no major problems this time. Here.' He took a cable that dangled from the table and plugged it snugly into the jack port of the device he wore on his arm, an integral part of his metal hand replacement. There was a soft *click* as the cable bedded into it.

His fingers danced nimbly across the keypad at his wrist and several bright runes winked into existence amidst the dancing display. Their own vessel was shown as a softly pulsing red light that moved in perfect time with the planet of Gildar Secundus. At Correlan's gentle coaxing, other symbols gradually brightened up.

Every ship that was presently deployed in the region showed up on the tactical hololith and Arrun pointed a finger to them in turn, naming each individually as he did so. In all cases, he named the ship before its occupants; a reflection on his position.

'The *Quicksilver* is closest to us. Our brothers of Ninth Company were to begin their journey back to Varsavia within the next few days. For now, however, I will inform them to resume their patrol.' Seeing the furrowed brows of the others, he elaborated, his face unmoving. 'Our ship may be incapable of quick response should the Resurgent fail at inauguration. We may need their support should such a thing occur.' He flashed the briefest of smiles. 'It is essential to always remain one step ahead of the enemy, particularly when there is no enemy visible.'

Arrun was aware of the sudden bristling of both the Techmarine and the Apothecary at the implication that the project may fail. He ignored them carefully.

The *Dread Argent* and the *Quicksilver* were only two of the Silver Skulls strike cruisers, the others all presently deployed elsewhere throughout the segmentum and beyond. Arrun resumed his register of the other ships still in the Rift. Most of these were Gladius-class escorts, many crewed largely by Chapter serfs. With the ease of decades of commanding the fleet, he drew up the outline of the redeployment.

Ryarus, the taciturn, stoic Apothecary had up until now remained silent. Now he tipped his head slightly and studied the redesign of the fleet. He made a laconic observation.

'Lord Commander Argentius is planning something.' It was not a question, but a shrewd observation. The sheer number of ships that Arrun was picking off from the display was extraordinary. When the orders were prosecuted and transmitted to the rest of the fleet, the presence of the Silver Skulls in the Gildar Rift would be cut by more than half.

'Aye. He probably is. Despite my repeated reports that something is not right in this system, he has chosen to downscale our activity here. We aren't to leave Gildar entirely without protection, of course. But yes.' Arrun stared at the hololith, his brow furrowing. 'Yes, he has something planned. It is not the place for me to question or begin to second-guess his judgement...'

He left the rest of the sentence unspoken.

Arrun turned from the strategium table to stare out of the ship's viewport and down at the world of Gildar Secundus. From here there was no way of recognising the volcanic nature of its surface. Far above the swirling atmosphere, there was a faint reminiscence of distant Mars. It was a uniform shade of murky red, as though someone had poured dust and ancient blood into the crucible at the time of its forging. Millennia of brutal eruptions during its cataclysmic formation had formed the distinctive jagged peaks and deep valleys that scarred its surface.

Hundreds of years had passed since the last active eruption and an exploratory geological mission had not only declared the planet was suitable for human colonisation, but had discovered rich deposits of the raw minerals needed for the refining of promethium which also bubbled to the surface in plentiful lakes. It was a double blessing from the Father of Mankind.

Far beneath them on the planet, thousands of Imperial citizens now dwelt largely in subterranean blocks tunnelled kilometres beneath the surface. Most worked the promethium refineries but as was the way with the children of mankind, they had an unerring habit of taking root wherever they could and making a life for themselves. After several years, agricultural domes began to output their produce and despite the best efforts of the planet's militia, there was a steady underground trade in obscura. Over the past years, it had become a thriving planet, the destination for many traders of the Imperium – and those serving themselves first. Despite its prosperity, it was first and foremost a human settlement and as such, had swiftly become a target for thieves, raiders and smugglers.

'Ryarus, Correlan... transmit the orders to the other ships,' he said. 'Advise the fleet to wait on my word.' With a brusque nod, Correlan shut down the hololith, unplugged the cable and left the room with Apothecary Ryarus.

Left alone with his chief advisor, Arrun turned from the viewport.

'Perhaps you would be good enough to once again divine the omens in this matter, Prognosticator.'

'Of course. But I must ask that you be very specific with your question, brother-captain.' Brand reached into a pouch at his waist and extracted a number of card-thin crystalline wafers. He shuffled them together as he spoke to Arrun, the surfaces of each brushing against one another with a faint whisper. 'The Emperor does not like to repeat himself.'

Arrun considered for a few moments. Since the inception of the Resurgent Project, he had used Brand's psychic connection with the Emperor to determine the appropriate course of action on many occasions. Thus far, the Prognosticator hadn't steered them wrong. But he had never asked the questions that he most wanted the answer to.

Until now.

'Are we doing His will by facilitating the creation of this... *thing*? Will we succeed?' he said, asking the question in a cool, calm voice. Brand let the captain's words fill the silence and die out, then inclined his head graciously before dealing out the pattern that would determine the answer to the captain's question. He dealt each wafer one at a time, relishing the familiarity of them beneath his fingers. He had come into the possession of his own personal tarot four hundred years before, and when his psychic abilities activated the illustrations hidden in their mystical depths, they were quite beautiful.

He closed his eyes, a flicker of blue warp lightning crackling between his fingertips as he extended forth the probing, questing tendrils of his psychic conduit with the Emperor of Mankind.

His voice barely audible, he mumbled the Litany of Conjecture and turned over the first card. Its crystal surface shimmered and flickered into life. He studied it thoughtfully, then passed his hand over it again.

'The Emperor. The most powerful card in the pack.' Brand looked up. 'Inverted.'

His heart had leaped at the first words, but had then sunk. Even Arrun who was not gifted with the foresight of the Prognosticators knew that the most powerful card in the tarot deck inverted was never to be taken as a good sign. An involuntary sense of unease ran like a chill of ice through his veins, trickling down his spine.

'Continue,' he said. 'I would know more.'

THE ENGINEERING DECK was a bustling hive of activity. Servitors, enginseers and Chapter serfs created a constant, dull monotone which dipped in pitch momentarily as Ryarus and Correlan entered. As the two warriors crossed from one side of the deck to the other, the throng parted silently to let them through. The ripple closed behind them in a smooth wave and the raucous, incomprehensible noise started up again.

There was little to no ostentation on board the Silver Skulls vessels, apart from the rich displays of the company trophies that were located in the chapels. The Chapter was not aesthetically barren of course; they took great pride in their body art and the tattoo artists, the Custodes Cruor, were regarded highly. Many of the Silver Skulls designed their own tattoos and a number of them were genuinely talented, gifted artists. The ancient Varsavian tradition of marking their bodies was considered the ultimate battle honour and every brother of the Silver Skulls Chapter wore designs that were completely unique to the individual. Some chose representations of great battles that were breathtaking in their detail.

In all cases, the last part of a Silver Skull's body to receive markings was his face. Only on ascension to the rank of captain were they allowed to receive that honour.

Passing through the bustle of the engine decks, Ryarus and Correlan headed for another room that was certainly not notable for any decoration. It was, however, notable for the many pieces of machinery strewn on every available surface. The smell of machine oil, burned promethium and lapping powder was all-pervading in here, its acrid odour permeating the air strongly. There was another Techmarine working who got up to leave when Correlan and his companion appeared. Correlan stilled him with a wave of his hand.

'Stay,' he said simply. 'You might learn something.'

This was Correlan's main workshop and the centre of the project that had taken over their lives. Cables and wires littered the ground and Ryarus picked his way through the treacherous obstacle course with a hint of a smile on his craggy face.

'I've never really quite understood how you can possibly work like this, Correlan. How in the Emperor's name do you know where things are?'

Compared to the ordered, spotless apothecarion where

Ryarus carried out his procedures, Correlan's workshop was a place of nightmarish bedlam. Machines had been stripped back to their bare souls so that the Techmarine might better tend to them. Often, these stripped-down machines simply lay where he had left them when another, more pressing project had demanded his attention. In the far corner of the workshop was his harness, the mechadendrites motionless and devoid of animation without the Techmarine's connection with them stirring them into life. The Techmarine treated Ryarus to an infectious grin, a stark contrast to his sour mood of earlier. Here, in what could be described as his natural habitat, the warrior was without a doubt at his best.

'A foolish question, brother.' His tone was playfully scolding. The Techmarine swept a pile of rolled-up schematics to one side. 'I know *precisely* where everything is, Ryarus, because everything will always be *precisely* where I left it.' As if to demonstrate the proof of this gargantuan, seemingly unbelievable claim, he moved aside several more mysterious objects, the purpose of which Ryarus couldn't ever begin to comprehend and picked up a data-slate. He waved it triumphantly at the Apothecary.

'You see?' he said. 'Precisely where I left it.'

As an aspirant, Correlan had demonstrated a remarkable talent with machines and an unerring ability to soothe troubled spirits. At times it was hard to believe that an individual in possession of such a fiery soul could demonstrate such patience with the stubborn servants of the Omnissiah. His training with the Adeptus Mechanicus on Mars had ended some five years previously and he had served under Captain Arrun for the entire time since his return. He worked hard and with great diligence and his prowess on the battlefield was executed with the same intensity that he delivered to everything.

Correlan was in possession of an honest, open personality and his emotions were always writ large in an unscarred, boyish face. His humours were often unpredictable but his abilities were without question. He had a tendency to insubordination and bad moods that made him tricky to handle; a trait which the Master of the Forge had frequently lamented.

'Emotions, Correlan,' he had said, 'are superfluous to the purity of the machine. You must learn to put aside such petty thoughts and feelings.' They weren't words that the young Techmarine had taken to heart. The Master of the Forge had let it pass, knowing that in time, circumstance and the growing sense of one-ness with the Omnissiah would mark changes in him.

Ryarus liked him. He liked the younger warrior's honesty and blunt nature and had taken Correlan under his wing in some respects, particularly during the course of the project.

More than once, Correlan's patience and faith in his own ability had been stretched beyond its limits and the Techmarine had been on the verge of admitting defeat. What they were trying to accomplish was beyond anything the Silver Skulls had ever attempted and there was no frame of reference for the depth of work needed: no research, no failed attempts that had gone before – and as the days and weeks had blurred into months, failure had begun to look like a very real option.

Whenever those moments had loomed, dark and miserable, Ryarus had been there to encourage and support the younger warrior. A real friendship had grown between the two, as different as they were, and a mutual respect that meant they worked together like they had been a team for decades.

Daerys Arrun may have been many things; arrogant and prideful amongst others. But he was also a great judge of character. It had been no chance arrangement that Apothecary Ryarus had been reassigned to Fourth Company at the inception of the Resurgent Project. His cool, level-headedness was the perfect counterpoint to Correlan's fire.

Correlan led the way to the far side of his workshop and placed his massive hand on the biometric scanner that was affixed to the wall. With a low hum and grinding of ancient gears, the door slid open almost reluctantly to admit them to the Resurgent's chamber. The room was located perfectly between the Techmarine's workshop and the apothecarion, allowing both Space Marines easy access whenever they were working.

This room was also cluttered – although this time it was with servitors rather than general debris. As the two entered, the machine-like chattering of the lobotomised Chapter servants swelled in volume. In their dull, emotionless voices, they delivered their reports. The noise would have been incomprehensible to anybody other than a Space Marine, but Correlan and Ryarus easily extracted the prudent and important information.

There was also a group of tech-priests picking their way awkwardly around the untidy area. Some were murmuring litanies that were barely audible over the noise of the servitors, whilst others were anointing various pieces of equipment with unfathomable shapes using fingers coated in sacred engine oil from a vial carried by one of their number. Everything they did was a complete mystery to Ryarus, but the earnest manner in which they behaved filled him once again with pride at his involvement.

Each one of them, from the lowliest menial all the way up to himself, had a specific purpose; a focus that related to the dominant feature of the room.

In the very centre of the room, encased within a transparent, narrow chamber; more of a tank which rose continuously from floor to ceiling was the Resurgent himself. A massive figure displaying the over-developed musculature and slightly equine face of the Adeptus Astartes was within, moving sluggishly within its confines. He was kept in a mostly rigid, standing posture, arms out by his side, by several clamps that minimised his body movements.

A gelatinous, sticky-looking liquid filled the tank, enveloping its occupant completely. It clung to his body, giving his darkly tanned skin an unnatural sheen. His arms and legs had long been severed from his torso at the elbows and knees and the machinery that had replaced them was not dissimilar to the arm and leg pieces of the Mark VII battle plate that the Silver Skulls favoured.

The human – if this was what he could still be considered – within the tank was now far more machine than anything and yet his face remained deeply human and astonishingly youthful. He was barely out of his teens. His skin was studded at regular intervals with jack-ports, exactly as Correlan and Ryarus themselves bore. These were the interfaces that granted a Space Marine the ability to connect to his power armour. But the boy in the tank had never been granted the Emperor's Ward, what other Chapters knew as the black carapace, the membrane that coated a Space Marine's bones and provided the valuable connection with their power armour.

The boy in the tank was incomplete. He was imperfect. He should, by all rights, be viewed as nothing more than a failure. Yet, to Ryarus's eyes, the boy was something else entirely. He was their future. He represented everything that they had worked so hard for over the past months.

His still-human eyes were closed. Even though he had long gained mastery of the Watchful Sleeper which allowed parts of his brain to rest whilst the rest of him remained alert and aware, old habits died hard. Perhaps, the Apothecary considered as he stared at the youth within the tank, he drew some comfort from the act of sleeping. He shook his head and crossed the room, resting his hand on the armaplas separating him from the Resurgent. He spoke a single word.

'Volker.'

At the sound of his name, the boy's eyes opened and he met Ryarus's gaze. A hint of a smile gave his face added warmth. Unable to move, he simply inclined his head in greeting. When his voice came, it floated from a speaker grille embedded in the front of his habitat.

'Apothecary.' His voice was still mostly human, with the slightest twang of artifice about it as the augmetic implants within his throat moderated the sounds. They didn't hide the soft tone in his voice, or the lightest trace of an accent that he still retained. 'You're late this morning.' The fluid surrounding him added a faint burbling to his words, but he was otherwise perfectly understandable.

'We were spending time at the captain's pleasure.' Without any further time spent on idle conversation, the Apothecary prepared to take the auspex readings of Volker's vital signs whilst Correlan began the onerous task of draining the youth's habitat so that he could exit the transparent holding tube.

Here then, was the Silver Skulls greatest technological project and most radical advancement of their existence. Here, within this specially designed tank was the future of the fleet. Here, within this tank was a technological wonder the likes of which the Silver Skulls had never seen. Here was the end product of a true marriage between man and machine.

Here, within the tank, was Volker Straub.

VOLKER STRAUB HAD been one of the most promising aspirants of his intake. Hugely charismatic and a gifted athlete, he was also a born leader. From the moment he had been brought from his tribe to the fortress-monastery on Varsavia, every soul his effervescent personality touched knew that his future would be bright. Here was a future Chapter hero in the making. He had undergone his earliest trials as champion of his group, never once defeated in hand-to-hand or blade training. He was bright, questioned everything and knew when to hold his tongue. It gave him great standing with his peers and more importantly with his elders.

Every implantation during the conversion process had gone like a dream. Every last thing about Volker Straub had dazzled the Chapter from his earnest nature to his startling wit and intelligence. He had been Captain Sephera's absolute favourite. The grizzled Chief of Recruits had written report after glowing report of recommendation and in advance of Volker's placement with the Scouts of Tenth Company, he had personally suggested that Volker receive a command at the earliest possible date. He had even offered to put his full personal support behind such a recommendation.

This aspirant is exceptional, he wrote. *Universally liked and with a capacity to think faster and with greater logic than many of his peers, I do not doubt that Volker Straub is destined for greatness.*

In all this, Volker never lost sight of who – or what – he was. He was an aspirant of the Silver Skulls Chapter. His loyalty was without question, both to his Chapter, his brothers-in-arms and to the Imperium. He was assigned to Sergeant Atellus in the Tenth Company and outperformed consistently. Every time the bar was raised, he met each new challenge with confidence and competence.

Then, two days before he was scheduled to undergo the implantation of his progenoid gland, the Prognosticatum intervened.

Nobody disputed that the Prognosticatum were the controlling force within the Silver Skulls. Comprised of the Prognosticators who were the Chaplain-Librarians who undertook a dual role and the Chaplains themselves, the Prognosticatum also boasted the elite Prognosticars. These were the Chapter champions; the heroes. They represented the very essence of the Silver Skulls.

Inspirational and powerful, this elite unit was formed of psychic battle-brothers whose prowess on the front line was second to none. Frequently, these were the psykers whose gifts tended away from the more esoteric divination and precognition that was so crucial to the functioning of the Chapter and leaned towards the more destructive in nature.

The most important decisions required by the Chapter were ultimately escalated to the Prognosticatum and the council was overseen by Vashiro, the Chief Prognosticator. Nothing involving a choice that directly affected the entire Chapter was ever settled without the rituals to cast the auguries. Every recruit, alongside his rigorous physical training regime and hypno-doctrination sessions was required to divine their future path at some point with a Prognosticator. This happened, traditionally, prior to the insertion of the progenoid gland. The most sacred of the implants, the Quintessence Sacred was the pinnacle of achievement.

Unlike many Chapters, the Silver Skulls were ignorant as to the lines of their heritage. The name of their primogenitor, the primarch whose genetic material had formed the pattern for their Chapter was unknown to them, the records lost many centuries before. Several centuries previously, the Apothecaries had performed countless genetic tests and suggested that the most likely line of heritage was that of the noble Ultramarines. But it mattered little. The simple fact was, they *did* exist and despite many great hardships, they thrived.

Four years ago, Volker had been on the edge of a bright future as a fully fledged battle-brother. Then the auguries had denied him the ultimate glory.

Had it really been four years ago? Ryarus remembered the decree that had been passed down from the Prognosticatum. Volker Straub was not to be given the progenoid gland that would allow him full ascension. It had been the most irrational thing the Apothecary had ever known be issued by them.

Denied that which he so desperately craved, Volker had formally requested Vashiro's permission to walk the Long Patrol anyway. Forming part of the final stage of a recruit's initiation, the Long Patrol saw the aspirants sent out into the feral wilds of the Varsavian tundra with no more than a combat knife to defend themselves with. Those who survived remained with the Chapter and ascended to the ranks.

Those who died were remembered with honour. Only those worthy enough to have reached the final stages of the process were permitted to walk the Long Patrol. It was better by far, Volker had said, than becoming a serf.

Again, he was denied.

Vashiro had explained to him that he was not to become a battle-brother which, at the age of sixteen and having undergone the arduous trials to reach this stage, left the boy devastated. Instead, he would continue with his physical training.

Volker was despondent. He had turned to the recruit's own Prognosticator for advice, for a divining of the future and all that he could glean was that his destiny lay down a different path to the one trodden by so many warriors before him. He received small reassurance in the insistence that everything decreed by the Emperor's Sight happened for a purpose – and that he was destined for greatness.

Nearly four years later, when Daerys Arrun had been approached by the Prognosticatum, the two had been twisted irrevocably together, the fate of Daerys Arrun and Volker Straub intertwining as one. The youth had gone with Captain Arrun gladly.

Now, here he was, having sacrificed his limbs, his freedom and his birthright in the name of progression.

'THREE MORE DAYS.' When Ryarus spoke, it was with complete confidence. A nod of agreement from Correlan cemented the estimate. Arrun, who had arrived in the chamber several moments before gave a brief smile of approval.

He found the answer surprising, but at the same time, pleasing. In the past weeks, whenever the captain had asked for a projected time of completion, a specific moment they could work towards when the Resurgent Project could go into its initial testing phase, he had always been met with uncertainty. The effects of connecting Volker too soon could be lethal, they had all agreed; not just for the Resurgent himself, but for the Dread Argent and the rest of its crew as well.

'The Resurgent Project will grant our fleet a much greater advantage,' Arrun said, reluctant pride creeping in his voice as he looked upon the assembly. He might not have been fully supportive of what was taking place, but he was fiercely proud of his team. All the anger he had felt earlier with regard to Argentius's unprecedented orders had drained away on receipt of the news that the project was almost into its final stage. 'I tell you this, my brothers. Assuming all goes as planned, Lord Commander Argentius will be pleased with how this project has gone. He will be pleased with all of us.'

He turned and considered the sleeping Volker, now once again returned to his semi-stasis.

'Mark my words. One way or another, we will be remembered

for this. Whether for good or ill remains to be seen. But nonetheless...'. Echoing Ryarus's earlier gesture, Arrun lay his own hand on the armaplas tank. 'We will be remembered.'

THREE
ENCROACHMENT

THEY MOVED SILENTLY through the stars, like sharks seeking out sustenance on their endless hunt through the oceans. Were it not for the periodic firing of their thrusters engaging to execute minute course corrections, the two ships could easily have been lifeless. Those bursts of activity, however, indicated that they were anything but.

There was nothing marking these two prowlers as friendly and neither was there anything to suggest that they may have been hostile. Nothing, of course, except for the very definite air of menace they seemed to exude in the manner of their transit. Keeping their movements in perfect harmony they performed a dazzling, deadly interstellar display of synchronicity.

They moved as one, slowly devouring the distance that separated them from Gildar Secundus.

These predators were in no hurry. There was no need, for they had time and cunning on their side.

Closer, they came.

Ever closer.

* * *

ALL WAS WELL.

For two days, nothing unauthorised had come through the Gildar system. The *Endless Horizon*, under the now decidedly less haphazard guidance of Luka Abramov, completed her deliveries and was escorted from the system. The *Endless Horizon's* captain had promised faithfully not to repeat his performance.

Other trade vessels continued to come and go and the *Dread Argent* did not need to leave her geostationary orbit. For this, both Apothecary Ryarus and Correlan were exceptionally glad. A stable situation was a preferable option at this juncture. Power systems could be more effectively diverted whilst the ship maintained orbit and the extra power in turn allowed for much more productive output into the project.

Ryarus considered this now. He and Correlan had worked slavishly for the past two days. The Techmarine had closed himself off for hours on end in his workshop where he became swiftly buried in the many schematics and plans that he had spent months drawing up. At this stage, a single error in judgement would spell disaster. His mood degenerated rapidly and eventually he was left to his own devices with only a number of servitors to aid him. Fortunate, Ryarus thought, that the mindless near-automatons had no emotions that could be laid bare under the Techmarine's lashing tongue. They would have been reduced to quivering wrecks within minutes.

For his part, the Silver Skulls Apothecary had spent time with Volker and had been satisfied that the boy was ready in both body and mind for the commencement of his new role. He had been absorbed, fascinated in the measure of his own success in terms of witnessing the precision of the augmetic enhancements. The replacement limbs were, in a sense, a practice ground; a way in which Volker could adjust to his body being grafted with technology. It was why the decision had been taken at the start to amputate at all. Replacement limbs hadn't been an entire altruistic thing. Getting used to controlling the augmetics trained up the dormant sections of Volker's brain, which would be vital come the inauguration of the neural network.

The Resurgent Project itself had been in stasis for a long time. A former Master of the Fleet had introduced the project to the Prognosticatum some four hundred years previously. He had been full of countless ideas and the concepts necessary to achieve the goal. He had even provided crude blueprints painstakingly drawn in his own hand.

He had been denied.

'The time is not right,' Vashiro had said, on consultation with the inner circle. 'We see merit in the idea, but until the omens are aligned, we cannot give you our approval.'

So the Resurgent Project had been effectively forgotten. With the inauguration of a new Master of the Fleet came the responsibility of knowing that they may be called upon to take the reins of the nascent prototype. Daerys Arrun's reaction on discovering this was going to fall into his remit had not been a positive one. Devoutly traditional, Arrun saw the Resurgent as an abominable thing, an effort on the part of the Silver Skulls to interfere with the status quo. He had obeyed only because he had to, not because he had any choice. He had assembled as perfect a team as he could muster. Thus, Correlan had taken over the mechanical part of the workload whilst Ryarus had taken responsibility for the biological.

Everywhere Volker went, even here on the training levels, a small retinue of tech-priests were not far behind, their voices as low and incomprehensible as ever as they chanted repeated litanies and blessings over the one they called the Great Honoured. Ryarus had drawn the line at the full contingent that attended him in the main chamber and had, extremely reluctantly, negotiated a party of four adepts.

Ryarus watched Volker carefully as the youth performed his daily exercises in the half-light of the training cages. The lighting in the area was intentionally dull, the lumen-sconces embedded in the walls giving off little more than a perfunctory glow. It was a habit of the Silver Skulls to train at various levels of light. Such practice better prepared them for combat in any conditions and helped maintain their ability to control their enhanced eyesight.

Volker had little need to consider his self-defence in the long term, of course, but Ryarus was acutely conscious that the exercise staved off the depression that the youth might otherwise have fallen into given his extended state of limbo.

During physical training, Volker could engage his mind on everything he had been bred for. It also meant that he was more self-sufficient than if he had been placed into an artificial coma and needed constant monitoring. This way, at least, the boy could maintain some sense of independence from the project that would ultimately consume all that he was.

The gloomy light cast eerie shadows of battling giants on the utilitarian walls of the ringed training tier. Along with Volker, there were a number of other Silver Skulls presently engaged in drills and training, barely more than indistinguishable silhouettes. Ryarus, though, would have known any of them at a glance. As ranking Apothecary in Fourth Company, all of them had passed through his care at one time or another. The sounds of blade against blade rang out, caught and funnelled upwards through the interior ziggurat of the *Dread Argent*.

Ryarus watched Volker's performance through half-closed eyes, his Apothecary's skills granting him the ability to assess everything about the youth's exertions in the training cage. He had coped well with his augmetic implants and had full control over them. It had been difficult for him, at first. Never granted the Emperor's Ward, or his own suit of power armour, the ability to interface himself with machinery on the level that the Resurgent Project demanded was always going to be a challenge. But it had been a challenge that Volker had adapted to with ease and satisfying proficiency.

Bare from the waist up, light combat fatigues covering his artificial legs, Volker fought with the skill and prowess of any of his peers. The muscles rippled across his back as he threw himself at the artificial enemy and he laid into the training servitor with great energy and enthusiasm. Given that he spent much of his time held motionless in the feed-tank, it must be liberating to be freed from his constraints, even if it was only for a few hours.

In a few short weeks, he would never move freely again. After the bonding took place, he would become as one with the *Dread Argent*. There was something sorrowing, even a little sinister about such a fate and yet the boy had never once tried to refute his destiny. The Prognosticators had laid out his future as dictated by the Emperor himself. No loyal member of the Imperium of Man would deny such an honour. Volker had always been more saddened by his denial to the ranks of the Adeptus Astartes than his ultimate sacrifice. Even with the loss of his arms and legs to the necessary augmetics that would serve as conduits to the ship's systems, Volker had remained upbeat and determined, optimistic beyond reckoning.

The Apothecary was fiercely proud of the success he had achieved during his time with Fourth Company. For the better part of two hundred years, his role had always focused far more on reducing the suffering of mortally wounded brothers by sending them to the arms of the Emperor swiftly and cleanly. He recovered the Chapter's legacy from the fallen so that future generations may strengthen their numbers.

There was a need for emotional detachment of course, yet the loss of each of his battle-brothers cut him keenly. His own honour tattoos were simple and deeply reflective of the soul beneath the skin, listing the name of every Silver Skulls warrior whose Quintessence Sacred he had reclaimed with his reductor. They would not be forgotten, not by him. Now, with the work he had undertaken with Volker, he had been given the chance to nurture, to create.

His own blood brother, Prognosticator Chaereus, had always claimed the ability to read the auras of others. Long since taken to the halls of the ancients, the psyker had always maintained that Ryarus's aura was that of a protector. 'Shield of the Emperor,' had been what he had actually said.

Fifty years dead.

Had it been so very long?

Ryarus rarely felt the weight of his years upon him, but when he did, they made themselves known heavily. The sorrowful and ignoble end his brother had met, torn to shreds by rampaging orks, had fuelled his own battle rage. Ryarus had cut down dozens of the greenskin menace single-handedly before a near-fatal shot to the chest had incapacitated him. Even then, his fading fury had kept him struggling to bring his bolt pistol to bear on the xenos. It was only the fact that his body had battled him down into unconsciousness that he had stopped at all.

Apothecary Malus himself had overseen his subordinate's recovery, an honour which even now remained unsurpassed in Ryarus's experiences. The Chief Apothecary of the Silver Skulls took personal pride and interest in all those who had followed his own calling, an ethic that Ryarus himself had unconsciously cascaded further down to his own juniors. He was greatly respected and admired amongst not only Fourth Company, but throughout the entire Chapter for his forthright nature and, of course, that legendary display of fearless tenacity against the orks – a story that was told over and over again.

Briefly caught up in his own memories, his humours tipped to decidedly melancholic. With a physical shake, Ryarus pulled his thoughts out of the past and focused instead on the future. He idly tweaked the plaited beard of white hair at his chin and considered the future made flesh in the training cage before him.

FROM THE SHADOWS, another figure watched Volker Straub. There was no pride emanating from him, though. It was a skinny, dirty little creature who knew he was already pushing the very borders of his luck by being anywhere near the training decks. But he had heard so many rumours about this 'Resurgent' that he had decided to take a look for himself.

The young man who guided the *Dread Argent* through the warp had been brought to the employ of the Silver Skulls by way of a hive-world where he had been running the streets, fighting for his own survival. Born into a family of the Navis Nobilite that had fallen far from grace, his parents had effectively sold him to the employ of the Imperium in an attempt to regain some sort of standing. They had sold him as a commodity and the insult to his person still smarted.

His name was Jeremiah, and he was *jealous*. He was jealous of the muscled, healthy youth fighting in the training cages before him. He was jealous of the encroachment on the only thing that he had ever felt truly belonged to him. the *Dread Argent* was Jeremiah's ship. At least, that was the way he saw it.

He was the one who had to soothe its troubled soul when it travelled through the warp. He was the one who had struggled for an acceptance that he still was not sure he had achieved.

He watched, winding a lock of lank hair around one finger. His eyes flicked over Volker and then shifted briefly to the Space Marine who was with him. He knew Ryarus. The Apothecary was one of the few Silver Skulls who had made an effort to display overtures of friendship. Jeremiah had shied away from it, not trusting the giants who now owned him. Besides, from what he knew of the Emperor's Angels, he could not shake the overwhelming feeling that the Silver Skulls were *wrong* somehow.

For all his flaws and his dubious sense of personal hygiene, the Navigator was astute. He had listened to the various conversations amongst the human serfs about the project and he had gathered the facts to him. He had learned that there was some division amongst the crew – Adeptus Astartes and human alike – as to whether the Resurgent was a good idea or not.

His sharp little eyes darted nervously as Ryarus got to his feet and moved towards him. He shrank backwards, willing the shadows to swallow him up. The Apothecary's eyes met his and there was the barest shake of the head and a faintly amused quirk of the lips.

'Come out, Jeremiah.' When the Navigator didn't move, Ryarus softened his tone a little. 'I am not angry with you.'

He could have run away, fled back to his private chambers where very few people ever bothered him. But the command in Ryarus's tone did not invite disobedience. Jeremiah took a step out of the gloom. In the flickering light of the lumen-sconces and lumen-strips he cut a pathetically scrawny figure. He barely came up to the Apothecary's waist, but he still held himself taller anyway. He waited for his inevitable scolding.

At twenty, maybe twenty-one years old at the most, he was the sort of gangly youth who gave the impression that he was constructed mostly of limbs. Coppery-coloured hair hung in lank, greasy strands around a pale face that boasted a straggly, unkempt goatee beard. He was thin and under-nourished and his watery eyes stared up at the Apothecary with a peculiar mixture of awe and defiance. His third eye was kept hidden beneath a grubby silk scarf he wore tied around his head.

'I am pleased you are here,' the Apothecary said, throwing Jeremiah off balance. He hadn't been expecting *that*.

'You… are?'

'Of course. There is someone I would like you to meet.'

Jeremiah's eyes narrowed and he moved slightly to look around Ryarus's leg at Volker. 'What if I don't want to meet him?' He spoke with a slight stammer that was more to do with his anxiety than any particular speech defect.

'I am taking a guess that you came here specifically with the purpose of seeing for yourself what the talk is all about. Yes, I pay attention as well, Navigator.' The Apothecary added the last on seeing the guilty look that slid onto the Navigator's face. 'Let me explain what we are trying to achieve.'

In the simplest terms he could find, Ryarus briefly outlined the essence of the Resurgent Project and the boy's face grew more and more expressionless as he talked. The Apothecary felt a surge of exasperation, suspecting that the grubby young man was largely filtering out the important elements and hearing only what he wanted to. When he had finished, a silence settled between them, broken only by the sound of Volker's grunts of effort as he trained.

Jeremiah blinked a few times and worried at his lower lip with his teeth. 'Took me ages to settle this ship down,' he said and there was possessiveness in his eyes. 'Don't like the idea of someone else interfering with that.' He swung his gaze upwards. What was it he had heard the officers say when he'd listened to them?

'Permission to speak freely, my lord?'

'Always, Jeremiah. Honesty is encouraged on board the *Dread Argent*.'

Jeremiah took a deep breath. 'I reckon as you're all mad,' he asserted.

'I see.' There was silence and then Ryarus spoke again. If Jeremiah had been anywhere near as wise as he liked to think he was, he would have detected the edge in Ryarus's tone. 'Would you care to elaborate on that interesting point of view?'

The Apothecary's expression hadn't changed at all, so Jeremiah clung onto the little wave of confidence that had made him say that. 'Yes. What you're talking about doing sounds to me like it'll be dangerous. What if he...' He waved a hand dismissively in Volker's direction. 'What if he can't bond with the ship? That can kill anybody who doesn't know how to do it.'

'Volker's skills are superlative.'

'You never touched the machine-spirit at the heart of a ship, did you? It isn't something you can teach or train. It's just something you can do. Or can't do.'

'Our Prognosticators have decreed that this young man is the perfect choice for the task. Do you dare to presume that you can go against the most powerful divinations provided to our Chapter by the Emperor himself?'

'I'm not challenging nothing,' retorted Jeremiah, sullenly folding his arms across his thin chest. 'I'm just speaking freely. You said I could. But if you aren't interested in what I have to say, then I'll just shut up.' Ryarus sighed inwardly. Jeremiah was difficult to handle at the best of times. He forced a smile onto his face, although after the Navigator's direct insult against the Chapter, the urge to crush the little worm's head in his fist was rising.

'No... no, Jeremiah, I am sorry. You are quite right to have your say. Perhaps, when the time is right, you will offer your aid. We would appreciate it.'

'Maybe.' The Navigator sniffed haughtily. 'I'll think about it.'

With that, the rodenty little man turned away and strutted from the training decks as though he owned them. Perhaps, Ryarus thought, in a strange way he *does* own them.

He was troubled by the Navigator's words far more than he cared to admit. It was not the first time that the Apothecary had heard the suggestion that what the Silver Skulls was attempting was bordering on the insane. Was that truth? Had they deviated so far off course? Had they become so removed from the Codex Astartes that even other Space Marines thought the same?

THE TWO SHIPS were still moving slowly in their plotted course towards Gildar Secundus. Within minutes, they would be detectable by long-range auguries, but for now, at least, they remained unnoticed and hidden.

The stolen, warp-tainted technology they harboured on board, however, allowed them to scan the *Dread Argent* fully. Data was received, reconfigured and transmitted down the chain to those who had requested it. Within scant seconds, there was virtually nothing about the operating capacity of Captain Daerys Arrun's pride and joy that the intruders didn't know.

They held position awaiting word from their leaders. Too soon and the entire plan would fall to pieces.

Timing. It was all about the perfect timing.

For endless minutes they waited, poised and ready to strike or run as ordered. They could not move further forward without falling out of range of the vox-relay that would send them their orders. The relay had been painstakingly set up over a long period of time and was innocent and innocuous enough that it had never raised suspicion. The Imperium was always doing whatever they could to enhance communications, particularly in a zone like this where interference was common.

A few more pressure-suited drudges working on a distant moon raised no eyebrows with anyone.

When the message reached them, transmitted simultaneously to the two vessels, the voice that gave the command was distorted and cracked.

It was a single word.

'Engage.'

With a burn of their thrusters, the two ships, both designated as Infidel-class vessels, pressed forward and began their final approach.

THE BRIDGE DECK of the *Dread Argent* was a whirl of activity. A slew of tech-priests were engaged in rites to consecrate the control lecterns in readiness for the Resurgent and their chanting voices cut through every other noise. The rumble of the far-distant engines maintained its omnipresence.

There was a sense of great optimism pervading everything. After months of abortive attempts to commence the project, Captain Arrun's sense of relief at the imminent execution of the project bolstered his mood and that in turn was infectious. Apart from the servitors who bustled around in their usual way, the Chapter serfs who performed the menial duties on the *Dread Argent* found themselves in a similarly enthusiastic state of mind.

Normally, Arrun found the monosyllabic chantings of the tech-priests almost too much to bear, removing himself from their presence before they began their daily rounds of the bridge systems. Today was different. Tomorrow, the *Dread Argent* would represent the most technologically and biologically enhanced radical move that the deeply traditional Silver Skulls had made in centuries.

Glory and honour was in his Chapter's grasp and despite his own doubts and misgivings, nothing could take that away.

* * *

CLOSER STILL, THEY came.

They were in sensor range now. If the *Dread Argent* was going to notice them, it would do so swiftly and take appropriate action. The plan had been drawn up and memorised so many times that there was no possible way it could fail.

The Gildar system would fall.

'INCOMING UNIDENTIFIED SHIPS.'

The words were spoken in an emotionless, flat monotone by the servitor at the sensor lectern and they cut through Arrun's mood with all the accuracy and cruel savagery of a chainblade. He rose immediately from his command throne and took the steps down to the pulpit where the servitor stood. It turned its head to him and fixed him with eyes that gave away nothing.

'Unidentified? No. That is unacceptable. Activate any working augur banks and sweep them for their designations immediately.'

'Compliance.' The servitor turned away, a faint hiss of hydraulics audible as it did so. The tech-priests were still chanting their apparently endless blessing and Arrun coolly bit back the urge to banish them from his deck. He turned to a young man seated at one of the control panels.

'Run the manifests and schedules. Determine what is due into the system today. I checked it myself this morning. There was nothing slated for either arrival or departure. Prepare to send out a response ship. These intruders will answer to me.'

'Yes, captain.'

Arrun balled his hands into fists at his side, furious at this unwelcome intrusion. These fools would learn swiftly what it cost to cross the path of the Silver Skulls. They would not be the first to learn that lesson.

A few more clicks and the servitor spoke again. 'Profile fits Infidel-class design. No identifiable livery.'

'Infidels?' The word immediately sent the hairs on the back of Arrun's neck standing on end. Once one of the favoured fighting ships of the Legiones Astartes, but now no longer used. Knowledge of their construction had long been lost and no Chapter of Adeptus Astartes or even the Imperial Navy had any remaining. At least, that was what Arrun had believed. Infidels were almost mythical. Any such vessels still flying were antiquities left over from the time of the Great Heresy.

'Confirm. Infidels. They are not responding on any known vox frequency codes. They are not transmitting verified data.' It chattered mechanically, turning to interface with the other console. 'Augury data confirms identification. Both vessels recorded as Infidel Raiders. Records are incomplete.'

Infidel Raiders. One of the escort vessels commonly favoured by a number of Traitor Legions of the Adeptus Astartes. The servitor made another chattering noise as it calculated distances. 'They are not yet in weapons range. They are holding position just beyond our ship's capability.'

'Clever,' muttered Arrun. 'Very clever.' He moved across the bridge to the schemata that were displayed as a shivering, unstable hololith. Just like that in the strategium, it showed the positions of the fleet currently deployed within the Rift. He turned to the tech-priest maintaining the image.

'Improve quality.'

The tech-priest nodded and, murmuring words to the Omnissiah, turned a few dials on the console that projected the image. It came into sharper focus and Arrun traced a line across the bottom section of the display. It rippled in the wake of his hand's passage and the tech-priest shot him an unseen look of irritation as it fiddled again with the dials.

'They crossed in through the fringes of the Rift,' Arrun said, more to himself than any of the others. 'It's used a lull in augury sweeps. Whoever this is, they planned ahead.' He turned to one of the humans standing close by. 'Muren, make a note of that and make arrangements to contact one of our smaller patrols to work that area.'

'Yes, captain.'

Arrun tapped at a small console, his fingers moving with nimble, practiced ease and on the rendered hololith before him, the flickering representation of the *Quicksilver* relocated from its current position to the point that it should have been. He similarly moved a number of the other ships to new locations on the plan and scowled deeply.

'We are the only ship in range should the need arise and unless they make a move from their current position...'

Arrun stood away from the plinth and turned to the occulus. At this distance, the two ships were little more than dots on an endless sea of stars.

If what the servitor stated was correct, they were Infidel-class. The escort ships were well known as being favoured by the Legions who had turned their backs on the light of the Imperium. That, combined with the continued lack of communication and the generally hostile manner of their approach suggested that they were more likely than not perfect fits to that profile. The mathematics needed no further thought. This, more likely than not, was enough to make a decision.

Arrun's brow furrowed and a surge of hatred bubbled up in the pit of his stomach. Cool, clinical detachment overrode his moment of anger and he began to bark orders. Every bellowed command was obeyed immediately, without question. Daerys Arrun ran a smooth, ordered ship and his crew, Space Marine, human and servitor alike, bowed before his will without hesitation. In a moment, the irksome chanting of the tech-priests had been blissfully drowned out by the overall volume of noise.

'Enemy craft are accelerating. Augury readings are returning power spikes in their forward lances.'

'Bring us around. We'll meet them head on. Run the design through the cogitator. I want every weakness brought up. Whoever they are, they're unannounced and uninvited. I will not stand for interlopers in my system.' He clenched his hand into a fist. 'Alert the gun decks. Load all cannons. Present forward batteries and prepare to fire on my word.' He paused briefly. 'Just in case.'

'Marks are continuing to increase speed, but they are no longer on a direct heading. They're still holding just on the edge of firing range.'

'This is the captain. All hands hear this. Take us out of geostationary orbit. We'll...'

'Captain Arrun?' The only questioning tone so far came from the Prognosticator at his side. Arrun turned. The Prognosticator was so quiet, he'd not even noticed the psyker's arrival. 'What are you doing?'

'They won't come to us, Prognosticator. So I'm taking the fight to them. They're piloted by traitors. I won't suffer their kind to continue their mockery of an existence.'

The Prognosticator looked out of the viewport. The two ships were moving ever closer. Brand stared at the screen as though his psychic powers could somehow reach through the womb of plasteel and armaplas that surrounded them. Indeed, having seen what his psyker advisor was capable of, Arrun didn't rate the chances of the ships had they been a very little closer. Brand's eyes burned with a momentary fervour.

'You should use caution,' he said in his whispering voice. 'The shape of the future is unclear to me. I should read the signs.'

'Understood, Prognosticator.' Arrun felt a moment's uncertainty at Brand's words. The Prognosticator's connection with the Emperor's will was not a thing to be taken lightly, but he would not permit this sortie to continue without intervention. He hesitated briefly. Protocol demanded that the Prognosticator cast the auguries, that they wait for the Emperor's guidance in this.

Daerys Arrun, however shrewd and brilliant his strategic mind may have been, was also exceptionally arrogant. He had neither the time nor the inclination to observe protocol in this instance. He took a deep breath and shot Brand a peculiar glance that was somewhere between defiant and apologetic.

'We don't have the time, Prognosticator. In this, you will need to trust to *my* judgement for once.'

If the other was shocked at this blatant disregard for what was undoubtedly the strongest of the Silver Skulls traditions, he did not show it. Instead, he turned away and took a seat to the right of the command throne. His hard green eyes gave away nothing of his reaction to the insult that had just been made to his face.

'Orders, Captain Arrun?'

Aware that he had just transgressed and that there would be a discussion on the matter later, Arrun turned away from the Prognosticator and nodded.

'Power up shields and begin loading prow cannons. Cogitator operators, begin calculating firing solutions' He took a deep breath. 'Reroute power from the Resurgent banks.'

'Captain, you will delay the...' Correlan's voice snapped over the ship-wide vox, but Arrun ignored it.

'Yes, captain.'

Scant seconds later, the huge strike cruiser hauled herself free of Gildar Secundus's orbit and began cutting through space, closing the distance between herself and the Infidels with ponderous majesty.

THERE HAD BEEN much trade activity in the Gildar system in the past few weeks. Many cargo vessels had come and gone, each without incident, each without question. Gildar Secundus was the usual destination but there were other, smaller worlds in the sector that received regular shipments from all across the Imperium.

None of them had been suspicious. None of them had raised any call for alarm. All of the ships that came into the system conducted their business swiftly and without lingering too long. It was possibly the presence of the Silver Skulls that encouraged such expediency, but it worked. They came, they transacted and they left.

But the ships did not always leave with the same numbers aboard with which they had arrived. Even this was not by itself cause for misgiving. People came and went all the time. Sometimes, larger vessels travelled through, bringing and removing regiments of young men and women to their assignments with the Imperial Guard in other systems. All these were entirely normal activities. Nobody paid attention when a ship came in with two hundred souls aboard and left with one hundred and eighty.

Had Daerys Arrun scraped beneath the surface, he would not like what lay there.

He would have found tiny things. But tiny things that came together to form a far bigger picture. A team of prospectors returning to the habs of Gildar Secundus from the plains had mysteriously disappeared. Local law enforcement officers reporting a spate of murders that shared no apparent reason or commonality. Mechanical failures that caused system shutdowns and rolling blackouts. All small things that happened with systematic regularity on Imperial worlds. There was nothing unusual in it. But thanks to tireless planning and effortless cunning, on the many worlds of the Gildar system, things were beginning to fall into place.

THE WIND HOWLED around the comms-tower which served the Primus-Phi refinery. It whipped up and bore the endless red dust with it. It pattered constantly against the armaplas of the window, scoring and pitting it. Not that the panel served much of a purpose; during these storms, it reduced visibility to nothing more than a dark red haze. Officer Evett shivered at the thought of going out into the howling dust storm and thumbed the rune that closed the armoured shutters. The interior lumen-strips flickered briefly as the heavy panels locked into place, but at least the eerie screech of the relentless gale outside was instantly muted.

'Your turn for the recaff run,' he grinned at his subordinate who lounged back in his seat with a groan.

'Is it really my turn? Really? I could have sworn that it was yours, sir. I grabbed us some of those seed bar things from the shipment, remember?' He raised his eyebrows and gave Evett a hopeful look, about as keen as the comms-officer to venture out into the unforgiving storm.

'Nope, definitely your turn. I picked up the lho-sticks. Recaff. Now. And don't forget to close that damn bulkhead properly or we'll be shovelling dust out of the vents for days.' Evett threw himself into his seat and propped his boots up on the console, confident that there would be little to disturb him until the weather improved.

'Fine. Just don't blame me if it's cold when I get back.'

Evett replied by stretching out an arm languorously and pointed at the stairwell. The engineer groaned and dragged himself down to the maintenance room. He struggled into an enviro-suit, rebreather and visor. The refinery entrance was only a few hundred metres away, but if he had to go out, he was at least going to go out prepared.

The small barracks on the ground floor that housed the militia detachment assigned to the tower was virtually empty, the troopers no doubt engaged on one of their endless and thankless patrols. The engineer didn't envy them tonight.

'Going out?' The voice came from Trooper Bessin, seated atop his bunk.

'No, Deeko. I'm all dressed up like this for my own personal comfort and entertainment. Why would you even ask that question?'

'Great,' the soldier smirked, unfazed by the dripping sarcasm. 'Grab me some lho-sticks while you're out.'

The engineer rolled his eyes, executing a theatrical bow. 'Anything else you would like while I'm out, Oh Glorious Lord of the Imperium?'

'Yeah, some dancing girls would be nice. And maybe a large bottle of something relaxing.'

'Amasec?'

The soldier laughed; a raucous sound. 'You and your amasec! It's a big Imperium. Why don't you find something a little more creative?'

The engineer's reply was short, crude and garnered another bout of explosive laughter from the off-duty soldier. The bulkhead marking the entrance to the tower was whistling softly in the wind and a few drifts of scarlet dust had blustered over the floor. The particulate matter would need to be swept out soon before it started to clog the atmosphere filters, but the engineer certainly wasn't about to undertake the onerous task. He stumped up to the access panel and punched a few runes.

A second later the heavy portal groaned and slid to one side admitting a blast of freezing wind and dust. Still grumbling in discontent and keeping his head down to avoid the wind, the engineer moved forward. He took barely five steps before he collided with something.

Entirely filling the entrance stood a hulking figure cast in blood and shadow. Too large by far to be one of his colleagues, the engineer raised his head up. Behind the visor of the rebreather, his eyes widened in shock.

The massive creature in the gloom moved slightly and the engineer caught the faintest glimpse of something shining in the sliver of light that came from the door. Transfixed by the fractal edge of the combat knife, Engineer Schafer felt the first, searing pain of the weapon as it opened his throat from ear to ear. Before he had even hit the ground, his life's blood had already begun to drain from the expertly opened gash.

He died quickly. He was one of the lucky ones.

'STARBOARD MARK IS accelerating to attack speed – her weapons are primed.'

On the *Dread Argent*, Arrun had taken his seat in the command throne. He leaned forward, his massive shoulders hunched with the tension of the moment. 'Focus your attention on that one, but do not lose sight of what her sister ship is up to.'

'She's training her guns on us, sir.'

The captain sneered. 'A genuine shame. I'm sure Correlan and his team would have liked the opportunity to strip that ship bare and expose her secrets. Shield power?'

'Deployed at sixty-eight per cent, captain. It's the best we can get.'

The *Dread Argent* was not without her own design flaws. She was old, but she was reliable. In the decades that Arrun had known her, she had never been perfect. He mused on it only briefly before everything once again became a babble of noise.

'Unacceptable. Divert more power from the port plasma coils.'

'Compliance.'

'Cannons loading.'

'Get me the Head Astropath. I need a message sending to the fleet.'

'Compliance.'

'And don't lose sight of that port ship. Continue tracking.'

'Augury glitch!' One of the human crew applied the ritual blow, slamming the palm of his hand against the end of the gas-lens scope that he was using to track the second Infidel. He swore. 'Tech-priest, I need you here.'

The tech-priest's subsequent chant, soft and barely audible underscored everything else that was taking place. Arrun's senses could separate and ignore it through a combination of years of practise and his own mental acuity. The tech-priest blessed the gas-lens viewer and stepped back. The serf checked its functionality and nodded. The tech-priest moved on to his next duty.

'Infidel Alpha still holding position.'

'Target Beta is powering up her weapons.'

'Shield power?'

'Shield generators now at eighty per cent, sir.'

Arrun drew a breath. Eighty per cent would have to be enough. They were an Imperial strike cruiser and the odds were heavily in their favour that they could withstand a bombardment from the Infidel and remain intact. But Arrun had seen odds defied before.

'What is it that this runt is trying to achieve?' Prognosticator Brand also leaned forward in his seat. 'Is it a distraction tactic, perhaps?' The question was entirely rhetorical, but Arrun turned to face him sharply.

'A distraction from what?' His tone was ice-cool and the unease he felt at the Prognosticator's suggestion was not at all welcome.

'An objective viewpoint, brother-captain. He has made his move and you have responded by deviating from your orbit.' Brand studied Arrun carefully. 'Do you think that may be intentional?' The Prognosticator got to his feet and moved across to the cogitator banks. His eyes scanned the data that was there. 'Is there anything – anything at all that might have slipped in behind our backs whilst they were turned?'

'I... haven't analysed the data yet, my lord...' The serf at the controls stared up at the Prognosticator anxiously. His eyes flicked to Arrun and back as the captain rose from his command throne and joined his advisor. The look on the captain's face was bordering on infuriated.

'What exactly are you suggesting, Brand?' The two giants towered above the serf and he visibly cringed at their proximity. The tension generated as the warrior faced the psyker was intense and uncomfortable for the others on the bridge. The sheer challenge in Arrun's tone was enough for the human serf to desperately want to get out of their way.

As it transpired, whatever the Prognosticator may have been suggesting would have to wait.

'Starboard Infidel has opened fire. I repeat – incoming lance fire!' The words were screamed out over the ever-present hubbub of noise in the deck.

'All hands brace for impact.' Arrun's brief anger with the Prognosticator was forgotten in the moment and he crossed the deck in several strides to the weapon bank. 'Return fire, Meron. Blast that bastard out of the stars.'

'Yes, sir.'

Meron's hand slammed down on the runic keyboards that operated the cannon launch systems and the *Dread Argent* spat her deadly forward payload across the vast reaches of space towards the Infidel.

The impact of the other ship's attack of chance went barely registered beyond a slight shaking of the Silver Skulls strike cruiser. The void shields crackled and rippled alarmingly. Arrun knew his ship well enough to note that a slight shaking meant a reasonable amount of damage had been absorbed. The Infidel would have no opportunity to shoot at them a second time; the missiles that the *Dread Argent* had launched would reach it and destroy it before that happened.

'Impact in three... two... one...'

Time stood still as the occulus blossomed with the glaring

white light of the Infidel as her plasma engines detonated. A vast shower of metal debris blasted outwards from the ship, some thrown as far as the *Dread Argent* itself. Arrun watched the destruction of the enemy vessel with ambivalence. They were strong little ships, certainly – but neither had nor never would be, a match for the might of the Imperium.

'Report.' Arrun's voice broke the silence. He knew what the answer would be, but protocol demanded it.

'Target destroyed.' The serf tapped his monitor screen as it flickered rebelliously at him. 'Confirmed. Target destroyed.'

'What of the port ship?'

'It's fleeing, sir. Should we give the order for pursuit?'

Arrun hesitated and turned his head sideways so that he could see the Prognosticator. Brand had resumed sitting back in his chair, his hood drawn over his eyes once again. It was an affectation, certainly, but it had the effect of lending the psyker an extra air of mystery he little needed. The Prognosticator's head shook. It was a barely perceptible movement, but Arrun knew it for what it was.

'No,' he said. 'No. We will let them go. The Fates have decreed that our job here is done. I do not believe they will be returning in a hurry now they have witnessed our capabilities.' The Master of the Fleet dragged a hand across his jaw thoughtfully. 'But conversely, we must not allow that to make us complacent. I want security on the Gildar system stepped up. I want regular reports from the main comms officers on those worlds. Arrange for the astropaths to spread word amongst the fleet within the Gildar Rift. Have them remain on full alert.'

Arrun strode across the bridge, orders continuing to fall from his lips. 'I want vigilance on all vessels into the system. Inform those shipping outbound craft that there are raiders operating in the area. Tell them to be on their guard. And send a further message to the home world. Inform Lord Commander Argentius that our return will be delayed a little longer.'

He turned to Brand. 'Those traitors are a poison that will not be allowed to spread in this system. You and I may not see eye to eye on some things, but this, I am sure, you agree with.' There was a burning hatred in his eyes. Arrun knew that Brand, just like him, found traitors amongst their own kin to be anathema. 'We will run them out of this system and those who do not run fast enough...' He turned back again to the viewscreen and his face twisted in a grim smile. 'Then they will suffer the consequences.'

HE WAS A creature of the stars, a creature of bloodshed and glory. His long-ago rebirth into a life of war defined him. It was what he had once aspired to become and what he now embodied. This enforced inactivity had been nothing short of torture. Yet his master had decreed he wait until the optimal moment. Taemar had served under his master's command for long enough to know that what he wanted, he got.

At least he was not alone. There were several of his comrades on this forsaken rock with him, all of whom were suffering the same effects of inactivity. For now, they were hidden, kept far away from the promethium refineries that dominated so much of the habitable areas of Gildar Secundus. They had put down on the planet several days before and as of yet, had received nothing to suggest the plan had been put into action.

'What is it that you seek, brother? Up there in the endless dark of night?'

The voice came from over his right shoulder and Taemar turned at the formal words and almost archaic tone. His shaved head bowed in a gesture of deep respect for the other.

'I merely search the stars for a sign, my lord.'

'Do you doubt that our master will signal us when the time is right? Patience is a virtue, Taemar. You of all people should know that. He will not rush a masterpiece that he has spent so long creating. It has only been days. It will be worth waiting for. The Silver Skulls are predictable and foolish, slaves to their precious routines. They insist upon allowing themselves to be governed by the skeins of Fate. Have a little faith in our leader's plans. Never doubt for one moment that he will play them right into our hands.'

Lord Apothecary Garreon of the Red Corsairs smiled. It was a slow, cruel smile that held no humour. He was taller than most of his comrades but with a rangy leanness that would have made him seem thin had he not been a Space Marine. Sharp, angular cheekbones stood out prominently in a scarred face whose most striking feature was the eyes. An impassive, unreadable dark brown, the colour of Garreon's irises were so dark that his pupils were barely visible. His hair was a tawny brown mane that fell to his shoulders, streaked through with grey that hinted at advancing years. It was a face that was filled with great intelligence but was also underlined with obvious cruelty. It told in the play of the quizzical way he tipped his head in a birdlike manner when he spoke. He always seemed to be questioning, even when he was simply conversing. It told also in the way his tongue would run across his thin lips when he was describing an experiment. One of the many battle scars that he bore pulled his expression into a permanent sneer that seemed to suit his manner.

Taemar had seen that face twist in thought and insatiable curiosity as the Lord Apothecary worked on one of his subjects. He knew how keenly intelligent Garreon could be. He was also acutely aware of how cruel he could be.

The Red Corsairs called him 'The Corpsemaster', not because he harboured any desire to see the dead walk, but because he took a pathological interest in the biology of the dying and the dead, both of whom provided him with a harvest of precious gene-seed. He believed, as had many Apothecaries throughout the history of the Adeptus Astartes, that the future of their brotherhood lay in a better understanding of human genetics and xenobiology. He performed regular dissections on enemies and Red Corsairs both – in some cases whilst his subjects were still living. He could keep his victims alive for a phenomenal length of time, reducing them to skeletal, still-living things that begged for a release that was an eternity coming.

Taemar resumed staring up into the star-studded skies

of Gildar Secundus. Huron Blackheart's plans were often impossible to fathom, but that was part of what made him so brilliant. Insane, certainly – but only when viewed from a certain perspective. 'If I might ask, Lord Apothecary, what is your particular interest in these deluded weaklings?'

'The Silver Skulls... hmm.' Garreon ran a long finger over his jaw in a thoughtful gesture. 'Predominately, their psykers. The particular genetic strain seems to grant them an uncanny ability to perceive the future. Whether it's a genuine precognition, a true link to the Emperor's will or simply clever sleight-of-hand and trickery on their part remains to be proven... but history would suggest that they are either well advised, or exceptionally lucky.'

His lips curled upwards into a smile. Taemar, still staring upwards, did not see it. 'Also, they are dying out. Their numbers grow ever smaller. They are a forgotten, far-flung, distant Chapter of the Adeptus Astartes. You don't recall the Astral Claws, do you Taemar? You were not one of my brothers when things changed irrevocably.'

Taemar made a grunt of affirmation. His roots had not been with the Astral Claws. Once, a lifetime ago, he had belonged to another Chapter. But the less he thought about his own betrayal, the less it bothered him. He'd fought and murdered his way through the Red Corsairs to the lofty position of one of Blackheart's champions. History suggested that this was no coveted position – death was his only reward and well he knew it.

'The Silver Skulls are stalwart warriors. They are fierce and savage in battle. I believe they should be...' Garreon tailed off, considering how best to end the sentence. 'I believe forming some sort of accord with them would be a beneficial arrangement.'

'You seek to turn them to our cause?' Finally, the Apothecary had Taemar's attention. He looked around. 'You think there is even the remotest of chances that they will do that?'

'They are arrogant. Proud. Yes, I believe there is a chance.' Garreon joined Taemar in seeking the stars above. 'There always is. Mark well the Silver Skulls, Taemar. You and your men seek to create death and destruction. But they will revisit such behaviour on us in kind. I ask that you try your best to bring me some live ones. I suspect that there is much they can teach us.'

'As you wish, my lord.'

ANOTHER SHIP SAILED the empyrean, its destination fixed and certain.

His personal chambers were always gloomy without so much as a lumen-globe to light the way. He preferred to spend his private hours in the shadows and the darkness.

The messenger, a grovelling, wretched slave by the name of Lem who had lost the drawing of straws, stood in the pitch darkness, trying to stem the quivering in his spine. Despite the fact that he had been sent down to deliver good news, they had still lost a ship. This would undoubtedly incur the master's displeasure.

It was silent in the chamber. But it was a loaded silence; the calm before the storm. The hesitation right before the explosive discharge from a bolt pistol detonated. The stillness of the air before a torrential thunderstorm. His master's discontent was a thing denied a voice.

Something brushed past Lem's cheek in the darkness and he flinched. His imagination. It was just his imagination. He squeezed his eyes closed and tried to control the trembling walls of his bladder.

All the while, the noise. A rhythmic drumming. The ring of metal on stone. *One... two... three... four. One... two... three... four...* Denied vision and thus unable to relate anything to the noise, Lem found it disconcerting.

After several long, agonising moments, he forced his eyes open again. He could barely make out the shape seated opposite him, nothing more than a bulky outline in the darkness, but now it seemed to move. The sound of scraping ceramite and the buzz and hiss of servos and hydraulics compensating confirmed his suspicion. The master was moving into a different position. He had remained silent during the delivery of the news and Lem had dared to hope that he might leave with his life intact.

'Excellent. A confirmation that all is as it should be. All our forces are gathered, everything is in order. We will take this ship.' The master's voice, a low, predatory growl, was thick with saliva, coming as it did through metal teeth that had long since replaced anything natural that had ever grown in his jaw.

They were only a few words, but Lem could feel the sheer menace implicit in them. He nodded – a futile gesture in this darkness – and backed towards the door. As it slid open on old, grinding gears, a sliver of light from the corridor beyond sliced through the room. It fell on the impossibly huge metal power claw of the leader of the Red Corsairs as he drummed it against the arm of his command throne. Lem caught a glimpse of glinting, razor-sharp teeth as though the master's mouth bared in a parody of a grin.

Then the door ground closed and left Huron Blackheart alone in his own darkness.

FOUR
TROPHIES

His MIND WAS open.

Prognosticator Brand sat in his private arming chamber, his eyes closed but every one of his senses on full alert. Like all of the Prognosticatum, he advocated meditation as a necessary method to clear the mind of emotional clutter and to ensure a free flow of psychic energies. Many of the Chapter's warriors also practised the method with varying degrees of success.

Brand had served alongside Daerys Arrun for a long time and the two had always been polar opposites. Where Arrun was spontaneous and rash, Brand had been consistently level and measured in his approach. For the most part, they complemented one another well. The basic differences in their personalities brought out the best in both of them. This time, however, Arrun's impetuousness had led him to blatantly cross a line that the Silver Skulls had drawn in the sand centuries ago. An insult directed at a Prognosticator was to insult their very way of life.

He would be here, soon. Brand knew he would. He could sense the captain's approach long before he turned up at the door. He could *see* the other warrior's consciousness, like a pinprick of radiant light moving through the map of the *Dread Argent* he held in his mind. Three tiers away now. He was close.

Brand sighed inwardly. Earlier, on the bridge, he had felt the shape of Arrun's barely contained anger. It had been a wild thing; a thousand birds battering endlessly against the cage constructed from his own iron will. Like many native Varsavians, Daerys Arrun was in possession of a fine temper. However, unlike some other Silver Skulls warriors, Arrun had learned to keep his temper largely reined in.

Two tiers.

It was easy enough to read Arrun. His anger had dissipated. He was still out of balance, but that primal rage had been replaced by something far less bestial. Something that Brand could not put a name to. Robbed of the correct word, he likened it to another series of emotions entirely.

Shame.

Regret.

Guilt.

Brand could sense all of these as the captain approached his chamber. He called out permission to enter before Arrun could even ask for it. The Prognosticator remained seated, cross-legged in the centre of his room, his back to the door, not turning to face his guest.

'Daerys.'

'Prognosticator.'

There was a lengthy silence following the formal greeting. Brand deliberately took his time completing his murmured litanies and praises before finally rising slowly to his feet and turning to face the captain. For a warrior who had faced countless enemies in his time, the well-respected captain of Fourth Company was looking decidedly nervous.

'You're fidgeting like an aspirant, Daerys.' Despite the severity of the situation, Brand was deeply amused at the manner of his captain's subservience. 'Be still. You are making me tired.'

When Arrun spoke, his words came in a rush, something

that only likened him still further to a youth a fraction of his age. 'I crave forgiveness, Prognosticator. The manner in which I spoke to you earlier...'

'You were in the middle of doing what it is that you were born to do. It does not matter.' Brand waved a hand dismissively. 'Between us, there is no bad feeling.'

'No, Prognosticator, no. It does matter.' Arrun ran a hand across his scarred scalp and his eyes met Brand's. 'We have been battle-brothers for many years. We are *friends*.'

'Aye,' confirmed the Prognosticator, watching Arrun carefully. His emotional state was uncannily out of balance. Not for the first time in recent months, Brand wondered if the erstwhile Master of the Fleet was spreading himself too thinly. Even the brightest and the best had their limits. Arrun was close to his. 'Aye, we are friends, brother.'

'I pushed the barriers of that friendship earlier. I showed you great disrespect.'

'Daerys, let it go. You are here now and you are apologetic. I accept that apology. It does not matter.'

'It *does* matter!' Arrun knew that he must sound like a raw, untried aspirant, but this was deeply important to him. He held his tone in check and took another deep, cleansing breath. The Prognosticator smiled inwardly. Arrun had always been like this. Quick to temper, much quicker to regret. Brand relented, not wishing to drag the agony out for his captain any longer than necessary. His role was not only to advise but was also to give proper spiritual guidance in accordance with his position as Chaplain-Librarian. Not all companies within the Silver Skulls had their own Prognosticator; they were a rare breed indeed. Chaplains within the Chapter were no less valuable or less respected, but it was undeniable that the Prognosticators and the rest of the Prognosticatum steered the Chapter's course.

'Very well, Captain Arrun. If it is so very important, if you cannot resume the prosecution of your duty without it, then you may have that which you crave. You transcended the boundary of respect that exists between the Prognosticatum and the rest of the Chapter. You are aware of that fact and I also know you well enough to be aware that any penance I dole out to you will be nowhere near as harsh as the punishment you will put yourself through.' The Prognosticator studied the captain thoughtfully. They had known one another for many years and as Arrun had already observed, they were more than battle-brothers. They were friends.

'I forgive you, Daerys.' He laid his own hand on Arrun's bowed head in benediction. 'Now let it go. It is done.'

Watching the relief flood through Arrun's body was like watching a balloon deflate. All the stress and tension flowed from his shoulders and although he still held himself rigidly to attention – a soldier's stance – he allowed himself to relax a little.

Within the Silver Skulls Chapter, those who represented the council of the Prognosticatum were revered second only to Lord Commander Argentius himself. Over the years, people had been put to death for less.

'Walk with me, brother-captain,' Brand said, after a period of peace had passed between them. 'I propose that you take some time in the chapel and restore the equilibrium to your troubled soul.' It was a simple offer, but one which Arrun gratefully accepted with an abrupt nod.

The two warriors fell into easy lock-step as they walked; the one grave-faced and shaven, the other with his long hair falling to his shoulders. The Prognosticator's expression was benevolent; almost kind. Yet his emerald eyes remained hard and impassive. He generated an invisible aura of calm that radiated to Arrun, settling his worries like a soothing balm. By the time they reached the chapel all of his earlier uncertainties had melted away.

The chapel was cradled in the deepest recesses of the mighty strike cruiser. It was a place of quiet contemplation and, as the Prognosticator had so eloquently put, the ideal place to restore balance to a troubled soul. Just the sight of the stone effigy of the far-distant Emperor of Mankind was always enough to calm the angriest of Silver Skulls. Just that visual aid that reminded them of their purpose. The reminder that all they did was in His name and was for the ultimate betterment of mankind.

There were a few other battle-brothers here, knelt in silent prayer. The area was strictly off-limits to the human crew, although servitors were permitted entry for maintenance purposes. This was one of the few places on the *Dread Argent* where a Space Marine could go to be reminded of who he was. It was a sanctuary and refuge and Arrun welcomed its comparative peace. Only the constant thrum of the ship's engines and the drone of the atmosphere scrubbers invaded the sanctity and they were welcome, familiar sounds.

Arrun moved to stand before the statue of the Emperor and touched a hand to his left cheek, where the sign of the aquila had been tattooed. It had been the first tattoo he had taken on achieving the rank of captain and whilst many other honours marked his body, it was the aquila that he was most proud of.

As was his way, he intoned the Varsavia Prayer to the Departed, a Silver Skulls tradition that had come to the Chapter from the long-dead shamans of Varsavia. The seemingly endless list of names he recited from memory were all brothers with whom he had fought alongside. Just as Apothecary Ryarus carried the names of the fallen in Gothic, copperplate script on the canvas of his body, Captain Arrun carried their names in his mind.

There were many others. So many Silver Skulls who had been lost to the enemies of man over the millennia. Those from other companies. Those he had known of by reputation but had never met. In his prayers, he remembered them as well.

He kept his voice low, out of deep respect for his fellow Space Marines who had come here to make their own genuflections. Yet it was still gratifying, as he reached some of the more recent dead, to hear his brothers murmur the names in unison with him. They were good men, all of them. Pride for his company and for his warriors fluttered in his breast and restored his sense of purpose.

Once his prayer was concluded, Arrun allowed himself

the rare luxury of letting his thoughts drift idly. He was soothed by the sound and rhythm of his own breathing and was rewarded with feeling the pulse of life through his own veins. His head remained bowed as he knelt before the vigilant presence of the Emperor and the words of Fourth Company's creed fell from his lip in a hushed whisper.

'Success is commemorated. Failure is only remembered.'

The lightest of breezes lifted the company banner from the wall, sending a shuddering ripple across its surface and distorting it. Arrun raised his head. Brand had moved to a darkened recess in the far wall of the chapel where a number of silver-coated skulls were standing on plinths. Each was adorned with a plaque detailing the name of the battle-brother who had taken the trophy and the date of the victory. A Chapter tradition, collecting the skulls of mighty enemies was more than just ostentation and pride. It was a measure of a company's strength and honour.

Fourth Company had many such trophies. Many of them had been taken by the captain, deaths delivered at the end of his favoured lightning claws. The Custodes Cruor, the Chapter's artisans, extracted the skulls from their former owners and coated them in molten silver. Each one was an exquisitely-wrought work of art, covered in spirals and whorls. Tribal markings, sometimes matching the tattoos of the brother who had slain the fallen enemy were embossed on the surface, marking each trophy as the rightful property of that brother's original tribe. Every skull was another mark of honour for the battle-brother who had taken it. Each one represented another vanquished foe.

For every skull there was a singularly unique memory. From the massive skull of the ork warboss to the slender, elongated one that still had part of its spine attached. That one had once belonged to a genestealer. Every trophy came with its own story. When not deployed on manoeuvres, or during the long periods of space travel that carried them to their next battle, the Silver Skulls regularly gathered to tell the stories of their conquests. Those with a flair for the dramatic could hold their battle-brothers captivated, regardless of how many times the story had been told.

Rising to his feet and absently dusting down his loose ship-board robes, Arrun strode across the chapel to join the Prognosticator. Brand was studying one of the skulls with a sombre expression on his face. His own name was engraved on the plaque beneath. He looked up at the captain's approach and a slight smile crossed his face.

'Your soul is more balanced now,' he observed. 'Your anger and control constantly vie with one another, Daerys. It is a flaw in your personality that hinders you at times. You have regained mastery of the anger once again. Excellent.'

'Aye, Prognosticator, they do sometimes come into conflict. I apologise once more for my behaviour. There was no excuse.'

'Stop apologising.' Brand ran one hand over the surface of his own trophy. The skull, as Arrun knew, was that of a Chaos Space Marine. A traitor of the Alpha Legion who had attempted to infiltrate the Silver Skulls many years past. Arrun knew that Brand harboured a special loathing for the conspirators who had turned their backs on the Emperor's light and embraced the Ruinous Powers.

'It would seem, brother, that I am not the only one troubled.' Arrun considered the Prognosticator. 'Do you wish to speak of it?'

'A... feeling. Nothing more. I have not spent time amongst the battle trophies for a while. And yet I felt a stirring of memory. With that memory comes a hazy sense of things to come. It is hard to describe to one without the Emperor's Gift. A *shape*, Daerys. With undefined edges. Chaos comes. Perhaps, perhaps not. Without time divining the matter it is never so easy to be sure. Other Prognosticators...'

Brand trailed off. Other Prognosticators were younger, cannier, more connected to the conduits of psychic prediction than he was. He had always known that he was not amongst the ranks of the Emperor's most favoured. His ability was... adequate. Nothing more. But it served well enough. His own perceived failings must never be revealed to any outside of the Prognosticatum. The entire Chapter looked to their psykers for guidance. If the fact that they did not all possess the greatest of skill became common knowledge, it would cause unrest. In this instance, adequate was enough.

'Let Chaos come, Prognosticator. We have defeated it once. We will do so again. We will be ready.'

'Yes.' Brand removed his hand from the skull. Should his slightly uncomfortable feeling become something more tangible, then yes. Fourth Company would stand ready to face whatever came at them.

He felt a surprisingly fervent hope that nothing would come. The Resurgent Project was close to completion. Like Arrun, his pride in the project was enormous and whilst his input had largely been minimal, his counsel had been invaluable.

Together, the warrior and the psyker left the chapel and began heading back towards the corridor.

The ship-wide vox crackled into static-charged life.

'Captain Arrun... your presence is required on the bridge, my lord.' There was a pause; little more than a heartbeat. 'We have a new incursion. Augury returns are showing no power to the newcomer's main plasma drives. She's just drifting. Looks like a derelict.'

Arrun's eyebrows rose. 'Perhaps you should learn to trust your feelings, Prognosticator.' Brand inclined his head, wishing that the brief taste of a possible future had not happened. The captain activated the vox-bead in his ear.

'On my way. Anything more you can tell me? Designation?'

'Yes, sir.' There was a faint hint of disbelief in the vox-operator's voice. 'Livery is that of the Space Wolves Chapter. We have run the ship's markings through the cogitators. We've made a positive identification.'

Brand and Arrun exchanged looks. The Sons of Russ had been known to periodically pass through the Gildar Rift, but they were always diligent about making their intentions known. The Silver Skulls had a long-standing comradeship with the Chapter. The two shared a number of similar traits. Arrun felt his ire begin to creep back. He would not be best

pleased with his opposite number for this breach of protocol.

'What is the ship?'

'The *Wolf of Fenris*, sir. She's transmitting a distress message.'

THE WOLF HAD been beautiful once. She had been a ship
without peer, a powerful creation which struck fear into the
hearts of the Imperium's enemies. As one of the strike cruisers under the command of the mighty Space Wolves, the
Wolf of Fenris was a harbinger. When she arrived retribution
almost invariably came in her wake.

Now, she was dying. A wounded leviathan drifting aimlessly before his eyes, she was bleeding her metaphorical
life out into the Gildar Rift. Holes were punched in her hull
indicating that there had been boarding activity. The scar-
ring and pitting of battle damage was clearly visible on her
exterior, even from this distance.

The moment Daerys Arrun set his sights on her, his hearts
sank and a small groan escaped his lips. The damage that
had been caused to the ship was bad enough, but it was the
thought of the desperate state their cousins must be in to
have limped from whatever battle that had reduced them
to this.

'Relay the transmission you received.' When he finally
found his voice, it was barely more than a whisper. His
hands systematically clenched and unclenched. By his side,
Brand stared impassively out of the viewport. His head was
thick with the psychic chatter that always accompanied
moments of uncertainty. Ripples of power coruscated across
the crystal mesh of his psychic hood as he filtered out the
tangled emotions of the *Dread Argent's* crew. Confusion,
uncertainty, trepidation... all of these were unwanted and
impractical emotions that served no useful purpose. One by
one, the psyker filtered them and kept his thoughts focused.

'Compliance.' The servitor's mechanical arms reached out,
connecting with the vox console to which it was slaved. It
operated its post with deft ease. After a few moments, a

broken and distorted message drifted across the bridge.

'... Agna... Space Wolves Chapter, Fourth Great Company. We were boarded and comprom... Strike force led by... fought them. Gnryll Bluetooth is dead. Our ship damag...' The message broke off into static and then resumed from the beginning.

'Is that all?' As silence settled once again on the bridge, Arrun's hands remained balled into fists. 'That is all that you can extract?'

'Affirmative,' replied the servitor in its monotone way. 'Transmission is thirty-six point seven seconds in duration. Seventy-six per cent of data has been corrupted by...' Arrun took a step towards it. Had it been truly human, it would have doubtlessly flinched at the giant's approach. As it was, it merely swivelled its head up to meet the captain's gaze and completed its sentence. '...interference from the debris field.'

'Filter the signal more effectively.' Arrun pointed a finger at the indifferent servitor. 'Extract more of it. Slave the augury cogitators for processing if it is more efficient.' He turned to the helm. 'Hold course for now. Try to reach Sergeant Agna on the ship-to-ship vox. By the Emperor's grace, some of the Sons of Russ may still be alive. It is our duty to lend our aid to them in this time of need.'

Arrun stepped back from the console allowing the servitor room to perform its charged task. 'Brand, round up the senior officers and meet me in the strategium. I think we need to discuss our best course of action.'

'As my captain commands.' The psyker's head lowered graciously, but Arrun had stormed off the bridge already. With another of those inward sighs that seemed to be more frequent lately, Brand headed off to find the officers, disappointed and discomfited that the captain's moment of calm had been shattered once again.

'WE CANNOT JUST leave them drifting through the Gildar Rift.' It was a redundant statement, but it was made anyway. 'At the very least, even if our cousins are all dead on board the

Wolf, we need to reclaim it.' The words were spoken with confidence, despite their almost innocent naivety.

Seven squad sergeants were seated at the huge table in the strategium, each one eager to prove his worth and each one with very different viewpoints.

'Thank you for that observation, Matteus. I'd not considered that eventuality.' Arrun shot a glowering look at the young sergeant, who sat back in his chair, duly chastised. Sometimes it frustrated Arrun that so many of the squad commanders were so young. The Silver Skulls numbers had been low for many years, but they were at least relatively consistent. It was inevitable that the older warriors would eventually be replaced. But these fresh-faced, eager warriors lacked so much experience. He bit back further sarcasm after a look from Brand. The psyker knew well what his captain was thinking. It was a regret shared by many of the older warriors. Brand's unspoken words drifted across his thoughts.

The old must give way to the young eventually, brother.

Arrun absorbed the psychic message instantly. They were words he and Brand shared regularly when they indulged in a rare moment of peace, seated together over a shared bottle of Varsavian wine in the captain's quarters.

'We need to make a decision swiftly, Prognosticator.'

He scowled slightly and dropped a data-slate on the table with a loud *bang*. 'It has also been brought to my attention that the comms officer at the Primus-Phi refinery did not file his report this morning. Whilst this is nothing to necessarily be concerned about, I feel that my instincts should take precedence in this matter. There is something not right about this. Too many oddities occurring at one time raise my suspicions.'

The captain turned to one of his sergeants. 'Porteus, I want you to take Squad Carnelian down to the surface and investigate.'

'Yes, sir.'

'Get under way now. I want you and your squad on a Thunderhawk and on your way down to the planet before we break orbit.'

Porteus rose and made the sign of the aquila, first to the Prognosticator, who returned the salute. He repeated the gesture for the captain whose distraction meant that he did not return it. He merely continued the meeting, effectively dismissing Porteus, who took his cue and descended from the strategium.

'As for the *Wolf of Fenris*... I propose we send two squads over. I will make a suggestion, but I would appreciate your consultation of the Emperor's will in the matter.'

Brand nodded. His tarot was already in his hands and he shuffled the thin wafers gently, his eyes roving over the assembled sergeants.

'Regardless of which squads you choose, I will go as well,' spoke up Ryarus. The Apothecary was seated at the far end of the table.

'I can't allow that, Ryarus. Not this close to the completion of the project. There are other Apothecaries on board. You will stay here.' Arrun cast an eye around the table. The sergeants were all leaning forward unconsciously in a desperate effort to bring themselves to Arrun's attention. He allowed himself the smallest of smiles. At least he would never have to ask for volunteers.

'Matteus, Hakan... you will take your squads across to the *Wolf of Fenris* with a recovery team. Once you have secured the ship, I will deploy servitors and tech-adepts to do what they can in terms of salvaging the ship and making it ready for transit. Ryarus, select two of your team to send with them. Brand, do you think we should send young Baeus?'

'I think given the Space Wolves general opinion on my psychic brethren, antagonising them may not be for the best. However, given the circumstances, a psychic presence may be essential. It will help scan for survivors.' His tact and diplomacy was admirable. He never once used the words 'rescue mission'.

'Excellent point,' Arrun replied. 'Well made. Baeus goes.'

In their past dealings, the Space Wolves had shown a strange sort of tolerance for the Prognosticatum of the Silver Skulls. Whilst they had no love lost for the psychic children of the far-flung God-Emperor, they found the divination methods of the Silver Skulls more in keeping with their own Rune Priests. It was still prudent not to antagonise them, though.

'Squads Kyanite and Iolite...' Brand considered the two sergeants thoughtfully as he fanned out the tarot wafers. His deft hands moved across them, their surfaces flickering as he allowed his mind to fall into an appropriate state to receive the Emperor's will. He selected several of the wafers and laid them out in a cross pattern.

All eyes were on the Prognosticator as he divined the future. He frowned a few times and moved one or two of the wafers into different positions, his head occasionally coming up from his task to consider the other sergeants. The images on the surface of the delicate crystals were not visible to those around the table. The Prognosticator's eyes seemed devoid of focus, so absorbed was he in channelling the Rites of Divination.

Eventually, Brand allowed himself to focus back on the present.

'Not Squad Iolite,' he said. 'Send Mohave.' His eyes darted to Arrun. 'And Ryarus.' In the heartbeat that followed, he added, 'it is the Emperor's will.'

Arrun considered defying the Prognosticator, but to do that would have been to go against everything that the Silver Skulls held dear and to deeply offend Brand for the second time in a day. Pinpoints of colour rose in his cheeks, but beyond that, he didn't let his anger show.

'Very well then. Mohave, not Iolite. You and Kyanite squads will deploy to the *Wolf* along with Ryarus. Assess the situation, get to the bridge and take the ship back under control. Grant our cousins as much aid as necessary. The Sons of Russ have stood at our backs many times. We will not hesitate to assist them now. Go prepared. That ship has been drifting for an unknown period of time. We know nothing about what happened, or its state. As soon as you can, check the condition of the Geller field generator.'

Arrun cast a meaningful gaze around the assembly,

checking for understanding. There were universal nods and murmurs of assent. 'Ryarus – do what you can to help their own Apothecaries. Do not linger, my brother. I need you back here swiftly. We are committed to seeing this damned project through to its end and I need my best men to be here to do it.'

'Yes, captain.' The Apothecary rose and descended the spiral stair from the strategium, heading for the apothecarion.

Matteus and Dasan inclined their heads and rose from the table to round up their respective squads and move to the arming chambers where they would begin the rituals of machine rites and weapon blessings. The remaining squad sergeants sat back in their chairs, disappointment obvious in their expressions. Arrun did not keep the smile from his face this time.

'Your turn will come, brothers. War will come soon enough for all of us.' Arrun had not yet made the announcement to the crew at large in relation to Argentius's wishes, but saw here a perfect opportunity to begin the dissemination of that information. 'When our work here is complete, we will be making a rendezvous with the *Quicksilver*. We are returning home.'

A murmur ran around the table. Being recalled to Varsavia was, as a general rule, a precursor to preparations for something on a grand scale. It was the most welcome news any of the sergeants could have hoped for. Just from the looks in their eyes and the enthusiastic manner in which they began talking to one another in low voices, Arrun felt a moment's reassurance. Yes, the old would eventually give way to the young. But the Silver Skulls were a tough breed.

They would prevail.

FIVE
CRY WOLF

Sergeant Dasan of Squad Mohave was a reticent soul. Like many of the Silver Skulls, he had grown to young manhood amongst a nomadic tribe. Many of these tribes had their own traditions and customs. In Dasan's tribe, unnecessary speaking before battle was considered borderline blasphemy. As such, he had a tendency towards being serious and silent, speaking only when necessary. It was the way of his people.

Sergeant Matteus on the other hand, was loquacious enough for the both of them.

Both were of an age; they had arrived at the fortress-monastery at Varsavia within a few short years of one another. They had trained together, fought together and received their promotions almost simultaneously. There was an old rivalry between them, but it was not malicious. It was the sort of rivalry that was encouraged by their superiors. A never-ending urge to be better than your peers drove you to greater and greater feats of strength and courage.

Right now though, Dasan would gladly have used every ounce of his strength to tear out his brother's voice box if it meant Matteus would cease his endless chatter. His brother filled the silence between conversation with unnecessary observations or words of self-perceived wisdom. Not for the first time since he had become friends with the confident, outgoing Matteus, the sergeant of Squad Mohave found himself irritated by the other. He even considered breaking his ritual silence to say something.

In the event, he did not need to.

'Still your endless tongue, brother-sergeant.' Ryarus's voice came from across the other side of the Thunderhawk. 'The only words that should be coming from your mouth right now are prayers and litanies.'

'Yes, Brother-Apothecary.' Matteus was duly chastened and fell into blissful silence. Dasan heaved a sigh of relief.

The two squads and the Apothecary were traversing the Gildar Rift relatively slowly. With the sheer quantity of debris and asteroids hurtling through the sector, it was a treacherous route that only a fool would consider attempting at speed. Their pilot, one of the Chapter's human serfs, was supremely good at what he did.

'Take us on a clear circuit of the ship,' Dasan said, his low rumble finally breaking the awkward silence that had followed Ryarus's harsh words to Matteus. 'That way, we may get a better idea of its condition.'

'At once, lord.'

Engines whining, the Thunderhawk banked sharply as it went into a turn to circle the prow of the stricken vessel. The starboard side of the *Wolf of Fenris* was, if anything, worse than the presenting port side.

'Boarding torpedo damage,' observed Matteus as he squinted through the tiny porthole-sized window above his seat. 'Evidence that they've been fired on – see all the scoring on the surface? Raiders, perhaps?'

'Our cousins are fierce warriors,' Dasan replied. 'They would not have fallen to an enemy easily, especially not disorganised raiders.' Matteus and Dasan exchanged looks, sharing a moment of consensus. Raiders generally attacked in small groups and usually homed in on small Imperial transport vessels. To consider raiders attempting to take on something the size of an Adeptus Astartes strike cruiser was laughable.

'Take us to the rear docking bay, Eryk.' Ryarus reached for his helm and tugged it on over his head. When he spoke next, all emotion and feeling was flattened from his voice.

'Squads Kyanite and Mohave... as the captain observed during the moot, this is to be treated as a hostile environment until evidence presents itself to the contrary.'

As he would be the senior warrior present, Arrun had turned overall command over to the Apothecary. Ryarus was steady of purpose and clear-headed. He would lead a search and rescue operation with smooth efficiency and not be distracted by the opportunity to deviate from the captain's orders in pursuit of some foolish glory quest. Dasan and Matteus were competent, capable warriors but they were content to defer to Ryarus's superior wisdom and experience.

Throughout the Thunderhawk, the only sound for a few moments was the soft hiss of helmet seals locking into place and the rhythmic creaking of ceramite-covered hands flexing and unflexing as the Silver Skulls ensured the correct functioning of the joints.

'If none of the crew still live,' Ryarus opened a vox-channel to both squads, 'then we stabilise the ship and we await the captain's further instruction. If our cousins are still with us, then we establish what happened and we either bring them back to the *Dread Argent* for treatment or if they are beyond mortal assistance, I will personally deliver them into the arms of the Emperor.'

He turned his visored head to scan down the line of battle-brothers. Both squads were presently at full complement, in itself almost a miracle. Each warrior wore his silver-grey armour proudly, the yellow-hued right shoulder pauldrons of Fourth Company glinting in what little light there was in the interior of the gunship. On their left shoulders was the emblem of the Chapter, a stylised skull cast in silver. Each squad's emblem had eyes picked out in the gemstone that gave them their name. Blue for Squad Kyanite; purple for Mohave.

Ryarus's eyes travelled back up the line once more. His ruby-red lenses gave away nothing of his thoughts, and he continued.

'From what we can see, many areas of the ship are going to be blocked by battle damage. There are obvious hull breaches which will cause spikes in your life support systems. Take note of your armour's warnings and good hunting. And, my brothers... if we for one moment suspect that there is warp-taint aboard, no matter how minimal, then we scourge whatever we may find. If for any reason we find ourselves outnumbered or outclassed, then – and only then – we leave the *Wolf of Fenris* and we give the order to have her destroyed.'

Every head dipped in acknowledgement. Steel-grey hands closed around bolter stocks and a faint murmuring of sounds filled the gunship's interior as each spoke his personal litany, often in the tribal dialect of their birth. Such connections to their lives before ascension to the ranks of the Adeptus Astartes were actively encouraged. The Silver Skulls were proud of their heritage and those who heralded from the Chapter's home world held onto the traditions and practices of their upbringing stoically.

'Bringing her round for docking now, my lord,' announced Eryk.

Ryarus nodded and allowed himself a moment for his own fervent prayers. The God-Emperor willing, their cousins would be living. It was pessimism to suspect otherwise. Ryarus, though, had always held true to a premise a former sergeant had taught him decades ago.

Never expect anything... and you'll never be surprised or disappointed.

THE INTERIOR OF the *Wolf of Fenris* told them as little as the exterior had done. There were scorch scars in the walls that suggested heavy fighting had taken place but it was impossible to say when this had happened. The air was thin and carried the stench of old, dried blood. The fading stains of it were spattered up the walls, across the steel decking and against the sides of the landing craft where they hung lifelessly in their grav-cradles. Spent bolter shells practically carpeted the ground underfoot and there were deep gouges in the side of a Thunderhawk that a closer inspection suggested could only have been made by a chainsword.

What little light there was came from emergency lumenstrips set into the sides of the hangar bay, but they wavered with a faintly audible fizzle. Sparks of electricity spat from ruptured power cables.

'I'd say we could confirm that there was a fight here, at least,' Matteus's voice came across the vox with its regular light-hearted tone and for once, Ryarus didn't snap at him to be quiet. Each Space Marine dealt with grim discoveries like this in their own way. The gentle attempt at humour did not jar at all; it was just Matteus's own method.

Dasan crouched and picked up a damaged bolt pistol. The barrel had been blown apart at the point the weapon had failed. Careful inspection revealed that it bore the crest of Fenris. All around, weapons lay where they had been abandoned; some damaged, others seemingly discarded.

There was not a single body in sight.

One of the warriors consulted the auspex he held in his hand. 'Life support systems are still on-line. Air is breathable but only just. I am guessing everything must have been automatically rerouted.' He shook his head. 'I cannot tell you any more without access to a working ship's cogitator. The vessel is running on emergency power but there is no way of telling how long that has been the case.'

'Is it possible that the Space Wolves trapped their enemy in here and vented them out to space?' Matteus, for all his inane chatter, could often be relied upon to postulate possible solutions to the inexplicable.

'It is a possibility, certainly. But surely the weapons would have gone too.' Dasan's logical thoughts put an end to that particular theory.

Ryarus cast a ruby-tinted gaze around the staging area. Runes ran across his retina and the auto-focus was working hard, picking out the rusty hue of the bloodied areas and the weapons that were strewn everywhere. The heat sensors in his visor showed nothing but his battle-brothers. He crouched and like Dasan, picked up a discarded bolt pistol.

A cursory examination showed that it was empty.

He dropped it back down to the floor again with a dull thud. Ryarus touched the purity seal at the hilt of his bolter.

'Mohave, we proceed to the bridge,' he said. 'Kyanite – begin proceeding to the engine room. Move with caution, brothers. This whole thing reeks of subterfuge.'

The lingering trace of blood was everywhere.

It streaked up the walls of the ship's inner corridors. It was smeared on the deck leaving virulent scarlet trails. Brother Temerus, one of Dasan's squad had tried, without success, to link into the *Wolf's* vox-net. All he had met in response to his hails thus far had been static.

With every step that they took, Ryarus's sense of unease grew. Whatever had happened to the *Wolf of Fenris* had been devastating and worse; whatever it had been that had committed such relentless slaughter may well still be aboard.

During the flight across from the *Dread Argent*, one of Matteus's many observations had been that a complement of more than twenty Space Marines had seemed excessive for a search and rescue operation. Ryarus had quietly agreed with the sentiment. Arrun was being over-careful.

Now, though, he mentally praised the captain's unerring sense of caution.

So far, they had encountered nothing but signs of battle. No bodies, no injured... nothing. A report from Matteus had detailed a brief diversion into one of the other staging areas which had turned up vast quantities of discarded battle plate. It had been massed into haphazard piles rather than carefully displayed and maintained as was the expected behaviour of a Space Marine. That was all that either squad had encountered.

The Silver Skulls made their way up from the aft section towards midships. The silence was eerie. No sounds of Chapter serfs or servitors, no distant clash of swords in training cages... there was nothing to be heard except for the heavy, metallic footfalls of Space Marine boots as they moved slowly across the fine steel mesh floors of the dimly lit corridors. The *Wolf of Fenris* creaked around them, the groans of super-stressed metal clearly audible without the usual rumble of the engine.

Tayln, one of Dasan's squad raised his head to listen to the sounds of the vessel. 'She sounds wrong,' he noted. As a promising Techmarine, he had not yet been despatched to Mars for his formal induction into the ways of the Mechanicus. As such, he had undergone his initial training at the hands of the existing Chapter Techmarines. He tipped his head to one side, listening. 'I can hear... *something*.'

'It's possibly a safe assumption that the engines were badly damaged in whatever battle the *Wolf* partook in, brother.' Dasan responded. Tayln held up a hand, stilling any further words from his sergeant. Later, much later, Dasan agreed fervently that it was only because Tayln had told him to be quiet that they had got the early warning of the assault.

'Listen, sergeant,' he said, his voice terse. 'I hear–'

The bark of a bolter stopped his words and every Space Marine present reached for their own weapon. There was no cover in this open, empty corridor and the flare of exploding bolter rounds bathed it in an unnatural glow that reflected off the highly-polished surface of the Silver Skulls armour. A round impacted on Tayln's shoulder and detonated, sending the young Space Marine staggering backwards.

Instantly, the vox came alive.

'Matteus, we're under attack up here...' Ryarus began to relay the information, but Matteus cut across him.

'We've got our own situation, Apothecary...'

'Squad Mohave – on me!'

With a combined roar of battle fury that had, in the past, stopped their enemies dead in their tracks, Dasan and his squad began advancing down the open corridor. Their bolters and their spirits were raised high as they unleashed the Emperor's wrath on those who had dared open fire on His chosen.

Ryarus stared at the reams of data scrolling in front of his retinas, his systems already adjusting from investigative to battle mode. The runes that had previously flashed white before his eyes began to wink urgently. He blink-clicked furiously, his eyes moving with rapid ease. He thumbed at the hilt of his power axe, ready to activate it at a moment's notice. For now, he opted to maintain a rearguard, holding back from the rest of the squad.

A gout of flame lit the corridor once again as Tayln unleashed the power of his flamer, and not far behind the roar of cleansing fire came agonised screams. Human screams.

Then came an abrupt silence that lasted several seconds.

'Dasan. Matteus. Report.' The responses came almost instantly.

'Human privateers, by the look of their clothing,' Dasan spoke first. 'No Space Wolf markings. These bastards weren't servants of the Sons of Russ.'

'Same here, Apothecary. We took them down easily enough.' Matteus sounded angry. Ryarus wasn't surprised. What did surprise him was the reality of the situation. The numbers must have been exponential to reduce the *Wolf of Fenris* to a drifting hulk. He kept his uncertainty in check. Both squads were already on edge. He did not wish to fan those flames any more than necessary.

'And the weapons they're firing?'

'Bolt pistols, mostly. Looted, perhaps. They're all dead now, anyway. But there's no way a group of humans this size could wipe out an entire ship of Adeptus Astartes warriors. They must be...'

The vox crackled, then went dead. From further ahead, around the bend of the corridor, a familiar Silver Skulls battle-cry was met with a sound even more feral and bone-chillingly menacing. Bolters began firing in earnest, the staccato sounds magnified many fold by the confined space. A sudden sun-burst flare lit up the corridor as another belch of red-hot flame spewed forth from Tayln's flamer. The glow remained steady this time as he trained it on whatever attacked.

The whine of a chainsword powering up added its voice to the fray and there was a grinding crunch as its adamantium teeth bit into ceramite and plasteel.

'Matteus! Damn you... the one time I don't want you to shut up, you go quiet on me! I need a report on Kyanite's situation as soon as you can.' Hurrying, he raced down the corridor to join Dasan and his squad. They were engaged in combat with other Space Marines. Some were wearing the grey battle plate of the Space Wolves Chapter, others wore armour that proclaimed allegiance – or at least a former allegiance – to other Chapters. In a frenzied moment, Ryarus saw the unmistakable yellow of an Imperial Fist and the bone-white of a White Scar. There were others too; some had defiled insignias that the Apothecary could not name. It mattered little. They were traitors one and all and they would all die.

Every one of them had one thing in common. The Imperial aquila across their chests were defiled and mutilated. Where their Chapter emblems had once been was a disfiguring red stain, a blotch of colour that obliterated their former fealty. A stain as red as the blood that had spattered the walls and floors of the *Wolf of Fenris*. Red as the blood that flowed through Ryarus's own veins. A blatant insult to the Chapters in question, it meant that those wearing the armour were allied to no loyal cohort of the Adeptus Astartes.

Ryarus had seen such armour markings before. He had fought against these warriors. He knew who they were. If the Space Wolves were already fighting with them, then any hope they may have had for their cousins was lost.

A chill ran through him at the realisation that in order to survive this situation they would have to kill their own brethren.

Not your brethren now. Not any more.

Traitors.

The two words that he barked across the vox carried a blatant undercurrent of disgust.

'Red Corsairs.'

Ryarus gripped the hilt of his power axe, screamed out guttural expletives in his native tongue and let the Apothecary mask drop for battle before wading into the fray.

The battle was brief and frenzied, an intense tangle of

limbs, weapons and exploding bolter rounds making it difficult to distinguish where one warrior stopped and another began. A battle rage gripped the Apothecary as he lay about him with his axe, fending off the encroaching warriors in the constricting corridor. The Silver Skulls had numbers on their side, but the Red Corsair warriors were ably supported by human raiders who were emerging from the distant gloom in a steady stream. They didn't present a major challenge, not to warriors of Adeptus Astartes calibre. But their small arms fire was a distraction the battle-engaged Space Marines could well do without.

Across the vox Ryarus paid close attention to the battle conversation between the two squads. The noise eventually faded out to be nothing more than background as he played his own part in the battle. He grunted and flew backwards as one of the Space Wolf warriors ploughed into him with a full shoulder charge, sending him barrelling to the floor.

The Space Marine who had attacked him was flaxen-haired with ragged rats-tails hanging around an unshaven face. The warrior went without a helm and the fury and hatred in his ruddy face was visible for all to see. He spat bitter curses at the Silver Skulls Apothecary as he dropped to place one knee on Ryarus's chest. The Apothecary was pinned, the Space Wolf being stronger by far.

A bolter was brought up to his head, the heat detectors in his visor screaming alarms at the proximity of the white-hot muzzle. This was it, then. This was how it ended.

As abruptly as the Space Wolf had floored him, the dissident Son of Russ was sent staggering by a Silver Skull who had been flung away by the maelstrom of battle. It was a moment of fortune rather than judgement and Ryarus seized the opportunity with all the ferocity of his gene-enhanced might. The crackling, energy-sheathed axe head buried itself in the traitor's chest and split it like old wood. The Apothecary dragged himself free of the gory wreckage of the Red Corsair and clambered to his feet as quickly as he could in the frenzied melee.

There was no point in thanking the battle-brother who

had knocked the Space Wolf clear. He was dead, his headless corpse the solid weight that had fallen into the battling pair and saved the Apothecary. Ryarus swore softly.

'We're outnumbered down here, Apothecary.' Matteus reported in. The sounds of battle were heavy across the vox.

'All units... begin a fighting retreat to the Thunderhawk,' Ryarus's gave the order in-between swings of his axe. 'Kill anything in your way. Matteus, keep trying to contact the *Dread Argent*. Tell them it's a trap.'

'Already on it, sir. They're filling the corridor behind us.'

'Concentrate on cutting your way through them. And get that message to Captain Arrun!'

'Yes, sir.'

'And no matter what else you do... don't stop. Fall back to the Thunderhawk and disengage. Do you understand me?'

'*Yes*, sir.' The faintest hint of annoyance was there in the tone and Ryarus almost smiled.

Almost.

Ryarus brought his axe above his head with all the force he could muster and slammed it with deadly accuracy into the skull of another Space Wolf assailant. He took no pleasure from the kill. He couldn't. This was not some foul xenos. This was a great warrior from a noble Chapter with a long and glorious history who had lost his way. In ending his existence in this manner, he was offering a service. It was the only way he could see it.

The retreat was slow but steady, the Silver Skulls managing to hold off the worst of the attack. But despite their best efforts, they were not winning. More of his brothers had fallen to the onslaught and there was no chance for respite. He yearned for a moment where he could check to see if they were dead or whether they were merely incapacitated. Worse still... if they were dead, he would be allowing their prized gene-seed, the Quintessence Sacred, to fall into the hands of these traitors. Denied the opportunity to recover the organs from the fallen was anathema to Ryarus's core ethic. To abandon the Chapter's legacy in this place was unthinkable. He was an Apothecary. He had sworn oaths to preserve the lives of his brothers and to preserve their heritage.

He forced himself to concentrate instead on aiding in the preservation of the living. It did not come easily.

At some point, the two squads merged; but the chaos in the corridor made it impossible to tell when that had happened. As they retreated up the corridor, Mohave and Kyanite squads dealt with the human element attempting to halt their egress, in some instances by crushing them underfoot. Skulls and spines gave way easily under their heavy tread. The screams of the dying and the stench of the dead was everywhere, permeating every fibre of the Silver Skulls beings... and it also had the effect of driving the already semi-feral Space Wolves Corsairs into a further frenzy of near berserker rage.

The situation was unquestionably dire. There was very little that could make it even more perilous. At least, that's what Ryarus's fleeting thought was, right before the ship's light levels began to increase, brightening to an almost dazzling brilliance. The chorus of screams was temporarily muted by the sound of plasma engines that had been gently thrumming on emergency power firing back up to full thrust.

The *Wolf of Fenris* was awakening.

'SHE'S POWERING UP!'

Captain Arrun looked up from his command throne at the words, his brow furrowing as he turned sharply to the viewscreen. The strike cruiser, which until now had been drifting aimlessly through the Rift was indeed taking on very visible and obvious life. Lights glowed in the viewports and contrails were starting to form in the wake of the engines as they switched gradually from emergency power to full. The massive ship began to nudge forward sluggishly.

There was a brief moment of jubilation. It ended abruptly when the next words were spoken. The console operator's voice shook as he spoke. 'Their weapons are charging. Sir, the *Wolf of Fenris* is preparing an attack.'

Arrun's reaction was instantaneous. He had allowed himself a moment's optimism; a spark of hope that Ryarus and his squads had been successful in locating and aiding the Space Wolves. He regretted that moment of laxity now. His orders came out in clipped, precise tones.

'Get the gunships ready to launch. Divert more power to the shield banks. Load the prow bombardment cannon. All other weapons batteries on standby.' His arms folded across his massive chest. 'If it's a fight that they want...' Arrun scowled, his scarred face darkening with anger. 'Then it's a fight that they will get. And we will fight them face to face. Aim to disable rather than destroy. We need that ship intact if we can manage it.'

'Yes, my lord.' The operative activated the ship-wide vox. 'Calling all hands, calling all hands, this is an Alpha-level emergency. All hands, prepare for combat. This is not a drill.'

'Send out fleet-wide astropathic messages to the other ships in the Rift. They will have been waiting for this. They should all be prepared to mobilise on my command. None of them should be far away if they've stuck to their prescribed course.'

'Yes, my lord.' The human serf couldn't keep the tone of impressed awe out of his voice at the realisation that the Silver Skulls Master of the Fleet had already laid the seeds of a counterstrike seemingly based on little more than intuition.

But then, there was a reason why Daerys Arrun had become Master of the Fleet in the first place.

'One step ahead,' he murmured.

Around the bridge, servitors and serfs scurried to carry out Arrun's orders. Theirs was never to question. Theirs was just to carry out the will of their masters. Despite a tendency to let his temper flare on occasion, the captain was both respected and even revered amongst the human crew.

'You are wise sometimes, Daerys,' remarked Brand from his position at Arrun's side. 'I occasionally wonder if you need me at all.' Arrun shot a glance sideways. Throne, but the Prognosticator could move silently when he wanted to. He had appeared seemingly out of nowhere. The captain shrugged, a barely perceptible movement.

'Of course I need you here, my friend. I need you to remind me how clever I am.'

They shared a moment of levity, but it was swiftly replaced by a mutual concern for the safety of their warriors.

Both wrestled with the other dilemma that faced them. If it came down to basic survival, if they had to destroy the *Wolf of Fenris* in self-defence, there would be many questions from the Space Wolves; something which would be hard to validate without proof that they were attacked first. Of course, were the *Wolf* to fire on them first, it would be recorded in the banks of both ship cogitators. It would still be excruciatingly awkward, though. This situation held far reaching consequences that both Silver Skulls were acutely and agonisingly well aware of.

'She's coming about.'

'Cannon crews are engaged.'

'All hands reporting ready.'

'As it should be.' Arrun switched his vox-bead to the ship-wide channel. His words carried throughout the whole of the *Dread Argent*, reaching every soul on board. He only had to speak a few simple words, but they would be enough. Fourth Company knew their captain well.

'Silver Skulls, be prepared to take up arms. And, my brothers – Primus inter pares! Never forget!'

Arrun didn't give the order to contact the squads and order them back. There was no point. His men were no fools. They would be doing that already.

If they still lived.

THEY STILL LIVED. But they were losing the battle.

They were not entirely failing in their mission, though. Not counting the humans who were swept aside like sacks of meat by the Silver Skulls, several of the Red Corsairs were now lying inert on the ground, either dead or incapacitated by ably placed bolter shots. Despite the visible evidence of their triumph, the rapidly diminishing runes on the inside of his visor screamed at Apothecary Ryarus, informing him that the Silver Skulls numbers were decreasing far too swiftly. There was no sign of any break in the onslaught, either.

The *Wolf of Fenris* had woken up; he felt the unmistakable jolt as she engaged her forward engines. He cursed and corrected his balance as the motion caused him to lurch slightly. The servos in his power armour compensated, keeping him upright but the sudden motion was an unwelcome distraction. His moment of unsteadiness proved enough for an opportunistic Red Corsair to take his chances. His chainsword cleaved through the Apothecary's left shoulder guard with a whine of servos and unmistakable crunching of bone. The ceramite plating split and clattered to the ground along with his axe. The Silver Skulls Chapter motif leered up at him from the floor. In a moment of misplaced irrationality, that somehow incensed him more than the injury.

'Apothecary!' The shout came from over to his right somewhere. A flare of pain blossomed in his shoulder, swiftly countered by the flow of drugs administered by the power armour. Although the chainsword had destroyed his pauldron and bitten into his bone, his body would work quickly to repair the damage. But he was blessed with two arms and although in battle situations he usually favoured his left, it didn't mean for one moment that he wasn't in possession of an equal level of skill with his right. Stooping briefly, the Apothecary picked up his axe again.

His opponent sneered at him as he hefted the axe's weight. Not waiting, the enemy brought down the chainsword in a fierce overhead smash, its teeth emitting a furious growl of hunger that would only be sated with the Apothecary's blood. Ryarus put his own weapon up to guard against the attack and there was the harsh, metallic screech of metal on metal. The chainsword bit ineffectually into the adamantium head of the Silver Skull's axe.

'Apothecary!'

He could hear the voice again; somewhere on the periphery of his aural awareness, but it seemed distant and unreal. He shook his head briefly to clear it of the fuzz that always accompanied a moment of pain. The burst of narcotics was familiar enough, but even for a post-human warrior at the peak of genetically enhanced perfection, there was a second or two of disorientation as his biology went to work.

He pulled back from the attack, then went at his opponent with renewed vigour. He felt a hand on his shoulder, tugging at him urgently and he shrugged it off angrily. Whether it was one of his own men or one of the Red Corsairs didn't matter. He did not welcome the physical contact, not whilst he was in the midst of battle.

Ryarus stared at his enemy through the red of his eye lenses. His power armour was gravely compromised and whilst he was an accomplished warrior, at this very moment in time, his opponent was physically superior.

The Silver Skulls had pulled back almost to the landing bay. He could hear the unmistakable sounds of weapons discharging, their echoes getting ever closer. Dasan's squad, being closest had reached the Thunderhawk first and were keeping the Corsairs pinned down with the gunship's heavy bolters. Even in his moment of distraction, Ryarus grunted approval at their methods.

His attacker launched at him once again and this time he was pressed back. It took every shred of his strength to keep the chainsword from biting into his helm.

'Keep moving back, Matteus,' he roared through the vox. 'I can keep this traitor engaged for a while.' He was not completely alone though; three or four other Silver Skulls were engaging in the rearguard battle with him. His heart soared at the fraternal sense of solidarity this gave him and his strength renewed, he shoved the Red Corsair away from him.

Matteus was dealing with his own situation. Whilst Dasan's squad were holding the wave of Red Corsairs back, his own men – or what were left of them – were setting krak grenades to blow the mag-clamps locking their ship to the floor. With the awakening of the *Wolf of Fenris*, all its systems had come back on-line, effectively cutting off their escape.

But they would not be trapped that easily.

The charges set, Matteus took advantage of the covering

fire of the heavy bolters to get inside the Thunderhawk. Already it was beginning its power cycle, making ready to leave. The Apothecary and the other warriors were at the landing bay door. They would make it.

Then, Matteus's spirits fell with an almost audible crash.

'Apothecary, behind you!'

Interposing himself between Ryarus and his escape was one of the single most massive Space Marines the Apothecary had ever seen. With a pockmarked face boasting a scarred but ruddy complexion, the warrior had dirty blond hair pulled back from his face in a topknot falling down past his shoulders. The many fetishes and runes that decorated his grey battle plate told Ryarus that here was another Space Wolves warrior who had turned his back on the Imperium.

In front of him, a blockage that he could not hope to defeat, not in his weakened state.

Behind him, chainsword teeth hungering for his flesh.

So this is how it ends. It was the second time he had thought that within the hour. Last time, it had not been the case. This time, he felt the truth of the moment far more keenly.

A humourless smile spread across his face beneath his helm.

'Go,' he voxed, hefting the weight of his power axe in his hand. He would not be removed from the Emperor's cause without putting up resistance. Matteus's head came down in an abrupt, curt nod and his voice, for once without humour, fed through the vox-bead in Ryarus's ear.

'Fight well, my brother. Primus inter pares.'

With those words, the Silver Skulls destroyed the controls to the staging area doors and they ground slowly closed with a shrill shriek of straining gears. As they slammed close, they left Ryarus and four others to stand their ground and buy the retreating squads enough time to complete their task and to get clear.

'Primus inter pares,' Ryarus repeated and turned his head briefly to the four Silver Skulls he now stood with. It was the right of every Space Marine to die gloriously – and they would hold here. Enough of their brothers would survive to regale their tale; an ending worthy of the favourite stories of Varsavia.

'Primus inter pares,' the Apothecary said again, his words echoed by the others. 'We are the Silver Skulls. We are first amongst equals.'

The smile behind his helm grew wider as he held his axe aloft. 'Time to die,' he said.

With a deep, bestial bellow, he rejoined battle with renewed vigour. He was filled with a determination to annihilate as many of the enemy as he possibly could before death finally caught up with him and claimed him for the Emperor.

THE TWO STRIKE cruisers were built to an ancient design and despite the differences in their colours and external livery, not to mention the very obvious damage that the *Wolf of Fenris* had endured, they were to all intents and purposes an equal match.

The *Dread Argent* was intact. She was well-crewed, robust and in peak condition. It would take a single word of command to obliterate the crippled Space Wolves vessel. Just one. But Arrun could not give it. Not until they either received word from the squads who had travelled across to secure it or if the *Wolf* fired on them.

Everything happened simultaneously. The Silver Skulls Thunderhawk burst out of the launch bay and began a hasty journey back towards the *Dread Argent*. A crackle of static broke through the bridge vox-operator's console and Sergeant Matteus's voice delivered the news Arrun had been waiting to hear. For once, the young warrior did not attempt to pretty up his words or indulge in unnecessary verbiage. That alone told of the gravity of the situation.

'Vessel is not salvageable. Red Corsair raiders. Clear *Dread Argent* launch bay, we are coming in fast and furious.'

Over the years, the Silver Skulls and the Red Corsairs had shared many encounters. The Gildar Rift had seen incursions from the would-be raiders many times but each had been successfully thwarted. But this was something new and untried. The sheer magnitude of what had happened to the *Wolf of Fenris* was devastating.

'Incoming munitions from their prow cannon and port-side batteries! All hands brace for impact! Repeat, all hands brace for impact!'

At this proximity, it would take next to no time for the *Wolf's* attack to reach them. Arrun barked out an order to return fire, but never quite got the full sentence out. The opening salvo from the *Wolf of Fenris* crashed over the *Dread Argent's* void shields, sending a rippling shudder through the hull of the vessel.

'Damage report!'

'Void shields are holding steady.'

'Is the Thunderhawk back on board?' Arrun turned to one of the servitors. 'Has it landed? Is it out of the firing zone?' He fired off the questions rapidly and the servitor responded in kind.

'Confirmed. Thunderhawk Delta Four has docked.'

The ever-present rumble of the far-distant engines was joined by the deep, throaty sound of the bombardment cannon preparing to spit her destructive load back at the enemy.

Arrun clenched his hand tightly, then unfurled his finger to point at the image of the *Wolf of Fenris* before him. 'Return fire. Blow her out of existence.'

A COPPERY TANG flooded his mouth as his body emerged from temporary stasis. The myriad wounds that lacerated his body beneath the power armour throbbed as his gene-enhanced physiology worked to knit together broken bones and seal wounds that had been caused by the blades tearing into him.

Breathe, Ryarus.

Like all of his kind, fear had been bred out of him. But that did not mean he couldn't experience other negative, detrimental emotions. He was in pain and although neural blockers kept the worst of it from consuming him, he knew it was impairing his judgement. He was confused and he was anxious. These were strange and unwelcome sensations. They were unfamiliar to him and he did not like it. Not at all.

Breathe, Ryarus. Steady yourself. Balance your humours.

They were familiar words. They were words that he spoke to those put into his care. From a habit borne in decades of service as an Apothecary, he allowed himself to remain calm, not to let the rage at his enemy consume him. For once, he practised what he regularly preached to others. It was a strange feeling to be giving himself such advice, but he took it.

It was good advice, after all.

Slowly, Ryarus. Let it come back to you in good time. Just breathe. Concentrate on the breathing. Feel each inhalation fill your lungs. Cherish each time you exhale another breath with which to fight the enemies of the Imperium. That's good. Just keep breathing.

It would have been the advice he would have given to any injured brother and he heeded it well. His breathing steadied and the pounding of his twin hearts began to stabilise. Clinical detachment took over. The fact that both hearts were beating gave a measure of the extent of his internal injuries. If he was wounded enough that his secondary organ was functioning, things were dire.

Utilising the skills of self-control, he regulated his breathing for a while longer until the soft *thud* of his second heart slowly faded to a barely perceptible rhythm. His Apothecary skills moved onwards, working outwards as he assessed himself with calm, methodical processes. The familiarity of the process was soothing.

His senses gradually came back to him one at a time, tuning him into his surroundings. He realised that his helm had been removed. A flood of scents tickled his olfactory receptors. Soft, acrid chemical smells that were well known to him. Antiseptic smells. Medical smells. He was in an apothecarion. He was not restrained. There had been little need to. He was injured enough that any attempt at escape would be futile. Even if he tried, he would not get far. The

Wolf of Fenris was an Adeptus Astartes ship. The traitorous crew on board would know all the escape routes he might have tried.

Ryarus turned his head, taking in more of his surroundings. To his left were two other Silver Skulls warriors in similar situations to his own. He couldn't tell from this angle whether their chests rose and fell. He had no idea if they were conscious or if they were even still alive. He had a sense that they were; the thought of why the Red Corsairs would choose to keep them living sickened him to the very pit of his stomach.

Better they were dead than this indignity. None of the Silver Skulls would ever turn traitor against their own. Their loyalty ran too deep. They would find some way to escape, or they would die fighting off their captors.

But there were unknown variables here. Perhaps they were being kept alive for the Emperor only knew what reasons. An Apothecary's concern for his charges welled in him and he let it take him. He tried to sit up, to go to their aid, but he could not. He murmured a string of curses.

'You're awake, then.'

The voice was deep, richly accented and came from somewhere over in the corner. The Apothecary lifted his head with concentrated effort, letting his enhanced optic sensors adjust to the murky darkness. A hulking figure stepped forwards from the shadows. It was the same Space Wolf he had fought in the corridor.

'What is your name, Apothecary?'

'I have no words for traitors. Do not presume to speak to me.'

The Space Wolf let out a humourless bark of a laugh and moved close enough so that he was in Ryarus's full line of vision. He was still clad in his blood-splattered armour and moved with an easy lope. His blue eyes were piercing and horribly devoid of all emotion. Ryarus's eyes were automatically drawn to the Chapter symbol on his shoulder where red paint besmirched the wolf's head. He focused on it as his captor encroached into his personal space.

'Are you not even interested in whether your brothers live or are dead?' The question seemed genuine.

'Better for them to be dead if you feature anywhere in their future.'

The traitor laughed, a huge boom that tore into the otherwise-silence of the room. Despite his efforts to retain his dignity, Ryarus flinched slightly at the noise. The former Space Wolves warrior ran a hand over his jaw, his fingers combing through the scruffy beard. The brief glimpse of humour dissipated as swiftly as it had come and his dispassionate gaze met that of Ryarus.

'My name is Vollsanger,' he said. 'There was a time when I spoke the very same words you utter now. At the beginning, when I was first brought here, I was loyal to my former masters. You *will* change your mind.' There was absolute certainty in his voice. Ryarus still said nothing, staring instead up at the ceiling. Vollsanger loomed over him.

'Your silence will win you no respect. Not here, Silver Skull. There is a way that you can garner that respect, though. A way that you can keep your life – and the lives of your battle-brothers – from being snuffed out... Ah! You look at me now. I found your weak spot, yes?'

'Tell me what I must do so that my brothers may live,' Ryarus demanded, his teeth clenched. 'Tell me what I must do so that they may be freed and together, then we will kill every last one of you where you stand.'

'What you must do? Ah, a simple thing, really.' Vollsanger leaned down and murmured the answer to Ryarus's question in a low voice. The Silver Skulls Apothecary let his eyes widen in shock. His expression rapidly moved to one of disgust and rage.

'Never,' he said. 'You may as well kill us now. That isn't ever going to happen. I won't ever serve the Tyrant. And I will *never* give up my birthright voluntarily.' He turned his head to the side and spat a mouthful of acidic bile at the mention of the name. It came out stained red with his own life's blood.

An expression flitted across Vollsanger's face that startled

Ryarus. It was pity; a reluctance there that surprised the Apothecary simply by its existence. A wild hope flared in him that even if the Space Wolves of this ship were lost to the evils that had brought them low there was a spark of their former nobility. But Vollsanger's words held no such pity.

'You will change your mind. In time. And if there is one thing the Corpsemaster can do well, it's persuasion.' Vollsanger's hand went unconsciously to his chest and Ryarus could only imagine what tortures the other Space Marine must have undergone, what horrors he must have been subjected to that had led to him committing the ultimate betrayal.

Something almost like sympathy rose in his gut, but the Apothecary quashed it instantly. He could not afford to feel sympathy, never for dissidents and betrayers. He had heard of the Corpsemaster, of course. All Apothecaries knew of Lord Apothecary Garreon of the Astral Claws. His research scrolls and early documentation were lauded for their extraordinary insight and understanding of Space Marine physiology. Even Ryarus had studied Garreon's earlier works.

The idea of meeting such a legendary figure might once have filled him with interest and reverence. Now it filled him with nothing but revulsion.

'I will leave you to ponder your options, Silver Skull. The Corpsemaster is presently engaged on the campaign, but I have no doubt he will be delighted that we have captured him another Apothecary. We need all we can get.'

'Go and crawl back to your fallen master. Go wallow in his debased heresy. I will never serve the Tyrant of Badab.'

A smile flickered over Vollsanger's face and almost absently, he patted the Apothecary's shoulder. He nodded, as though expecting such a response. 'If it counts for anything, your brothers live still.' The former Space Wolf moved away from Ryarus's sight. 'We killed none of them. You are all worth far more to us alive than dead, but dead will do if necessary.'

With those words, he turned and strode from the apothecarion. Ryarus could feel the reactions of his body, striving its hardest to swiftly bring him to fitness. He touched a moment of despair. He couldn't imagine for one moment that even if he healed quickly there was a lot he could do about his present situation.

All the Apothecary had left was his free will and it was likely that the Red Corsairs would do their best to rob him of it.

SIX
BETRAYAL

TIME SEEMED TO slow to a crawl from the moment Arrun gave his command to return fire on the *Wolf of Fenris* right up to the moment it was carried out. A hesitation lingered unpleasantly in the air as the bridge crew exchanged confused glances. There had been little time to fully explain the situation and all they could see was that they were firing on a ship belonging to another Chapter.

'I said, return fire!' Arrun's temper flared in the split moment of hesitation. In six short strides, he had crossed the bridge deck to the unfortunate young man he had directed the order at. 'Why are you not obeying my orders? I–'

'*Wolf of Fenris* is increasing speed. All current cogitations suggest that the *Wolf of Fenris* is setting herself on a likely collision course with the *Dread Argent*. At current speed and bearing, the *Wolf of Fenris*...' A servitor's dull tones began to report the situation and Arrun spun to stare at it.

'Be silent!'

The captain's voice carried across the bridge with considerable power and command. His bellow was the single loudest thing at that moment. Coupled with his sheer presence, every soul on the bridge stopped what they were doing and paid attention to the huge warrior standing at their very centre.

Then, as was a fundamental part of its programming in the wake of its lobotomy, the servitor broke the momentary silence that had fallen in the wake of Arrun's fury to acknowledge his order.

'Compliance.'

It bowed its head and resumed silent duties at its station. Arrun's eyes and focus flicked immediately to the viewscreen and the indolent human who had not carried out his orders was temporarily forgotten. The young man breathed an unchecked sigh of relief at the servitor whose timely words may have just ensured his head remained attached to his shoulders. He need not truly have worried. The sight of the other ship's thrusters firing now held everyone's attention.

As the servitor had so correctly observed, the ship was powering up to run towards them. It didn't take a lifetime's naval experience to predict that they were rapidly approaching ramming speed.

'My lord?' The young officer at the console spoke tentatively, reluctant to bring the captain's gaze back on him for fear of what retribution that may bring with it. 'Your orders?'

Evasion would be impossible. A vessel the size of the *Dread Argent* was not going to move swiftly out of the collision course that the *Wolf of Fenris* had set.

'Right now, I would prefer to unload every single weapon that we have at them. But... no. For now, hold our position.' Arrun's expression darkened. 'I will not turn tail and flee. We can tear into them well enough with the prow bombardment cannon. Be prepared to engage weapons on my command.'

Several chimes of acquiescence rang around the bridge and Arrun stalked back to his command throne. The Prognosticator was watching him carefully. Arrun's brow furrowed. Brand was not really watching him at all. He had a strangely detached look about him. He was staring *through* the captain, his inner sight locked on something only he could see.

'Brand?'

The psyker was apparently lost in some sort of trance. Arrun felt his stomach lurch. A Prognosticator's conduit with the Emperor could occasionally keep them ensnared for longer than usual, leaving them in a blessed state of semi-awareness. Arrun's frustrations increased. This was not the best of times to lose his advisor. He glowered at nobody in particular. To jolt Brand from his state could be danger- ous. He would have to wait until the psyker came back to him.

It was not long before Brand displayed awareness once again. The Prognosticator's green eyes blinked rapidly as he shifted his thoughts back into the same timeline and reality as his captain.

'Did you see something?' Arrun's temper had already dissolved at the look on Brand's face. A shivering thrill of anticipation ran through him. Had his Prognosticator received an Emperor's Gift? A true moment of foresight that could ensure the difference between loss and victory? Such moments were considered amongst the greatest of a Silver Skulls Prognosticator's service – and the service of those with whom he shared his visions.

'I see many things, Captain Arrun.' Brand's voice held a strange, almost dreamy quality. Gone was the steady bari- tone that normally accompanied his words. In its place was something slightly higher-pitched. A beatific little smile quirked the Prognosticator's lips upward. 'In this instance...' He stared off into the middle distance again. 'Those who have forsaken their colours. And I see dawn. Midnight. Sun- set. These three will bring much strife in their wake. They seek to destroy. There is no room for compassion in the bat- tle that lies ahead. Ultimately, you will have to override your thirst for vengeance.'

He focused back on Arrun. 'You must keep your head, Daerys, or the price will be considerably greater than any- thing you can imagine.'

Arrun absorbed everything that Brand said with an insatiable hunger. The psyker delivered his vision in a series of barely comprehensible riddles, but where would the challenge be if the Emperor lay down a path of destiny in plain words? The Silver Skulls held tightly to the belief that whilst the Emperor's will guided them, they retained free rein in the interpretation of the dreams and visions.

There had been times during the Chapter's long and illustrious history when that interpretation had proved to be incorrect... but such errors of judgement were few and far between.

'Is there any more that you can tell me?'

'I see... three. Three of them. I do not quite have the measure, the scope of the vision... its very shape eludes me.' Brand's voice gradually returned to normal as he prised himself away from the psychological constraints of his meditation. 'That is all I have for you right now. I would need to divine the matter further to give you a full answer. The overwhelming sense I felt is that of betrayal, however.'

Arrun nodded. It went with the territory. The Red Corsairs, guided by a leader whose lust for power and greatness had spelled his own downfall, were traitors to a man.

'We can deal with this situation. We have strength, numbers and the power of the Imperium on our side.' He looked up. 'That is assuming that the enemy doesn't just run through us first.'

'We will survive this encounter. The *Wolf's* claws will not catch us. Not this time.' Brand shifted his gaze to Arrun. 'You do well to hold your ground, brother-captain. Standing proud in the face of such defiance will result in the survival of us all.' He gave a slow nod, sure of himself in this matter.

'I have never once questioned your advice in the many years we have served together, my friend. I am not going to start now.' Arrun looked up at the looming vessel. 'Evacuate non-essential areas. Lock down the bulkheads and all crew prepare for possible collision.'

* * *

THE FULL DUPLICITY of Huron Blackheart's scheme was still to unfold, but in low orbit, far beneath the stand-off between the two strike cruisers, another act was playing out.

Squad Carnelian had travelled down from the *Dread Argent* in companionable silence, oblivious to any of the drama occurring above them. Their destination was the communications tower to the north of the Primus-Phi refinery on Gildar Secundus. Their orders had been straightforward enough. Land, ascertain all was well and remain on the planet until they were summoned back to the *Dread Argent*. Not exactly taxing – but, as Sergeant Porteus reasoned, it was a chance to run through a few environmental training exercises with his squad. The uniquely formed mountain ranges of the planet would allow for some considerable opportunities. Training cages could only allow for so many scenarios after all. Nothing beat live exercises and terrain training.

The sergeant's moment of thoughtful contemplation was invaded by a sudden lance of white light that speared past the nose of the Thunderhawk. Catching sight of the pulse of energy out of the corner of his eye, Porteus had only to turn his head slightly to recognise what it was. By then, it was far too late.

Moments later, it happened again. The second lascannon shot struck its target this time, searing a crippling wound in the flank of the gunship. From his position at the controls, the human pilot was bellowing out curses and litanies to both the Emperor and the machine-spirits to keep them aloft.

'Counter-measures! Counter-measures!' Porteus roared to the pilot as he smacked his harness release buckle. 'Where is that coming from?'

'The shots are coming from the turrets on the promethium refinery! Aiming guns... firing...'

There was the chatter of the Thunderhawk's weapons as the slaved servitors engaged and then there was a disorienting, rocking explosion caused by another shot which completely obliterated the starboard engine. It tore itself away from the wing in a shower of smoke and debris and tumbled to the surface below.

Any hope the pilot may have had of keeping control of the ship was ruined. The Thunderhawk was thrown off its trajectory and began a deadly corkscrew spin, plummeting downwards. Unbalanced, Porteus smashed into the side of the cockpit, his armour scraping with an unpleasant squeal against the hull interior. He lurched forward again. The warning sirens were blaring unnecessarily and he harboured a sudden raging urge to tear them from the walls.

His gauntleted fingers scrabbled for purchase and his fingers tightened around a weapons rack. He scrambled back into the main body of the gunship, shouting orders to his men to put on their helms and to prepare for a crash landing. Apart from Berem the pilot, an augmented human who had served Squad Carnelian for many years and the gun servitors, all aboard were Space Marines. The majority of them stood a good chance of surviving a controlled crash. The others were collateral damage. Clinical and harsh though that view might be, it had to be taken.

The third shot vaporised the cockpit and Berem was lost along with it. The interior space filled up immediately with rushing wind and choking smoke. The burning remains of the Thunderhawk plunged downwards, comet trails of fire and smoke marking its passage. Next to him, the squad's Prognosticator was speaking fervent words of passionate zeal, words designed to fill the hearts of Squad Carnelian with fire and courage. All of the squad's voices raised in conjunction with his until they were all speaking the Chapter's litanies, their voices perfectly in rhythm.

The surface of Gildar Secundus loomed large in the sergeant's vision and he broke off his recitation. The next words that he spoke were largely drowned out by the catastrophic introduction of the tortured hull to the unyielding mountain rock.

'Brace for impact!'

* * *

'BRACE FOR IMPACT!'

The *Wolf of Fenris* was going to hit them. The two ships were going to annihilate one another.

But it did not.

The tiniest of mathematical calculations that had been input in the *Wolf's* helm several minutes earlier was enough to bring the ships agonisingly close. Yet in spatial terms, 'agonisingly close' was still an astonishing distance away.

'She's preparing to fire her port batteries.'

'Run out our own. They want to take a broadside swipe, then we will give them one of our own back.'

'Aye, my lord.'

Relentlessly pounding at each other, the two behemoth vessels ran parallel for a time. Void shields trembled and shrieked at the proximity, flooding the space between them with crackling, arcing discharge. The energy that each ship's shields generated sought to repel the other with equal ferocity.

Macro shells that were easily the size of battle tanks, streams of plasma so potent that they could boil hab-blocks and huge calibre laser fire filled the spatial gulf, stippling the void shields of both with thousands of tiny impact craters, each desperately seeking to claw its way through.

'Our shield generators are starting to fail. They're still holding for now, but we can't take much more of this.'

'She will hold.' Arrun's confidence and faith in the *Dread Argent* was absolute and those on the bridge accepted his quiet assurance without question. She was taking a beating, yes, but like the Chapter who utilised her she was made of stern stuff.

It was apparent to even the untrained eye that the *Wolf of Fenris* was not faring quite so well. Not all of her guns were operational, probably as a result of whatever had happened to her. As such, the fiery venom that she spat at the *Dread Argent* was nowhere near indicative of her true deadly force. The Silver Skulls ship, on the other hand, was at peak performance.

The punishing assault finally collapsed the last of the

Wolf's shield banks and the multitude of projectiles from the *Dread Argent* began tearing at the armoured skin, now raw and exposed. Venting gases, armour plating and bodies spiralled into space as the Silver Skulls arsenal chewed breaches through the port decks, leaving nothing but blackened scars and frost-rimed corpses in its wake.

The Space Wolves ship was critically damaged – but even an assault of this magnitude had failed to blunt her tenacity. It wasn't until after the last shot was fired and the guns fell silent that the reality and truth of the matter became fully evident. They had been tricked.

The *Dread Argent* was now far out of Gildar Secundus's orbit, having left it to intercept the apparently drifting *Wolf of Fenris*. This had put the other ship now directly behind them accelerating with alarming pace towards a planet now devoid of the Silver Skulls defence. Turning around was a slow, cumbersome process. It had been a cunning ploy. It had worked.

But there was more to it.

'Augury contact,' said the console operator. Arrun turned his head, only to realise that the operator hadn't finished. 'Another augury contact. Three. Four!' Panic came into his voice and Arrun strode across the bridge and stared at the screen himself.

One after another, ships were being disgorged from the warp and emerging into realspace. Translating deep in-system to the Gildar Rift was the kind of risk that only a fool would take. There was a catastrophic risk of collision. The captains of these vessels were either fools, desperate... or they were fearless.

Longer range sensors began to announce the arrival of still more ships, not translating quite so close and the truth of the matter became horribly apparent. Arrun's fist came down in fury on to the console.

Seven ships. Eight. More. Every single one of them was heading directly for Gildar Secundus. Not a single one of them would be hindered by the patrolling *Dread Argent*... because the *Dread Argent* had swallowed their bait without hesitation and was no longer in position and patrolling.

Far too late, Arrun realised what had happened. Shouts from various console officers overlaid one another in discordant anger, a counterpoint of horror and disbelief that all ultimately sang the same song.

'We have been outmanoeuvred,' marvelled Brand as the console operators reported the disturbing news. Arrun treated the psyker to a venomous glower.

'No, Prognosticator. We have not been "outmanoeuvred". If you would, perhaps you will recall that I put out an astropathic call to the other ships in the Rift. They will be here in a matter of hours as soon as I give the word. The *Manifest Destiny* is amongst them. With a battle-barge on our side, these traitors don't stand a chance.' He turned his attentions back to the crew. 'Bring us about. None of these ships can cause us any real harm, not yet. In the main, they're nothing more than frigates, destroyers... maybe a couple of escorts. If necessary, we will pick them off one at a time.'

Arrun's voice held both the tone of authority and the ring of steel. His fingers toyed idly with the belt that cinched his tabard at the waist. A thrill of anticipation ran through his veins. Soon he would be back into his wargear. The promise of battle was upon them. They would slaughter these raiders to the last man. They would cleanse the Gildar Rift of this taint. Once the *Manifest Destiny* arrived, they wouldn't stand a chance.

The battle-barge, one of two the Silver Skulls boasted, was his usual command. It was quite capable of enough firepower to wipe these intruders from the face of the Gildar Rift with a few barrages of its main weapons.

'Brother-captain.'

Sergeant Matteus's voice broke across his thoughts. In the frenzy of the moment, Arrun had all but forgotten the returned Thunderhawk. The young warrior's voice was reasonably well modulated, but the strain implicit was felt by all.

'Speak, brother-sergeant. What's happening over there?'

'It was the Red Corsairs, sir. They took the *Wolf of Fenris*.'

Arrun nodded slowly. He should have suspected as much. The loss of the strike cruiser was a blow to the Space Wolves and a great source of fury for all loyal battle-brothers. Information travelled so slowly throughout the Imperium of Man, given the great distances, that it was entirely possible Terra itself wasn't even yet aware of this turn of events. Despite the gravity of his own present situation, he made a mental note to set an astropath the task of sending the news as soon as possible.

'Give me a quick report. How many of you have returned?'

'We lost eight, sir. Apothecary Ryarus among them.'

'No...' Brand breathed the word instantly. 'No! He must still be alive. He *has* to still be alive. The Emperor did not see eternal darkness for him during my divinations.'

'Alive or not, Apothecary Ryarus is in the hands of the archenemy. You and I both know what that means, brother.' Arrun's own crushing disappointment at the loss of such a key member of his project team had to be put aside for the moment. 'If he lives still, he will be given a choice. Swear allegiance to Blackheart, or die. Much as it pains me to say it, I would wish for his swift death, Prognosticator. I wholeheartedly believe that he will do the same.' His face darkened. 'Unlikely as it is, I would not want to ever come up against one of my own brothers in a battle.'

Whether Ryarus lived or not was not even worthy of debate. Given the cutthroat nature and attitude of the Red Corsairs, one thing was certain. Ryarus was lost to them. It was a blow on more than one level. First and foremost, they had lost a brother. An Apothecary at that – and a blessed good one. His key involvement in the Resurgent Project was another reason. There was a brief, wild thought that perhaps the Prognosticator's insight would suggest a cessation of the project. For the first time since he had been pulled into the whole thing, Arrun realised that this made him feel concern far more than hope. He was in too deep now. He did not *want* the project to stop.

Either way, he knew that he would have to keep his regrets at bay until the current matter was dealt with. He was still smarting, deep down, that the *Wolf of Fenris* had been used as a lure to draw him out in the open. At least they were still in one piece. It was a small mercy, but a crucial one at that. Perhaps, the Emperor willing, they would be given the chance to return to the stolen strike cruiser for Ryarus and the others who had been lost.

But now they were caught quite literally between a rock and a hard place. Arrun was going to have to play the game a little longer.

WHAT HAD ONCE been a proud Thunderhawk gunship was now nothing more than a twisted, molten knuckle of metal, its fist plunged into the ground of Gildar Secundus. Black, acrid smoke poured up in thick columns, twisting and curling into the dusk of the planet's night sky. Broken conduits fizzed and popped whilst ruptured fuel lines dribbled their contents out onto the ground in some sort of cheap mockery of the promethium refinery several kilometres away.

Porteus dragged himself to his feet, shaking his head to clear it of the buzzing in his ears. A glance around told him very little but the obvious; Brother Simeon had died shortly after the point of impact, unable to make any noise beyond an agonised gurgle. One of the Thunderhawk's structural girders, a massive thing, had torn from its mountings and impaled the unfortunate psyker from behind. It had torn through his chest and his body hung there, limp as a broken doll, congealing blood dripping slowly and stickily from the hole that had been punched right through him.

Blood now dribbled down the front of his blue battle plate, the armour that marked him as different from the rest of the squad. It pooled beneath him in a sticky mass on the floor of the gunship. Porteus turned his head away briefly, touched by a moment of profound grief for the loss of one of his closest friends. His swift death had ensured that his suffering was minimal.

That was to say, Porteus *hoped* it had been swift.

The Silver Skulls who formed Squad Carnelian variously knelt or lay on the ground, as stunned by the landing as the sergeant had been. Porteus tore his eyes from the dead psyker, whose face was hidden from sight by the helm he wore.

'Status report,' the squad sergeant said. 'Who's still with me here?' Removing his helm, he hawked up a mouthful of bile. It came out stained red. The air was thin here, suggesting they were at a reasonable altitude. How they had not been impaled on the reaching fingers of the mountainside defied all odds. The Thunderhawk had come down in a dusty patch of scrubland somewhere in the heart of the mountains; within a range that on the local maps of Gildar Secundus was called the Steeple. Brown, sickly-looking plants sprouted out of the rock here and there, clinging desperately to life, although many of them were smouldering having been caught in the toxic fumes and fire of the wreck.

Porteus had no idea how he had survived the crash and he did not care to linger on the how of the situation. Right now, he had to establish the condition of the living. The dead he would take care of later. Dire situation or not, the psyker had not only been his friend and his battle-brother. He was a Prognosticator – and there were rites that had to be observed, lest the Emperor's wrath descend upon them. At the thought, Porteus made the sign of the aquila, his thumbs interlinked across his chest.

By the Emperor's grace, only Simeon was dead. Their armour was in varying states of disrepair and there were a few broken limbs which were not worrying. They would heal swiftly enough. Keyle, one of his surviving squad members, found an unbroken auspex somewhere in the remains of the Thunderhawk. With a mumbled and decidedly clumsy prayer to its dormant machine spirit, Porteus was able to force it to awaken. It didn't offer much to alleviate their situation, but it gave them an idea as to their current position in relation to their intended target zone.

They had been sent down here to complete a mission and they would execute that command to the bitter end. Every attempt they made at ground-to-ship communication failed.

'Interference from the Rift, probably,' Keyle suggested.

'Although there may be some sort of blocking signal being utilised by whoever tried to shoot us down.' One of the newer members of his squad, the young warrior had sustained a minor injury to his head. A clotted stream of dark red was on his face, issuing from a jagged cut in his scalp.

'"Probably" isn't a word I want to hear at this time, Keyle,' replied Porteus. 'There is no time for woolly thought or fleeting guesses. We need to establish why it is that the refinery was firing on us. There is an obvious answer, I feel.' Porteus did not frequently act in accordance with his gut instincts; something he had inherited from a previous commanding officer. The sergeant had always been very much of the opinion that assumption was the providence of fools... and the dead. Forgetting that rule was the way good warriors died. Despite the situation, Porteus's lips twitched in a smile. Gileas hadn't expressed his blunt view in those exact words; his choice of language had always been far more colourful and definitely more descriptive. But it was close enough.

Looking around at the squad in their dented and damaged suits of power armour and assortment of injuries, Porteus checked a sigh. 'We will have to scout it out ourselves and establish the situation. We also need to get to the comms tower on the north of the refinery. Here.'

He knelt in the dust and began drawing a rough diagram using a combination of the auspex and his own mental map of the layout as reference. 'We were supposed to land here... a few kilometres away from the communications array. The tower itself is a little north of the refinery. We were knocked off course. By my estimation, we're about...' He marked a point on the crude map. 'Thirty, maybe forty kilometres to the west.'

He glanced over at the body of Simeon. They had no Apothecary with them which meant that as ranking commander present, the job of recovering the Chapter's legacy fell to him. It was a messy, but necessary job. It was hard enough to lose a brother in such an inglorious way – far worse that it was their Prognosticator. The fact that they had lost their link with the Emperor's will was a poor omen indeed. But they could not stay here. There was every possibility that whoever had shot them out of the sky would send out scouts of their own to make sure that the job was complete. Unlikely, given the mountainous terrain, but still a consideration.

Porteus tore his eyes away and addressed the squad. 'The terrain is going to be difficult, but we can allow it to work for us rather than against us. It will help us mask our approach more effectively.' He straightened up. 'Let's get moving. I want a full weapons check, then we salvage whatever we can from the wreck and burn he rest. We don't need it falling into enemy hands. Swiftly, brothers. Night is coming in fast and we should take that as another advantage.'

The squad began to carry out their sergeant's orders without question. Porteus joined Keyle in the belly of the Thunderhawk and ripped aside broken panels and wreckage until he located the emergency medical supplies. At some point during their rapid descent, the equipment had been thrown into complete disarray. No matter where he looked, there was no reductor to be found. That meant that he would be forced to commit the doubly heinous sin of carving out Simeon's gene-seed with nothing more advanced than the sharp blade of his combat knife.

Porteus took a deep breath. It felt almost like a violation, a disrespect to the dead Prognosticator; to be recovering his Quintessence Sacred in this barbaric way rather than an Apothecary performing the task with the reverence and skill it deserved. But needs must. The progenoid gland must be recovered so that the line of Silver Skulls could continue. The genetic stores of the Chapter were already greatly depleted.

With Keyle's help, he moved Simeon's corpse from the ungracious position it had ended up in. They slid the dead Prognosticator clear of the girder and his body freed with a grotesque wet *slurp*. The girder had punched right through his back, cracking open the fused ribcage from behind. Whilst it made Porteus's job easier, it was still an undignified mode of death.

I wonder if he saw this coming?

It was a blasphemous thought and Porteus quashed it immediately, ashamed at his own inner musings.

With the Prognosticator laid on the ground, it was a swift enough job to remove the progenoid, but to Porteus's dismay, it was ruined. The girder had torn through half of the organ leaving it ragged, a useless thing. It merely added to the heavy sense of foreboding the sergeant already felt at the loss of their psyker and he returned the damaged gland to the gaping hole in Simeon's corpse. It would be incinerated along with the rest of his brother's body.

All that remained was to strip away Simeon's battle plate. They would not be transporting it with them, but they could not perform the rite of cremation whilst he remained encased in its shell – and whatever bits and pieces they could salvage could be used by those who still lived. As he removed the other's helm, Porteus was surprised at the expression on his battle-brother's face. In death, Simeon had the faintest hint of a smile on his lips. His eyes were closed and he looked for all the world like he were meditating. The expression was achingly familiar. The sergeant lay the helm to one side and spoke a few words from one of the Silver Skulls many funerary litanies.

Kneeling in the fading light and dust of the mountains, Porteus felt anger bubbling deep inside him. As he stood, he accepted a flamer from Keyle. Igniting it, he aimed it at Simeon's lifeless body. The words of vengeance dropped from his lips before he could stop them.

Around him, other voices joined his own and repeated the oath. Each felt Simeon's loss as keenly as he did and Porteus took pride in the knowledge that every last one of them would exact that revenge by his side.

The flames licked around the Prognosticator, burning ferociously. It would take time to fully dispose of the body and time was something that the squad had precious little of. Night had fallen completely now and the sky was studded with the many stars that made up the constellations of the Gildar system. Porteus looked up into the glittering tapestry and a smile ghosted across his face. He could almost hear

Simeon explaining the importance of looking to the stars for guidance. It had been his preferred method of untangling the web of future events.

As the stink of charred flesh permeated the air, Porteus hefted the weapon and nodded.

'Helmets back on. We're moving out now.'

THEY WERE AT stalemate, for now at least.

More ships had entered the system. Escort vessels, more Infidels... but as of yet, nothing as large as the *Wolf of Fenris*. The strike cruiser had presented a clever ruse. Bait to lure the Silver Skulls out into the open and even now, Arrun cursed himself for taking it like a naïve child. Even as he had dealt with the repercussions of that, further things were occurring.

In carrying out his orders to commune with the rest of the fleet, the astropaths had initially experienced a terrible psychic interference that had left most of them wailing and weeping bloody tears of pain. They had been driven to greater efforts by the whiplash tongue of the Head Astropath however, and eventually, one of them had managed to penetrate the raging currents of the empyrean, pierce her way through the psychic static and project her message. She had died straight afterwards, the sheer force of effort curdling her brain with psychic feedback and causing her to haemorrhage, but the message had been sent. Several others now lay in degrees of useless torpor, of no use to the astropathic choir or, indeed, anybody any more.

'Word has been sent to the fleet as you ordered, my lord,' reported the Head Astropath who had been duly summoned to the bridge. Fear rippled from him in waves that caused Brand to stare at him in disgust. If Arrun was aware of it, he didn't indicate it as he nodded and dismissed the human psyker.

The astropath scurried from the bridge in relief, Brand's eyes boring into him all the while.

'He possesses a mediocre talent at best,' the Prognosticator observed. 'How he rose to his position defies belief. We should consider a replacement when this is over.'

Brand's easy confidence that the situation would be resolved satisfactorily was surprising, but not unexpected. Arrun was standing at the hololithic display that projected their current situation in the Gildar Rift and he was not liking the picture it painted.

'We could hold out well enough against the escort ships,' he said as he stared at the flickering images. 'But by the time we are well positioned for attacking them, the *Wolf of Fenris* will undoubtedly have begun to come about and be seeking to enter the fray. We can deploy our gunships, but without heavy support...' Arrun scowled. 'They won't last long.'

'What I would be more concerned about,' suggested the Prognosticator, 'is exactly why it should be that none of them, apart from the *Wolf*, have made any sort of aggressive gesture towards us yet.' He joined Arrun at the hololithic display and studied it thoughtfully, his eyes picking out one ship after another.

'The thought had crossed my mind. Right now, though...' Arrun took a step back. 'I'm more interested in understanding exactly what it is that they are doing. Or, more precisely, what they are not doing.' Other than the broadside attack by the *Wolf of Fenris*, not a single vessel had made so much as a threatening move. No weapons were firing at them. The ships were just there. Waiting.

Arrun glared at the display as though he could rectify the problem by staring it down. 'There is much to consider. I have fought the Red Corsairs many times, but this is something new. They've never sent a fleet this size into the Gildar Rift before.' He leaned forward onto the pedestal on which the sector map was projected and met his Prognosticator's gaze head on.

'On top of that, I still have to consider the impact of Ryarus's death on the Resurgent Project.' Brand noted that the captain chose to consider the other Silver Skull dead rather than consider the alternatives. It was a logical choice and the Prognosticator approved.

'He kept copious notes, brother.'

'But the bond he built up with Volker... the boy trusted

him implicitly. Do you think he will be so willing to make the final sacrifice without that?'

'He is Varsavian through and through. He wishes to serve the Chapter in the only way he can. I would not concern yourself as to Volker's conviction. The other Apothecaries will pick up where Ryarus left off.' Arrun found himself smiling bitterly.

'I presume you have already divined whether or not we should continue with the Resurgent Project?'

'Yes. And we must not stop. Not now.' Arrun sighed, resignation weighing on his shoulders heavily.

'You have absolute conviction we will come out of this situation, don't you?'

'Of course I do,' said the Prognosticator, surprised at Arrun's words. 'The Emperor guides me. The Emperor protects.'

'The Emperor protects,' Arrun acknowledged. He lifted his eyes to the viewscreen and his posture stiffened.

'Whatever they were waiting for,' he said, moving into the centre of the bridge deck. 'I think we're about to find out.'

There was a ripple, a distortion beyond them; more ships translating in-system. Only this time, it wasn't something small and comparatively insignificant. This time, the vessel that emerged from the warp, slowly and menacingly moving towards them, was bigger even than the *Wolf of Fenris*.

Arrun knew this ship. He knew it well. 'The *Spectre of Ruin*,' he said, staring at it.

'You know this vessel?'

'Aye, brother, I do.' Arrun's spine straightened and pure hatred filled his eyes. 'It is one of the chosen transports of the Tyrant of Badab. I suspect, my brother, that Lugft Huron is on board.'

SEVEN
BLACKHEART

ONCE, HE HAD been Lugft Huron, Chapter Master of the Astral Claws. Then the Imperium had forsaken him. The Imperium had tried to deny him what had been rightfully his and the Imperium had tried to strike him down when he made the decision to take it anyway. Lugft Huron had faced down the amassed forces that the Imperium had thrown at him and he had survived. But the cost had been beyond measure.

The long ago siege on the Palace of Thorns, and the final assault on his throne room instigated by the thrice-cursed Androcles of the Star Phantoms had been costly and it had been bloody. The wounds Huron had received had been critical and had it not been for the subsequent, tireless efforts of all of the Apothecaries and tech-priests who served their master with unswerving loyalty, the Tyrant of Badab would have been no more.

Against all the odds, the Tyrant lived. He survived levels of physical stress and pain tolerance that would have killed lesser warriors. He had been so heavily augmented and enhanced that it was true to say that the Space Marine known to the Imperium as Lugft Huron had died that day and Huron Blackheart had been born.

There were rumours, but there were always rumours, that he was literally not even the same man. He knew who he was. He was content in his identity. It was he who lived with the agony of his continued existence. What did he care if the rest of the universe speculated and disagreed? Let them. Whatever and whoever he was, he had died once already.

It had been both a physical and metaphorical death; the Tyrant's disgust at the lies of the Imperium combined with his status as an outcast renegade had led him to sever any and all ties to his own past. Lugft Huron was a being he cast aside without compunction; caught as he was in the iron grip of vainglorious madness. During the long period of his delirium, in the days he clung to the spark of life with tenacious fury against overwhelming odds, he engaged in negotiations with unseen powers he never openly acknowledged and he made countless deals of which he never spoke.

He was granted rebirth. Eight days after he was struck down by Androcles, the former Master of the Astral Claws rejoined the physical plane and spoke to his loyal men once more. They thrilled to the reality of his impossible return, rejoicing in his restored presence. The very fact he had survived certain death awoke the spark of fanaticism. He soaked up their adulation and his arrogance knew no bounds.

In acknowledgement of who and what he had become, he took the name 'Blackheart' to his breast and decreed that the name of the Astral Claws be forever stricken from their lips and memories. They had desecrated their power armour, defiling the aquila and painting over the sigil of their once-noble Chapter. In time, others had flocked to Blackheart's banner. Cultists who revelled in the Red Corsairs brutality. Space Marines from other Chapters who felt that they had been wronged in some way. Some were convinced to serve Huron Blackheart in lieu of owed payments on substantial debts. There were those who truly believed in what he was doing, or who could be persuaded to believe in it very quickly.

Blackheart and his men, it was said, could be surprisingly persuasive when the mood took them.

For the most part, the Tyrant himself remained a figurehead, rarely leading the standard raids and boarding actions that formed the backbone of his Red Corsair's activities. He remained in solitary contemplation of his dark fate. Apothecaries and tech-priests attended him as required, ensuring his augmetics were well maintained and doing whatever they could to relieve the constant pain. But every so often, something would pique his interest. At these times, he would step from his throne room as though he had never been away and he would once again indulge his voracious appetite for power.

When he chose to take command, he did so with the same charisma and power that he had demonstrated in his heyday. He was an unstoppable, powerful force with an ability to plan for several possible contingencies and adapt his ideas at the very last minute. He was considered to be a scourge and he revelled in the moniker.

The activities of the Silver Skulls in the Gildar Rift had engaged his curiosity and the old, unslakeable thirst for things that were not his own had bubbled to the surface. He had monitored them for long enough. He knew their patrols, understood their methods and he had decreed that the waiting was at an end.

Today the Red Corsairs would strike.

ALL ACROSS THE Gildar system, the arrival of the *Spectre of Ruin* heralded the rousing of a rebellion that had been sleeping peacefully for several long months. The hydra heads of insurrection and incursion that had been so carefully and strategically placed reacted to the moment of the flagship's arrival with precision timing.

Their poisonous strikes were swift and struck true, seeing vital Imperial structures brought to their knees with alarming alacrity.

Gildar Primus, the airless mining world orbiting closest to the sun, saw sudden raids on atmospheric generators which caused more than a dozen hab-domes to be starved of oxygen. Countless workers and defence troops died in breathless agony without ever knowing the reason why. Defence forces mustering in response to the disaster found themselves cut off by the airless, frozen domes. They stood helpless, unable to react as the Red Corsairs, safe from the ravages of the atmosphere, took control.

The hydroponic gardens of Gildar Quintus suffered terribly. Once fruitful and yielding vital foodstuffs that served not only the Gildar system but were exported to Imperial worlds beyond, their bounty withered and died as the poisonous chemicals introduced into the feed lines by human Red Corsair infiltrators seeped forth their toxic fumes.

For every world a different plan. Civil rioting broke out across the Gildar worlds, engaging the planetary defence forces and keeping their attention from the true threat that loomed beyond the planet's atmosphere far above them.

As Porteus and his squad had discovered on their way to the surface, Gildar Secundus was already dealing with its own situation. But it wasn't the only planet that was under threat. Across the eight major planets of the Gildar system, the arrival of Huron Blackheart meant that loyal Imperial citizens were finding themselves drowned in the relentless tide that he had brought. Red Corsairs raiders, Adeptus Astartes and humans both received the call to arms from their revered leader and they did exactly what they were instructed to do.

Everything happened quickly. Far too quickly for any kind of fast response. The Gildar system was falling.

The full extent of Huron Blackheart's complex strategy was only just beginning to come to light. They were schemes that were so twisted, convoluted and duplicitous that they had passed by even the uncanny predictive capabilities of the Silver Skulls greatest Prognosticators.

* * *

'MY LORD APOTHECARY.'

If Huron Blackheart was capable of expressing any kind of pleasure, this was as close at it came. The hololithic display from the *Spectre of Ruin* flickered before Garreon, poor in quality, but a welcome sight nonetheless. He and Taemar had been tasked with this most important element of Blackheart's ground plans and the one which had been in effect longer than any other. Their infiltrators had been in place for months. Taking control of the communications tower at the given moment had been a work of almost breathtaking simplicity.

Once the communications tower had been taken, it had been the easiest thing to broadcast the message sent by the *Spectre of Ruin* across the system, heralding the start of the attack. The promethium refinery had fallen swiftly into the Red Corsair's hands, the Corpsemaster himself dealing much of the death that was evidenced before him.

Broken, bloodied bodies of Primus-Phi's outer defence guard lay in dismembered ruin everywhere. The stench of death was dulled a little by the falling rain – but not to Garreon. He could still smell death and it fired his blood and his soul. Red Corsairs moved within the exterior compound of the refinery, some manning the cannons, others merely looting the bodies of the dead for anything of value.

'My lord.' The cadaver-like face of the Corpsemaster twisted in a brief smile. 'I trust your arrival in the system has thus far been unimpeded?'

'As if there was any doubt.' The Tyrant's growl was grating and harsh as it was torn from the replacement larynx and metal teeth. 'These worshippers of the corpse-Emperor will soon come to learn the futility of resistance. Even now, they prepare their paltry defences. I welcome this. It will be an amusing distraction.'

A rhythmic grating suggested that Blackheart was laughing. 'But tell me, my Lord Apothecary, my most glorious Corpsemaster, are my plans progressing well?'

'Aye, my lord. Our human allies did not disappoint us. They took the communications tower easily enough. The defences here at the refinery were weak at best.' A slightly twisted smile. 'They were easily bested. I confess, I found the brief engagement almost disappointing. But there was fine bounty to be taken from it.' He referred to the piles of dead from whom he could take any amount of genetic material to use in his experiments.

The Corpsemaster hesitated briefly, then grudgingly continued. 'Taemar led quite an impressive raid. He fights well, even with his inglorious heritage.' The Corpsemaster's face twisted in a supercilious sneer. 'I have never been too proud to admit when I am wrong. You have chosen your lieutenant well. Even if he is not one of our very own.'

'Curb your disdain, Garreon. Has he returned to the *Wolf of Fenris*?'

'Yes. He departed as soon as the signal was received and the moment the *Wolf* was in range.'

It had been a masterstroke. The positioning of the *Wolf* had been vital. It had needed to be within teleport range of the planet in order to both deliver the call to arms that had launched the Red Corsairs into action – and to receive Blackheart's second-in-command as he returned ready for the next phase.

'Excellent.'

'He sent a most interesting communication on his return. I am led to believe that there is a particular reward awaiting me on our ship. The capture of a number of Silver Skulls warriors.' Against any sense of control he may have had, the Corpsemaster began to salivate at the thought of access to a much-coveted Chapter. The secrets to be unlocked would engage his attentions fully for months to come. He raised a hand absently to his lips and wiped the drool away from his chin.

As though sensing what his Apothecary was thinking, Blackheart gave another of his grating, inhuman chuckles. 'I deeply regret making you wait before you can indulge your insatiable curiosities, my Lord Apothecary. But this will be over soon. As soon as I have taken the *Dread Argent*, I will be joining you on the surface and we can take what we need and plenty more of that which we do not. You will ensure you hold it for me?'

It was oddly plaintive; the request of a spoiled child and as he had always done, the Corpsemaster indulged his lord and master outrageously.

'You must learn not to doubt your most faithful, my lord. Primus-Phi is ours now. Already we have destroyed a ship sent down by the Silver Skulls to investigate. We have a confirmation that all that remains is a hulk of metal. The refinery guns are firmly under our control and the wealth of this place is all ours.'

The noise that came from Blackheart could only be described as an excitable giggle. The depth of madness implicit in the sound was extraordinary, but the Corpsemaster had grown used to his master's growing instability over the decades. The noise ceased as abruptly as it had begun.

'You are to be commended.'

'Thank you, my lord.'

'WE HAVE VERY few options, brother-captain.'

Daerys Arrun was staring out of the viewscreen, his eyes fixed on the battle-barge as its immense proportions grew ever larger. It was enormously frustrating; the feeling of being the prey instead of the hunter. Brand's simple words forced him to turn away from the *Spectre of Ruin* and to look at the Prognosticator. There was a smouldering rage barely contained beneath the surface of the Silver Skulls captain and from the way the veins stood out in his neck and forehead, he was working exceptionally hard on keeping it quelled.

'We make our stand,' was all he said. 'They outnumber us by too high a factor. We can only pray to the ancestors that the Tyrant does not know the rest of the fleet is inbound. If we can make a stand until then...' He turned his head towards the *Spectre of Ruin* once again. 'If we can make a stand until then, we can have a chance.'

'We could consider Volker.'

'Yes, we could consider Volker.' The tone of Arrun's voice

suggested that it wasn't a consideration that was particularly high on his list of options. 'But without Ryarus, it would be a gamble at best, destructive for us all at worst.'

'The gamble may become our only option.' Brand scratched his jaw. 'Bear that in mind. Better by far that the *Dread Argent* is destroyed in the attempt than to let her fall into enemy hands.'

There were many ships outside, effectively pinning them into position. Yet they all remained unmoving. Were it not for the occasional firing of a stabilising thruster from one of them, it could have been a scene frozen in time. They made no move to fire upon the *Dread Argent* which to Arrun suggested only one thing.

The Red Corsairs wanted to take the ship.

'Over my dead body,' the captain murmured to himself.

'The God-Emperor willing, it won't come to that, brother.' Despite his low mutter, Brand had heard him.

Their brief exchange was interrupted as the servitor slaved to the communications console spoke up. 'Incoming transmission over the ship-to-ship vox-net,' it droned.

'Silver Skulls vessel *Dread Argent*, hold your position. Slow your engines and prepare to be boarded.'

The voice was grating and inhuman, almost mechanical in sound. But there was still a lingering trace of humanity there as well. It was sneering in its tone, making a mockery of the words with which the Silver Skulls themselves used to deal with intruders. The implied insult did not go unnoticed, but Arrun remained silent. He did not have to wait long for confirmation of his suspicions. The enemy clearly had no desire to drag out the suspense and for that, Arrun was almost grateful.

'As you have no doubt realised by now, I am Huron Blackheart, Master of the Red Corsairs. Your vessel will shortly belong to me. I would suggest that it would be in your best interests to give up any foolish thoughts of resistance or some kind of dramatic last stand. I am well aware of the Silver Skulls tendency to heroics and truly, Captain Daerys Arrun, there is no point. What happens to your crew at this point is up to you... although I suspect this will be your personal final battle.'

Every soul on the bridge of the *Dread Argent* listened to the words as they dropped through the vox-net, their acidic nature and understated threat carrying much more weight than an outright boast. There was a barking laugh and Blackheart's rumble resumed.

'What, nothing to say, Captain Arrun? And you have been so talkative in the past! Such interesting transmissions.'

'You will not take my ship, traitor.' Arrun finally spoke up and Brand nodded quiet approval at the level tone of his voice. 'The Silver Skulls will never betray the Imperium. You will not succeed here. We will prevail.'

'I rather hoped you would choose to resist,' the response came. 'Had you meekly surrendered, it would have robbed us of an ideal opportunity for some much-needed sport. Later, when I am ripping out your pathetic chapel in the heart of my new ship, I will spare a thought for your spirited attempts at defiance. Who knows? I may even make a trophy of your skull to adorn my new chambers. Or perhaps I will let you live long enough to watch as I desecrate that which you hold so precious. I will–'

'Kill the link.' Arrun's rage was towering. 'Kill it. Now.'

'Compliance.' As the servitor severed the audio link from the *Spectre of Ruin*, the lingering sound of Blackheart's inhuman laughter could still be heard.

The look of impotent fury that was locked on Arrun's face could have adorned a war-mask. Yet behind his blazing eyes his mind was calculating and coming up with an alternative strategy with expediency. The evidence that he had been outmanoeuvred loomed large on the bridge hololith, mocking him, and the sight of it did nothing at all to salve his wounded pride. Yet he would never allow this ruthless warmonger the swift victory he so obviously craved.

The Silver Skulls would never lay down arms in the face of the enemy. Huron Blackheart was a madman to think they might be persuaded otherwise.

The bridge silenced to a hush as the crew anxiously

awaited the orders that would send them into battle.

After little more than several heartbeats, Arrun nodded and raised his head.

'Reduce shields to minimal power. Divert everything we have to the engines.' A few eyebrows raised in confusion, but he ignored them. 'Ahead full speed. Full burn. Hard and fast as you can muster.' An officer hastily relayed the orders and within seconds the angry thrum of the plasma reactors could be felt vibrating through the hull.

'If we try to run with such weakened defences, then the Tyrant will burn us from the void in seconds,' Brand stated. There was no reproach in the Prognosticator's words; more a sense of bafflement at his captain's strategy.

'I know,' Arrun replied, 'in fact I'm counting on it.'

'Explain.'

'It's obvious.' A sardonic smile crossed Arrun's face. 'He doesn't want a ruined hulk, he wants a trophy. As such, he will aim to cripple rather than destroy us. Once he's achieved that, he will descend and pick us apart from within. He has played us from the very beginning. But now?'

The smile on Arrun's face became something different. 'Now... I intend to do the same to him. It is time to level this playing arena.' It was a dangerous gamble, but given their situation there was little choice.

Brand nodded his agreement, understanding the reasoning behind what appeared to be little more than a random decision. Seeing the mixed, worried expressions on the faces of his crew, Arrun wordlessly cursed the Tyrant for his cunning. Caught as they were, with their backs on the frigate blockade that lay between them and Gildar Secundus, they had no choice. They had to keep the *Dread Argent* held together and in their possession long enough for the rest of the flotilla to arrive.

Arrun knew that his crew would trust his orders. He had never made random decisions during his time in command and he was not acting randomly now.

Thrusters burning hot with the increase of power, the *Dread Argent* began its desperate lunge for freedom. As Arrun had predicted, within moments of their move, the guns of the *Spectre* unleashed a murderous volley. What the slave crew of Huron Blackheart's massive vessel lacked in skill they more than made up for with enthusiasm and before the *Dread Argent* had truly begun to make any headway its shields had collapsed under the barrage.

Half a second later a brass-wrought shell the size of a battle tank tore a savage hole in the armoured engine housing. Immediately, liquid plasma, the ship's life-blood began to spill into the void. Wounded, the mighty thrusters sputtered and died, their raging fury dulling to a sullen orange glow.

Their quarry brought to heel, dozens of barbed boarding craft detached from the belly of the Tyrant's flagship, swarming their way towards the limping vessel like ants racing to a carcass.

On the bridge of the *Dread Argent*, Captain Arrun watched their approach with grim satisfaction. The deck was bathed in flickering crimson light and several banks of cogitators belched smoke and sparks, their slaved servitors fused and ruined.

It could have been worse, Arrun considered, but did not articulate. The Tyrant was reaching out and taking the bait.

'Is there still power to the reactors?' The captain laid a firm hand on the shoulder of the tech-adept hovering by the nearby console. The young woman looked up at him, then pressed a few buttons, turned a few dials and engaged some levers. Eventually, she nodded, although it was hesitant. There was something akin to reproach in her eyes. The ship, her *charge* had been damaged after all – but she fully understood the compromise. She crisply relayed the information he wanted and he gave her a grim, self-satisfied smile.

'We have breaches in the enginarium and several primary conduits have fractured. The emergency venting has served its purpose, however, my lord. To the eyes of others we appear wounded – but we retain precisely sixty-seven point three per cent combat efficiency.'

Arrun nodded. 'It will have to be enough. Now, come just a little closer, you mongrel pack of traitors.' He watched as the cloud of tiny runes on the flickering hololith closed around his beloved ship.

'Our burst of acceleration has carried us beyond the stern of the enemy vessel,' an officer informed him. His uniform was scuffed and he sported a shallow wound to his scalp, no doubt suffered during the barrage, but the young man carried himself with admirable confidence given their dire situation. The captain made a mental note to see that he was commended when the crisis was over.

'Excellent,' he glanced again at the cluster of runes that now almost surrounded his ship and smiled grimly. 'Now... bring those insects down and all power that we can muster to the engines.'

The strike cruiser was famed for the ferocity of its guns, mighty cannons that hurled shells from orbit to crush cities and sunder continents. Like many ships however, it was studded from prow to stern with hundreds of smaller turrets that were most frequently employed to keep debris, missiles and other small projectiles at bay. Lascannons and massive rotary guns filled the space around the *Dread Argent* with a lethal storm of energy and shrapnel that cut the surrounding raiders to pieces with ruthless efficiency.

Simultaneously, the vast engines roared once more into life, propelling the cruiser from its lethal predicament and out of reach of the arsenal of the encroaching *Spectre*. The sly gambit by the *Wolf of Fenris* was now revisited upon the Red Corsairs flagship as they put the enemy to their back. From his command pulpit Daerys Arrun fancied he could hear the furious roar of Huron Blackheart as he was cheated of his prize.

'We have time on our side now,' he said to the Prognosticator who had forsaken propriety and was grinning wildly at his captain's cunning. 'It will take them as long as us to come about and attack and they *will* do that. We can use that time to our advantage and prepare for them. The Emperor willing, the rest of the fleet will be upon those traitors shortly. Arrange for the highest ranking Apothecary on board to meet me in Correlan's workshop.' Arrun stepped to the console and considered for a few moments.

'This is Captain Arrun,' he said, activating the ship vox. 'All Fourth Company who are not yet geared for battle should make their way to the arming chambers with expediency. The Tyrant of Badab has designs on this ship and we are not going to let him take it without exacting a price in blood he will long remember. That is, if he even survives at all when we are through with him. We will prevail, brothers. Primus inter pares! To the fight!'

The Prognosticator murmured the company's motto along with the captain and the two warriors swept from the bridge deck to prepare for battle.

RED SNOW WAS falling.

At this altitude, so high up in the mountains, precipitation from the heavy cloud cover over Gildar Secundus fell as snow, thick and cold. It coated the armour of the Silver Skulls, swiftly obscuring their Chapter sigils and dulling the orange carnelian gems in their pauldrons. As it made its way down through the atmosphere, it changed swiftly to sleet and rain. Up here though, the flakes floated serenely downwards, blanketing the jagged mountain tops. The flakes were stained with red, pollution and dust from the promethium refinery, wending its way back to the ground.

Sergeant Porteus brushed the rust-coloured snow from his shoulders as he led his squad cautiously through the peaks. The path here, such as it was, made for arduous passage. Every one of them had given thanks to the ancestors and to the guiding hand of the Emperor that their ship had dumped them unceremoniously on an outcropping. Another kilometre in any other direction and the Thunderhawk would have been pierced by the thrusting mountains. Had that happened, then *all* of them would have been destroyed utterly. So in exchange for the reward of continued existence, Porteus was more than prepared to undergo a little hardship.

It was the kind of environment that few could ever claim to feel comfortable in and yet there was something startlingly and mournfully familiar about the mountains. The fortress-monastery of the Silver Skulls was itself located deep in the heart of Varsavia's northern mountain range. It was a harsh, inhospitable place that only the most tenacious and hardy souls would brave. Most of the Chapter's young aspirants and novitiates saw their first view of the fortress-monastery from the window of the transport that carried them there. A select few, though, had climbed their way to the top of the mountains alone. This was an impressive feat even for an Adeptus Astartes, let alone the handful of children who had made it.

All of the Silver Skulls were required to undertake something of a pilgrimage prior to their final conversion and deployment into the Scout Company. The long, lonely trip to the far-flung Prognosticator Temple where individual auguries were cast had necessitated travelling in mountains that were no easier than this. Strange, how it brought back such largely forgotten memories. It was clear from the conversation he was listening to across the squad's vox that it wasn't just a memory-jogger for Porteus; the other members of Carnelian were sharing quiet reminiscences. Occasionally, despite the situation, one would chuckle lightly.

Porteus did not cut across the conversation. With the death of Simeon, there was unsettling talk amongst his battle-brothers of poor omens. Without the guiding hand of the Emperor's Chosen walking alongside them, the Silver Skulls felt uncomfortable. So Porteus allowed the easy banter to continue. They needed to hold on to whatever drove them forward. Porteus felt Simeon's loss as keenly as they did, but he kept it clamped down. There would be time later for the appropriate rites.

The sergeant knew that once they located the source of the threat, all of their scurrilous whispers would dissolve in the one outlet that would allow them to release their pent-up anger. Battle.

Every brother of Squad Carnelian burned with the same desire to exact retribution on those who had dared commit the twin crimes of shooting them out of the sky and murdering one of their most revered. Any unfortunate who found themselves on the end of that particularly well-honed blade of fury would not fare well.

For now, though, things remained subdued. It was as though the snow itself somehow muted them.

The sergeant checked the various data feeds that he was receiving in his helmet. His positioning systems were compromised by the proximity of the mountains, but he did what he could to plot a course through the treacherous peaks. He even attempted some of the navigation by the old Varsavian method of using the stars; but the thick cloud cover that had descended rendered much of the night sky lost to his sight. By both Porteus's own reckoning and that of his power armour, they were heading more or less in a straight line towards the Primus-Phi refinery.

Direction was not his primary concern right now. What was giving him pause for thought was the problem that they would undoubtedly need to consider the practicalities of descent. These weren't well-travelled mountains; they were forging a complicated path by climbing and descending where opportunities presented themselves. At some point, they would have to drop down further. It was unlikely that there would be a path downwards from this altitude. There would be no easy way to descend. Suited in their battle plate as they were, they could easily withstand falls of some reasonable distance – but it would not be the most desirable method. They would end up with potentially damaged and compromised armour, something which they could ill-afford.

Porteus once again reminded himself of the fact that they were still alive at all and the squad moved on without him verbally expressing his concerns. If he could not allow himself to believe that they were guided in this venture by the Emperor, he could not expect his squad to. So for now at least, he kept his own counsel.

They moved onwards.

* * *

THE ARMING CHAMBER was a riotous discord of noise. A large area of the embarkation deck that had long ago been set aside for this specific purpose, the chamber was always busy with the comings and goings of the Silver Skulls. During times they were not engaged in war, the Space Marines would come here to work out imperfections in their armour. Each battle-brother took great pride and care of his battle plate knowing that not only was his life at stake if he did not, but that it was to bring shame on the Silver Skulls to appear as anything other than perfect. It was always teeming with activity, the shouts of one brother to another commonplace.

Now, though, the shouts of Fourth Company warriors could barely be heard, drowned out by the whining and shrieking of the riveters being used by a swathe of servitors. Machining the Space Marines into their power armour was not a difficult job, but it involved critical attention to detail, something the servitors were eminently practical at.

Each individual segment of the ceramite plate had to be anointed and blessed by a tech-adept before it could be connected with adequate care and an assurance that not a single socket was loose. One false connection could knock out the suit's core systems in a potentially fatal way.

'May your blessed battle plate awaken, brother-captain,' intoned the tech-adept standing before Arrun. He laid a hand on the captain's arm and closed his eyes. 'They are girding themselves for the fight to come. Bear this precious gift of the Omnissiah into battle well and let the warrior spirits sleeping within guide your hand.'

Having so spoken, the tech-adept moved to the next battle-brother in the line, making room for a second who spoke further blessings to the spirits housed within the armour asking for harmony with the warrior who carried them forth.

As the shell of ceramite began to take shape around him, Arrun welcomed the return of its weight. He relished the familiar, and yet slightly unpleasant, feeling of the suit's nodes entering the points in his black carapace like probing tendrils. His gene-enhanced body and the armour had long ago attuned to one another and as he flexed his now-gauntleted hand, Arrun revelled briefly in the sensation of feeling invincible.

With a shrieking whine, the final rivet was driven in, studding his gauntlet to the vambraces and he stepped down from the arming podium. He took a brief moment or two to unconsciously alter his carriage; the design of the power armour necessitated a change in posture after time wearing his shipboard clothing. His back straightened and the servos at work in the armour adjusted to his movements after barely a nanosecond's delay.

Brand was already clad in his cobalt blue armour; the visual reminder that he was forever set apart from his brethren, the armour that marked him out as a psyker. He stood to one side of the arming chamber, his face set and stern, awaiting his captain's pleasure. As Arrun approached, Brand inclined his head in greeting.

'Brother Naryn is on his way to the apothecarion,' he said as the two of them fell into a matched stride. 'As is Techmarine Correlan.'

'You understand, Prognosticator, that engaging the Resurgent must be the absolute last resort?' They did not walk with the same easy pace that they had employed so recently when they had walked together to the chapel. There was controlled expediency in their stride now.

'Yes, brother-captain. I am well aware of the additional reservations you have now that Ryarus is not involved. But Naryn has an impeccable record as both a warrior and an Apothecary. I trust him to pick up Ryarus's work without any difficulty.' Brand's tone was measured.

'Have we heard from Porteus at all regarding the situation down on Gildar Secundus?' Arrun preferred to turn the conversation back to strategy rather than the inevitability of the conclusion of the project. He was all too aware of the issues that would be faced were the Red Corsairs to gain control of such a critical Imperium stronghold.

'Our communications are continuing to experience

difficulties. I believe that the Red Corsairs are employing some form of jamming technology alongside whatever psychic interference it is that they've been broadcasting.' Brand himself had dared to test the psychic waters between the two ships and had come out of the experience with a headache. It was no wonder so many of the astropathic choir were dead – or useless. Whatever psychic support Huron Blackheart had brought with him was considerable.

'There is too much space and too many hostiles between us and him in order to provide him with effective support at this time.' Arrun rubbed his chin thoughtfully. 'In addition, I require every battle-brother aboard to stand in defence of this ship should we be boarded. No, not should. When.' Arrun looked at Brand and the Prognosticator nodded slowly. 'Not to mention that for now at least, we have moved ourselves out of position. Right now, the risk of sending more brothers to the surface is too great. Porteus is a good man and an astute warrior. He will cope.'

'A wise decision.' Brand nodded.

'Has there been any change at all in the Tyrant's position?' Arrun would never allow himself to speak the name that the leader of the Red Corsairs had chosen to bestow upon himself. To the loyal members of the Imperium, he was and always would be the Tyrant of Badab. The Blood Reaver. A traitor who needed to be brought to justice.

'Nothing. Although three further ships have come up alongside the *Spectre of Ruin*.'

'Three more?'

'Executor-class.' The words were enough to stop Arrun dead in his tracks, as Brand had known they would. 'All of them.'

'Executor-class?'

'Yes, brother-captain. We've not yet established their lineage, but they are most definitely Executors.'

'Damn him.' At the mention of the three ships, there was an unmistakable admiration in Arrun's tone; a professional interest in the vessels rather than in their current owner. 'Damn him to the bottom of the Mare Argentium. Those things were thought to have all been lost. And he has been keeping them to himself. Well, add taking them back to our list of objectives. Right after killing Lugft Huron and taking his skull as a trophy.'

'Employ caution, Captain Arrun.' The Prognosticator arched an eyebrow at the tone of his captain's voice. 'The Tyrant of Badab is no fool. He is insane, certainly, but he has thus far anticipated every move you have made.'

'Thus far, I grant you.' The two Space Marines resumed walking. 'But with luck, the arrival of the rest of the fleet will give us tactical and numerical superiority.'

'In my experience,' said the Prognosticator quietly, not truly wishing to prick the bubble of arrogance that the captain had formed around himself, 'there is the Emperor's will, that which myself and my brother Prognosticators divine. Luck, chance... All of these things that suggest a deviation from the Emperor's pre-ordained path simply do not exist.'

The lights in the corridor that pulsed a dull red as the ship remained on high alert picked up every line, every scar on Arrun's face as he took this statement to heart. It was a matter he and Brand had spent many a time discussing and he had never satisfactorily come to an agreement with the Prognosticator over it. Now, of course, was hardly the time to engage in philosophical debate.

Another alert siren began to sound. The bridge officer's voice came over the ship-wide vox, crackling and breaking up slightly.

'Proximity warning. Another vessel is entering the system. Augury lock in four... three...'

'Time to see if the gamble has paid off,' said Arrun quietly.

'Two... one... We have contact. I repeat, we have contact. Scanning for identification... receiving ident. My lord, it's the *Manifest Destiny.*' The note of excited relief in the officer's voice could not be missed and the captain's spine straightened still further.

'No such thing as luck?' said Arrun, triumphantly. 'I beg to differ. I will see you on the bridge. The battle is just starting and I want to be there for the first shot. Take whatever time you need to divine the Emperor's will and report to me.'

He pressed his fist across his chest in salute and strode away from Brand. The renewed surety and confidence in his walk was evident for all to see. Several battle-brothers, passing through the corridor on their way from the armoury stood to attention, making the sign of the aquila and gazing after their captain with untold admiration. When he was at his best, Daerys Arrun inspired his men to greatness just by his presence alone.

Brand hoped it would be enough this time.

EIGHT
ENGAGEMENT

TO ARRUN'S EYES, the *Manifest Destiny* was a thing of beauty and as he strode onto the bridge, the battle-barge loomed large in the viewscreen. The captain's heart swelled with pride at the sight of his own ship. The *Dread Argent* was a huge ship, but the Silver Skulls battle-barge, implacable and grim, dwarfed her into insignificance.

Almost immediately, the captain fell into an efficient exchange of information with his bridge officer.

'We are reading massive spikes in power from the Red Corsairs fleet. They're arming weapons. There's been no communiqué from the *Quicksilver* as yet, I'm afraid, sir. For now, at least, it's just them and us.'

The arrival of the *Manifest Destiny* was a blessed welcome; a turn in their fortunes that would, without question, go a long way towards evening the odds in this conflict. But even then, they were still considerably outnumbered and outgunned. If... Arrun corrected himself. Not if. *When* the other strike cruiser arrived, then as far as he was concerned, victory would be assured.

'Get me a vox-link to the *Manifest Destiny*. We must discuss our strategy. Make it swift and patch it through to me in the apothecarion once you have her. There are matters I must attend to.'

'At once, Captain Arrun.'

One of the slaved servitors reported that the *Spectre of Ruin* was starting to move slowly forwards, evidently beginning to make its turn. Arrun frowned. The vessel was colossal and it was going to take some time for her to come about fully, a manoeuvre that would be made even more complicated given the amount of debris that needed to be carefully avoided. Once she had negotiated her way through that hazard, she would undoubtedly bring her prodigious fore arsenal to bear. In the meantime, they could expect a burst from her broadside batteries on the way.

'Our shields?'

'If we continue to divert power from non-critical systems, shield banks will operate at a constant ninety-six per cent until damaged,' the servitor reported. 'Damage sustained to this ship following previous attack by the enemy vessel *Wolf of Fenris* was minimal. There is a minor hull breach on deck six, but it is under containment. Statistical chances...'

'Enough. Yanus, corroborate damage reports and dispatch appropriate teams as you see fit.'

'Already begun, sir.' Pre-empting his captain's next question, Yanus continued. 'The *Wolf of Fenris* is maintaining position for now. She's entered a high orbit of Gildar Secundus, but augur returns aren't showing anything coming from her. Superficially at least, it looks like she's barely capable of maintaining her own momentum. I suggest we may have caused enough damage during that pass-by to keep her out of the fray for now.'

It was all strangely calm and ordered. Every member of the crew knew their places and knew their duties. This was what they spent most of their lives in training for and now that their time had come, each was as eager as the other to rid the Imperium of a menace that had long been allowed to go unchecked.

'As you were, Yanus. I pass bridge command to you. The *Dread Argent* is, as of this moment, under your control. Keep me updated.' The very faintest flicker of a smile played around Arrun's lips. Both he and Yanus knew that the formal handover was little more than words. There was a need for a strong commanding presence amongst the bridge crew and whilst he was overseeing the activities of his company, Arrun could not take that role. The bridge crew liked and respected Yanus and the officer had commanded several times in his lord's absence.

He still straightened at the words, though, and a flush of pride coloured his cheeks.

'Yes, my lord.'

Nodding curtly to the bridge commander, the captain made his way without impedance to the apothecarion.

Naryn was already there with a number of servitors and assistants, putting together narthecium packs ready for deployment with the various squads as they prepared for battle. He looked up at the sound of Arrun's approach and stood rigidly to attention.

Like many of the Silver Skulls, Naryn favoured wearing his hair shoulder length. Unlike many of the Chapter though, his hair was a deep, burnished copper colour. It had always marked him out amongst the largely blond or dark-haired Silver Skulls and indicated his family heritage from one of the non-Varsavian recruiting worlds that they had begun to use. With that colouring, he was likely from the ash wastes of Garanda II. He had an expressive and intelligent face with large, inquisitive eyes and those eyes fixed on the captain with great enthusiasm.

'Apothecary,' Arrun greeted. The other returned the greeting in kind and wasted no time at all in launching into an animated discussion.

'I have studied Ryarus's notes regarding the Resurgent Project in great depth,' he said, indicating the data-slate on the table behind him. 'I was fortunate enough to be one of his assistants during the earlier part of the project and I–'

'If you have to put the Resurgent Project into action, how confident do you feel that you can achieve it without error or disaster?' Arrun cut across the Apothecary's words. He had neither the time nor the inclination for a protracted discussion about Naryn's competencies or suitability. The fact that Brand had recommended him was more than adequate. Now was the time for expediency.

'I...' Naryn was thrown temporarily, but regained his composure just as swiftly – something which did not go unnoticed. 'I am very confident, Captain Arrun.'

'Good,' replied Arrun. 'Because it is very likely that you're going to have to prove that your faith in your own confidence is justified. I would suggest that this is likely to happen sooner rather than later.'

Anything Naryn had to say regarding the matter was pushed into insignificance when the vox-bead in Arrun's ear chirruped. He held up a hand to forestall anything Naryn might have said and turned away from the Apothecary.

'Daerys.' The voice sounded distant; coming as it did from the *Manifest Destiny*.

'Sinopa.' A warm smile flickered over Arrun's face. 'I take it you've not broken my ship whilst I've been away from her?'

'I haven't,' came the genial response. 'Which is more than I can say for what you have done to that one. What is it that has happened, brother? Your bridge officer informs me that damage is minimal, but the *Dread Argent* is a mess from the outside. And something about the *Wolf of Fenris*? I confess he seemed a little flustered by my questions. What has occurred here?'

'Treachery of the worst kind, Sinopa.' Arrun turned to Naryn and indicated that the Apothecary should follow him through to Volker's chamber.

Returning his full attention to his fellow captain, Arrun continued. 'The Red Corsairs. That is what has occurred here.' He had no need to explain any further. 'Right now, you are in command of our best chance of success. The Tyrant is likely to start launching attack ships at us any time now in an effort to cause as much damage as he possibly can. Prior to my retort to his opening gambit, I do not believe he had plans to actually destroy us. In the wake of that, however, I would not put it past him to soften us up more effectively.'

Arrun took a moment, then spoke with an edge in his voice that only hinted at the steel in his heart. 'He said he wants to take the *Dread Argent*, but you and I both know that we cannot possibly allow that to happen. You understand what it is that I am saying here?'

Naryn finished giving instructions to his assistants and, picking up the data-slate from the bench, fell into step with the captain. He glanced up at the last sentence, easily understanding the message implicit in the instruction. He was quite correct, of course. The *Dread Argent* and the Resurgent Project were far too valuable to ever fall into the hands of the enemy. Every last warrior of the Silver Skulls Chapter would agree. The sacrifice would be immense, but essential.

Naryn vowed softly to himself that if he had any input into the matter, it would not come down to such a choice.

Arrun ran a hand across his jaw. Sinopa had not yet responded to his last statement. He knew precisely why it was. Undoubtedly, his battle-brother was consulting with his own Prognosticator. Finally, after several moments, the crackle of the vox brought his reply and a confirmation of his suspicions.

'I understand, brother-captain. And though it both aggrieves me and goes against my better judgement, I will not hesitate to comply should there be no other alternative. But then, and only then. Brother Ikek agrees that it must be so.'

'Excellent, Sinopa. Yanus has temporary command of my bridge – give your orders to him directly. But as your commanding officer in this matter, as Master of the Fleet, I have just one order at this time.' Arrun lifted his head and Naryn saw the glint in the captain's eyes. The Apothecary felt a familiar pre-battle thrill of anticipation run through him and he whispered a soft litany to himself. Arrun's eyes met his and there was something hungry, almost predatory in them.

'Annihilate them.'

THE BATTLE BEGAN slowly; almost painfully so. Every single one of the ships engaged in this combat were leviathans, built for long-distance travel or for delivering punishing retribution to transgressors on planets far below. All but three of the vessels were sluggish to respond.

The three Executor-class vessels that had come into the system like dogs at the heels of their master peeled away from the *Spectre of Ruin's* larger shadow. They performed turns that were tight and graceful and now faced the *Dread Argent*. Their very presence was menacing and as they powered up their thrusters, their initial movement was slow and jerky, necessitating sharp movements to avoid the debris. The field of junk had been freshly stirred up in the wake of the sudden rapid thrusts of two enormous warships. Despite their early glacial pace, they swiftly gained speed and were soon accelerating with all haste towards the battle-barge.

Simultaneously, the *Spectre of Ruin* opened fire with her dorsal guns. The Red Corsairs ship was nowhere near at full turn. Consequently, the assault became more of a warning shot across their bows than anything else. The missiles ripped through the spatial void and clipped the *Dread Argent* on the aft side. The huge ship shuddered and groaned under the impact, but the shields held.

'She's aiming to cripple us,' came the astute observation from one of the crew and Yanus grimaced his acknowledgement. Huron Blackheart had made very clear his intentions not to destroy the strike cruiser, but that strategy would likely only be the truth until the whim of a moment changed his mind. At any time, the leader of the Red Corsairs might grow bored or indifferent to the situation. They could never hope to fully plan a counter-strategy. Military research and history had taught every naval officer in the Imperium that Huron Blackheart's methods were erratic and unpredictable.

'Minimal damage. Shields holding.'

The Executors tore past the fore viewscreen of the *Dread Argent*. They moved with a grace that belied their age and design. Vessels of ancient lore, all of the Executors had been missing, presumed lost, for centuries bar one or two never-confirmed sightings. Now, here they were in all their mythological glory. Three of them. They may have been grand cruisers in their own right, but the lance boats moved with far more speed and with relatively tighter control than their sluggish, bigger counterparts.

One of them on its own presented a considerable threat; their flanks bristled with banks of energy lances and huge calibre plasma cannons designed specifically to shatter shields and pierce hulls. Such a phenomenal amount of weaponry could deliver a punishing amount of damage to any unfortunate vessel that strayed into its path.

Three of them working together was a nightmare made flesh and was, in many ways, more of an immediate threat than the sheer explosive power of the *Spectre of Ruin* itself.

Despite their very visible threat and menace, they were beautiful to watch. At such a time, aesthetic wasn't something that seemed even remotely appropriate and yet even Yanus had a certain professional interest in the Executors. Any identifiable designations had long since been defiled and as the ships passed heart-stoppingly close, Yanus could make out nearly every individual battle burn and metal scar that they carried. They were brutal things. Brutal and efficient.

They were extraordinary.

Yanus forced himself to pull his thoughts away from admiration and to concentrate on the matter.

'Open fire on the Executors.' Sinopa's voice came across the vox. Yanus nodded absently, then realised that Sinopa wasn't on the bridge with him. He cursed himself softly for the moment of distraction.

'Yes, lord.' He relayed the message to the gunnery crews standing by far down in the gun decks and the *Dread Argent* spat shells of loathing from her fore bombardment cannon towards the middle Executor.

'Reload.'

The orders were relayed through the ship to the better part of a full kilometre away. Deep within the armoured and stifling confines of the magazine, an army of servitors and Chapter serfs sparked into immediate, obedient action. Colossal racks located beneath a shielded canopy lowered pressure-heated shells onto the mass of conveyors that lined the interior of the ship. These shells were hauled into the cavernous breaches by a combination of archaic technology and serfs. The noise was deafening; the shouts of the humans, the stuttered input of the servitors and the hiss from the missiles all competing and vying with one another in an effort to be the loudest.

Once the projectiles were secured into position, the rising whine of a hundred banks of generators added to the noise, filling the air until it rose to a pitch that could no longer be heard by anyone other than the aurally augmented. When the missile was fired, the forces created by the generators propelled the massive shell towards its target.

Had there been any sort of atmosphere to carry it, the sonic shock created would have undoubtedly pulverised flesh and shattered stone. But in the silence of space, the launch was marked only by an explosive halo of vapour which ringed the cannon muzzle as the Emperor's wrath left the *Dread Argent* seeking its target.

From initial order to execution, the process took a little under a minute. In a pitched battle, even this was too long. Once the ship was engaged in earnest, the crews would have to show a marked improvement and well they knew it. Their lives – and the lives of all on board – depended on it.

Their job was simply to load. Other things, such as aiming and engaging the circuits that propelled the missiles happened far away, on the bridge. The Executor had already been designated 'Target Beta' in response to the rapid, quick-fire exchanges taking place between the two Silver Skulls vessels. Referring to it as 'the middle ship' was somewhat superfluous in the situation and in the three dimensional vastness of space.

In a rare moment of poetry, something quite contradictory to his current nature, Huron Blackheart had renamed the trio of devastating ships something far more extravagant and ostentatious. *Hope's Sunset, Midnight Solitude* and *Nightmare's Dawn* were the monikers he had almost lovingly bestowed upon them. He would have poured scorn on such an unimaginative naming convention.

Each one of the Executors was indistinguishable from the other to the untrained eye, yet each one had a very specific role to play. He had employed them in a number of campaigns and they had always triumphed.

The *Dread Argent's* payload burned through the blackness of space, a glowing trail of fire in its wake. But ship-to-ship warfare under duress, and when coupled with an area as densely packed with obstacles as the Gildar Rift, would never be an exact science. As such, the shot did not detonate on its target, instead glancing with no visible effect that burst against the Executor's shields. As the smoke cleared, it was obvious that it was not only the *Dread Argent's* shields that were holding steady.

'Reload,' ordered Yanus.

The three Executors veered sharply as they bore down on the *Manifest Destiny*; one continuing on its direct assault run and the other two breaking away in seemingly impossible synchronicity, each heading to either side of the battle-barge. They were planning to bombard the Silver Skulls flagship from three sides.

Yanus silently cursed the necessary delay of reloading and felt impotent and helpless as he stood watching the three Executors open their attack on the battle-barge.

The officer, a failed aspirant of many years past, had dedicated his life to gladly serving alongside the Silver Skulls in whatever capacity he could manage. He was every bit as fierce and loyal as one of the chosen. This had not gone unnoticed as was evidenced by the fact he now stood in command of an entire Adeptus Astartes strike cruiser. Yes,

Yanus may have failed but through years of hard work and dedication, he had received his due reward. Now he felt the pressure of command weigh him down.

'Keep concentrating your weapons on Target Beta.' Sinopa's voice across the vox was dark and rich, calm and measured. 'The *Manifest Destiny* will deal with the other two. Fire at will. Prepare to withstand a fierce barrage from their guns. I do not doubt for one minute that they will turn on you in an instant. The augur arrays are picking up the imminent arrival of a number of our own escort vessels. They will help distract the enemy.'

'At your command, my lord.' Yanus turned to face the bridge officers and relayed the other's orders. Sweat was prickling his brow and running down his sun-darkened face in a glistening line. He reached up and wiped it away. Allowing such weakness to be shown before the others would not do and Yanus was a proud man.

'There is another attack incoming from the *Spectre of Ruin*.' Yanus swallowed and nodded. He allowed himself the briefest moment of doubt, wishing that Arrun was here and that this heavy responsibility was back on his lord's more-than-ample shoulders. Then he straightened his back and held his head up high.

'Maintain power to the shield generators. As soon as the strike dissipates, track and fire on Target Beta again.'

There was a faraway, dissonant rumble as the second missile detonated far to the rear of the *Dread Argent*. At this great distance from the physical location of the strike point, it was felt as barely more than a slight shaking. But this in itself was enough to indicate what had happened. Several red lights began to flash with some urgency on the consoles and Yanus eyed them with the sort of expression he normally reserved for upstart young crewmen. The announcement when it came held no surprise.

'Shield bank alpha failing. Generators down to seventy-five per cent. Compensating.'

Yanus nodded. Another two or three partial hits would disable the shields completely. A direct hit after that would destroy them. They could only reroute power to the shields for so long before they burned out the systems completely. The Tyrant was trying to force them into complete surrender.

The bridge officer knew full well that would never happen. Not whilst Daerys Arrun still drew breath.

PORTEUS HAD BEEN right. The descent from the mountains had been gruelling and perilous. Prior to their deployment, Simeon had cast the auguries and they had been excellent, according to him. Yet here they were; their Prognosticator dead, their route lethal and right now, at the end of this most perfidious journey, they faced the seemingly impossible.

Further minor injuries, little more than cuts and bruises, had been sustained during their climb down the mountains, but fortune had favoured them. There had been a number of sheer drops where they had not had any choice but to let themselves fall. Despite these inconveniences and a series of broken or dislocated bones that began to heal during the journey, they had descended without too much difficulty.

It had been good in a way; the firm belief that this mission was meant to succeed had been restored in the squad and they moved with renewed purpose and determination towards the target. They would honour Simeon's divination. They would trust to his judgement and to his confidence, even though he was not here to reiterate it.

The communications tower was hardly worthy of the name. A basic, two-storey structure, it was heavily shielded, with defences that were designed to hold out against an orbital attack. The topography and shielded location of the Primus-Phi refinery meant that its builders and defence planners had arrogantly held no suspicion that it might be vulnerable to any sort of ground assault. Such a blind oversight had been the core factor in ensuring that the building had fallen quickly from the hands of the Imperium into the Red Corsairs' ownership.

Huron Blackheart's plan had been simple in theory, but in its execution had proved extraordinarily brilliant. With the

Wolf of Fenris in orbit acting as a strategic relay, Gildar Secundus had become the key communications lynchpin for the ground actions of the Red Corsairs. With the aid of the strike cruiser's greatly enhanced long-range vox, all of the Tyrant's instructions could be relayed from here.

Bereft of information, Porteus knew none of this. All he knew for certain, as he surveyed the communications tower from his vantage point between a natural cleft in the mountains, was that there were Imperial traitors wearing defiled armour coming and going. There were many of them within the compound – far too many for him and his squad to take on with any hope of victory. But the communications array itself seemed to be manned by the Red Corsairs' slaves. They would be far easier to deal with.

That was the first obvious advantage in the situation, but certainly wasn't the greatest. The communications tower was built some distance from the rest of the refinery. The massive facility was still within sight, but its distance from the tower was a clear bonus. A small militia garrison was situated at its base, with only a single clear entrance. From the burn scars, broken masonry and corpses littering the ground, it was evident that the guard had made a determined stand in their attempts to hold the tower.

It didn't take a huge leap of logic for Porteus and his squad to deduce what had happened; at least here at the Primus-Phi refinery. They remained oblivious to the torrid battle raging out far above them, focused as they were on dealing with their own situation.

The sergeant's mind was working swiftly as he studied the scene before him. He was certainly practical enough to realise that there was no possible way they could hope to retake the facility. He cast a brief eye over at it. It was a huge sprawl of industrialisation, spread across the natural valley in virtually every direction but that which led into the mountains. The crawling tangle of pipelines, stacks and ferrocrete buildings were all a uniform slate grey, dull and eminently practical. Steam and smoke billowed out from the stacks in equal quantity, carrying forth their unique brand of snow-reddening pollution into the atmosphere. Everywhere there were puddles of stagnant, stinking water.

Screams came from somewhere over to the right of the compound: agonised, terrible screams that were torn from a throat not designed to express such anguish. They didn't end abruptly, merely grew weaker before ceasing altogether.

Movement caught the sergeant's eye and he blink-clicked his visual display to zoom mode. Targeting reticules immediately came into being and he gazed past them at one of the Red Corsair, he could make out. He was talking to a refinery worker. Closer examination reviewed that 'talking' wasn't quite the word. The raider was threatening the man who was obviously and very gamely attempting to resist. Porteus felt no sympathy, but a moment's pity for the man as the renegade Space Marine delivered a backhand that would no doubt have killed him in an instant. Although the deduction was nothing new, it was evident that this section of the facility was in enemy hands. From what Porteus knew, which was not very much, this was a small-sized operation in terms of staffing; remote and largely independent. A strike force of Adeptus Astartes would have taken it easily.

He registered a moment's curiosity that they had not simply slaughtered all the workers. It broached the question: why?

Interesting.

'Brother-sergeant, what are your orders?'

Porteus turned away from the refinery and back to his squad. 'We cannot hope to take the refinery,' he said, stating aloud what they all knew. 'We do, however, need to get a message to the *Dread Argent*. I presume our efforts to do that are continuing to fail?'

Keyle shook his head. 'There's a signal jam. I would guess that it is actually being emitted from that tower though,' he added. 'The interference is particularly strong here.'

'From that tower. Is that so?' Porteus smiled grimly beneath his helmet. No, there was no chance they could hope to take back the refinery. Not without a huge influx of additional infantry. All attempts to contact the *Dread Argent* were proving futile. Had Simeon lived, he may have been able to connect with the astropaths on board, but they were denied that opportunity in the wake of the Prognosticator's death. For now, they needed to focus on one step at a time.

That first step was going to be to wrest back control of the communications tower. Once that happened, they would have to move as swiftly as they could to get the message back to their company that they were in need of support.

It was all they had to do. It was a big, seemingly impossible 'all', but they were Adeptus Astartes. The impossible was what they excelled at.

At this level, the snow had become driving rain that drummed off the armour of the Silver Skulls, forming dirty, polluted puddles at their feet. Through the precipitation, the lights of the refinery were blurred and wavering, almost unreal. They could hear the low exchange of voices, but even with their enhanced hearing, improved still further by their helmets, they could not make out specifics.

Porteus looked up at the sky. The inky blackness of the Gildar night was fully upon them now and if they were going to make any sort of move to reclaim the communications array, night would give them the best possible cover and greatest advantage.

WHILST THE BEHEMOTHS of the two opposing Chapters traded their opening salvoes, the fighters and gunships that both had launched were weaving their way through the spinning debris of the Gildar Rift. The lethal route had already claimed a number of casualties on both sides; although the Red Corsairs were perhaps faring worse.

A battlegroup of Thunderhawks which had burst from the front of the *Manifest Destiny* ploughed through an expanding cloud of gas and wreckage that had, up until mere moments ago, been a squadron of Doomfire bombers. The first unit to have been scrambled on the Silver Skulls battle-barge's arrival in-system, Seventh Strike had been stalking the hazardous space lanes whilst more of their brethren spewed forth into the void surrounding the escalating conflict.

Designed and modified by the Chapter's tech-priests and Techmarines, these close-support variants of the ubiquitous Space Marine gunships were of a slightly sleeker design and boasted las-weapons in place of the more common heavy bolter mounts. Clutches of high explosive warheads hung beneath the stubby wings. The ships punctured through the dissipating smoke and raced onwards towards another one of the seemingly endless stream of traitor craft that poured from the shadowed interior of the *Spectre of Ruin*.

Piloted by human serfs – the Adeptus Astartes battle-brothers considered too valuable to deploy into a dogfight – Silver Skulls were nonetheless stringent about the training their pilots undertook. Each one was exceptionally talented at what they did, in receipt of intense, relentless instruction.

The vox-net linking the Thunderhawks to one another was alive. Some of the transmissions filtered back to the bridge of the *Dread Argent* where Yanus was listening grimly.

'Pursuing target... just out of range...'

'You've got one on your tail. Do you need–'

'No. No, it's all right. I can lose him in the debris field.'

There was a pause, then a flare of light burst forth as a Red Corsairs Doomfire misjudged a turn. The overcompensation caused it to collide with an asteroid, a chunk of rock that was easily half its size. It never stood a chance of avoiding its doom. The moment of victory was short lived as the pilot who had lured the Red Corsair raider to its end spoke again.

'There's another three of th–'

Another detonation blossomed and the pilot's communication went dead.

Through the expanding aurora, another Silver Skulls craft emerged, its weapons blazing. The lascannon carved a dazzling blue path through the void and the engine housing of the furthermost Red Corsairs ship was ruptured. Burning fuel spilled into space, spitting and boiling away. As the Thunderhawk screamed past, the helmsman caught the briefest of brief glimpses of the pilot and gunner of the traitor ship, both roaring in impotent fury as he burned past them.

A moment later, the Doomfire was lost in a cloud of plasma as its drives detonated.

'They're still coming!'

'And they will be met in kind! Punish them for their insolence, for the Silver Skulls and for the Emperor!'

The words were simple but stirred the blood. The Thunderhawks renewed their attack run with gusto. Two more of the Silver Skulls ships were lost within scant seconds to the continued fire of the Red Corsairs. Another was lost due to a moment's overconfidence on the part of the pilot, who misjudged his distances. He was clipped by a spinning piece of debris that had once been the wing section of one of his own fleet. The ship went spinning wildly out of control. The only saving grace was that as it came to a stop, it did so embedded in one of the other Red Corsairs ships. Both of them were vaporised in an instant.

The pace of battle was fierce and relentless, but the Silver Skulls pilots were keeping the worst of the pounding at bay. Were it not for the undoubted skill and efficiency of their efforts, things would have been far worse.

Despite the fleeting moments of triumph, the Silver Skulls were still heavily outnumbered. The rest of their fleet may be inbound, but they needed to arrive sooner rather than later.

'THEIR DEFENCES ARE holding, lord.'

The bridge deck of the Spectre of Ruin was dimly lit and crewed predominately by Red Corsairs Space Marines. Ships power systems were far too valuable to waste on things like maintaining bright lighting when they had vision that could see into the infrared. The power was far better diverted to the engines to increase the velocity of the turn they were making. The fact that there were lumen-strips at all was a grudging concession to the human contingent.

Standing stock-still in the middle of the bridge deck, Huron Blackheart stared out of the fore occulus of the battle-barge. If it had not been for his heavy, rasping breathing, he could well have been a statue placed there to honour the dread Lord of the Red Corsairs. At the helmsman's words, he whipped his head to the right, spittle flying as he roared a string of furious, guttural curses. Daerys Arrun had outmanoeuvred him once already. He would not do it again.

'How long until we have a firing solution?' His voice grated, the vocal cords straining over metal augmetics. The Red Corsair to whom he spoke showed no fear in the onslaught of his commander's wrath and consulted the ship's augurs.

'Soon, my lord.' The Red Corsair remained totally calm in the face of Blackheart's spitting fury. 'The dorsal cannons have been brought to bear...' He glanced back at the augur arrays. 'The broadside batteries still do not have their range. Not yet.'

'Soon?'

'Very soon.'

'Boarding parties to embarkation decks. We will take them down from within. They cannot hope to hold that ship against my men. The minute we come about, unleash.'

He headed towards the console. Despite his massive bulk, he moved with a predator's grace; almost a prowl. He put a gauntleted finger on one of the switches, opening a vox-channel to the *Wolf of Fenris*.

'Taemar. Execute the plan at your leisure.' Blackheart closed his hand into a tight fist. 'Break them. Destroy them. I want their ship and I place the responsibility into your hands.'

'About time.'

Blackheart's scarred, disfigured face twisted at his first captain's words. Taemar was a bloodthirsty warrior from a bloodthirsty Chapter. He would delight in the slaughter he would create this day.

'I want the *Dread Argent* as my trophy before the day is through. Make it happen. I want you to bring me Daerys Arrun alive.' He paused, flickering embers of malice glittering like jewels in the depths of his mismatched eyes. 'If, of course, it is reasonably practical to take him alive. I will show him that nobody can stand against the might of the Blood Reaver. Your reward will be great if you accomplish these things, Taemar. As will your punishment should you fail in this.'

'Yes, lord.' The hunger and impatience in Taemar's voice perfectly mirrored that in Blackheart's own.

'Open fire on the battle-barge as soon as we are able. If we can take that as well, so much the better. But right now, it is that strike cruiser I want. '

His augmented eye flared red deep in its socket. There was a sudden sound, like the fluttering of wings and the Tyrant raised his head. He felt the settle of a familiar weight on his shoulder. He could not see it, but that was its nature. Nobody could see it, not properly. Only glimpses of... *something* out of the corner of one's eye. To look directly upon it effectively rendered it invisible.

Its presence was welcome, however. When the hamadraya was not with him, he was mighty. When it was, then he was invincible. Such was his arrogance.

'I want it. And I will have it.'

'IT'S TOO SOON. Far too soon.'

Correlan stood, young and defiant in the face of his captain, not even attempting to keep his expression neutral. He folded his arms across his chest. Fully armoured, now wearing his harness, Correlan had the height advantage. But Arrun had dealt with many arrogant young warriors in his time and he was neither the slightest bit intimidated nor in the least impressed at the display of attitude.

'I gave a direct order, Techmarine. I want you to work with Naryn and I want the Resurgent Project on-line within as short a time frame as possible.' Arrun's ice-blue eyes burned as he stared down the younger warrior. 'We are holding the enemy at bay, but there is no saying how long that will be the case. You will do as I order you and you will do it now. I am your captain and you will not defy me like this.'

The Techmarine's mechadendrites twitched with some mental impulse that Correlan was barely keeping contained, snaking briefly around him in a defensive gesture. He shook his head. Several of the ever-present tech-priests looked as though they would step forward and protest, but at a signal from Correlan they held their position and they held their tongues.

'I mean no disrespect, captain, but you do not understand the sheer magnitude of what you are asking of me. There are protocols and rituals that must be observed; individuals that need to be present. If we are lax on even one element of the process, the machine spirits may not accept him and the consequences of that–'

The second shot from the *Spectre of Ruin* struck at that point and everyone in the Resurgent chamber stumbled, except Volker himself, who was secure in his restraints. The young novitiate's eyes were closed and he looked for all the world like he was meditating peacefully.

Correlan continued where he had left off as though he had not even been interrupted. '...could be grave indeed. Not to mention the sheer biological issues surrounding the project. If we try to engage the subject with the systems at this stage in the process, he will experience mental stresses the like of which you and I couldn't even begin to fathom!' Correlan was hugely animated as he spoke, his hands weaving about. The tendrils on his harness moved with him, adding further emphasis to his words. 'Captain, even Vashiro himself would struggle with this if he wasn't given the right preparation time.'

Arrun glanced up at the youth restrained in the chamber, then back at Correlan. 'We don't *have* preparation time, Correlan. The wolf is quite literally at our heels. You will work with Naryn and you will find a way. This is not a request. I am warning you. Do not make me repeat myself a third time. It is an order.'

Correlan's mouth opened again, but the look that Arrun shot him was so furious that he clamped it closed again. The young Techmarine was not afraid to speak his mind and for that, he knew he engendered equal responses of respect and frustration from his superiors – but he would never openly disobey a direct order. He limited his disapproving response to a scowl and he nodded abruptly.

The Apothecary had taken a step back to avoid being a part of the heated debate between his battle-brothers but now that the worst of it seemed to have dissipated, he moved forward again with his data-slate in hand. He engaged every ounce of diplomacy he possessed and he gauged it accurately. His words put a thin veneer of calmness back over the situation.

'I took the liberty of compiling an implementation checklist based on Ryarus's notes. I am sure that with Brother Correlan's assistance, we can achieve what you ask of us as swiftly and with as few hindrances as possible. I really need you to help me in this, Brother Correlan. Nobody else knows the project as well as you.'

The gentle compliment was enough to mollify the Techmarine and he took the proffered data-slate, scanning his eyes across it. Within moments, the two of them were locked in technical conversation.

Arrun left them to it. He shot one last glance at the apparently sleeping Volker Straub. The boy would soon be introduced to his full potential. He fervently hoped that the Prognosticatum had been right when they had picked him out from his peers.

The captain made his way to the assembly tier, usually alive with the sounds of the training cages, but now thronging with fully armoured battle-brothers who stood to attention in mute respect as he passed. They maintained an attentive stance as their captain made his way to the dais where his chief advisor already stood. Arrun lived for these moments; the times when he could speak the words that would spur his company on to great things. This was something usually reserved for either the Prognosticator or Chaplain, depending on which a company had with them at the time. Captain Arrun, who would have become a Chaplain had he not demonstrated such aplomb and skill in the field of strategic planning, had always preferred to take responsibility for his company's inner fires. The Silver Skulls had thus lost a great Chaplain, but had gained a frenetic, powerful warrior who had risen to become Master of the Fleet.

The Chapter relied heavily on their Prognosticators to carry the word of the Emperor into the heart of battle. Over the centuries, their reliance on the Librarian-Chaplains had become such that Chaplains were few and far between now.

Arrun, though, was superb at stoking the embers of battle fury into raging infernos. Brand gladly allowed him the room he needed for this task, knowing that Arrun's charisma and zeal was greater than his own.

Here stand my brothers, Arrun thought as he allowed his eyes to roam the ranks of assembled warriors. Apart from those who had been killed or wounded on the recent deployment to the *Wolf of Fenris* and the men of Porteus's squad, Fourth Company was almost at full complement. The best part of a hundred good warriors who would make a stand for the Emperor and who would bring further glory to the name of the Silver Skulls.

My brothers. My charges. My responsibility.

He shot a glance at Brand who opened his hands wide in the gesture that meant he had divined the Emperor's will and that Arrun's plan of action was to continue without question. Uncharacteristically, Arrun was glad that there was no lengthy discussion on the possible alternative options. Time did not favour them. His eyes raked the assembled company and he spoke. His voice was low, but carried easily with a power that could not be ignored.

'The Tyrant of Badab is closing the net, brothers,' he began. Several of the Silver Skulls made the sign of the aquila at the words; a Chapter custom that was firmly believed could ward off evil. 'But he will never contain us. Lugft Huron was once a master of strategy, but in his warp-tainted madness, he exposes chinks in his armour. He says he wishes us to surrender, yet he must know that we never will. He opens fire on us. His words are meaningless.'

Arrun allowed himself to laugh aloud; a hollow noise that held no humour at all. 'I say this to you now, battle-brothers of Fourth Company. This Tyrant has had his day. He is no being of terror to be feared, least of all by the Silver Skulls.

He is a desperate madman whose taint tarnishes a system under our protection. It is our job, no, it is our *duty* to remove the stain he brings.'

His words were stirring the enthusiasm and energy in his men that he knew they would. Quiet ripples of untapped potential welled up in them and he tapped it relentlessly. He believed every word he spoke with almost fevered passion and that feeling flowed down through his men.

'When the time comes for us to stand and fight against him, we will do so with everything we have. We will give the Red Corsairs no quarter. We will scrub every remnant of these foul traitors from the Gildar Rift. For the Emperor! For Argentius! For Varsavia! We are the Silver Skulls! And you all know what that means!'

'We will prevail!' Nearly a hundred voices cried out the ritual response, their voices caught and filtered upwards through the interior of the *Dread Argent*. The sound reached the human crew on the bridge and fired up courage there.

Arrun nodded and allowed the zealous moment to die down before he continued. He lowered his voice just enough to lend an air of mystery to his tone. Brand watched him, marvelling at his oratory deftness.

'We are taking a step into the unknown. Even as we speak, the Resurgent is being primed for awakening. We must believe that it will succeed. Because we will not fail. That is not our way.'

For the first time, Arrun discovered that he meant every word he spoke. Could it be that his belief in the Resurgent was finally coming to the fore? Was it that all the doubts and uncertainties, all the opposition he had shown had been wrong and all that had been needed was the right moment to awaken his faith in Volker Straub?

'Whatever happens, the rest of the fleet is inbound. Even if we are fated to fall under the onslaught of the Tyrant, our brothers will ensure that his celebration is curtailed. Prepare yourselves.'

His final words were met with a mighty roar from the

assembled company. They would meet whatever was thrown at them with stoicism and might. As the roar settled again, Yanus's voice came across the vox.

'Captain Arrun... they are coming,' was all he said.

NINE
DEADLOCK

HIS DEATH LOOMED above him, twisting and glinting like a sword hanging on a silken thread. Given his current predicament, the unfortunate refinery overseer couldn't help but review the easy life he had led so far. In the twinkling of an eye he suddenly knew a million regrets; all the wasted years, the countless errors he had made – some crucial, others inconsequential – the women and financial deals that he had let slip through his fingers... but most of all, he regretted the fact that he was here right now. He thought, bizarrely, of his parents and his younger sister, none of whom he had seen in over thirty years. He should really have made more of an effort to keep in touch.

A quiet sob escaped him.

Turning at the noise, the Corpsemaster treated the overseer to a smile that seemed as though it had come from the very depths of the Maelstrom itself. His skull-like face always seemed to be fixed in a rictus grin anyway; but the thin lips were twisting upward.

During the brief battle for domination of the refinery, the workforce had put up fierce resistance. It had all been to no avail. Even the trained armed forces had lasted a pathetically short time. The Red Corsairs human infiltrators had mostly been slaughtered along with the rest during the frenzied attack, but they could easily be replaced. Slaves, after all, were plentiful enough and easy enough to breed.

The overseer was restrained on a table in what had, until a few short hours ago, been one of the refinery mess halls. His ostentatious, richly embroidered robes that had denoted his station had been stripped from his body and he lay naked and shivering as the day he had been born. All around him were the signs of the Red Corsairs relentless assault. His workers lay dead and torn apart around the mess hall. The smell of blood and urine and faecal waste from exposed bowels was strong. Had he not already thrown up everything that had been in his expansive belly, he would still be vomiting. As it was, he merely retched silently.

The Corpsemaster turned away again and considered a selection of equipment on the table. When he spoke, his voice carried over his shoulder to the unfortunate man. 'My battle-brothers will be busy for some time securing this facility and fortifying it against the inevitable attempt at a counter-attack. This delay in our plans suits me perfectly as it gives me the opportunity to indulge in a little... experimentation.' He took up one of the instruments he had laid out and held it up to eye level, twisting it so that it gleamed. 'Normally, by the time they cross into my path, the only human subjects I receive are dead already. Much of my live experimentation has to be carried out on my injured brothers. And believe me, I find humans just as interesting as my own kind.'

Fat tears of terror rolled down the overseer's face and he squirmed miserably. His voice, when it came, was barely recognisable. It came out as a squeak, shaking and frightened. 'I will tell you anything you want to know. Codes to the cogitators, security frequencies... anything.'

'You will?' The surprise in the Corpsemaster's voice caught the overseer off guard. The Red Corsairs Apothecary moved closer, delight apparent on his hideous, twisted face. 'That's excellent! Then you can tell me which of your DNA strands give you those green eyes, and which of them mean that you have two kidneys, or why it is that your liver functions. Why it is that you dream, what it is that you see when you sleep. You can tell me these things?'

All the time he had been speaking, he had moved in closer until the overseer could smell the oil in the servos of his power armour. This close up, the skin of the Space Marine was puckered and pockmarked with tiny craters and scars from many decades of warfare. There was a hunger in his eyes and the overseer knew without question that his life was forfeit.

'Well?' The Corpsemaster repeated the question in a gentle, almost encouraging tone of voice. 'Can you tell me these things?'

Mutely, the overseer shook his head.

'A pity. For you.' The Corpsemaster took his flesh cutter in hand. 'I will have to find out these things for myself, then.'

The overseer learned, to his ultimate cost, that pain could last a long time before it killed you. Tragically, he would never pass on that knowledge.

THE DREADCLAW ASSAULT boats and boarding torpedoes were almost lazy in their motion as they moved towards the *Dread Argent*. The *Spectre of Ruin* had finally come about enough that its gaping maw could release the assault like a swarm.

The damage that would be caused to the hull of the Silver Skulls strike cruiser alone would be considerable, but both Chapters had assessed the likelihood that not every one of the boarding vessels would reach its target. Even as they were launched, the guns lining the *Dread Argent* were powering up, ready to destroy as many of them as possible before they ever got close enough to cause any threat. The *Manifest Destiny* could offer them no help. They had troubles of their own.

More of the Silver Skulls fleet was beginning to translate in-system, arriving as ordered from their outlying patrol routes. Mostly escort ships and light cruisers, but their additional fire power was critical at this stage. These newcomers were already fully occupied dealing with the Executors bearing down on the Silver Skulls fleet battle-barge. The three ships were delivering a punishing attack that was starting to tell in the *Manifest Destiny's* failing shields and erratic return fire. The void shields continued to respond to the Executors' attacks with a miasma of swirling colours that rippled across the invisible barrier between the warring ships.

So the *Dread Argent* was, for the time being, on her own. If the Executors continued their assault, then that was the way it would stay, too.

Thunderhawks and Swiftdeaths continued in their seemingly endless, balletic dance of death, contrails of flame and fury intertwining as they battled one another amidst the lethal backdrop of the Gildar Rift. Under cover of their attack, the bigger Doomfire bombers were weaving their reckless way towards the Silver Skulls. Periodically, one of the Thunderhawks, freed from battle with a Swiftdeath, turned its guns onto one of the assault boats or torpedoes. Their powerful weapons detonated the unshielded and defenceless shuttles with ease. For every transport that was destroyed, more debris was produced; pieces of armour-plate, corpses frozen in death and more, rushed in to add to the disorder.

Several Space Marines disgorged from the shattered pods survived thanks to their enhanced physiologies and the additional sanctity offered by their armour – but it was a poor triumph when bare seconds later they were obliterated as a chunk of plasteel hurtled into them. If their bones weren't pulverised by the impact, then their armour shattered, cracking open like a shell and exposing them fully unprotected to the vacuum of space. They were equipped to survive for a short period in the void, but very few would do so.

Conversation between the *Manifest Destiny* and the *Dread Argent* was fast-paced and urgent. Yanus had to accept that he was effectively in sole charge of the strike cruiser whilst the battle-barge dealt with the Executors. One of the three was already critically damaged, flames belching from its engine housings and whilst its inevitable destruction would even the odds a little, the damage it could cause when it exploded might be insurmountable.

The strike cruiser's point defence weapons came on-line and a steady stream of fire started up from the guns studded at regular intervals across the hull. They hammered explosive round after explosive round towards the incoming boarding vessels. The fortunate ones that made their way through the onslaught and struck the *Dread Argent* were far fewer in number than had been deployed, but the imminent onslaught was massive.

'They're splitting up their attack,' Yanus reported through the ship vox to Arrun.

'Their most likely targets once they are aboard are going to be the enginarium and the bridge,' Arrun said to his assembled warriors. 'Matteus – you are in charge of the defence of the bridge. I will take two squads with me to the engine decks. The rest of you deploy as necessary between the two. Be ready to move with alacrity to breach points as they are detected. Squads Onyx and Garnet – you are best suited to this task.' The sergeants of the two assault squads nodded their understanding.

Arrun glanced around. 'Above all else, protect the apothecarion and Volker. Be ready for anything, brothers. The *Dread Argent* must not fall into the hands of the enemy.'

The Silver Skulls followed their captain's orders immediately and without question. Silently, they deployed, a mismatched group of humans moving out alongside them. Weapons had been passed out to the non Adeptus Astartes contingent down in the armoury. The captain of Fourth Company knew that they would fight every bit as fiercely as any of them. He turned and considered the Prognosticator.

'Get the bridge sealed,' he said, although there was hesitation in his voice. 'As of this moment, it is under your control. Unless that door is breached, it will not open again unless it is either at my word or at your own command. You know that they will try to take it. Do not let it happen, brother.' Brand inclined his head and joined Matteus. Arrun looked from Naryn to Correlan.

'You all know your duty and what must be done if we are overrun. Take up your positions and begin work. Be prepared to activate the Resurgent on my word.'

The mechadendrites on Correlan's back reared up like hissing snakes and he scowled. 'Aye, captain. I hope to Throne it does not come to that. For all our sakes.' The two of them swiftly headed off for the apothecarion taking with them the last hope of success for the project that Arrun had.

He checked the magazine in his bolt pistol and set off at a light run after the rest of his battle-brothers.

A shudder rocked the ship as the *Spectre of Ruin* opened fire one last time on them, reducing their shields to nothing. The resultant wailing sirens and pulsing lumen warning lights heralded the next stage of the attack. Arrun's apprehension at the situation with his beloved project was washed away in a wave of battle adrenaline, heightened by a sudden flow of stimms from his armour. He pulled on his helm, its silver half-skull denoting his rank and he took up his bolter. He had consciously elected to use a bolt pistol and his chainsword in the confined spaces of the ship corridors. They suited the purpose far more than would his usual choice of power claws.

A clutch of torpedoes had run the gauntlet of debris and gunfire and sunk their fangs into the aft section of the strike cruiser. They were now relentlessly grinding and drilling their way through the hull of the Silver Skulls strike cruiser. The first breach was imminent and the Space Marines were ready for them. The torpedoes bit and chewed through strategic points along the side of the *Dread Argent*. Several more were destroyed by Silver Skulls fire even as they tried to make their entrance, prised like limpets from a rock with melta charges and heavy weapons.

'First contact in ten… nine… eight…'

* * *

TAEMAR'S AXE HUNGERED.

The champion of the Red Corsairs paced the length of the room, unable to stand still such was his impatience. His axe was clasped tightly in his fist. It was a massive, double edged two-handed weapon that suited his visceral, bludgeoning style very well indeed. Soon it would satisfy its hunger with the blood of the Silver Skulls. Soon he would sate its desperate thirst. It was a weapon that no other could wield with such vicious perfection and this was all because of the additional talents that Taemar brought to its use.

He ran a gauntleted finger down the razor-sharp blade with a screech of ceramite that set the teeth of the slaves in the room on edge. None of them could see his face beneath the helm that he wore, but Taemar was smiling. It was not a pleasant expression. It was the ravenous, toothy smile of a predator about to be released on the hunt.

Even as his weapon lusted for the kill, so did he. Impatience got the better of him.

'When?' Taemar stormed up to the slave who was monitoring the augurs and cogitators. The man trembled visibly at Taemar's proximity and spoke with a voice that tried to be bold.

'You will know the second I do, my lord,' he promised. 'We need to finish taking down their shields and the forward team need to reach the...'

'I know the plan, slave. Do not presume to lecture me.'

'No, my lord, I would never...'

Taemar made a move as though he would cuff the slave around the face, but stayed his hand at the last. Instead, he leaned forward until the expressionless face of his helmet was level with that of the operative. He gleaned great satisfaction from the fact that the man was shaking visibly.

'Never answer me back if you value your life. You are a slave. You will speak when you are spoken to and not before. Are we clear?'

The man nodded vigorously. Taemar patted his face hard enough that there would be bruising and returned to his ceaseless pacing. He was like a caged lion, desperate to be unleashed.

Taemar had fought against the Chapter before and his twin hearts thrilled at the thought of the battle to come. The Silver Skulls may have been Imperium lackeys, but they were fierce fighters, warriors who acquitted themselves on the field of battle with almost legendary savagery. They were skirmishers rather than line troops, and a skirmish was exactly what they would get now. In his past battles against them, the Silver Skulls had never given ground.

He had been charged with the all-important task of taking the bridge. Blackheart had led the same charge when they had taken the *Wolf of Fenris* and to hand this honour to Taemar was great. He was diligent in the discharge of his duties and he was eager to please. He would not fail.

But the waiting was tortuous.

'FIRE ON DECKS sixteen through forty,' droned the servitor in response to Sinopa's demand for a status report. 'Plasma lines have ruptured and there are electrical fires in several locations. Containment teams have deployed. Situation under control. Situation under control.'

Unsure exactly who it was that the servitor was trying to convince, Sinopa turned and addressed another servitor. 'Our shields?' The lobotomised slave stared down at the cogitator before it.

'Holding at fifty-five per cent.'

Sinopa gripped the arms of his command throne. Fifty-five per cent was quite considerable given the punishing salvoes they had already fended off from the Executors. One of them was on the verge of defeat but unless more heavy support came for them soon...

'First torpedoes have struck the *Dread Argent*,' another nameless servitor reported. 'Their shields are reduced to inoperable.'

'Daerys, my brother, Throne be with you.' Sinopa murmured the words softly, then turned his attention back to his own dire situation. For now, they were struggling to deal with the cruisers. It was no easy feat. Had they been able to concentrate all their firepower on one of the Executors, they could have destroyed the target with consummate ease. One cruiser would have presented no threat against a battle-barge. Three of them were potentially devastating.

But they had to keep the three of them at bay and the only way they could do that was to split their firepower. It was working – after a fashion – but it was by no means ideal.

'Continue firing. Those ships need to be brought down.'

'Compliance.'

'Torpedoes locked with the *Dread Argent*. Will achieve maximum and effective hull penetration in seven... six... five... four...'

The *Manifest Destiny's* guns opened once again and the next round of battle commenced.

'WHATEVER HAPPENS, YANUS, you need to maintain command of this ship for as long as you can.' Prognosticator Brand spoke harshly – perhaps more harshly than he had intended – to the bridge officer. Yanus had been startled at first when the deputation of full battle-ready Adeptus Astartes had marched onto the bridge, but the surprise had rapidly turned to relief at knowing the Space Marines had them covered.

'Yes, Prognosticator,' he affirmed, dutifully, snapping off a smart salute. 'Truth be told, we are an easy target right now. Our shields are reduced to nothing and all the time we are being breached, we cannot hope to get even a modicum of power back to them.'

'Just continue training the guns on whatever you can,' the psyker replied, his voice distorted by the battle helm he wore. 'Take out targets of opportunity and, as soon as you are able to do so, take a swipe at the *Spectre of Ruin*.' The psychic hood rising up from the gorget of his battle plate was already sparking with eldritch fire as he readied his mental abilities. Intricate filigree designs of silver curled around the blue breastplate of his wargear, designs that mimicked the tattoos he bore beneath. Several silvered human skulls hung from a chain at his waist; trophies the Prognosticator had taken himself from amongst cultists. He had a particular hatred for human traitors – but any Space Marines who had turned against the Imperium were far more deserving of his loathing.

It never failed to surprise Yanus that Brand, so genial and wise when he was going about his everyday business, became a warrior of such fearsomeness when the call came. The psyker radiated an unmistakable aura of majesty and command, engendering great respect from all those Silver Skulls who had been granted the chance to fight alongside him.

He is an inspiration, the officer thought. *He embodies everything that we are told to admire about the Adeptus Astartes.*

The Prognosticator turned his helmeted head towards Yanus as he skimmed off the man's surface thoughts. He chuckled, lightly. It was a strange sound given the circumstances but its warmth was a peculiar sort of comfort.

'Thank you, Yanus. May your ancestors guide you in this upcoming struggle. I sincerely hope that we get to swap stories at the end of it.'

Yanus felt a moment's guilt at the ease with which the Prognosticator had plucked his surface thoughts from his mind, then he bowed deeply and turned back to the onerous task of keeping the *Dread Argent* steady. Warning sirens were now sounding throughout the ship as hull breaches turned into imminent attacks. Brand, with effortless ease, directed Matteus to take care of the outer defences and retaining only a handful of warriors on the bridge punched the door controls that would bring the reinforced bulkhead slamming down. The bridge was, from that point onwards, effectively sealed against attack. Any Red Corsairs raider who made it this far would have to contend with several squads of Space Marines, then get through the heavy barrier of the door.

In the unlikely event they achieved that, then they would discover the wrath of a powerful psyker.

In a moment of wild relief, Yanus was glad that he was *this* side of the door.

'THREE... TWO... ONE... contact!'

The first torpedo that successfully disgorged its load of raiders onto the decks of the *Dread Argent* was met with instant fierce resistance. Before the enemy had even disembarked, the Silver Skulls had opened fire with bolt guns and flamers. The explosive rounds mostly bounced off the torpedo, exploding as they did so. Frag grenades were activated and thrown forwards as well. All of these counter-measures increased the difficulty of exiting the boarding craft.

The majority of the cultist raiders, insane and foaming at the mouth, to engage with the battle were cut down on their exit, their bodies torn apart by the frag grenades and the detonating bolter shells that razored through their flesh with ease. The Red Corsairs Space Marines, on the other hand, were an entirely different matter. They withstood the initial cordon of fire and broke through to the next line.

With bellowing screams of allegiance to their traitorous leader, the Red Corsairs, dressed in desecrated, scavenged armour, tore into the Silver Skulls with no hint of trepidation or uncertainty. They were absolute in their commitment to the battle and even as they died, they took great pains to ensure they delivered just as much damage as they took.

Across the ship, more torpedoes were boring through the hull. Throughout the corridors and walkways of the strike cruiser, dozens of small battles were taking place. Ship's servitors and Chapter serfs fought alongside their Adeptus Astartes masters and countless fell at the hands of the raiders.

For every last one of them Daerys Arrun witnessed fall, he swore a new oath of vengeance until his blood was boiling with the fierce battle rage that all Silver Skulls experienced. He tore apart one cultist with his chainsword, dismembering the man with two precise strokes of the weapon. His armour was spattered with blood and gore, the teeth of his weapon coated in more of the same. All around him, each one of his battle-brothers fought with the fury and might of five. He hurled himself back into the fray, his blade a blurring whirl of motion.

They would never take his ship. The *Dread Argent* represented more than everything he had worked for for such a long time. It represented a future for the Silver Skulls Chapter that he had longed to secure. He would never allow it to fall into the hands of Lugft Huron. When he and his company had dismissed these pathetic attackers, he would find the Tyrant and he would take his head as a trophy.

The thought of such a victory drove him forward once again into the thick of the battle. His chainsword sang as he cleaved heads from shoulders, shattered ceramite casings and denied these would-be thieves further egress into his ship.

The vox-bead in his ear crackled into life and he began receiving reports of similar incursions taking place throughout the *Dread Argent*. Every story was the same. A mix of human and post-human raiders in each boarding torpedo. The Red Corsairs were evidently using their slaves as cannon fodder. It was cowardly behaviour and entirely to be expected. At least, Arrun thought grimly, this way they were able to slaughter the cultists and the Red Corsairs at the same time. The warriors who survived were slowly gathering their numbers together into a single fighting force that was snaking its way to the core strategic points of the ship.

Is this how the *Wolf of Fenris* fell? Arrun wondered as a well-placed blow with his chainsword stopped a howling cultist in his tracks. In a single, unbroken move, he turned and fired his bolt pistol at point-blank range into the face of another who had run screaming towards him. Is this how the Sons of Russ lost control of their ship? It seemed impossible to believe. Daerys Arrun had fought alongside the Space Wolves Chapter on many occasions. They were fierce, noble warriors. The rebellious, near-blasphemous thought flickered across his mind that perhaps their cousins had given in to the fight. He knew it couldn't have been the case. He had known the *Wolf of Fenris's* master. Bluetooth would never have given up without a terrible fight. Neither would he.

It was entirely feasible that unless they were to capture and question any of the surviving Space Wolves, they would never truly come to understand the truth of what had happened on board the *Wolf of Fenris*. The chances of such an individual surviving the furious, confined battleground of a starship corridor however, was slim to non-existent.

A flare of light burst into the corridor as a photon grenade was detonated and whilst the helms of the Silver Skulls adjusted immediately, their armsmen were temporarily blinded, forced into a semi-retreat up the corridor. The brief lull in the sounds of gunfire and chainblades seemed almost surreal. As the flare died, a hulking figure stepped from the open end of the torpedo into the corpse-strewn heart of the combat. It wore a bulky pack connected by an armoured feed to the huge weapon clasped in its hands.

Without any hesitation, the Red Corsairs Devastator turned towards the defenders. His finger squeezed tight on the heavy bolter's trigger and cultists and Silver Skulls alike were cut down mercilessly, first by the impact and then by the explosions of the stream of bolts that thundered towards them. The corridor filled with screams, curses and vaporised blood and suddenly the Silver Skulls found themselves giving unwanted ground.

THE PLAN WAS simple, but as was often the way, simple proved to be the most efficacious.

After several minutes of watching the communications tower, it became apparent that the Red Corsairs, in an unfathomable moment of arrogance, had decided to place only minimal defences on the structure. A few slaves who had been armed with standard automatic weapons and comparatively primitive melee weapons. There were only three Red Corsairs Space Marines that Porteus could identify. It was almost ridiculously under-defended, given its obvious strategic importance. Evidently, the raiders were engaged with the ongoing tasks necessary to ensure the refinery remained within their control and as such had spared minimal force for this task. They probably did not have long before that situation was rectified.

They had to move quickly.

Of course, the sergeant had no idea just *how* important the tower was. Still oblivious to the terrible battle that was going on back on board the strike cruiser, Porteus's stated objectives were simple. Capture and hold the tower long enough to transmit a distress call. They had to do it with all haste and they had to do it now.

'Move out,' Porteus voxed on the squad channel. 'Ancestors go with you.'

'And you, brother,' came the replies, one after the other.

It felt strange, initiating a plan without confirmation from Simeon, or any other Prognosticator. Strange – and also strangely liberating. Again, it was an odd, unwelcome thought and Porteus berated himself for indulging in such ideas.

The thundering rain had tailed off and now fell in a misty and precipitous drizzle. Night had fallen completely now. The cover of darkness wasn't something they could hope to use to their advantage now that they were out of the mountains; the many lights of the Primus-Phi refinery along with the orange blaze that burst forth in periodic spumes from the flare stacks were bright enough to negate any benefit darkness may have offered. Their flickering, jumping shadows as they approached would be as much warning as would be needed.

Approaching the communications tower was going to be more about timing and opportunity than about any sort of stealth.

Not, Porteus mused briefly, that there was much chance of ten Space Marines in full battle plate employing that much stealth to begin with. What they did have in their favour was the element of surprise. With a little bit of forward planning, and a lot of cunning, they could deftly turn the situation to their advantage. If there was one thing the

Silver Skulls had in plentiful quantities, it was cunning.

They had split into three small groups and, using the comparative cover of mountain darkness, two groups had encircled the militia station in an approximate horseshoe. The plan was really quite simple. Two of the groups would form a distraction and the third group would storm the entrance.

A burst from the flare stacks was the cue that they needed to make their move and Porteus sent a single static burst across the vox bringing the plan into action. As soon as the burning orange glow faded to a sallow orange light, three massive shadows were thrown across the wall of the low building as the first group of Silver Skulls moved in.

There were shouts and bellows of alarm and surprise and moments later the sounds of gunshots began to fill the void of silence. As soon as the first three were ensconced in the skirmish, Porteus sent another two bursts of static. The second group moved in swiftly and the defenders of the comms tower were engaged on both sides.

'Now,' he said to his own group of warriors. Chainswords and bolters held high, the four of them pounded across the compound. Blades swung and weapons were discharged and the fight became suddenly and rapidly very intense. Porteus's team had covered enough ground in their dash to reach the entrance of the building. The sergeant reached for a frag grenade on his belt and pressing the activation stud, threw it in through the open doorway.

Tick, tick, tick.

Three seconds. That was all it was. But it felt like an age before the grenade detonated with a faintly muted *boom*. The worst of the sound was effectively muffled by the thick ferrocrete layers of the militia defence building. The few unfortunate humans who had been inside and had survived the explosion were cut down the moment they emerged. Some of them may have been original troops who had been retained as new slaves for the Red Corsairs. Porteus had no time to discriminate.

The Traitor Space Marines were going to prove harder

to dispense with, but Porteus had to trust to the first two groups to handle the situation. He and his men had to get to the control room and resolve the issue of their jammed communications. There was no doubt that the Red Corsairs would already have voxed for assistance from their fellows, but if the Silver Skulls held onto the shred of luck that had kept them from dying in the death-plunge of the Thunderhawk, then this gamble, insane though it was would pay off.

Roaring in battle-fuelled rage, the four Silver Skulls burst into the militia building, bolters live and ready to meet any threat that met them within. Their weapons swept the circuit of the room rapidly.

They encountered nothing. The thermal imaging on Porteus's helmet suggested that those who lay on the floor, still living after the explosion of the fragmentation grenade, were rapidly joining the ranks of the deceased. One or two tried raising rifles weakly and firing on the Space Marines, but their battle plate protected them fully, the projectiles harmlessly bouncing off. Porteus could hear heavy footfalls above them; running. Too heavy to be human, more likely to be Red Corsairs Space Marines.

'We have incoming,' he voxed to his brothers. From outside, the sounds of battle could still be heard. The battle-brothers outside would be able to hold the entrance for a reasonable length of time, but once the Red Corsairs backup arrived, their time would be cut murderously short. 'Take them down.'

His prediction proved correct as two Red Corsairs loomed into the doorway. Both – to their ultimate cost – were not wearing helms and Porteus knew a moment's gratification at the look of shock on their faces as they encountered the Silver Skulls.

Space Marines were built to survive the most extreme temperatures. Their bodies could heal the most atrocious wounds and they could get up after losing limbs and keep going as though they had merely scraped their knees. But even Space Marines, with all their genetic enhancements, hypno-doctrination and years of battle training could do

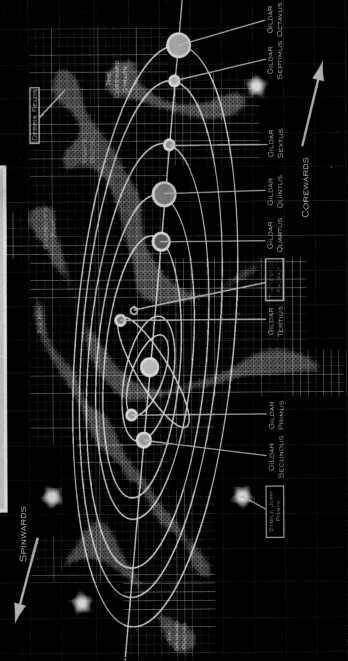

THE GILDAR SYSTEM

DEBRIS FIELDS

THE COREWARD STRAITS

GILDAR OCTAVUS

GILDAR SEPTIMUS

GILDAR SEXTUS

GILDAR QUINTUS

GILDAR QUARTUS

THE TERTIUS ANOMALY

GILDAR TERTIUS

GILDAR SECUNDUS

GILDAR PRIMUS

STABLE JUMP POINTS

SPINWARDS

COREWARDS

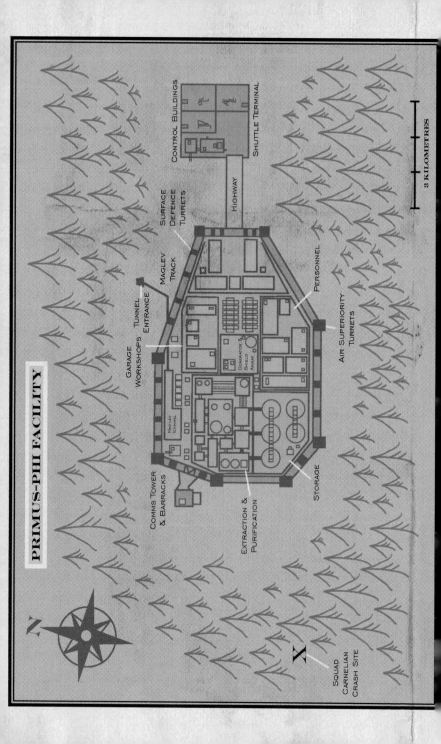

PRIMUS-PHI FACILITY

N

3 KILOMETRES

CONTROL BUILDINGS

SHUTTLE TERMINAL

HIGHWAY

SURFACE DEFENCE TURRETS

MAGLEV TRACK

TUNNEL ENTRANCE

GARAGE WORKSHOPS

PERSONNEL

AIR SUPERIORITY TURRETS

GENERATOR & SHIELDS ARRAY

MAGLEV TERMINAL

COMMS TOWER & BARRACKS

EXTRACTION & PURIFICATION

STORAGE

X

SQUAD CARNELIAN CRASH SITE

PRIMUS-PHI / TALONPORT REGION
GILDAR SECUNDUS

Talonport Flats

Acktrasin Plains

Agri-Habs

The Steeple

Machron Ash Wastes

Salinmarsh

The Vaults

N

Legend:

HILLS AND MOUNTAINS
SALT MARSH
ASH WASTE
LIGHT FOREST
MAGLEV

1. PRIMUS-PHI
2. SECUNDUS-PHI
3. TERTIUS-PHI
4. TALONPORT CITY
5. SECUNDUS-THETA
6. HYDRO-PLANT MONUS
7. HYDRO-PLANT BILUS

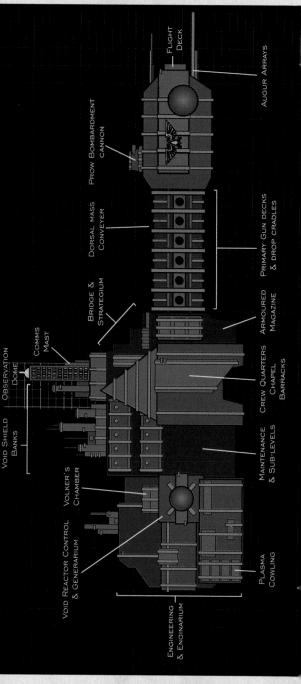

THE DREAD ARGENT

VOID SHIELD BANKS

OBSERVATION DOME

COMMS MAST

VOLKER'S CHAMBER

VOID REACTOR CONTROL & GENERARIUM

ENGINEERING & ENGINARIUM

PLASMA COWLING

MAINTENANCE & SUB-LEVELS

CREW QUARTERS CHAPEL BARRACKS

ARMOURED MAGAZINE

BRIDGE & STRATEGIUM

DORSAL MASS CONVEYER

PRIMARY GUN DECKS & DROP CRADLES

PROW BOMBARDMENT CANNON

FLIGHT DECK

AUGUR ARRAYS

little about a bolt pistol fired at point-blank range right into their face.

The first enemy's bellow of fury was cut abruptly short as the bolt pierced the soft skin of his temple and lodged in his brain where it exploded barely a heartbeat later. He fell to the floor twitching, blood and grey matter mixing from the jagged remains of his skull, before he lay still, his traitorous tongue forever silenced by Sergeant Porteus of the Silver Skulls.

To his credit, the other Red Corsair put up a strong fight. But he was unprepared and not fully armoured and the might of four furious warriors soon ended any thoughts he may have entertained of a heroic last stand. He shortly joined his dead brother on the bottom stair of the communications tower.

THE BRIDGE WAS on fire. With the collapse of the void shields, electrical overloads and exploding cogitator banks had erupted into a series of small infernos that the bridge crew were straining to keep contained. For now at least, they were managing.

The formerly well-structured and ordered bridge of the *Dread Argent* was now descending on the wings of celerity into complete pandemonium. Through it all, the Prognosticator stood, staring at the bulkhead. He had filtered out the panicked voices and terrified thoughts of the human bridge crew and had allowed his mind to reach out beyond the protective plasteel door to see what he found.

What he found out there disgusted him. The vicious, iron-forged minds of a Chapter of once-noble warriors, corrupted by a single warrior's insatiable greed and lust for power. Brand pushed out further, beyond the ship itself into the void beyond and he encountered something unprecedented.

A mind easily recognisable as that of an Adeptus Astartes, but a mind that was now so warped by the hunger it held for power... Brand blinked involuntarily. It was detestable to him. It was a beacon of darkness amongst the shining minds of his loyal, Imperialist brethren. All of the unfamiliar minds that twisted and wormed into the psyker's thoughts were unpleasant, but this one mind was unlike anything he had ever encountered. Insane, possibly. If not, then certainly well on the way to that state. Power-crazed? Yes, perhaps – but Brand, who had fought against a good many corrupted governors, cultists and countless slews of his own Chaos-warped brethren knew that mental state well.

A feral growl started deep in his chest and he let it fill his thorax with its vibration. It was good to know this anger. It served to remind him what he fought against. But that mind... it was like a black hole, sucking all the positivity out of the immediate area, filling the hearts of those at his back with dark thoughts and urging them to darker deeds. It was anathema to everything the Prognosticator knew; everything he lived and fought for.

There was more. The mind that met his head-on across the empyrean was something more than just that of a warrior. There was warp power there, too. Minimal, certainly, nothing near the strength of the Prognosticator's own. But it was unprecedented nonetheless.

There were words for a being who possessed a mind like that.

Traitor.

Psyker.

Sorcerer.

As though focusing his attention drew the interest of his target, Brand felt the unmistakable sense that he was being scrutinised right back. He fancied he could see the Red Corsairs psyker grinning wickedly. The connection was made and caught in the macabre fascination of the moment, Brand did not break it.

'My name is Taemar,' said the other psyker, straight into Brand's mind. *'And I am coming for you.'*

'New engagement being reported by Squad Onyx,' one of the servitors announced, briefly pulling Brand out of his contemplation of the encroaching horror. 'Raiders have reached the bridge corridor.'

'Throne of Terra,' said Yanus, looking over at the servitor, worry etched on his pale face. His thin, greying hair, usually so well-combed and ordered was in disarray, an external indicator as to his stress levels. Brand weighed his weapon thoughtfully. The force staff seemed an odd choice – but only to those who had never seen the psyker fight with it. Yanus wasn't able to hide the shake in his voice and Brand did not feel disdain for his uncertainty. 'Squad Onyx are holding them at bay for now, my lord.'

Of course they were. Emareas and his squad were Assault Marines, and like most of their similarly jump pack wearing brothers, were fierce, angry fighters to whom the confined horror of the corridors would be an opportunity to express that passion for battle fully. They were not equipped with their jump packs; there was no use for them on board the ship. But even without the machines that made the squad such a boon on an open battlefield, all of the Chapter's Assault Marines best represented the sheer ruthlessness and savagery that the Silver Skulls were famed for.

Sergeant Emareas was fierce, fast and furious and he would keep the raiders from the bridge for as long as he still lived. If he was killed, or if Onyx were cut off from the fighting, then there would be nothing left to stop that grim, dark mind from coming to face him in person. Brand had come up against the Red Corsairs enough times now to know that for every major incursion, Blackheart had a new lieutenant. A psyker, though... that was a first. It put a new slant on any potential battle as two of the Emperor's psychic children could easily kill one another before the enemy even passed over the threshold of the bridge door.

Through the heavy bulkhead, the encroaching sounds of battle came closer and closer. The roar of chainswords, the shouts of the fighting warriors. Emareas voxed through to the bridge, his words punctuated as he thrust and parried with his weapon.

'...three of them... made it through this far... carrying...'

At this proximity and with his psychic powers so honed they were practically humming, Brand took the words straight from the sergeant's mouth. '...a teleport beacon. By the Emperor!' The Prognosticator turned his head to Yanus. 'Move your people away from that bulkhead.'

'But I–'

'Do it, Yanus, and do it now.' Brand activated his own vox-bead. 'Sergeant, you must not let them activate it. Do whatever it takes, but do not let them reach the bulkhead. Keep your distance. Do not let them activate the...'

The warning had come too late. Despite Squad Onyx's best efforts, despite the bolter shells that were now puncturing power armour and tearing into flesh, the last Red Corsair left alive was running with the remaining ounce of his life. He pounded on, grimly determined to reach the goal that he had been given. His life was forfeit, he knew that – but if there had been any doubt at all, that ended in the moment when, in his dying seconds, he brought his fist down on the teleport beacon he carried clutched to his chest.

For a moment it seemed as though nothing had happened. At Brand's warning, Emareas had called his men to a halt. Whilst they continued firing on the Red Corsair, nothing stopped him reaching his goal. Then a small and almost innocuous light began winking on the device like a malevolent eye.

'Shoot it. Fire on it!' Emareas trained his weapon on the device and squeezed the trigger. Too late. Even as he fired, an expanding field of warp energy began to balloon from the beacon. The Red Corsair clutching it in dead fingers was swallowed almost instantly, as was Emareas's bolt shell, his body simply vanishing from existence. The bubble of energy, invisible and yet buckling the corridor in a perfectly traceable passage spread as Emareas and his team backed down the corridor.

'In the name of the Emperor,' Brand said, planting his feet firmly on the steel mesh of the bridge deck, 'this will end here.' The members of Squad Malachite who were with him formed up at his back. The Prognosticator's head was screaming in protest at the proximity of the warp field, but he dared not shut his mind off to it lest he lose a vital advantage over the enemy. Behind him, the serfs had their hands clasped to their ears, the noise that accompanied the warp field finally reaching levels that could only be heard by the ears of the Adeptus Astartes and then beyond even that, reaching a pitch that only the foulest daemons of Chaos could respond to.

An abrupt silence and the bulkhead door began the *pink-pink* of super-heated metal. Where the lone Red Corsair had been at its epicentre there was now nothing but a perfectly concave impression in the deck where the warp field had formed. There was plasteel so hot that it was melting – and a hemispherical opening in the bulkhead itself. The vestiges of the warp field finally collapsed. It turned in on itself and then, there was no longer one, but eleven Red Corsairs raiders standing on the bridge of the *Dread Argent*. They stood, back to back, some facing out to the corridor, others facing inwards to the bridge.

Huron Blackheart's intrinsic knowledge of the interior of a strike cruiser had served him well yet again.

The intruders wasted no time at all in engaging the stunned Assault Marines in battle. Emareas and his squad responded immediately and battle was re-joined. Brand slammed his force staff down on the bridge deck and blue sparks of warp power crackled up its length. His eyes flared with the surge of energy and his psychic hood burned with a rage that could at last be given voice.

'Primus inter pares!'

THE BOWELS OF the ship were crawling with the traitors as they attempted to mutilate and burn their way through the serried ranks of loyal Silver Skulls and Chapter serfs. What the Red Corsairs slaves lacked in functional weaponry, they more than made up for in sheer numbers. Whilst they had fielded an impressive force, there were still less of them than the Silver Skulls. However, with the sprinkling of heavy weapons that they had brought with them, they were more than holding their own.

Despite the ferocity of their attack, they met with equally fierce resistance not just from the Silver Skulls, but their loyal servants. More than one of the cultists was lost under a flurry of blows from anything that the Chapter serfs could arm themselves with. Amongst their number, the skinny little Navigator prowled, armed only with an omni-tool that he had picked up on his way to join the fighting.

It may not have looked much of a weapon, but Jeremiah had already caved in the heads of three Red Corsairs cultists. Blood joined the grime on his shabby clothing and his face burned with fury. He cast around himself, seeking another victim and saw the back of a robed cultist attacking several serfs.

'Get off my ship,' he screamed, bringing his weapon to bear again. He hurled himself bodily onto the cultist. He was comparatively tiny and his thin frame meant that he weighed very little but the sudden attack unbalanced the cultist. He whirled desperately trying to shake his assailant free, but Jeremiah had no plans at all to let go. Raising the omni-tool, he brought it down again and again on the cultist's skull until he felt the grimly satisfying break of bone. The cultist sank to his knees and died in terrible agony, the *Dread Argent's* Navigator still attached to his back like a limpet.

Jeremiah sucked in several lungfuls of air. It had been a long time since he had expended so much energy.

'Get off my ship,' he repeated in a threatening tone, raising the omni-tool yet again.

DEEPER THEY PRESSED. There was a relentless tide: Space Marines, cultists and human pirates of every shape and size. The numbers were inconceivable. For now, at least, they were being kept from the main enginarium – and the precious home of the Resurgent Project. For now, they were holding a defensible position.

Defensible maybe, but certainly not desirable. Daerys Arrun's rage was smouldering just beneath the surface. Within seconds, his mood darkened still further as he received not one, but a whole chain of vox transmissions. The first came loud and clear from Emareus, sergeant of

Squad Onyx. The rest of the voices tumbled over themselves as the signal jamming that had been coming from Gildar Secundus via the *Wolf of Fenris* was finally broken. Many voices began to flood the vox-net and Arrun filtered out the pertinent points amidst the babble. Amongst them was one that he did not need to hear.

'Red Corsairs have infiltrated the bridge.'

'Squad Tabasheer already on route.'

'*Quicksilver* inbound.'

'...Porteus on Gildar Secundus. Distress call. I repeat, distress...'

'Squad Iolite containing breach in mid-section.'

'...refinery has fallen into enemy hands. Red Corsairs... anybody recei...'

The growl that had been building up in Arrun's chest since the first sighting of the *Spectre of Ruin* broke forth and he levelled his bolt pistol, firing off a series of shots that struck down several of the slaves. There was no longer time to carefully consider the pros and cons of the ultimate decision that now loomed hugely before him. It was time to commit himself to making it. He dropped back against the hull as las-blasts and bolt shells whistled past, perilously close to him.

'Naryn. Correlan. Status report.'

'We are at ninety per cent engagement, sir. Volker is...'

'Make it one hundred. Bring the Resurgent on-line.'

Arrun switched channel before Correlan could start his protest and transmitted a brief message to the stranded sergeant down on the planet. 'Porteus, I understand. Received you. Hold your position for as long as you can.' The captain fired more shots from his bolt pistol, then flung aside the spent magazine, reloading even as he talked. 'We will be with you soon.'

TEN
TURNING OF THE TIDE

Psyker battling psyker.

It was the sort of battle that was born out of legend and here it was, taking place on the bridge deck right in front of Yanus's eyes, even as he dealt with his own dire situation. As a young man born into one of the Silver Skulls vassal families, he had grown up with the same degree of awe and reverence for the Chapter's Prognosticators as the Silver Skulls themselves. A psychically arid world, Varsavia's heroes who were born with the ability of the Emperor's Sight were considered blessings from the God-Emperor of Terra himself.

The two of them had swiftly become locked in a blistering melee, the force staff that Brand favoured ringing as its metallic length connected with Taemar's rune-inscribed axe. Physically, the two warriors were more or less equally matched. Taemar had the slight advantage of youth, but Brand had the added bonus of at least three decades more experience – and the fact that he was not half-insane.

Blue, gossamer strands crackled between the two weapons as they connected, spitting eldritch fire in all directions.

Taemar hooked the head of his axe over the staff and pulled hard, temporarily knocking Brand off balance, but the older Silver Skulls warrior found his footing deftly. He raised the staff above his head and easily parried Taemar's second furious swing. The two Space Marines leaned in to one another, their helmeted faces almost touching. Not a word left the speaker grilles, but they were engaged in a conversation that only they could hear.

'You will die here, traitor.'

'Less talk and more fighting, lapdog. Your god is long dead. Your ship is ours; your gene-seed is forfeit. It will not be *me* who dies here. Now ready yourself for battle and prepare to meet your demise like a warrior, not an insect.'

With those words, Taemar unleashed his first psychic attack. It was almost tentative, probing; aimed at testing the strength of his opponent's defences rather than an offensive attack that could cause any real damage. The paltry effort met the solid construct of Brand's mental bulwarks and went no further.

He may have tried to disguise his original allegiance by obliterating the sigil of his former Chapter, but the core colours of his armour proclaimed that Brand's opponent had once been one of the Executioners. Behind him, his twisted battle-brothers were keeping Emareas and his squad well and truly occupied. Having opened fire on the bridge crew immediately following their arrival, it had not taken them long to burn through their ammunition.

The Red Corsairs were not interested in preservation of the ship's condition. They were barely interested in their own self-preservation. They discharged their weapons without discretion or care for the delicate bridge instruments. It was reckless; they did not have regular supplies of ammunition and weaponry. They took what they found and they did what they could to make every round count. As soon as the last shell was spent, they had discarded their projectile weapons and were now fighting with blade and fist.

Bodies of loyal Silver Skulls Chapter serfs and broken servitors, their electrical implants fizzing and popping lay strewn across the floor. Led by Yanus, those who still lived-were juggling the twin demands of keeping the ship running with a skeleton crew and defending themselves. Fortunately, barring their leader, the Red Corsairs were occupied with the Assault Marines in the corridor – who were even now being joined by those from the bridge and others who were making their way forward.

It was a tight, frenetic battle, confined to the area immediately inside the bulkhead and it meant that Taemar and Brand's epic fight was free to roam around the bridge wherever it so desired.

Their weapons connected time and again, each pre-empting the other's strike repeatedly. All the while, both were gathering in their respective considerable abilities, ready to unleash the power of the warp on the other.

Centuries of battle training had long taught Brand to assess an opponent's vulnerabilities and weaknesses and already he believed he had the measure of the Red Corsair who faced him. Too eager to kill, caught up in the moment and not thinking several steps ahead... these errors in judgement would be his downfall. Brand had already foreseen several ends to this battle, a combination of his own strategic mind and his gift of foresight. The Emperor had given him a number of choices. It was up to him now to steer the battle in the most effective direction.

Brand swung his staff in a low, wide arc, forcing Taemar to step back. The Prognosticator raised a hand, palm outward, towards the Red Corsair sorcerer. He could feel the shape of the warp power forming in the back of his mind, shapes that were almost comforting in their familiarity. Words of fealty to the Emperor dropped like jewels from his lips and he felt the rush of power as he unleashed a bolt of energy at his enemy. His body thrummed with the ecstasy of it.

Reacting with alacrity, Taemar moved with preternatural speed, raising his own hand and swatting the bolt out of the air as though it were nothing more than an insect. The force of the psychic impact pushed both warriors back away from each other, a mentally induced wedge that separated them.

But it was only a temporary thing. Again, they struck at one another.

All the while, Brand could sense Taemar's fury; could hear the other psyker's crazed laughter and it sickened him to the core. That a loyal and noble brother of the Adeptus Astartes, one who had belonged to such a great Chapter, could have fallen so far...

A thought crossed his mind; the seeds of an idea embedding themselves and the Prognosticator leaped backwards away from his attacker. He hurled another bolt of psychic energy at Taemar and turned, bounding up the staircase that led to the strategium at its pinnacle above the bridge.

With a roar that was the first sound the pysker had made out loud since his arrival on the bridge, Taemar tore after his prey.

VOLKER LAY ON his front in the supporting cradle that would ultimately become his permanent home. His eyes were open and he was fully conscious and very aware of everything that was occurring around him – and specifically, to him.

He blinked, startled as a tech-priest crouched beside him and drew a series of binary symbols on his face with an oiled finger. Dutifully repeating the words of the litany offered to him by the priest, Volker's voice shook only very slightly.

The cradle that supported him was a network of cables, purity seals were attached to every part of it. It had been consecrated and re-consecrated so many times that surely the machine spirits could not deny them. Mechanically, the project was proceeding well. The tech-priests had expressed their acquiescence that the process was going ahead and had moved to obey Correlan's summons within minutes.

Biologically things were not so reassuring.

The young man's body had already undergone a considerable amount of stress, but his biometric readings had remained stable and he had even made one or two light-hearted comments whilst Naryn had been systematically severing his nerve endings. Very soon after, Correlan picked up where the Apothecary left off and replaced those nerve endings with fine wires that he inserted with great care, threading them inside Volker's neural system. There were hundreds of tiny incisions, and at the completion of each connection an adept stepped in and cauterised the wound with an arc-brander, lacing the flesh with a lattice of electoos.

The pain must have been terrible, even with the numbing stimms that were all they could use. They could not render Volker unconscious at this stage of the process because they needed him to tell them that things were working. He had to be alert and he had to be awake at the moment of truth. Without it, he could not take control. He cried out once or twice, but always bit it back. His stoic acceptance of his fate was a boon and a great incentive to those who were operating on him.

It was not a process that could easily be hurried and it was exceptionally fortunate that by the time Arrun's order was barked through the comm-bead in Correlan's ear, they were in a position where they could step the pace up. Correlan had begun to protest, but had realised that Arrun had switched channel. Swearing softly, he had wiped a bloodied hand across his face. He had worked tirelessly during the course of the Resurgent Project and had hoped to take his time over the binding process. This was not purely altruistic of course; he did care that Volker didn't suffer too much but also the process was delicate and rushing it could end in disaster.

'You are doing fine, brother,' Naryn reassured the young Techmarine. The Apothecary had learned very quickly during the intense bonding process he had been forced to undergo with Correlan that the exterior mask of swaggering arrogance was just that. A mask. Correlan had spoken barely a single word to either Naryn or Volker during the surgical process, concentrating so hard that the veins in his head stood out.

It didn't help that they could hear the sounds of bolter fire outside the chambers. Still reasonably far away – but approaching, nonetheless.

'Fine may not be good enough,' the Techmarine had responded. 'But it is the best I can offer.' He shot a look at the Apothecary that told of his anxiety and doubt. 'Give me a biometric reading.'

The Apothecary passed his auspex over the prone Volker and nodded. 'Accelerated heart rate, but nothing beyond expected parameters. Biometric signs are perfect.'

The harried Techmarine nodded. 'Then I am engaging the third rite.' Correlan took a deep breath and stepped back from the cradle, turning to a control panel. He punched a few buttons on it and fervently murmured prayers to the machine-spirit that he had harnessed during its creation.

The tech-priests repeated his prayers, surging to stand close to Volker. Each one of them laid a hand on the cradle and recited blessings over and over until Correlan thought the scandalously unthinkable and wished they would all just leave him to complete this in peace. He chewed his lip and closed his eyes briefly.

For all the overconfidence that his youth gave him, Correlan was an undoubted prodigy of the Adeptus Mechanicus. He had excelled during his training on Mars, demonstrating a love of design, a natural affinity for the fickle machine spirits and an outstanding grasp of the necessary rituals. All these strengths had served him well during the course of his tenure on the project. The device that now lowered from the ceiling was the end product of several years work in which he had been but one link – although a crucial one – in the chain and now all those modifications he had worked on with such great attention to detail and care were coming to fruition. He had slaved over them in his own time, what little of it he had. He never participated in the social gatherings when his brothers indulged themselves with stories of their past greatnesses. He was too busy working hard for their future success.

The very real fear of failure weighed heavily on his shoulders.

Humming softly as it lowered, the cradle was nothing more than a neatly arranged number of cables and connectors that lay dormant and unmoving. As the Techmarine pressed a few more buttons, the cradle woke into a seething, writhing mass of electrical life. It was oddly reminiscent of the Techmarine's own mechadendrites.

The chanting of the tech-priests grew to a crescendo and they all looked on, awestruck at the sight of the seemingly living, breathing thing. It was a marvel of technology and the Omnissiah had seen fit to grant it existence. Something akin to holy fervour grew in Correlan's breast and his fears were quashed. This was what he had been building up to. This was his moment. In the next few minutes, he would either fail or succeed. There was no grey area.

'Connections live,' he reported, looking at the built-in auspex on his wrist. 'All systems appear optimal.'

'Biometrics remain stable.'

The brief exchange was odd, the Techmarine thought in a rare moment of introspection. Technology and biology coming together to work on something that was, ultimately, technology and biology coming together. He pulled his mind from the distracting thought and moved to take hold of the cradle. He carefully removed the first of the end connectors and angled the cable so that it was ready to marry up with the port that had been embedded in Volker's spine. Almost instantly, a tech-priest reached across to anoint the cable. It took all of Correlan's patience not to swat him away. This had to be done. It *needed* to be done.

'Once the first cable connects, the others will follow automatically,' he said, quietly, more to Volker than to Naryn. 'It is similar to the method we use to connect to our power armour. I'm sorry, Volker, but you will very probably experience some pain as they make their connections.'

Volker nodded, apprehension on his face, but courage there still. He quietly began to recite the Catechism of Fortitude. Naryn scanned the young man one final time and then took a step back.

'He remains stable. It is now or never.'

'Best be now then.' Correlan smiled thinly, but nobody

returned it. 'Engaging connection,' he said, a slight tremor in his voice as he brought the cable to Volker's spine. It snaked forward, a questing, hungry tendril and then slid into the lowest of the ports that were studded up the Resurgent's back. There was a faint *slick* as the cable seated and then the cradle came to active, urgent life.

Correlan watched its progress wordlessly. Before each cable implanted itself, a tech-priest ensured that there was a dab of sacred oil on its tip. Whether this aided the physical process or not, he could not say; but such consecration and devotion as was being poured into Volker Straub was unprecedented.

One after the other, the cables thrust themselves into Volker's spine. The process was not gentle and to the youth's credit, he only let out the faintest of cries. Naryn, watching with something between concern for his patient and fascination at the process, monitored his output closely. Again, apart from the expected increase in Volker's heart rate, he bore the process well.

Five, six, seven cables all made their connections into Volker's body and then another eighth cable, this one a little thicker than the others seated itself at the very bottom of his skull. This time, Volker's pain found itself an outlet and the young man screamed in anguish.

'The third rite is complete,' Correlan said, staring down at the outcome of all those months of careful research and tireless work. He looked at what he had wrought. Agony so intense that the boy suffering it could barely take it. Yet he still lived. Admiration overrode Correlan's doubts and he moved back to his bench, picking up the final connection.

It occurred to him, although he did his best not to linger on the thought, that if he had paid more attention to his own litanies and prayers; had he not allowed his attentions to be diverted to the beauty of the blueprints, the ecstasy of creating things with his hands... if only he had spent more time in devotional worship of the Omnissiah, then perhaps he could have alleviated some of Volker's suffering. The guilt was his to bear and he bore it stoically.

'Mind impulse unit,' he said, keeping his focus. 'With this gift may you commune with the machine. Connection...' He pressed the device to the back of the thrashing Volker's head, blanking out the screams as best he could. '...engaged. The fourth rite... is complete.' He stepped back again and shot a look over at the Apothecary. Naryn was looking concerned, his dark eyes fixed on his patient. Introducing drugs to Volker's system before and during the connection process had always been an impossibility. Trying to forget the accusatory look he had gotten from Naryn when he had explained this, Correlan studied the readings on his auspex. After several moments of Volker's screams which had by now faded into soft, agonised moans, he nodded.

Correlan closed his eyes briefly. He suspected very strongly that the sound of Volker's suffering would be something that he would remember for the rest of his life in service to the Imperium.

The Apothecary sucked in a breath as he stared down at Volker's biometrics, which were spiking wildly. 'His stresses are bordering on the dangerous, Correlan. Much more and we will have to abort the procedure. Much more, and he will die.' The Techmarine nodded grimly and opened his eyes again.

'You can give him pain relief now,' he said. 'Forgive me, Volker.'

Naryn stepped forward and injected painkillers directly into Volker's neck. It would take several moments for them to take effect. The Apothecary was acutely aware both of the urgency of the situation and the encroaching sounds of battle outside their protective bulkhead.

'Has it worked?' Naryn's question, when it came, was clipped and shorter perhaps than he had meant it to be. Volker at least had settled again. The young man's eyes were closed, but his lips were moving as silent prayers and litanies came to the fore. Correlan's eyes were riveted to the output auspexes. After a moment or two, he shook his head.

'It hasn't worked?' Naryn was startled at the sense of disappointment that welled.

'No. I mean, yes. Yes, it has worked. I'm just...' Correlan looked up, his eyes wild with delight and triumph. 'Connection is complete. All that remains is to position the cradle and connect the MIU to the ship's systems. As soon as I perform the ritual of unbinding, he will have full access to the ship.'

'Make it swift, brother. I don't think that the captain will tolerate much more tardiness in this matter.' Naryn was firm in his resolution and his confident tone gave Correlan the reassurance he needed. The Techmarine gestured to some of the menials and servitors who were bustling around and who had up until now been largely unused. They hurried forward and began the manual task of raising Volker from his prone position to the vertical upright within the tube that had housed him previously. The cradle of connectors on his back was hooked up to the wider ship's systems. As soon as everything was ready, the armaplas tube would seal shut back around Volker.

'Captain Arrun, this is Techmarine Correlan.' With his burst of renewed confidence, the young Space Marine opened up a connection to his captain.

'Go ahead. Tell me what I want to hear. If you cannot oblige, then do not bother me.' Arrun sounded harried and his tone was tight. The unmistakable sounds of fighting could be heard as an underlying background to his words; the roar of chainswords and the sound of bolters being discharged.

'The last rite is complete. We will be going live imminently.'

'Good. Arrun out.'

That was all that Arrun had to say on the matter.

His pomposity slightly deflated, Correlan moved to flick the switch that would lock the cradle and engage the full connection with the MIU. He paused as a soft voice cut through the noise of the chamber.

'Apothecary Naryn?'

The voice was Volker's and the Apothecary turned to him immediately, crouching so that his face was levelled with that of the Resurgent. Volker offered a tired-looking smile.

'If this works, will you get word back to my family on Varsavia? Tell them what I became? Promise me.'

'I promise you, Volker. And Brother Correlan and I will tell your tale on the journey to many a campaign. Yours is the sacrifice of a hero and we will never let it be forgotten.'

Volker closed his eyes once, then raised his head as much as the sandwich of the two cradles would let him. When he spoke again, it was to say the last words that he would ever utter as Volker Straub.

'I am ready.'

He smiled at Correlan and Naryn and the Techmarine threw the switch that would close the cradle, seal the tube and unlock the Resurgent's access to the ship's core systems.

With a hiss of servos, the tube sealed closed, with Volker within. The Resurgent's eyes looked down on those scurrying beneath him, like some kind of benevolent god. A beatific smile flickered across his face and then he threw his head back. Runes flickered into life on the surface of the tube and scrolled down at the level of Volker's eyes. Clearly visible from outside, the runes were not dissimilar to those that the Space Marines saw on their retinal displays when they wore their helmets. Volker's head came slowly forward and his eyes followed the reams of text as his brain gradually merged with the primitive machine spirit heart of the *Dread Argent*.

He spasmed for a few brief seconds, then the smile broadened. Every system on the ship bar the main generators powered down and the vessel was plunged into darkness.

THIS WAS DEATH. They were the words that first came into Yanus's mind as the lights went out, engulfing them totally. The air, always stale and recycled became bitter and the officer judged, accurately, that life support systems had gone off-line as well as every lumen-strip. All that could be seen were the strobing muzzle flares of bolters being fired in the corridor and above them, the red glow of the lenses in the battling Space Marine's helmets. They continued to fight without showing any awareness that anything had changed.

From his vantage point on the bridge, Yanus could make out the moving figures of the two psykers, outlined in silhouette thrown by the crackling nimbus of their force weapons which continued to connect time and again. Four red helm lenses gave away their positions as they ascended ever higher.

A blaze of orange light cast by the activation of a flamer out in the corridor threw the whole bridge into sharp relief for a moment, casting grisly shadows of beheaded servitors and corpses that lay across the shattered cogitator banks where they had fallen. They flickered eerily in the firelight and then the weapon shut off again, bringing the unwelcome return of the deadly darkness.

Yanus was going to die of asphyxiation here on the bridge of the *Dread Argent*. He had always expected to die in the service of his Adeptus Astartes masters, but this was inglorious. He crouched down, his hand resting on the hilt of the combat blade he wore strapped to his thigh. He would not die flapping like a fish on the deck. He would die fighting.

That was presuming that the *Dread Argent*, uncontrolled and now drifting in the Gildar Rift was not destroyed first, of course.

Despite the certain knowledge of his own imminent demise, Yanus remained transfixed at the battle raging above him. The two psykers had fought their way up the staircase to the strategium and, thanks to its armaplas design, he could see them, lit by the blue warp fires. The soundproofing properties of the material meant that they could not be heard. But the exchange of words above him was intense.

'WHAT USE IS wisdom if it only comes with age?'

The words were spoken out loud by Taemar, the first coherent sounds he had properly uttered since he had engaged in battle with the Silver Skulls Prognosticator. 'Look at yourself! You are failing. You are wounded – and you are old. Your own doubts plague you. Your foolish trust in your dead god is all for nothing. You will lose this battle and if my master decrees it, you will live. You will live and you will be made to watch as my brothers and I take your ship for our own.'

There was a certain element of unfortunate truth in Taemar's taunts, but Brand did not let them bother him in the slightest. The Red Corsair's jeers did nothing. They didn't anger him further, they didn't tap into some deep-rooted sense of shame, they were just words. Despite the power of words, Brand did not let them affect him.

A chance blow from Taemar's axe had found its way past his guard, cutting into the shoulder joint of the armour covering his left arm. He had felt the blade bite through the servo cabling and coolant had sprayed like arterial blood. It had anointed him and his opponent swiftly in a slick coating of oily, dark liquid.

When the ship's systems had gone down, Brand's helm had instantly switched to infrared vision. Apart from a slight skip as his sensors adjusted to the new lighting levels, and a slight increase in the amount of oxygen mixed into his in-built life support, he barely noticed. The fight with Taemar was occupying all of his attention. He did not answer the other's rhetorical questions, choosing instead to treat his opponent with the disdain he felt the traitor deserved. His force staff came around as though he were aiming for Taemar's midsection, but he feinted at the last moment and instead struck the Red Corsair in the armoured knee. Warp energy flared, confirming what Brand had suspected. Taemar's guard was down. His warp shield was either exhausted or his opponent's sheer arrogance had simply meant that he no longer maintained it.

He had no desire whatsoever to engage the Red Corsairs sorcerer in conversation. He had little need to; his very actions spoke far louder than any words he could bring himself to speak.

They moved across the expanse of the strategium's floor, their weapons flaring in the velvet darkness and lighting them in profile as they engaged in their deadly dance. For all his constant jibes and apparently ceaseless talking, Taemar was a superb warrior. What Brand had thought – in his own arrogance, he grudgingly admitted to himself – would reach a swift resolution was taking far longer than anticipated.

'You could give yourself up to us,' the Red Corsair hissed through the grille of his helmet. 'We have much in common, your Chapter and the Red Corsairs. We are both small in number... betrayed by the Imperium...'

Brand finally allowed a retort to leave his lips. It was a preposterous suggestion. 'The Silver Skulls have always been loyal to holy Terra. Thus it shall ever be. We share nothing with dogs like you and your twisted master. The Imperium has not betrayed us, traitor.'

'The Imperium betrayed *all* Adeptus Astartes, you fool!' Taemar snarled furiously and Brand could picture him beneath the helmet, spitting in rage. 'You owe them *nothing*! If you would just swear allegiance to Huron Blackheart...'

'That will never happen.'

Their weapons connected yet again and this time it was Brand's turn to lean forward until their faces were almost touching.

'I may die here, Taemar of the Executioners, but it will be a death most worthy.' It went against everything Brand believed in to call this filthy traitor by his name and former affiliation and yet he knew it would be the cruellest blow he could throw.

He raised the force staff and began to channel everything that he had, everything that he was, into it. He shook his head, almost sadly. 'How is it that you have fallen so far from grace and glory, Taemar?' He used the other's name, the name that had been whispered into his mind on the other's arrival on board. He sensed the sudden moment of confusion this caused, but Taemar swiftly covered it. Brand persisted. 'What could have happened to turn your face and heart from the Emperor's sight? When did reason give way to such madness?'

Unlike Taemar's attempts to goad Brand, the Prognosticator's skill allowed him to cut through the Red Corsair's defences like a red-hot knife through unresisting flesh. The set of Taemar's shoulders betrayed his renewed fury and he snapped his head back, away from Brand. Helmed and hidden he may be, but the impact of Brand's words on him was clear.

'I chose this path myself, Silver Skull. It was my decision to make.' The weapons came apart once again with a snapping of warp energies. 'Others fall prey to moments of weakness and linger over regrets and lost causes. The Red Corsairs never fall. We are in the ascendant. Our star is rising.'

'Not any more, Taemar. This ends for you. Now.'

With heavy emphasis on the final word, Brand brought his force staff down on the surface of the floor with a powerful strike. Sparks spat and bare seconds later, the rigid armaplas that had always supported a full complement of company sergeants and a heavy, priceless table began to crack like ice on a frozen pond. Filigree splits began snaking across its surface, each laced with blue warp energy. The cracks expanded and spread. Anticipating what was about to come, Taemar let out a feral howl of rage and lunged for the Prognosticator. But he was too late. Much too late.

Brand brought his staff down again and the floor shattered into a thousand glittering shards. Taemar's hands closed around the arm of his opponent and both of the Space Marines and the heavy table tumbled to the distant bridge below.

As he fell, Taemar's body twisted desperately as he attempted to get himself into the position that would likely cause him the least damage. A fall of such magnitude would all but destroy his power armour and likely leave him with broken bones, bruises and a risk of internal bleeding. Red warning lights flashed in front of his retinas and he swore loudly at them. He reached for the bolt pistol clamped in its magnetic holster on his thigh. He drew and fired, the shell shattering the Prognosticator's battle helm, but causing nothing more than a few shrapnel wounds. He fired again, and again. Both shots found their mark, the explosive shells blasting craters in his opponent's armour. It was little consolation.

The heavy, bejewelled table hit the deck first, killing several unfortunate crew members who had already been injured and had been unable to scramble from the falling warriors. The heavy wood splintered and broke on impact, the beautiful jewels that had once made up the map of Varsavia fracturing free and showering the deck in a rain of exotic drops of colour. It was lost on those who were still left in the darkness of a ship's failed systems, but to Brand, as he fell, it was a most extraordinary sight. The rainbow shards were all stained peculiar hues of red through the filter of his eye lenses.

Taemar hit the floor next, landing on his back. His fusion pack buckled with the impact, spraying superheated gas in all directions and splitting the ceramite shell of his armour. The internal systems registered the shock as a final, chaotic spray of runes before going completely dead. His expertly-crafted power armour may have saved his life in this instance, but it was far from over. This was the least of his concerns however. He had a fraction of a second to move before Brand descended on him like an avenging angel, his staff raised in readiness to deliver the Emperor's final judgement.

'So will end all traitors. The Red Corsairs will never take this ship.'

The words arrived in Taemar's mind at the same time as Brand's staff thundered mercilessly into his fractured breastplate, blowing both it and the flesh beneath into pieces. Shards of armour and scorched meat rained for a brief moment, accompanied by the ozone stench of psychic discharge.

The Prognosticator remained vertical for a few seconds and then, as his body finally reacted to the shock of the impact and injury, collapsed on top of the ruptured corpse of the Red Corsair. His hands released their grip on the force staff, but it remained standing proud, embedded in what remained of Taemar's chest.

* * *

'REPORT! I NEED a report!'

Arrun had reacted to the shutting down of systems on his ship with less than good grace. He was making his way towards the bridge, his enhanced eyesight and helmet providing him with clear, unobstructed views of the way ahead.

Correlan's voice crackled across the vox. 'All critical systems have shut down throughout the ship. Repeat, we have a system failure.' Reception was poor; his voice was broken and distorted, holding onto the vestiges of the short-range vox-net before it too shut down. 'Resurgent Project has failed. Working on bringing emergency sys–'

Correction, Techmarine Correlan. The Resurgent Project has not failed.

A sudden silence fell following the words. Every soul on board the *Dread Argent* heard it; Silver Skulls and Red Corsair alike. It was an inhuman voice, its timbre altered forever by the artificial means of its production. It issued from every single vox-grille, every micro-bead and address system throughout the strike cruiser. It echoed around the spaces in-between. It pervaded all.

It sounded calm and rational – and yet its humanity was nonetheless blunted by its synthetic tones.

Emergency systems... detecting. Rerouting power. Bridging failed connections. Emergency systems will come back on-line imminently.

The *Dread Argent* lurched violently and the hull began shaking. Arrun was thrown ungraciously against the corridor wall and he swore loudly. He was barely feet from the bridge corridor now. Emergency lumen-strips flared briefly, then died again.

'Correlan. Report. Now. What is happening to my ship?'

'Volker is happening to it, brother-captain. He is... assimilating the system controls. Integrating himself into the ship's consciousness.'

'You said it had failed.'

'I thought–'

Emergency systems fully rerouted. Power diverted. Life support, emergency lighting. Activating. Diverting all core systems to restore shields.

The voice ceased and then the sensors in Arrun's helmet readjusted as the low coils of the emergency lumen-strips warmed and bathed the ship in a soft, ambient glow. The captain had no time to think on the situation however, because he was now within eyesight of the bridge. Between him and the ship's command chamber was a mob of fighting Space Marines. He waded into the fight, chainsword screaming and bolt pistol barking.

'Nice of you to join us, Captain Arrun,' said Emareas as Arrun fell in beside him. 'Something has happened. I think that we have broken the back of their assault. They are starting to lose cohesion.'

'Loss of their leader.' It was a hypothesis based on the many times he had fought against traitors like these. Arrun aimed his pistol and squeezed off more shots. Emareas's words were correct; the Red Corsairs were falling back but they were falling back in the direction of the bridge. Of the original strike force that had transported in, there were only four still fighting. Any hope that they had of maintaining control over the bulkhead was rapidly diminishing and they were trying to fall back. Krak grenades were making an appearance and Arrun urged his assault squad onwards. The Silver Skulls would put paid to this threat once and for all.

'Correlan... instruct Volker to bring our shields back online as urgently as po–'

You do not need to go through him, Captain Daerys Arrun. I can hear you. I am already calculating a solution to the problem.

'It worked.' Arrun laughed aloud, despite the situation. 'It *worked*!'

His triumph and joy was short-lived, however. 'Prognosticator, situation on the bridge?'

There was no reply and for Arrun, that was far, far worse than anything that had happened so far. Two more calls for his advisor returned nothing and he had no choice but to fear the worst.

* * *

I am alive. The Omnissiah be praised.

I am alive. The Emperor be praised.

It's dark. It's so dark. I don't know where I am. I don't know who I am. But I am alive. I think. I feel. I must be alive.

I am alive, certainly, but I do not know who I am. I do not know what I am. I have a name. I had a name. I am... I was... Volker Straub.

+++ I do not know you. +++

It was not a voice. Not really. It was a *feeling* more than anything. A sense of confusion and suspicious mistrust that could best be expressed with what he remembered. Words. This new form of communication was unlike anything else.

On the periphery of his hearing there was the sound of chanting. A strange sound and he could not place it. It was almost musical in its tone. Musical, lyrical, impassioned... prayers to the machine spirits. Yes. He remembered the tech-priests. He remembered them. With that memory came others, a rush of them one after the other.

I know my name. I know who I am.

+++ I do not want you. +++

Hatred, rejection. A staunch denial to accept an otherwise truth.

I am Volker.

+++ Leave me. +++

Querulous and uncertain – it was all the shades of red. Anger, tinged by a pink halo of fear.

+++ You are not familiar. Leave me. +++

I know who I am and I know who I was. You and I are one. I will not leave. Do not fear me.

More feelings and images flashed before whatever it was that now passed as his consciousness. A peaceful coexistence with one other – the ship's Navigator. The machine spirit of the vessel was truly afraid of this intruder. As such, the humanity remaining within Volker Straub softened in his approach.

I am more than the others, now. I am something else. I am greater. I have reached my potential. I am something new. I am something better. Together, we are ultimate.

There was still denial, resistance, and Volker gently soothed.

It is the way things must be for the future. We need to work together. It is the will of the Emperor himself and the greatest of blessings from the Omnissiah. The Prognosticatum have ordained that this be so.

The change these words effected over the mechanical mind of the ship was spectacular. Like the warriors whose prayers and thoughts echoed through its corridors and hangar bays, it knew its place. The fear melted away, replaced by a warm glow. A sense of pride. A sense of honour.

+++ If it is the will of the Emperor, then I must concede. +++

The being that had once been Volker felt the ship's virtual embrace. He felt himself sink into its endless depths and the two became one. There was a lingering sense of uncertain doubt and as though to reiterate the bond, he tried it out for size.

I am the Dread Argent.

+++ I am the Dread Argent. +++

We are one.

We are awake.

We hear you, Captain Daerys Arrun.

We obey.

ONE EXECUTOR WAS utterly destroyed, a hit from the *Manifest Destiny's* primary cannons having obliterated the bridge almost instantly. It had been a chance hit and Sinopa knew it well. But the Emperor's favour had smiled on them, just as the Prognosticator had said it would.

Of the remaining Executors, one was now completely removed from the battle having taken a hit which had effectively disabled its main weapon banks. Whilst it continued attempting further fire from its secondary guns, the damage it delivered was negligible. One continued to pound at the battle-barge, but with the effective removal of just one target, their chances of defending themselves increased exponentially.

With the continuing arrival of more of the smaller Silver

Skulls ships into the battle, the Red Corsairs no longer had the advantage of numbers. Huron Blackheart had been left with no choice but to recall some of the ships that he had placed in the blockade around Gildar Secundus and they tore into the fray with fresh blood and sharp teeth.

Many of the Doomfires had also been recalled, those that were still able limping desperately back to their parent craft. Several of them were picked off as they tried to retreat, but others made it back to the bigger vessels that had brought them here. Some headed to the *Wolf of Fenris*, still in slow orbit around Gildar Secundus, others headed straight for the *Spectre of Ruin*.

On the bridge of the *Manifest Destiny*, Sinopa's heart lifted at the sight of the fleeing ships. Huron Blackheart's plan was failing. The Silver Skulls were winning the battle. Yet whilst the immediate threat of the Executors was reduced to practically nothing, there was a new situation that demanded their attention.

'The damaged Executor is accelerating. Its current vector heading suggests...' There was a pause of barely a heartbeat. 'It intends to ram us,' Sinopa cursed loudly. Clearly the remaining crew of the cruiser had determined that if they were going to be reduced to a burning chunk of debris that would forever drift along in the Gildar Rift, then they may as well do as much damage as possible on the way out. It was a bold, desperate final measure. It was also, though it pained him to admit it, exactly what Sinopa would have ordered had the roles been reversed.

There was no way that they would be able to manoeuvre the huge ship away from the Executor's planned course. The best they could hope for was damage limitation. It was gunning whatever remained of its engines and steering towards a head-on collision, aiming to destroy itself by hurtling down the throat of the battle-barge. The *Manifest Destiny* would not move very far if they engaged engines now, but it could be enough to prevent major damage.

'Status of our shields?' Sinopa knew what the answer would be, but there were protocols. Protocols must be observed.

'Shields are down.'

Sinopa nodded grimly. 'Then we have to take our chances. Engage engines. Move away as much as we can.'

Combined with the damage of an exploding vessel on the hull of their ship, the continued fire from the remaining Executor would neutralise them altogether. The Thunder-hawks were firing heavily on the approaching vessel, trying to disable it before it made contact with the Silver Skulls battle-barge. The grand cruiser's shields had long since collapsed under the relentless fire from Sinopa's ship and parts of it were starting to fracture and break up.

'Collision imminent. Five minutes.'

'All hands, brace for impact. Fire teams prepare to deploy on my mark.' Sinopa's hands curled around the arm of the command throne. If the *Manifest Destiny* were to fall now, then the *Dread Argent* would not be far behind her. 'Open a channel to the *Dread Argent*. Explain our situation. Tell them...'

Sinopa stared at the occulus, at the churning drama of ship battle that was taking place outside the sanctuary of the ship's hull. 'Tell them that we will do the best we can to continue lending support, but that we may well be out of action following this. Tell them also...' Sinopa's dark face twisted in a smile. 'Tell them that we will bleed every last drop from them before we go.'

'Four minutes.'

Another shot from the still-intact Executor shuddered across the ship. With their shields gone, they were taking damage and Sinopa knew true frustration. They had been winning. They had been at the point where they could have taken out Blackheart's Executors. But now the tables had turned. His hands curled into fists.

The burning prow of the stricken grand cruiser loomed large through the occulus, a deadly spear levelled at the heart of his ship. There was no doubt at all that it would cripple the proud vessel. Sinopa fancied that he could see tiny, burning figures spilling from the blazing wounds torn in the hull of the ship, but logic told him that it was nothing more than debris being forcibly ejected by decompression.

The view was abruptly eclipsed by an eruption of light so brilliant that the screen dimmed to compensate. After a few seconds it slowly returned to transparency revealing an expanding cloud of plasma where, mere moments before, the enemy craft had been. A few shattered and twisted pieces of the wreck pattered harmlessly against the armoured hull of the *Manifest Destiny*.

'Report!'

'Augur reports new contact.'

The look on the officer's face as he turned to Sinopa was one of sheer joy. Unadulterated, unbridled and thrilled.

'Sir, it's the *Quicksilver*. She's translated in-system.'

Sinopa nodded, delighted by the news, but not allowing himself the luxury of assuming all was going to be well.

'Incoming transmission.'

'*Manifest Destiny*, this is *Quicksilver*. Siege Captain Daviks extends his cordial greetings and asks if you require any further assistance, or if you wish to take care of the matter yourself.'

It was just like Daviks to send such a message and despite himself, Sinopa grinned wickedly. The Siege Captain would not have been in command of the vessel, but as the ranking Adeptus Astartes aboard would have certainly have been granted permission to broadcast whatever he wanted.

'Concentrate all guns on the remaining Executor,' he told his bridge crew and looked up at the occulus and the beautiful shape of one of the last remaining Executor-class grand cruisers in the entire Imperium of Man. Such a prize. Such a wonderful vessel: so rare and mythical. And Huron Blackheart had produced three of them seemingly from nowhere.

Now Sinopa was going to destroy them.

The Emperor's grace had indeed favoured them. Once the Executors were no more than a memory, the rest would be academic.

'Fire all weapons,' he said, his voice barely more than a whisper. The servitor slaved to the main weapons array whirred slightly as it turned to the console.

'Compliance,' it acknowledged.

The captain of the enemy vessel had evidently decided that the destruction of its sister ship tipped the odds very much against him. He had altered course and had already begun to flee towards the protective shadow of the *Spectre of Ruin*. Shells and plasma fire clawed at its shields as it accelerated away, though a few lucky shots scorched the hull. The battle-barge itself had also begun to retreat, its titanic engines burning hard towards the scattered screen of escort vessels.

Two battlegroups of destroyers and frigates nipped at its heels as it forged ahead, but were forced to disengage as the remainder of the traitor fleet closed in. The *Manifest Destiny's* guns roared their defiance and in a blazing flash of a reactor breach, the Executor was destroyed. The tide was well and truly turned.

The arrival of the *Quicksilver* triumphantly heralded the arrival of the rest of the ships that had been alerted before this attempted incursion began. Messages flew between the captains; throughout the Gildar Rift, the Red Corsairs attack fleet was being gradually forced back out of the system.

You do not belong there.

We can see you. We can feel you, stalking my decks. We can sense you, attempting a stealthy approach to the enginarium. Another few feet. Just a little more. That's right. There is nobody in the corridor. Your way is clear. A few more feet. You are very clever, yes? You have managed to find a way through the belly of the ship; a way not protected by the warriors.

So many of you. Our sensors detect you. The machine spirit at the heart of this fine ship knows what you are. You are Adeptus Astartes. But you are all wrong. Everything about you is an insult to the glory of the Imperium. You are the ultimate traitors and you are going to be cleansed.

A few more feet.

+++ Open airlock. Maintenance sub-deck Alpha Two. +++

You are clinging onto whatever gives you purchase, but you know the futility of it. Your death is imminent. Embrace it. Die like the warriors you purport to be.

+++ Venting complete. +++
+++ Seal airlock. +++

ALL ACROSS THE *Dread Argent*, Volker Straub was proving the Prognosticatum's faith in him to be justified and correct. Everywhere, systems were coming back on-line. His adaptation to manipulating the ship's systems was incredibly swift. The process of venting the enemy into space could have been carried out by the bridge crew, but they had not performed it. The ship itself had.

It was thinking autonomously.

Everywhere, airlocks opened and vented Red Corsair pirates and cultists alike out into space. Arrun received report after report detailing where those who could not be disposed of so easily could be found. Teams were deployed to mop up the lingering remains of the threat.

On the bridge, the lights had come back up to reveal a scene of grisly horror as the tattered remnants of the human crew gathered around the fallen psykers. Splinters of armaplas were strewn around them, carpeting the floor of the bridge. The dead and dying were everywhere, but through it all, Yanus continued grimly commanding what remained of his crew.

The Silver Skulls Prognosticator, against all odds, stirred slightly as Daerys Arrun arrived on the bridge, anxiety in his face for the fate of his Prognosticator and his friend. Brand's breathing was ragged and he reached up to remove the tattered remnants of his helm, his white hair spilling across his shoulders.

'I fear that any chance of this traitor's skull being added to my collection is nulled,' he said. Blood dribbled from the sides of his mouth, but it was superficial. He was damaged beneath his ruined power armour, certainly – but he would heal in time. Arrun clapped his advisor's shoulder and rose to face Yanus whose face was pale but determined.

'The *Spectre of Ruin* is on an escape vector and is preparing to leave the system,' he reported. 'Several of the smaller ships have already fled like the cowards they are.' There was a pause, a hesitation in his voice and Arrun read it accurately. His glowing red eye lenses fixed on Yanus as he waited for the officer to complete the sentence.

'They have deployed drop-pods and landing craft across the system.'

ELEVEN
OBSTACLES

THEY WERE SURROUNDED. But as long as they drew breath, they would never give up the fight. Porteus and his squad had already held the communications tower long enough to disable the jamming signal that the Red Corsairs had been sending. The moment that had been successfully overridden, they had successfully transmitted to the *Dread Argent*. His captain had ordered him to hold his position and that was exactly what he and the squad would continue do.

The rain was coming down harder now, drumming against the roof of the tower relentlessly, providing a pounding, accompanying beat to the fight that was taking place. For now, the Silver Skulls were still maintaining control of the situation, but their grip was tenuous at best and fragile at worst. Their advantage was being lost with every passing second. As soon as the first shot had been discharged, the Red Corsairs had come running.

This location was strategically vital to both sides and although it would be a hindrance, its destruction would do great damage to the enemy's cause. Porteus was largely counting on the Red Corsairs appreciating such a fine point and forcing himself to focus on the hope that they would not attempt to destroy it. But the traitors were such a confused mass of different Chapters, a melting pot of vastly different backgrounds with a complete lack of ethics or sense that there was no predicting what they might do.

From outside, the sound of orders being shouted could be heard; some came from human voices, others were issued in deeper tones that were evidently those of the Red Corsairs. Glancing briefly at his squad, Porteus checked the magazine in his bolt pistol and mag-clamped it to his thigh. He took his flamer from across his shoulders and hefted its weight easily, shifting his stance so he was standing firm.

'We hold here,' he informed the others. 'For as long as we are able.' Without question, the entire group took up positions near the door.

The vox noise from the six warriors engaged in fighting outside was intense and difficult to properly filter. At least Porteus was able to monitor their personal readings through the information feed in his helmet's visor. Data scrolled constantly across his retinas and his expression darkened as at least three of the runes glowed between healthy white and a deep, unfriendly red. Three of his squad were incapacitated – although not dead. Not yet, at least. The three Silver Skulls still standing outside the tower were still fighting. They wouldn't stop fighting until they were told, or until they breathed their last.

'Keyle, Ignus, on me.' Porteus turned. 'You two remain here. Hold this array for as long as you possibly can.' Porteus led the way down the creaking staircase, his flamer held close to his chest. They would provide whatever extra support was required and with the Emperor's will, would keep the Red Corsairs from entering the facility.

An ululating battle-cry sounded from somewhere just outside the building and the report of firearms was unleashed once again. The enemy were drawing closer. Porteus's flamer burst into life as the ignition light flared. It would take nothing more than a squeeze of his finger and he could produce holy, purifying fire that would cleanse all in its path.

'In the name of Argentius,' he roared, his defiance obvious in every syllable. 'Die!'

The three Space Marines pounded across the ground floor of the tower and burst out into the torrential downpour. Porteus turned the throttle on the flamer and the gout of burning promethium erupted into a roaring inferno.

The close-quarters fighting was intense and they were greatly outnumbered, but their sheer determination and raging fury ensured that for now they were able to keep a healthy distance between themselves and the raiders. The open ground between the tower and the refinery was littered with the dead and dying of both sides. A carpet of ragged, bloody corpses revealed the terrible toll the stoic Silver Skulls had inflicted upon the treacherous cultists, but strewn here and there amongst the mass the bulky, fallen form of one of their own could be seen. The Red Corsairs were driving their slaves into the killing field in an effort to exhaust the ammunition of the entrenched Adeptus Astartes. It was slow and ruthless, but a winning tactic for all that.

As Porteus watched, a pair of cultists raced in from the refinery gates and hastily began assembling a tripod upon which to mount a heavy weapon. Well placed shots from his brothers turned the pair into ragged, ruptured corpses before the job was even half done. A quick cast around the compound confirmed that his squad had done an excellent job of holding things at bay, and even now, even with the wounds they had borne during the attack, continued to carry and prove themselves with ferocity and grim determination.

'Give no quarter!' Porteus ordered across the vox. 'Hold your positions. Punish these traitors for daring to set foot on Imperial soil!' Those who were still capable, still standing and still very much fighting confirmed receipt of the order and within a few moments, the Silver Skulls were defending the door. Porteus cast a grim nod at his injured brethren. Down, but not out. Commendable, but no less than he expected. The sergeant's flamer fizzed slightly as it began to wane under the endless precipitation, but the bolters in the hands of his battle-brothers were still functioning and until they finally ran out of ammunition were still doing their job.

A distant scream of atmospheric retro-jets was heard and the Silver Skulls raised their heads, fresh hope stirring in their bellies.

'Drop-pods,' murmured Keyle. 'Thank the Throne.'

'Aye, brother,' said Porteus grimly. 'We will thank the Throne once we know that these newcomers are actually on our side. Otherwise, there will be precious little to be thankful for.'

ARRUN WAS TORN. The *Spectre of Ruin* was already on the fringes of the Gildar Rift, preparing to enter the warp. He knew that Huron Blackheart must be on board that ship. It was an opportunity being handed to him on a plate and it felt almost as though it were too good to miss. They could engage in a pursuit; leave the *Manifest Destiny* and the *Quicksilver* to mop up the ground assaults. He struggled with the matter for scant seconds before his decision was made. Decades of faithful, loyal service and endless hypno-doctrinations made the choice for him. His loyalty, his *duty* was to the Imperium first and foremost. It did not help; he acknowledged that what remained of his fleet bore significant damage. For the first time since Daerys Arrun had taken the position of Master of the Fleet, his precious charges had been forced into limping away from battle. The decision not to pursue Blackheart was, therefore, one borne of necessity. Had he had the choice...

He did not have the choice. Huron Blackheart would not be his. Not today. He had to rid the Gildar system of these traitors. It was his duty and his responsibility.

As though adding insult to injury, as if losing a chance to capture the prize of Huron Blackheart, the *Wolf of Fenris* broke from its orbit around Gildar Secundus and tore its way through the void, sustaining major damage from the Rift's endless fields of debris as it fled. Arrun watched its departure, his heart heavy. Carrying the news of its loss to the Space Wolves would not be an enviable task.

Brand had been taken down to the apothecarion with countless others who had sustained injuries during the boarding action. Initial reports on his condition were positive. The Prognosticator required a few grafts and there was possible damage to one lung that may require intervention surgery at a later date, but he would survive. Remarkably, the majority of injuries sustained were not severe or immediately life-threatening. Of the close to one hundred Silver Skulls on board, only eighteen were deceased or were temporarily incapacitated beyond anything that could be dealt with expediently.

Porteus's squad were on the surface, which reduced the company's numbers still further. Fortunately, they now had the *Quicksilver* and the *Manifest Destiny*, which provided them with at least three other companies.

But eighteen dead was eighteen too many.

Already he had lost good warriors to this incursion. He would purge this taint and he would deliver the Emperor's retribution swiftly. With the exodus of the *Wolf of Fenris* came the brief, searing knowledge that any hope they had of recovering Apothecary Ryarus was gone. The loss of his friend and battle-brother was perhaps the deepest wound amongst the many that the captain had taken so far during this bloody battle.

Several of the serf crew, continuing to fight alongside the Silver Skulls, had cleared the *Dread Argent* of the Red Corsairs who remained. Not a single one of the intruders had been taken alive. Wherever the raiders roamed unchecked, Volker's new-found consciousness demonstrated ruthless efficiency in dealing with them: venting the Space Marines to the void, or closing off areas and shutting down life support where the Red Corsairs slaves tried the stealthy approach.

Many of the Red Corsairs escort vessels that had formed the blockade around Gildar Secundus were also showing signs that they were planning on following the *Spectre of Ruin* and the *Wolf of Fenris* out of the system. The guns of the *Quicksilver* and the *Manifest Destiny* made the gauntlet run far from easy for them and more were satisfactorily obliterated as they tried to flee. Several of the escort vessels employed an unexpected move of throwing themselves deliberately between the Silver Skulls fleet and the retreating Red Corsairs battle-barge. They absorbed the lion's share of the pounding punishment meant for the *Spectre of Ruin* until they too were shattered into pieces. Their sacrifice was not in vain either, as the distraction had given the *Spectre of Ruin* enough time to achieve an escape vector. More drop-pods were ejected from the huge hulking ship as its dread shadow passed over the planet. Accelerating, using the planet's gravity well to aid its exit from the system, the *Spectre of Ruin* rent its way through space, disappearing into the empyrean as though it had never been there.

It made no sense. They had apparently deployed countless raiders and vessels across the entire system, judging from the continued flood of messages that were now pouring through the unhindered communications system. Yet they were sending their means of escape away.

Huron Blackheart was throwing away the lives of his warriors either through insanity or spite; but then not a single strategy that he had employed thus far had been predictable in any way, shape or form. Daerys Arrun found that unsettling.

It was not long before the guns stilled completely and all that remained of the battle that had raged for several hours in the heart of the Gildar Rift were fading, dying contrails of smoke and fire and many broken ships. Dotted amongst the destruction drifted corpses, some whole, some shredded or broken. All of them tumbled through the void, faces forever frozen in their last throes of death.

Arrun immediately opened a vox-channel to the *Manifest Destiny*, conversing with Sinopa in short, clipped sentences that barely concealed the rage that he was feeling. Sinopa himself reported minimal losses, although the *Manifest Destiny* had taken some quite considerable damage. The conversation between the two captains was tense, even strained, particularly for two battle-brothers who had always been so close.

'We need to deploy ground troops, Daerys. We cannot allow the enemy more time to further entrench themselves. They need to be rooted out and they need to be purged.'

'I do not dispute the logic in that statement, Sinopa. What does not sit well with me is the fact that we have no idea how many Red Corsairs have been sent down and to which locations. We are blind here.' Arrun ran his hand over his shaved scalp, his face set in a rigid scowl. 'My proposal is that we send a strike force down to join Porteus and retake the promethium refinery as our first priority. I will contact Daviks and he can join me here. His expertise will be invaluable in planning such an attack.'

'Aye. You'll get no argument from me on that front, brother.' Although equally tense, Sinopa's mood was in stark contrast to the Fourth Company captain's tone. Where Arrun's fiery rage told through the simple cadence of his voice, Sinopa was calm and measured. His continued calm eventually helped bring Arrun's mood down and he was able to set aside the grief and anger. There would be time enough to mourn those who had fallen in the ship's defence. Sinopa deferred to Arrun's overall command in his position as Master of the Fleet and when the orders began to pour thick and fast, his compliance was assured.

'Sinopa, review any data that our ships have been able to glean regarding numbers of ships and pods sent down by the Red Corsairs. Daviks and I will concentrate our forces on Gildar Secundus. I leave it to you to coordinate the offensives on the other worlds in this system that have been afflicted by this madman's taint. As soon as we are able, we will lend you our aid.' He slammed his fist into his thigh. 'Expedience. They will be eliminated and they will think twice before they dare set foot in Imperial space again. The Silver Skulls *will* prevail – and we will show them the futility of their actions.'

His confidence was infectious and Sinopa's instant assent buoyed Arrun's energies once again. The momentary loss of control he had suffered when he had been unable to fathom the twist of Blackheart's plans had been horribly unfamiliar. He had always been a man who held the reins of power tightly in his hand. Now they had been passed back to him once again and he would end the matter once and for all.

In the meantime there was a matter awaiting his attention in the heart of the ship. Since his bonding with the *Dread Argent's* machine-spirit, Arrun had been acutely aware of Volker's presence everywhere. He was unsure whether that consciousness was genuine, or whether it was just the knowledge of what Volker was becoming that prickled his senses; made him feel that the youth was somehow watching him.

In the confident satisfaction that everything was finally back under the control of the Silver Skulls, he left the decimated bridge once again in the hands of Yanus and made his way through the ship's corridors. Everywhere he walked he saw lingering evidence of the attack: the Chapter serfs, aided by the Adeptus Astartes, were removing the bodies of the fallen raiders, but their presence still remained. Here a broken pauldron. There a spent, abandoned pistol. Blood smeared the corridors and deck and craters were burned in the walls where grenades and shells had detonated. The smell of accelerant from the flamers used in defence of the *Dread Argent* was strong.

The *Dread Argent* had taken considerable damage to her hull during the battle but all of the containment bulkheads were fully functional. Volker – Arrun could not stop thinking of him as such – had demonstrated a phenomenal capability to cope with the myriad ship's systems.

Arrun entered the area where Volker was now housed. The chamber, which until he had been permanently linked had rarely seen visitors, was now buzzing with frenetic activity. Servitors had been set to monitor a variety of bio-feed outputs that were spewing forth from the cogitator banks. Arrun paused and took the scene in. Before him was the culmination of years of research and perseverance. Arguments against the project had been many and vociferous; but he had won through in the end.

Naryn was absent from the scene. Finding himself as the ship's ranking Apothecary, suddenly thrust into a promotion he had never anticipated, his duties caring for the fallen took precedence over the situation. He was overseeing the processes of recovering gene-seed from the fallen and attending to healing where it was required. Correlan was there, of course, fussing around the servitors and marking things on a data-slate he held clutched in one hand. He looked up as Arrun entered and gave him a tight, terse nod.

'Captain,' he acknowledged. 'You'll forgive me for not stopping, I hope? Things are... difficult here.'

'You have done well, Correlan,' Arrun said, taking the Techmarine's words as his cue to fully enter Volker's chamber, his boots ringing on the deck. 'The Lord Commander will be pleased to hear of your efforts.' The carefully chosen words of flattery weren't completely hollow or designed to placate the edgy Techmarine; Arrun was truly impressed with the way in which Correlan had conducted himself when it had mattered most. 'Now tell me how he is doing.'

The usual entourage had thinned out noticeably now. Once the Resurgent had joined with the blessed machine, the tech-priests had scaled down their attendance. It had taken some time for them to complete the rituals of thanks and even Correlan had joined in those prayers. The relief he had felt was strong and he felt that offering up his gratitude was the least he could do. The faintly sweet smell of incense still lingered and traces of oil shone on the exterior of the chamber.

'He is adjusting to the situation with considerable ease, brother-captain.' The deep crease-lines of worry on the Techmarine's face had lightened noticeably at Arrun's words and he handed over the data-slate. Arrun glanced down at the reams of technical data and looked back up at Correlan.

'Give me a brief summary,' he said, mildly. 'With the emphasis on the "brief".'

'Of course, of course, my apologies.' Correlan set the data-slate down on the desk, then snatched it up again before one of the servitors took it. He shouted a few words of instruction to the lobotomised slave and beckoned Arrun over to Volker's tank.

Now permanently ensconced within the armoured tube, Volker was so still that it was hard to believe that he lived at all. Unlike the mortally wounded warriors who were bound for the greatness of a Dreadnought body, the fluid that surrounded Volker was completely translucent. It was mirror-calm: no ripples, no bubbles and the figure within was rigid.

Cables and wires ran in every direction from the youth, through specially bored intakes into the armaplas for the purpose. They curved upwards, all connected at the same point in a position some way above Arrun's head where they were then wired together before being swallowed into the ceiling and the ship's systems directly.

'We have not yet established full motor control,' said Correlan. 'By which I mean we are unable to fully hand over the piloting of the ship to him. For now, at least, we need to use the helmsman.' The Techmarine's tone was apologetic but the look he shot at Arrun held the faintest hint of reproach. 'We did not have time.'

'You have time now, though, Correlan. Take it.' Arrun's attention was riveted on the naked figure within the tank and he moved forward to consider it further. His scarred, tattooed face twisted in pleasure at the result of so many long years of work.

'There is another issue I should raise with you.' Correlan hesitated, not wishing to provoke Arrun's ire any further than he already had done today. 'Whilst running system diagnostics and working through the litanies that will take us to full integration, we realised another matter that needs to be dealt with. We... genuinely forgot to take it into account when we were planning.' Correlan looked grim. 'He told us quickly enough, though.' The Techmarine's anger faded away to be replaced by something that could have, in a human, been considered discomfort. 'There is a hurdle that is proving hard to jump.'

'Ah,' said Arrun, turning his attention away from Volker.

'I believe I know where you are going with this. Ryarus expressed concerns to me shortly before he left for the *Wolf of Fenris*. You are referring to the Navigator, am I correct?'

'Aye,' came the reluctant reply, then Correlan's frustration came out in an explosive burst of irritation. 'I cannot get him to see reason, brother-captain. He refuses to come up here to speak with Volker. I have been polite. I have cajoled and even threatened him, but he still defies me. Conversation with him is impossible.'

For the first time in what felt like an age, a sparkle of amusement came into Arrun's eyes. 'Now then, Correlan,' he said, gently. 'You have wrought a miracle here today. I have every faith in your ability to achieve the impossible.'

'A MESSAGE FOR you, my Lord Apothecary. From Lord Blackheart.'

The Red Corsairs warrior bowed his head in deep respect as he stood at the doorway of the hall. He glanced past the other's shoulder to the subject on which the Apothecary had been working. The unfortunate overseer had been splayed open, his ribcage prised apart to expose his innards. The stench of blood in the room was powerful.

'Proceed.' The Corpsemaster's hands were coated in a sticky red layer. He put down the wicked-looking blade that he had been using to carry out his grisly task and turned to face the messenger.

'Taemar has failed our cause. The Executioner is dead.' There was an unmistakable sneer on the face of the Red Corsair. Taemar had never truly garnered that much respect from his peers, not even when he had repeatedly demonstrated his prowess on the battlefield and his uncanny ability to dispose of any competitors for Blackheart's favours.

'Unfortunate,' said the Apothecary. 'He showed tremendous promise for a short while. No matter.' With those words, the champion's fate was brushed away. He gave the messenger a slightly disdainful look, which sent shivers down the warrior's spine. It didn't matter just how fearless in battle he was. The Corpsemaster's gaze could chill the hardest and most stoic of hearts. 'I am sure our leader will find himself another new champion soon enough.' A distant sound of gunfire and shouting caused a look of annoyance to flicker across the Apothecary's sallow features. 'What is the gunfire in aid of?'

'A small unit of Silver Skulls are attempting to hold the communications tower,' came the slightly apologetic reply. 'Seems that the destruction of their force to the surface was not as thorough as we might have hoped. They will not be bothering us for much longer. The situation is perfectly under control. You need not concern yourself.'

'I expect nothing less. Well then, what does my Lord Blackheart want of us now?'

'We are to proceed to securing secondary objectives,' continued the messenger. 'Everything is in position.' The Corpsemaster nodded, evidently pleased by this news.

'Then I must prepare myself for battle,' he said. He began to move towards the door, then stopped, gesturing to the overseer with his head. 'Dispose of that. I may need to use this area later.'

'There is more to the message.' The Red Corsairs warrior could not keep the disgust out of his voice, not so much at the thought of removing the revolting corpse of the putrid, fat overseer, but more that the Corpsemaster saw him as nothing more than a lackey.

'There is more?'

'He says he will see you sooner than expected.'

A slow smile spread across the Corpsemaster's face.

'Excellent,' he said.

IT STANK IN the Navigator's chamber. Cartons of barely eaten and half-rotted food lay around, spilling their contents out on the floor. The lumen-strips were turned down to a permanent low as was its occupant's preference. Whenever Correlan had found reason to come here in the past, he had always been put in mind of a rat eking out its wretched existence. There were no windows; no starlight or any other sense of being anywhere but in a prison.

'Jeremiah?' Correlan's gene-enhanced eyesight adjusted easily to the gloom and he cast around, looking for the Navigator. 'I have no time for this. Get out here, now.'

The little man had always had a tendency to hoard and hide; the first evidenced by the stinking, rotten food. The second was almost pointless. He could not hide from the Adeptus Astartes. Not when Correlan had eyesight that could pick up the tiniest movements.

He still tried, though. Old habits were hard to shake.

Correlan scowled in exasperation. He had no time for this foolishness, but Arrun had suggested to him that patience and even kindness might pay. He attempted to put a kindly tone to his voice.

'Jeremiah? We need to speak.'

Arrun had delegated the job to him as Correlan had suspected he might. In fairness, the captain was too busy now with the job of ensuring the continued safety and redeployment of the fleet to concern himself with trivial matters – and he was certainly far too busy to deal with petulant youths.

'Jeremiah!' Forsaking kindness, Correlan's tone became commanding. He caught the scurrying movement from somewhere to the rear of the chamber and strode forward. He was so massive, with his harness still attached, that he barely fit into the low-ceilinged room. One of the mechadendrites snaked forward, reaching into the little nook his physical self could never hope to reach and there was a squeak of rage as the pincered appendage closed around his tunic collar.

'Out here, boy. Now.'

Correlan tugged with the mechadendrite, wrenching the Navigator free from his little bolthole and out into the dimly lit chamber. The scrawny figure stumbled, falling to his knees. Correlan released his grip and stepped back, allowing the boy a little time to pick himself up and regain whatever he had that passed for dignity.

'The ship needs me.' It was the Navigator's usual opening line whenever any of the Adeptus Astartes on board had reason to bring him to task. It had become his defence and he hid behind it with all the tenacity of moss clinging to a rock. 'You can't hurt me.'

Correlan stared down at the thin figure. He could have picked Jeremiah up and crushed him with his hands alone. Indeed, at the moment, the Navigator's repeated refusal to help them integrate Volker fully into the system made that prospect almost unbearably tempting. Correlan didn't even pretend to understand how the bond the Navigator and the *Dread Argent* worked and he cared still less. All that mattered was getting Jeremiah's full compliance to work with Volker.

Correlan knew little about the man other than that he had come to the *Dread Argent* less than a year before and in that time had struggled to operate on any sort of social level with the giants who were now his masters. He spoke as little as possible to any of them and kept himself away from the rest of the crew, aloof and indifferent, unpopular and unliked. Correlan had to grudgingly admit that he was not a bad Navigator however; and it was this reason and this alone that had ensured his continued tenure aboard the *Dread Argent*.

'Volker tells me that you are resisting him,' Correlan said, keeping his expression cold and impassive. 'This is unacceptable.'

'You didn't ask me.' Jeremiah got to his feet and dusted himself down imperiously. He somehow succeeded in making himself even filthier. He wore a ragged tunic over black trousers. His feet were bare beneath them and he padded back towards his nook. He met Correlan's stare with an easy confidence. He was so sure in his position and his perceived importance that he had no fear of the Space Marines. When he spoke, he did so in clipped sentences, used to being by himself. Words cost effort and he had long ago learned to expend as little energy as possible.

Yes, Jeremiah had no fear and perhaps unfortunately for him, he rarely showed any respect, either.

'You should have asked me first,' he continued. 'I worked hard.' He wiped his hands on his dirty tunic again and glowered. 'I worked hard to build my bond with the machine spirit in this ship. Nobody helped me. I had to do it myself. He's a stranger. I don't know him. I don't like him. I don't want to help him. The Apothecary was going to talk to me, but he never came.'

'You were given every opportunity to be a part of the process, Jeremiah. Apothecary Ryarus tried to give you the chance to be involved and yet you declined. You cannot now start to refuse to cooperate. I need you to come with me now and to speak with Volker.' He folded his arms across his massive chest, but the snake-like mechadendrites at his back did not quell their writhing, giving away his anger.

Jeremiah smirked up at the Techmarine and repeated his earlier words. 'The ship needs me. Volker doesn't. If he's so clever, let him figure out the warp drives for himself.'

It was the absolute last straw. The arrogance. The sheer arrogance and smug tone in the boy's voice irritated Correlan whose day thus far had not gone at all well.

'Treat him with patience and kindness,' the Fourth Company captain had advised, but things had gone far beyond that now. Correlan was neither a patient nor a kind soul by nature and his temper flared.

'You would stand there and ignore a direct order from your betters? You are a fool, Jeremiah.'

'Perhaps,' replied the boy in a strangely philosophical tone. 'Perhaps I am. But either way, you don't frighten me, Silver Skull. Without me, you are blind in the warp. Without me, you can't ever hope to complete your project.' He fixed his watery eyes on Correlan and smiled guilelessly. 'You all need me.' His smile turned into a beam that displayed several broken teeth.

Correlan took three steps forward and with a lightning fast movement, reached out and picked the youth up bodily, this time with his hands rather than the tendrils of his harness. Jeremiah squirmed and squeaked, fighting such rough treatment with commendable ferocity. He had grown up on the streets of a hive-world and it showed now as he continued to wriggle helplessly in the Techmarine's grip.

'Enough of this,' Correlan said, his voice grim and carrying more than a hint of threat. 'I'll give you a simple choice, boy. Either you come with me of your own free will right now and give Volker what he needs, or I will carry you there myself. Failing that, then I will carry you to the nearest airlock and throw you out.'

'You wouldn't,' gasped Jeremiah, still struggling. The Techmarine caught the scruff of the Navigator's tunic and raised him to eye level, giving him a baleful stare.

'Do you want to test the veracity of that statement, Jeremiah?'

Their gazes remained locked for a few short moments and then all of the little Navigator's fight went out of him. He sagged weakly in Correlan's grip and hung his head.

'All right,' he conceded. 'I'll give you what you need.'

'Good.' The Techmarine set the grubby Navigator back down on the floor and stood aside to allow him to scurry past. Not for the first time since he had been assigned to the *Dread Argent*, Correlan wondered just how on earth Jeremiah had lived as long as he had. He shook his head and followed the boy down the corridor.

TIME WAS RUNNING out for Porteus and his squad. Of the eleven who had taken the communications tower, only six remained standing and two of those were upstairs ready to fight the final battle and hold out to the last. The others were dead or dying, their lives fading away on this blasted rock. But still Porteus fought on. His flamer had long since sputtered out and died through lack of fuel. There was something cruelly ironic about that, particularly given the proximity of the promethium refinery – but he had abandoned the flamer, drawn his chainsword and carved his way through several of the Red Corsairs who had dared come close.

His armour was barely protecting him any longer. Several close-range bolter shots had soon reduced the ceramite shell to little more than a weight that pulled him down and was more of a hindrance than a help. The coppery taste of blood was rich in his mouth and he didn't need the helm's insistent, flashing runes to tell him that he had taken internal damage.

An agonised scream from over his right shoulder told him that Keyle had finally fallen under the onslaught of a massive Red Corsair clad in desecrated Space Wolves armour. Porteus was the last one defending. His two battle-brothers waited at the top of the tower, ready to defend the array for several minutes longer. Right now, though, every weapon was trained on him. He gripped the hilt of his chainsword determinedly and he stared defiantly at the enemy through the shattered lenses of his battle helm. Let death come. He had served well and he would die well. He would not surrender. The thought never even crossed his mind.

But death did not come for Porteus. Instead, he heard one voice above all the others. A soft, whispering voice that was so low that it was barely more than a susurration on the very edge of his awareness. Yet it carried above the driving wind and rain, cutting through the battle shouts of his enemy. The words it spoke contained far more menace than any of the red-hot bolter muzzles that had been pointed at him.

'Keep this one alive for now.' The whispering voice held an unmistakable tone of command and Porteus turned his head, trying to locate its source. 'Restrain him and bring him to me. He could prove useful. No doubt the heroic Silver Skulls will soon rush to take back what they consider to be theirs.'

'Yes, my lord.'

Several warriors in the defiled battle plate of the Red Corsairs swarmed towards Porteus, but he would not be taken down so easily. Planting his feet firmly on the ground, he filled the entrance of the tower and let them come.

His left arm dangled uselessly at his side, the cracked and broken ceramite of his armour painted crimson with blood; some that of his brothers, most his own. Surveying the carnage his valiant stand had wrought, Porteus allowed himself a glimmer of satisfaction. The first traitor to reach him died beneath his screaming blade. The second staggered away missing a hand, while the third spun away blinded. Porteus was still swinging his sword and roaring in righteous fury when the crashing rapport of a bolt pistol punched him from his feet and into all-encompassing darkness.

TWELVE
COUNTERSTRIKE

THE STRATEGIUM ABOARD the *Quicksilver* possessed none of the grand ostentation of the *Dread Argent*. But it was adequate. It was more than adequate. Plainly and sparsely furnished, this was a room where siege plans were drawn up. This was a room where Adeptus Astartes worked out ways and methods of destroying entire cities. The heavy, plain wooden table dominating the room was scored with countless lines where captains and their men over the years had drawn up plans of attack on vast diagrams and plans.

Despite being so similar on the outside, the interior of the *Quicksilver* was nothing like its sister ship. It was claustrophobic almost; a complete contrast to the airy, open ziggurat style of the *Dread Argent*. The strategium was located off the bridge and on his arrival, Arrun and three of his company sergeants had been led there by one of the Ninth Company Devastators. He was joined in time by the Company's Prognosticator who had been sent ahead to greet Arrun and his men. Inteus was young, as were so many of the Silver Skulls these days, and following the formal greetings had turned thoughtful and intense eyes on Arrun.

He had offered more in the form of conversation, but once the formalities were complete had spoken with much less stiff tones. 'Siege Captain Daviks extends apologies for his absence,' he had explained, 'but he will be along in a little while. He is gathering what schemata and available data he can locate on the refinery and the outlying buildings.'

The absence of his own Prognosticator was keenly felt in the presence of this young psyker. Like all the Silver Skulls, Arrun had the greatest of respect for those battle-brothers who wore the cobalt-blue of the Prognosticatum, but he could not help feel unsettled in Inteus's youthful presence. He did not take a seat as offered, but instead paced the length of the room. The three squad sergeants he had been able to spare to bring with him took seats at the table and kept their silence, occasionally sharing grim glances.

Arrun would have been happier in many ways if he had not left the *Dread Argent*. He had been reluctant to do so given that Volker was still in his fledgling hours in control of the ship. But the plans had to be drawn up and discussed and without a strategium, the *Quicksilver* was the natural choice. Daviks, of course, as Siege Captain was far better placed to lead the assault that would inevitably have to take place.

It came as no surprise to discover that the Ninth Company captain was gathering everything together already. The Siege Captain's nature had always been to pre-empt the needs of a mission. He had demonstrated such a propensity for this that the Prognosticatum had tested his skills on more than one occasion, suspicious that he may have had latent psychic ability. Of all his brothers amongst the other company captains, Arrun had always found Daviks to be the most serious and earnest. Nobody could ever recall seeing the Ninth Company captain at ease. He was in a perpetual state of tense readiness; a spring coiled and ready to strike at a word. Solid and dependable, nigh on as impregnable as the defences he had designed during his tenure, Daviks was frequently deployed as the ambassadorial face of the Chapter. His earnest brand of solidity loaned an aspect of seriousness to the Silver Skulls that Argentius liked to present to the universe beyond the borders of Varsavia.

If Daviks was put in charge of overseeing your assault, the other captains had often said, semi-jokingly, then you could conquer worlds in hours and entire systems in days – as long as he had the plans. Daviks was at one and the same time an engineer of sturdy fortresses and the architect of their destruction.

Finally Arrun ceased his pacing and took a seat at the table. He steepled his fingers beneath his chin. He stared up at the walls which were papered in countless purity seals, fastened to the walls at the end of a campaign. It was a red and white sea of embossed seals and fading parchments dating back into the Chapter's long and glorious past.

For his part, Inteus was all but silent. The Prognosticator sat at the far end of the table, already fully clad in his blue wargear. No matter how many times Arrun looked away and then stole a glance at him, the psyker was looking back, a serene smile on his face. Arrun got the very definite sense that the younger Silver Skull was playing a game to amuse himself.

'Did the *Quicksilver* take any heavy losses during the fighting?' In the end, Arrun spoke simply to fill the silence. The younger Space Marine shook his head.

'By the Emperor's grace, we were spared. Our late arrival was unfortunate and yet at the same time, a blessing it would seem. We were on the furthest reaches of the sector at the time your astropathic message was received, heading for home. Of course, we turned about and made for the Gildar system with all haste.' His voice was strong and confident. 'It took some time for the will of the Emperor to make itself clear to me.' He touched a hand to the rune bag at his waist. 'Enginseers have reported little more than superficial damage. I am glad to note that the same cannot be said for those Red Corsair traitors.'

An infectious grin lit up the Prognosticator's fair-skinned face. The sudden demonstration of warm affability took Arrun completely by surprise. He had grown far more used to the gravitas of those he had shared the battlefield with over the years. The calm and controlled Brand, the haughty indifference of Bast of Eighth Company... Vashiro himself, even. All these men were stoic, serious and even a little aloof. The warmth that came from Inteus was unexpected, but under the circumstances, not unwelcome. He found himself relaxing a little.

'Daerys Arrun. You are not dead yet, then?'

The rumble of Daviks's voice from the doorway pulled Arrun's attention away from Inteus and he rose to his feet, crossing to the door to grip his fellow captain's arm in his own.

'No more than you, my brother,' he said. It had been some time since he had seen the Siege Captain but Daviks had not changed. Still as grim of face and solid of build as he had ever been. Looping whorls of red ink marked his face and neck, visible above the bulk of his wargear. He turned and gestured to the serfs who hovered in the corridor behind him and they rushed in, spilling armfuls of data-slates and schemata on the table. Arrun raised one eyebrow at the quantity of information. Daviks noted the expression and one of his shoulders lifted in a slight shrug.

'The best I could do under the circumstances,' he said, without any hint of irony. 'With some work, the tech-adepts aboard were also able to patch me into the cogitator banks in the refinery stronghold. They were resistant to my taking a look around, but with a little manipulation and coercion they gave up their secrets soon enough.' Daviks lumbered fully into the room and bowed his head respectfully towards Inteus, who had also risen to his feet at the arrival of his captain. 'Prognosticator Inteus.'

'Brother-Captain Daviks.'

'Have you told Daerys of your vision?' Arrun's eyes darted immediately to the Prognosticator who looked a little disconcerted. 'Have you told him what it was that you saw that delayed our arrival?'

'I have not. Not yet, anyway.' Inteus wrinkled his nose in a manner which suggested that he had been withholding information until the most appropriate time. Daviks shrugged his massive shoulders again.

'Then perhaps you might care to regale him whilst I turn this mess into something we can effectively use.' Daviks said nothing further and moved to the table and began sorting through the piles of data-slates and information wafers almost as though the other warriors were not there.

Arrun turned his attention to the Prognosticator who was looking distinctly uncomfortable at his captain's blunt manner. 'Would you perhaps elaborate on this, Prognosticator?'

Inteus reached up and scratched at the neat, sandy beard that covered his chin, his eyes regaining that same intensity that he had shown on Arrun's arrival. He pulled a rune from the bag as he spoke, twisting it absently in his fingers. It did not bother Arrun at all; he was used to the other Prognosticators of the Chapter and each one had their own method of concentrating what could sometimes be skittish thought. In time, he composed himself and stood.

'I cast the auguries on receipt of your order to mobilise, Brother-Captain Arrun,' the Prognosticator said, his tone formal and all hint of geniality buried under an instant layer of seriousness. It suited him, added weight to his words and any uncertainty Arrun had felt at the Prognosticator's comparative youth dissolved in the face of such a familiar confidence. He nodded approvingly at Inteus's words and the psyker continued.

'The runes have never lied to me in my years of service,' Inteus continued and he stopped rolling the one he held between his fingers, closing his palm around it in a fist. 'They read that the orders were excellent, that the portents were good and with the Emperor's favour secured, we set course.'

A strange expression flickered into Inteus's eyes. Too young and inexperienced yet to have acquired any facial tattoos of his own, every emotion played across his unlined face. 'During our journey here, I was sent a vision. I have not yet fully divined its meaning. Such visions are rare for me and I have little practise at interpreting the signs the Emperor sends.

His meanings are often subtle, sometimes even obscure.'

He met Arrun's gaze directly and showed no sign of hesitation. 'At best, I extrapolated a warning.'

'A warning?' Inteus kept his clear gaze steady. Arrun noted the slight change in the cadence of his voice; a particularly dramatic method of delivering the Emperor's word that all the Prognosticators seemed to adopt. In a human, it would be called melodious. But there was nothing pleasant about it. The words left Inteus's mouth weighted with severity.

'Rage should always be tempered with reason.'

'What does that mean?'

'I cannot say, brother-captain. There is no easy way I can describe how these messages work. I can only take it to be a warning and I can only suggest that it leans towards wariness of blind vengeance.'

'Lugft Huron has killed many fine battle-brothers this day,' retorted Arrun. 'He has slaughtered them for nothing more than his own gratification. You cannot tell me to avoid exercising my right for retaliation in this matter, Prognosticator. What am I supposed to do? Ignore him? He killed my Apothecary...' At this, Daviks's head came up.

'Ryarus?'

'Aye, brother. One of the best. He led a boarding party to the *Wolf of Fenris* and did not return.' Arrun's hands closed into fists. The loss had left a yawning chasm in his world; not just the presumed death of his battle-brother, but the perceived failure at preventing it and the impossibility of being unable to return for him. All these things bore through the armour of self-righteousness that Arrun surrounded himself with. Every one of them cut him to the quick. He did not like what he could not control. He had never liked that.

Daviks gave a small sigh. 'That is... unfortunate. He was a fine Apothecary and a superb warrior. We will not see his like again. Our loss is the ancestor's gain.'

The taciturn Daviks shook his head, the only concession to grief that he was likely to show and resumed his work.

'Aye,' retorted Arrun. 'He was all that. And I cannot simply sit by and watch as the Tyrant of Badab mocks our Chapter.

He will meet my blade of retribution and he will fall beneath it. Or I...'

'...will die trying,' finished Inteus, his voice soft. 'I see you understand the import of this.' He sat back in his chair and spread his palms out in a gesture of supplication. 'That is the warning, brother-captain. It is up to you how you choose to interpret it.'

Arrun felt his mood, already dark, slipping further and acknowledged the Prognosticator's words with an abrupt nod. 'My death,' he said, addressing his words to the table at large, 'would be a small thing if it saw an end to his tyranny.'

'With the greatest will in the world,' Inteus resumed playing with the rune in his hand and leaned forward once again. He glanced back up at Arrun. 'I hope it does not come to that.'

'HE LOOKS STRANGE.'

There was a sharp intake of breath from the three attendant priests. 'You speak grave heresy,' one of them said in a scolding tone. The Navigator took precisely no notice of the robed adepts to his right. He had always found the techpriests to be more than a little terrifying and he dealt with them in his approved method of ignoring them.

'Why's he got all that glowing stuff all over him?' It was a simple description of what was actually right before his eyes. The adept spoke up again, his faintly mechanical voice proud and pleased.

'He bears an inscription that we branded into his body. His whole being is a dedication to the Omnissiah. His connection with the *Dread Argent* is delicate and the wardings will protect him; help him find his way to True Oneness. The power of the machine lights up the runes. It is a most glorious state.'

'Don't understand a word of what you just said. Interesting, I'm sure. He just looks like he's glowing to me. Don't know anything about no Omnissiah.'

Jeremiah's nose was practically pressed up against the rune-covered surface of Volker's tube. Correlan reached over and pulled him back again, as a servitor dutifully wiped the greasy nose-smear off the front. The Navigator, who rarely came out of his chambers, was acting with all the childishness that he usually demonstrated. He had been delighted by all the pieces of machinery lying around. Correlan had watched him like a hawk from the moment of his arrival, half-suspecting the rat-like little man would attempt to steal something.

'He looks strange,' Jeremiah repeated. 'Not like last time I saw him.'

Hello, Jeremiah.

Correlan observed the Navigator's reaction to the voice with wry amusement. Even he was still finding the way Volker's voice seemed to leak out of every proverbial pore of the *Dread Argent* slightly unsettling. Jeremiah's immediate response to Volker's semi-mechanical greeting was to drop the gear housing he had been fiddling with. The metal casing clattered to the table loudly, a cog assembly breaking and sending parts spinning everywhere. Correlan winced slightly. The Navigator whirled around and stared about in surprise.

'Did you say something?' The accusatory tone in his voice was directed at Correlan who shook his head and nodded towards the figure in the tank. Jeremiah turned and stared. Volker's eyes, which had been closed, were now wide open. Disconcertingly, they did not fix on either the scrawny Navigator or even Correlan, but seemed to look beyond, to a point in the middle distance. A dreamy, beatific expression was on his face.

Hello, Jeremiah. Volker repeated his greeting and the boy swore colourfully. He took a step towards the tube, but did not touch it. *We are gratified that you have brought yourself into our presence.* It was stiffly formal; an unprecedented aftereffect of the joining that Correlan had not even considered.

'Well now, I've seen some strange things, but this is...' Jeremiah peered suspiciously at Volker. 'What are you?'

We are the Dread Argent. *We are also Volker Straub. We... are. Let that explanation suffice. Although we can provide you with the simplest possible comparison.* Volker blinked, slowly and languorously. *We are not dissimilar to a Dreadnought. A fusion of man and machine wrought by the hands and minds of the Chapter. Is that not right, Techmarine Correlan?*

The Techmarine nodded, pleased at Volker's choice of comparison. Of course, the basic methods he had employed did indeed draw comparisons to the technology used to inter a warrior in the sarcophagus of a Dreadnought. But in this instance, the joining of Volker and the *Dread Argent* was far more invasive and far more complex. When the integration was fully complete, the idea was simple. Lightning-fast reactions and orders that could be channelled directly to the machine spirit of the *Dread Argent* without the necessary intervention of third parties. Volker could command the ship to fire and as long as the guns were loaded and replenished, she would fire. He would be able to plot firing solutions by using the auguries as though they were extensions of his own senses.

When the full wiring grid was complete, he should be able to steer and turn the ship with far greater control and effectiveness than the helmsman could ever manage.

Jeremiah presented a stumbling block in that he was particularly protective of the *Dread Argent's* machine spirit. For several months, since his engagement, Jeremiah had been the one who had closest contact with what passed for the ship's sentience. Now there was someone getting as close – if not closer – and he felt threatened by the fact. He had engaged Correlan in conversation once, claiming that the great vessel's 'machine soul', as he had put it, was not unlike that of an eager pup.

Correlan had not liked the analogy. He saw the *Dread Argent* as something far more austere and grandiose. 'An eager pup' was far too frivolous.

Volker moved slightly, sending a series of ripples through the amniotic fluid that surrounded him. The skinny little Navigator tipped his head to one side and watched him in fascination.

'Does it hurt?'

It was a surprising question and Correlan wasn't entirely

sure he wanted to hear Volker's reply. The youth had reassured him that the initial pain was long passed, that he had transcended beyond it. Volker considered for a moment before answering, then laid a hand on the inside of the tube.

It is uncomfortable, but we are getting used to it. We feel a sense of disquiet. 'Hurt' is something which fades in time. What we feel... we feel the cold of the void on our skin. We taste the eternal emptiness and we see the energies that sweep from the stars. We are finding that understanding is a slow process, Jeremiah. But we are proud. It is an honour to serve.

The words were beautiful, almost poetic, but they were lost on the Navigator. A simple soul, with simple needs, he merely wrinkled his nose. 'You sound like him.' Jeremiah gestured over his thumb to the Space Marine who scowled slightly at the continued lack of respect the little bastard was demonstrating. 'He's always on about duty and respect and all that sort of stuff. Me...' Here, Jeremiah broke off and tapped himself proudly on the chest. 'I just like being here. I like guiding the ship through the warp.' He leaned forward and whispered conspiratorially. He didn't particularly lower his voice and Correlan heard every word he said. He kept his face stoic and unemotional, however. 'I like being *needed*.'

And that is why we need you too. We need you to work with us, Jeremiah.

There was something soothing and almost gentle in Volker's mechanical tone and the Navigator chewed on his lip thoughtfully. Then he looked down at his stubby, dirty fingers with the chewed nails.

'It's all I have,' he said and the honesty of his tone was disarming. 'Wasn't good for nothing 'til they brought me here. Don't want to give it up, you see?'

Jeremiah... you would not be surrendering your position. We would work alongside you. We are capable of doing many things and our senses can reach far. But for all this, Jeremiah, we lack what you possess. Our senses cannot penetrate or understand the shifting tides of the empyrean. We cannot proceed without you. We need you, too.

Jeremiah looked up and peered at the shape ensconced in the tube. His head tipped on one side. 'You're just saying that.'

No, we speak nothing but the truth. Your skill and expertise are required. The Dread Argent *knows you and so, by extension, we know you. We ask that you extend to us your trust.*

The silence that grew between the two of them was lengthy and Correlan found himself holding his breath. Kindness and patience, it seemed *had* been the best approach because the Navigator slowly nodded his head. Jeremiah's watery eyes turned to Correlan and the Techmarine was half-amused at the ferocity implicit in the glance shot in his direction.

Jeremiah. Volker spoke again and there was something almost urgent in the way he spoke. *The ship and I have formed a tentative bond, but I cannot complete the process. Not alone.*

'Are you scared, Volker?' Jeremiah put a hand to the tube again.

More than you can even begin to comprehend. I am scared, yes. But I am honoured to do this thing for the Silver Skulls. Please, Jeremiah. Help me to do this thing. Don't let the Dread Argent *consume me completely. We… I… do not want that to happen.*

The Navigator considered Volker carefully and seemed to weigh things up in his mind.

'I told the Apothecary that they were all mad doing this thing. I don't think that now. No, not mad at all.' His watery eyes grew as hard as diamonds. 'Cruel. Selfish. But not mad. Not so much.' He thought for a little while longer, then turned to Correlan.

'All right,' he said. 'But because Volker asked. Not you.'

Correlan didn't bother to hide a sudden amused smile. Perhaps it was relief that this exchange had gone so swiftly and easily. Certainly it had not been as lengthy and protracted as he had estimated. Perhaps it was a deep-seated spark of humour at the feisty little Navigator's continued defiance. Whatever it was, it mattered little. Jeremiah had agreed to cooperate and that was all he personally cared about.

The Navigator's words of insult against the Chapter were quietly noted and stored away for future reference. Jeremiah was given a certain amount of leeway now due to his required services. He took that leash and ran as far as it would allow him. Eventually one of the Silver Skulls would pull it taut and rein his attitude in. Of that, Correlan had no doubt.

He inclined his head. 'Of course, Jeremiah.'

'DIRECT INSERTION IS not an option.' Daviks tapped the plans laid out on the table and looked around the room. 'The enemy has tight control of the defences within the refinery and fine as our battle-brothers may be, they would be cut apart long before they were able to fully deploy.'

'Your recommendation, Daviks?'

The Siege Captain frowned and scratched his nose in thought. He considered the plans on the table before him. 'If we deploy all our units to this shuttle terminal in the east, we will be visible for quite some distance.' He drew a trajectory across the plans with another finger and tapped it down firmly. 'The refinery's position, nestled as it is in the mountains is an obstacle, but none of the difficulties here are insurmountable. The highway from the terminal to the refinery is well maintained and can take our ground support. Brothers Pallaton and Apenimon are awakened and will be fully prepared.'

'The venerable brothers will deploy with Fourth Company,' Arrun nodded. The Dreadnoughts would undoubtedly prove to be one of the key components in the success or otherwise of the Silver Skulls counterstrike. 'They will more than make up for the shortfall in numbers we have in infantry.' Daviks raised one eyebrow. Arrun had not elaborated on the company's losses incurred during the ship battles and it was not in his nature to press a point. If the information was felt at any time to be salient or relevant, then it would emerge.

Daviks returned to the matter at hand, straightening his back and standing up. 'We have enough heavy weaponry in our arsenal to burn the facility beneath us to nothing more than a pile of ashes if we so desire. But the last thing we want to do is level the objective. We can provide you with heavy covering support for as long as it takes. We must place our missiles well, though. Sending such powerful fire into a promethium refinery... well, I don't believe I need to elaborate.'

'Aye.' Arrun nodded and studied the plans thoughtfully. Built into a natural bowl in the mountains, the refinery was remarkably defensible. Apart from the road that came from the shuttle terminal, there was no other obvious direct way into the refinery apart from above. All the treated promethium that was destined for other parts of the Imperium had always been shipped down the road to the terminal. Arrun tapped this structure now.

'What of this?' he said. 'Should we blockade the road? You could land the heavy artillery at the terminal and prevent any sort of escape strategy that they might have put into place.'

'Absolutely.' Daviks nodded. 'From that distance, none of those vehicles will be able to lend any sort of support to you at the refinery, but if you can draw the Red Corsairs out of the mountain's cradle, then we can deal with them very quickly.' Again, he drew lines with his finger across the chart. 'Undoubtedly we will find resistance there. The Red Corsairs must have landed at that location to begin with. But if we hold that highway, there will be no exit for them.'

He rubbed at his jaw. 'It concerns me a little. It makes me wonder whether they have a second escape route planned out. But with the information I have managed to obtain, I cannot see how or where.'

Arrun studied the plans carefully. 'I will deploy my assault squads from the air, one to the north, the other to the south. They can be dropped in deep cover within the mountains and they can work their way to the refinery on foot. Once they are in position, their objective will be to disarm the guns and aerial defences. That will allow us to send the gunships in with a lesser degree of danger.'

'A sound idea.' Daviks nodded sagely. 'Once the turrets are stilled, the retaking of the refinery will become little more than a matter of time. It was a rash, foolish notion on the part of Blackheart to think this was in any way a plan at which he could succeed.' Daviks shook his head slowly. 'The people of Gildar Secundus have become lax in their defences. Perhaps they simply became too comfortable with their own perceived safety.'

'Idleness breeds heresy, brother. They have undeniably paid for their complacency in this matter.'

'Perhaps,' Daviks sniffed his disdain. 'It will not be a mistake they make again. Let us hope that this unfortunate incident is dealt with swiftly and effectively and that their replacements are more vigilant in their defence of such important Imperial assets.'

'I do not doubt that they are already regretting their laxity, Daviks. That is a discussion for later, however.' Arrun's brow drew together in a frown. 'Let us dispense with the traitors first, then we can proceed with the investigations as to what it was that went so wrong. I only regret that my duties as Master of the Fleet will keep me aboard the *Dread Argent* to ensure the cowards don't try to send in any further reinforcements.' He closed his hands into fists and growled softly. 'At times, much as I appreciate the honour of my position within the Chapter...'

'Hungry for a fight, brother?' Daviks interjected, his craggy face twisting into an expression that could almost pass as a smile.

'Against the Red Corsairs?' Arrun fixed Daviks with a cool gaze. 'Against the Tyrant of Badab? Are you not hungry for the same?'

'Starving, brother-captain.' For the first time since they had come aboard the *Quicksilver*, Daviks grinned wickedly.

'WAKE UP, SERGEANT.'

The voice was soft, almost whispering and Porteus clambered from the pit of unconsciousness with frantic desperation. Recall came and he groaned; a curious noise that expressed his pain and grief at the loss of his battle-brothers. He remembered a heavy weight falling onto him as Keyle had been cut down. He remembered holding his ground for as long as he was physically able; until a well-placed shot had penetrated his battered and damaged power armour and pierced his primary heart. His body had dropped him into healing stasis and now he was...

There was no indication as to where he was. He was no longer outside and he was lying on a cold, ferrocrete surface. He was restrained, his hands bound behind his back. A brief test of the restraints confirmed that whoever had trussed him thus was experienced in holding an Adeptus Astartes. Of course they were, he thought, bitterly. They were once loyal Space Marines themselves. They would have all the necessary methods to keep a warrior under their control.

He hawked up a mouthful of blood and spat it out. He raised swollen eyes that would not open fully to the owner of the voice that had invited him back to the land of the living.

The pitted, scarred face of the Corpsemaster smiled benevolently down at him and patted his cheek in a fatherly way. Porteus pulled his head back from the touch. 'You see? He wakes. An excellent constitution.'

Porteus knew who he was – or at least knew of him. The Corpsemaster was well-documented in the many records and visuals that all the Silver Skulls were required to study. His face was as recognisable as though he were staring at his own reflection.

The Red Corsairs Apothecary busied himself with putting away equipment and Porteus shifted position. Pain sang in every nerve ending and he attempted to mentally assess his condition. His power armour had been removed and he was dressed in nothing more than the black bodyglove that he wore beneath. A mental check of his own body drew his attention to the source of the pain. The bodyglove had been torn apart to reveal a raw, freshly sealed wound in his chest.

The Corpsemaster watched him and added a commentary. 'You were seriously injured,' he said, sounding almost delighted about the fact. 'Once the rest of your squad had been dealt with, I repaired the worst of the damage to your primary heart.' His tone was so cheerful and friendly that it disorientated the injured Silver Skulls warrior. 'Come now, sergeant. Do you have no words of thanks for me?'

'I have no words for traitors.' His own voice sounded strangely husky. The slow awareness of pain around his body suggested that he had probably taken a further shot to the throat. 'You would have done well to kill me when you had the chance. Because when I am free, I will visit that fate upon you.'

'I think not, sergeant.' The Corpsemaster reached down and patted his prisoner's cheek again. 'Once you stand before my Lord Blackheart, once you come to understand the lies of the Imperium, you will serve his cause. Just as many others before you have done.' The Corpsemaster held up a jar in which a single, bloodied pulpy mass could be seen. 'And if you don't, it matters little to me. I have what I want.'

Porteus stared at the jar. The progenoid gland. The most precious of all his Adeptus Astartes organs was in the hands of an enemy. The traitor must have removed it whilst he was dealing with the injury. Several wild thoughts ran through Porteus's mind. How long had he been here? What had happened to the two battle-brothers left guarding the array? The sergeant raised himself to his knees and lifted his head to stare at the Corpsemaster in furious defiance. His situation, had he but known it, mirrored that of the one Ryarus had faced aboard the *Wolf of Fenris*.

'I will never turn my back upon my brothers,' he said, meeting the Apothecary's amused gaze full on. 'I will never betray my Emperor and I will die before I swear allegiance to Lugft Huron.'

'Greater warriors than you have attempted to resist the truth,' retorted the Corpsemaster, moving to set the jar containing Porteus's precious gene-seed down. 'Why do you feel that you are different? All of them see the truth in the end. All of them come to understand the lies of your Corpse-God. You misunderstand our motives, Silver Skull.'

'I will never turn my back upon my brothers,' Porteus repeated. 'When they come for you...' His words had an electrifying effect on the Corpsemaster who whirled to face him. All the surface calm that the Apothecary had previously exuded fled to be replaced by the mask of a madman.

'Are you speaking of those same brothers who even now leave you to your fate at my hands? Where were they when you and your pathetic squad attempted to infiltrate and disrupt our plans? Where are they now? Nobody is coming to your aid, sergeant of the Silver Skulls. Your fate is sealed. You will either join us or you will die. There is no third option.'

'Then you may as well save your words, traitor.' Porteus lifted his bloodied face and met the Corpsemaster's fevered gaze. The calm indifference that was now apparent in the Apothecary's expression infuriated and unsettled him. The Corpsemaster's moods swung as erratically as anything he had ever experienced. The sergeant's hands, clasped firmly behind his back by the strong restraints, clenched and unclenched, as did his jaw. 'You talk too much. You should kill me now.'

'I think not. You have much value to us at the moment and I would certainly not want to risk my lord's ire by dispensing with you prematurely.' The tone was almost reproachful, even amused.

'My brothers will be here soon,' said Porteus with easy confidence. He nodded at the jar containing his gene-seed, the organ that the Silver Skulls, like all the Adeptus Astartes, venerated above all others. They called it the Quintessence Sacred for a reason. It was the quintessential element of what and who they were. It was the genetic legacy of many generations, whose memories and knowledge lingered in some small way in the DNA threads that wove through the bodies of those gifted.

Porteus had heard many tales of battle-brothers who, on the verge of death, touched and tasted the memories of their forebears. In quiet moments of meditation, he had sometimes felt the shape of something... of *someone*, but he had never been able to fully grasp it. '*The shape of glories past*', Vashiro had called it once, that feeling.

'Ah, yes. Your brothers. The noble Adeptus Astartes of the

Silver Skulls Chapter.' The Corpsemaster nodded sagely and ticked off his words on his fingers as he spoke. 'Fierce warriors. Noble and relentless, fearsome in battle. Deploy only on the word of their psyker brethren. Unusual in that regard. And yet what did your psychic brothers have to say about Gildar Secundus?' The Corpsemaster spread his hands in query. 'What prevented them from seeing us here?'

Porteus said nothing. The question had crossed his mind many times since Simeon's death. Surely the Prognosticator would not have travelled to his own demise so willingly? He remembered whispers, forbidden words passed from battle-brother to battle-brother. Words that were bordering on blasphemy. Words that he should never have listened to. Words directed at the Prognosticatum and the power they wielded over the Chapter.

Doubts. Suspicions. Fallacies.

'But where are your brothers now, sergeant?' The Corpsemaster looked around as though he expected an entire company of Silver Skulls to be there. 'Why have they not come to save you?'

The question was rhetorical and did not allow time for a response. The foul traitor continued. With every word he spoke, Porteus's hatred became something more tangible. His fury and rage was all he had, now. He took it and shaped it. In the event he freed himself, he would use that weapon, formed in the heat of his fury and he would tear out the Corpsemaster's hearts.

'Ask yourself the question "why", sergeant,' the Apothecary said, picking up the jar containing Porteus's precious gene-seed and twisting it as he studied it. 'Ask yourself why it is that your Prognosticators are continually making poor choices and giving advice that leads to your Chapter's slow, systematic destruction. They claim to interpret the Emperor's will...'

He set down the jar again. 'Had you considered that the Emperor has no will to interpret? Because the truth is... the Corpse-God to whom you are all so enslaved does not care for you.' A smile, cruel and self-assured twisted his lips. 'The Silver Skulls are a dying breed, sergeant. Much as the Astral Claws were before my Lord Blackheart realised the Imperial truth was nothing more than a lie.' The Apothecary's pockmarked face twisted in savage delight. 'You and your Chapter are dying, sergeant. Actually and metaphorically.'

'The Silver Skulls will prevail.'

The adage was old, words that had become the Chapter's unofficial motto of sorts. Porteus had always believed in it with all his heart, but now the doubts planted against the veracity of the Prognosticators took hold. In a low voice, he began to recite the Litany of Hate, certain that doing so would strengthen his resolve.

'Will they, sergeant? Or has the time come at last for you to accept defeat graciously?' The hideous, mutilated face moved so close that Porteus could feel the other's rancid breath on his skin. His flesh crawled involuntarily. 'Perhaps the time has come for you and your brethren to finally throw off the shackles of the Imperium and become all that you know you can be.'

'The Silver Skulls will...'

'Prevail. Yes, yes, so you said. And maybe they will. But you, sergeant?' The Corpsemaster shook his head and waved his hand dismissively. 'Very soon you will have to make a choice. It will be up to you whether you personally prevail or not. Think about that for a while. I have work to do.'

With those words, the Corpsemaster strode out of the room, shutting the door firmly behind him. Porteus stared after him. It was only a door. It was made of wood, nothing more. He could break through it as though it were paper. If he were able to free himself of his restraints, he could tear this place apart. Just the opportunity to lay his hands on the Apothecary...

For the first time in his life, Porteus was genuinely plagued by the twin demons of doubt and uncertainty that had long lingered in the back of his mind. The Corpsemaster's words had fed them and although his words of defiance had been spoken truly, there was now the tiniest nugget of irresolution.

Become all that you know you can be. The Corpsemaster's final words haunted him and left alone, all that Porteus could do was brood on them. He had spoken truths that Porteus knew he had denied for many years. The Silver Skulls numbers were rapidly depleting. More and more experienced battle-brothers were lost with only young men to take their place. Once, the Silver Skulls had been a powerful presence in this sector. Once, the Silver Skulls had partaken in a raid on Commorragh.

Now...

Porteus yearned suddenly for the comforting blackness of sus-an sleep. His world was on its head, his fate in question. But he would never willingly betray the men he called brother. Of that he was certain.

THIRTEEN
BAIT

'THIS IS CURIS of Squad Carnelian to the *Dread Argent*.'

The broken words came virtually unheard across the strike cruiser's busy vox-net and went unnoticed for several minutes. In amidst the constant barrage of voices that had flooded the system since the comms tower had ceased sending the jamming signal, Brother Curis's voice was lost somewhere in the incoherent babble. It was only after he had announced his presence on several more occasions that it was isolated by a servitor who was filtering through the entire network.

'Brother Curis of Squad Carnelian is attempting communication,' the slave said in a dull monotone. 'I have acknowledged his signal.'

'Isolate the transmission,' said Arrun moving to stand directly behind the servitor's terminal. 'Get me a stable connection to him. I must know what is going on down there.'

'Compliance.'

The servitor turned dials to adjust the modulation and frequency of the weak transmission that was being broadcast from the surface of Gildar Secundus. Eventually, Curis's voice was modulated and adjusted enough so that he could be heard clearly. It was still broken and distorted, but the words could be filtered out enough to get the gist of what he was saying.

'Come in, *Dread Argent*. I repeat. This is Brother Curis of Squad Carnelian.'

'We have you, brother. We hear you. Speak.'

'Captain Arrun?' There was relief immeasurable in the warrior's voice. 'Thank the Emperor that we succeeded in damaging their communications blockade.'

'Report, brother.' Arrun could not keep the irritation out of his tone. There was no time to linger on any unnecessary pleasantries. He needed as accurate an appraisal of the situation as he could get. The very fact that Curis, one of the more junior members of Porteus's squad, was the one who was making contact at all told a very definite story. The young warrior's next words confirmed those suspicions. Every syllable thudded leadenly into place.

'Squad Carnelian has fallen, captain. To the best of my knowledge, I am all that remains.'

'How is that so? How is it that you have survived when the rest of your squad did not?' There was the merest hint of accusation in Arrun's tone, although he knew that Curis was as stalwart and stoic as any of the other Silver Skulls in his squad. If the other Silver Skulls warrior picked up any sort of implication in the words, he did not let it translate across the vox. Between crackles of static and broken sentences, he continued his report.

'Brother Emetrius and myself were charged with holding the equipment at the top of the communications tower. Sergeant Porteus and the remainder of the squad were holding the entrance. When Porteus fell...' There was a pause in Curis's recital and Arrun sensed the rage implicit in the other's voice. 'Emetrius and I made the conscious decision to cause as much of a distraction as we possibly could. Amazing what a few strategically planted explosives will do to several ranks of cogitators and hololiths. It has not done the signal any good, but I spent some time trying to patch into a different frequency. I think that the raiders have a backup transmitter somewhere.'

Curis paused for barely a heartbeat. 'Regrettably, I don't believe there any survivors from the Red Corsairs who tried to stop us we could ask to confirm it.'

A flicker of a smile ghosted across Arrun's face. The gallows humour of the moment was surprisingly welcome.

'We did what we could and we made a strategic withdrawal. We needed to bring word to you and in Sergeant Porteus's absence, we made that decision. I succeeded in getting clear. Emetrius did not. He was taken down by a traitor whilst we made our retreat. His sacrifice ensured I am here now, giving you this report and you can rest assured that he successfully dispensed of several more of the enemy before he was taken. He walks with the ancestors now.' Another one of those brief pauses and the barest hint of uncertainty. 'I trust my captain does not feel that I have acted in any way improperly?'

'No, Curis, I do not. You did what you could, brother,' said Arrun, although the embers of his annoyance were fanned once again. Squad Carnelian had been one of the best tactical squads in the company and they were now gone. Another fine unit of his company's warriors destroyed as a direct result of the machinations of Huron Blackheart. Keeping his temper under control the best he could under the circumstances, Arrun focused on the situation at hand.

'What is your exact location, Curis?'

'I retreated south-west. Back into the mountains,' replied the other. 'I have not activated my locator beacon in case the Red Corsairs can track it. The numbers of Traitor Marines and cultists alike seems to be growing. There are more arriving almost constantly now. A steady stream of them. They are congregating in the compound. Massing their forces, I think.'

'Your plan?'

'To infiltrate to the best of my ability and learn whatever I can about their intentions and their firepower.' Despite the gravity of the situation, another smile twitched on Arrun's face. Curis was showing great initiative and acting very much in his sergeant's style; which as far as the captain was concerned was more than acceptable.

'I will be deploying support within the hour, Curis. Gather whatever intelligence you can, regardless of how little or seemingly unimportant it may be and report back. Do not engage with the enemy if you are discovered. In this instance, death at their hands is not a preferable option. Do whatever it takes to keep yourself out of their sight.' He paused. 'Consider that an order.'

'Yes, Captain Arrun.' A flutter of hesitation. 'I think you should also know... the Corpsemaster is here. I have heard them talking about him and from what I have overheard, he is stationed within the refinery.'

A dark, angry scowl creased Arrun's face and he balled his hand into a fist, bringing it down on the damaged console hard enough to startle the Chapter serfs who were busy clearing up the broken table and other wreckage brought about by the fight between the two psykers. To a man, they backed away from the enraged Space Marine.

'Let me reiterate my previous order,' Arrun snarled. 'Much as it pains me to say it, if you see him, do not engage. Much as I would like for you to terminate his evil, I can't afford to lose this link with you. I doubt that you will get close yourself. Rest assured, brother, that we will make eliminating their precious Apothecary one of our primary objectives once we deploy. Report back to me when you have news.'

'Yes, captain.' The link was severed and Curis was once again on his own down on the planet's surface.

Arrun took a deep, calming breath.

'I am going down to see Volker,' he said in a quiet, dangerous tone. 'I want all arms and ammunition to be distributed and the entire company ready to deploy in ten minutes.' He lifted his eyes and met those of Matteus. 'Make it happen, brother-sergeant.' The trust he was placing in Matteus was not random or completely unfounded; the young sergeant was proving himself to be smart, savvy and entirely competent. 'Speak with those Prognosticators who remain.

Ensure that the omens are good and that the auguries cast a favourable outcome. Once they have given their blessing and assent to our counter-attack, report back to me and not a moment before.'

'Yes, captain.' Matteus bowed his head and made the sign of the aquila across his chest. He spun abruptly on his heel and left the bridge with alacrity, practically radiating determination. Arrun gave a few remaining orders to the skeleton remains of his deck crew and followed Matteus from the bridge. His destination, however, was very different.

+++ INCREASE POWER to port-side rear thrusters by seven per cent. Maintaining position. Entering geostationary orbit in five minutes. +++

'Volker?'

+++ Engines performing at eighty-two per cent of optimal power. Rerouting conduits from non-essential systems. Praise be to the Omnissiah. +++

'The Omnissiah be praised.' The resident priests intoned the words as soon as Volker spoke them. Arrun murmured his own prayers, although he had no idea if he was saying the right things. He slowly moved up to the figure in the tube and laid a hand on its surface. Far from being cool, there was a nascent warmth beneath his touch. He turned his head to the Techmarine who was still monitoring a number of readouts.

'Should it feel this warm?'

'The warmth you feel is the embrace of the Omnissiah.' Arrun glanced at the tech-priest. He had not addressed him, but he felt that the comment deserved a response.

'Then Volker is blessed indeed. You have outperformed yourself. He is not the only one so favoured.' The tech-priest inclined his head, pleased with Arrun's choice of words. The captain smiled thinly and looked at Correlan, directing the same question to him.

'Aye, captain. The warmth you feel is also in part due to a chemical reaction caused by the fluid we are using to maintain the biological remains of Volker. It will not harm him, I promise you.'

'The *remains*?' The word was cold and callous, spoken in the same factual way that the Techmarine approached everything. Correlan set down his data-slate and looked up at Arrun properly.

'Yes, sir. By the minute, there is less and less remaining of Volker; at least in his original guise. His consciousness has connected with that of the ship's far more swiftly than I anticipated. Already he has begun to gain mastery of the flight controls. The project has gone far beyond successful. You should be proud.'

'I wish to speak with Volker, though.'

+++ Altitude adjustment in progress. +++

Throughout his entire exchange with Correlan, the metallic grind that had become Volker's voice had been giving a gentle, running commentary on what actions he was performing. Correlan gestured to him.

'At the moment, he is not making all of those decisions himself. This is still very much an assimilation phase. He is working on information transmitted through the neural implant that connects directly to the helm.'

'And if I wish to speak to him?'

We will be with you presently, captain. +++ Engines performing at eighty-seven per cent of optimal power. Maintaining surplus energy reroute. +++

The transition from a conversational tone to one of mechanical monotony not dissimilar to that of the servitors was seamless. Correlan considered the youth for a moment or two, then continued his conversation with the captain.

'In time, he will be able to make such basic decisions by himself. Decisions as to appropriate moments to apply thrusters, or to adjust altitude without any intervention from the helm. Eventually, the helmsman will be able to hand over full control of the ship to him. In situations that demand fast reactions.'

'During battle, you mean? Or in stormy sectors?'

'Yes. Exactly as per your original designs, sir.' Correlan nodded and took up the data-slate again. 'I have instructed the servitors to run a battery of tests whilst I am on the planet's surface. At this point however, I am pleased to report that everything is as it should be.'

Arrun nodded. 'Your presence on the surface will be welcomed, brother. We have received word from Squad Carnelian. They are all lost to us, bar brother Curis. We fight in their name and that of those we lost on the *Wolf of Fenris*. I want the engagement to be swift and merciless. There is only one true objective and only one conclusion to this battle. The death of the traitors.'

Correlan rumbled his acknowledgement and obvious approval of the strategy. Arrun continued. 'Your skills will be invaluable when we retake the refinery. We will need a full status breakdown of damage so that we can ensure repairs are undertaken where required and also a stock take of equipment. The Red Corsairs are likely wanting either to steal or hold the refinery to ransom. The latter we can deal with quickly through concentrated application of the Emperor's vengeance.'

'It will be my pleasure to deal with the last thing on that list, sir,' said Correlan with a sudden, infectious grin, 'and it will be my honoured duty to carry out the others.' Arrun nodded, almost absently, and turned back to Volker. Disconcertingly, the youth's eyes were fixed directly on his.

You wish to speak with us, captain? We must ask you to make all haste. We must concentrate on restoring full power and shields are operating at a fraction of their capability. It necessitates our prompt attention and we–

'I will not take much of your time, Volker,' interrupted the captain. 'I wish only to speak with you before you become too...' He hesitated, not wishing to cause offence. A brief smile found its way onto Volker's lips.

We understand. Our view is much altered, Captain Arrun. We see... beyond human boundaries now.

'Be that as it may, Volker, there is nonetheless something which I must say to you before I do not get another chance.' Arrun studied the boy within the tube for a moment or two. 'Your actions, your sacrifice and your bravery... Everything you have undergone to reach this point is worthy of any battle-brother of the Silver Skulls Chapter. You may have been denied the right to ascend to the ranks of the Adeptus Astartes, but I make you this promise. Your name will be passed back to Vashiro to be entered in the Book of Remembrance. As soon as this matter is settled, the astropaths have been instructed to send a message home to Varsavia. You will be entered into the Book and be remembered for all time as a Chapter hero, Volker Straub.'

For a fleeting moment, the expressionless face behind the tube lit up in pure, unadulterated joy. The remaining vestige of Volker's humanity had heard and understood Arrun's words and he knew sheer, overwhelming delight at the accolade. The moment was swift and passed quickly as his new consciousness filed the new piece of data away for future reference.

We exist only to serve, Captain Arrun. +++ System Kappa Delta four-three-zero rerouted. Increase rear port thrust. Blessings of the Emperor upon... +++

The inhuman, mechanical narration resumed and the connection with Volker was severed.

Arrun remained with his hand against the tube for several more moments and then moved away. They had gained a phenomenal asset through this venture, but the cost, visualised as it was within the cocoon of embryonic fluid, had been high.

'Those moments will become fewer and far between,' observed Correlan who had remained silent throughout the exchange. 'In time, Volker will cease to be... well, Volker.'

'He will always be so to me,' murmured Arrun. 'May the Emperor guide your hand in the battle below, Correlan. On your return, we will discuss the future of the fleet – and perhaps more pertinent to you personally – your role within it.' It was as close to words of thanks that the captain was ever likely to utter to the Techmarine and Correlan nodded soberly.

'His light willing, it will be so.'

Arrun paused as though he would add something else and

then strode from the chamber, lost in contemplation that was at one and the same time triumphant and thoughtful.

'Is ALL IN readiness?'

'Yes, my Lord Apothecary.'

'Good.' The Corpsemaster surveyed the road approaching the refinery where many vast figures clad in the various assorted colours of the Red Corsairs were approaching. 'These reaches of space may once again belong to the Imperium, but they will find us harder to remove on the surface. Our ground troops are hungry for battle and the refinery's guns are trained on the skies above us.'

He smiled. It was not a pleasant or even friendly expression but was filled with a hatred that had burned for many long years now. A hatred directed at all the loyal servants of the Imperium.

'This day,' he said, more to himself than the warrior who stood with him. 'This day we will bring about the beginning of the end for the Silver Skulls. Those who do not die here will, in time, become ours.' Easy assurance and confidence dripped from every word. His companion nodded agreement, more than convinced by the Corpsemaster's vision. The Apothecary's smile broadened and his spindly finger pointed.

'See there,' he said, his gaze locked on one of the approaching figures. 'Our Lord Blackheart comes.'

'ALL SQUADS ARE in position,' reported Matteus as Arrun approached. 'I have spoken to our company's remaining Prognosticators and additionally have communicated with Prognosticator Inteus. It would seem that the Emperor's will in this matter is perfectly clear.' He turned his helmet over in his hands and gave a fierce, predatory grin. 'We are ready to deploy as you ordered.'

'Excellent,' replied Arrun. He moved up to consider the squad sergeants who were gathered before him. 'I grant overall command of the tactical squads to you, Matteus. Daviks is overseeing the operation. He will initially be stationed at the shuttle terminal. His company will provide support to your attacks and the Ninth Company Dreadnoughts will walk with you.' The others nodded their unspoken approval at the choice of command structure and none of them could keep the delight from their faces at the news the two ancients would march into battle alongside them. It was the brightest news they had received on a day ridden with so much tragedy.

Arrun turned his attentions back to the assembly. As ever, his position as captain meant that he was expected to speak encouraging words to inspire his company to greater feats. For a few moments, the words simply would not come. He felt a terrible, sinking void in the pit of his stomach. It was what he had always presumed to be a bad feeling. Without Brand to reassure him, he could not afford to linger on it. Inteus and the other Prognosticators were clearly confident. He had to put his trust in them. It was the Silver Skulls way.

'Brothers, hear this. It is the will of the Prognosticators that we proceed with this course of action,' he said, confirming that the auguries had spoken in favour of a battle. These words themselves had an electrifying effect on the assembled warriors. Arrun looked from eager face to eager face and tried his hardest not to feel a modicum of concern at the youth of his company.

'Your primary objectives are clear,' he said. 'Captain Daviks and his Devastators will breach the refinery defences. You will then sweep and clear the facility of traitors. First priority is to re-establish security of the Primus-Phi refinery and bring it back under the yoke of the Imperium. Secondary objectives are the elimination of any residual Red Corsair forces, particularly their Chief Apothecary, also going by the name of the Corpsemaster. As a united, strong Chapter the Silver Skulls will purge the Gildar system of this taint. Now go to your drop-pods and your gunships. Go forth in the name of Argentius. Execute the Emperor's will to the greatest extent of your abilities. Trust to your battle-brothers and we will return victorious to Varsavia, our bellies filled with fire and our hearts full of stories of our accomplishments.'

With a resounding cheer, the Silver Skulls warriors dispersed. Matteus was the last to leave, making the sign of the aquila across his chest before he headed to the drop-pod that would soon carry him and the remnants of his squad to the mountainous surface of Gildar Secundus.

'And may the Emperor guide your hand well, my brothers,' Arrun murmured after them.

THE ARRIVAL OF Huron Blackheart had seen a marked change in the behaviour of the Red Corsairs. Until the Tyrant of Badab had strutted through the massive front gates of the refinery with the self-assurance and arrogance that dictated everything he did, their enthusiasm had been mediocre at best. Two of his Terminator elite bodyguards attended him and their massive presence was almost as intimidating as the Tyrant's own.

His Corsairs were never idle, of course; they were every bit as disciplined a fighting force as the Imperium's best. The quiet but ever-present menace of the Corpsemaster ensured compliance amongst the slaves and even saw a certain curtailment of the aggressive in-fighting that so marked the Red Corsairs at times.

Now, though, the entire refinery was a veritable hive of activity. Every last one of the traitors was going about his business with eager energy, attempting to catch their master's attention whilst being especially careful not to incur his wrath. Word of Taemar's death had spread swiftly. The master would eventually have to choose a new champion which meant that his attentions would be wandering to his men.

His anger had been terrible to behold. The near-destruction of his fleet had not been any feature of his original plan and the fact that the Silver Skulls had pulled their forces together in such an organised and devastating way had left him not best pleased. Within fifteen minutes of his arrival at the refinery, he had executed two of his own slaves in what could only be described as a fit of pique. He had raged and fumed his way through the refinery, criticising everything and everyone he passed until he had reached the Corpsemaster. Then, and only then, his anger and rage had finally begun to ebb slightly.

'How many?' was all he had asked. 'How many have you taken so far?'

'Just the one still alive,' the Corpsemaster replied mildly. 'A squad sergeant.'

'I want those warriors,' Blackheart said, his hand clenched tightly into a fist. His voice, grating and harsh through the metallic jaw and teeth, was inhuman and every word delivered with mechanical precision. 'The Silver Skulls must be brought into the fold of our cause. I want their strength. I want their foresight and I want Daerys Arrun's ship.' His augmetic eye whirred and glinted in the flickering half-light of the Corpsemaster's temporary apothecarion. His massive claw curled in on itself in a mechanical mockery of his own hand as it clenched. The Corpsemaster had witnessed that claw tear through Space Marines as though their power armour were paper. He had seen Blackheart decapitate and dismember his way through battle after battle.

The Corpsemaster's eyes caught the faintest flicker of movement and he turned his head sharply. The being continued to defy his attempts to see it but even the Corpsemaster was aware of its presence. It carried with it the musty stink of decay. There was the vaguest hint of wings, but there was no noise.

Death comes on silent wings.

A strange creature. It chose to be seen when it desired and it did not always maintain the same form. As far as the Corpsemaster had ever been able to tell, the farther from the Maelstrom Blackheart travelled, the more ephemeral the thing's corporeal form became.

Denied in his attempts to see the entity, the Corpsemaster turned his head back towards his lord and master. His fascination with the Silver Skulls was undeniably bordering on the obsessive. His interest in their Prognosticators was understandable, of course. For all his ferocity and might, Huron Blackheart was a deeply superstitious warrior, who tried to find omens and portents in many things. His inability to read or understand such signs was another personal failing that fed his mighty rage. He would never have admitted as such, but the Corpsemaster knew him well. His tone became soothing.

'They will come, my lord. There is no doubt about that. This refinery is far too important to their foolish Imperium for them to simply leave it in our hands. When they come, when they take the irresistible bait that we have laid before them, we will kill those we must and we will take those we can.'

Blackheart considered him for a few moments, then gestured over his shoulder. 'Walk with me, Garreon.'

'As my lord commands.' The Apothecary bowed deeply and respectfully. It was good to see Blackheart so vigorous and full of vitality. It was a stark contrast to the days he lingered in a state hovering somewhere between life and death, barricading himself against the endless pain that came with his condition. This lucid time would not last. It never did.

The two Red Corsairs cut a curious tableau as they walked out of the refinery into the compound. They were almost complete physical opposites, despite the obvious similarities caused by their shared heritage. The massively armoured bulk of Huron Blackheart made the Corpsemaster seem almost frail. Both warriors went bare headed and the grizzled mane that crowned the Apothecary's head was in stark contrast to Blackheart's half-shaven, half-metallic head.

The Lord of the Red Corsairs armour was remarkably well-tended; at least, as well as it could be given the number of ceramite cracks and weapon damage it had sustained over the years. It was frequently maintained, although with his foul moods Huron got through more artificers than most. A number of tokens and fetishes hung from his waist; at least three human skulls and even a wizened human hand that had been perfectly preserved. Also at his waist, he wore a long vial, crafted from thick glass and encased within a fretwork of ornate metal. Nobody knew what was in that vial. Nobody had ever asked.

His very aura was menacing and as they walked, those

who were not Space Marines moved swiftly to put themselves out of his way and out of his thoughts.

The velvet darkness of the Gildar Secundus night was beginning to bleed through to the grey of pre-dawn. A pinkish tinge on the far horizon hinted at the arrival of the morning, but the scent of rain remained in the air. Inhaling deeply, Huron Blackheart's augmetic eye whirred and clicked a few times. In-built sensors tracked the ionic particles in the air. An ability to predict meteorological conditions was often a massive advantage on any battlefield.

'There's another storm in the air,' he observed.

'This planet has more than its fair share of them, it seems,' acknowledged the Apothecary. 'Tiresome weather patterns and a poor ecology. I am glad that your plan is not to remain here longer than is absolutely necessary. I grow bored of the Gildar system.'

'You grow bored of the system, old friend? Or is it simply that your impatience is getting the better of you? At least one of the Silver Skulls waits your undivided attention on the *Wolf of Fenris*. I am sure that you can hold your instruments steady for a few more hours.'

'You know me too well,' lamented the Corpsemaster. 'Still, I admit that it is an intriguing prospect. I confess I am looking forward to seeing what it takes to break one such as they.'

'You are filled with more cunning than any other I have ever known, Garreon. I am sure that your investigations will prove most fruitful. And the more we learn about the Silver Skulls, the better our chances of embracing them within our fold become.'

'They are unlikely to appreciate the gesture, my lord.' The Apothecary's pinched, puckered face stared out across the jagged peaks. 'They will not see it for the glorious opportunity that it is. I fear that their hearts are too set. Too engaged with the outmoded concept of nobility. Their minds are far too pliant to the will of the Corpse-God. But there is a weakness, oh yes.'

He turned his head from the horizon and looked up at his commander. 'There is doubt in their hearts as to the veracity of the Prognosticators. If we can feed that doubt, if we can turn it from something innocuous and uncertain into something tangible, we may be able to divide them from within.'

'An interesting prospect, Garreon.' Blackheart drummed the claws of his artificial hand against the thigh plate of his armour, then raised the index finger of his other hand to the skies.

'See there,' he said, and there was immense satisfaction in his tone. 'They take the bait, my old friend.'

Streaks of light were illuminating the pre-dawn sky as the drop-pods and gunships of the Silver Skulls Chapter burned into the lower atmosphere. A cruel, twisted smile played across the Tyrant's face. 'As I planned,' he repeated in a satisfied voice. 'They come.'

'CONFIRMATION, CAPTAIN ARRUN. Fourth Company deployment has commenced. All units are now en route to planet's surface.'

The monotone of the servitor reverberated around the walls of Arrun's arming chamber. The captain nodded absently, before voicing acknowledgement of the fact. He had already paid a brief visit to the chapel where he had knelt before the statue of the God-Emperor, attempting to bring a little calm to the turbulent waters of his soul. It was a lamentable fact, whether he liked it or not, that his lofty position as Master of the Fleet meant his responsibilities lay here, aboard the *Dread Argent* rather than facing the hated enemy on the ground. He had murmured soft words of prayer and quiet apologies to the distant God-Emperor of Mankind for even considering abandoning his duties.

He was sure that the God-Emperor would understand his moment of laxity, but he chastised himself softly nonetheless. It was every Space Marine's right to be filled with the yearning desire to prosecute the Emperor's will; but he had duties to his Chapter as well.

Of course, he now had additional duties and responsibilities to the young man forever sealed in a transparent coffin far from this place of repose in the engineering decks. It had been through his machinations and manipulation that Volker and the *Dread Argent* had become one. It would be his guidance that saw the project through to full completion.

He found pride in that thought and his misgivings settled a little. His skills and talents would undoubtedly be far better served here. Should the need arise, his own deployment could be engineered without any trouble. As long as the portents agreed, of course.

Considering this took his thoughts down a new branch. Brand's recovery was progressing well and whilst the highest-ranking Prognosticator would not be taking the field with the company, his underlings were more than competent to fill the void left by his absence. He remained critical but stable and was accessible for advice and guidance. Arrun felt some small relief in that knowledge. The two of them had fought side by side for so many decades that to think of a permanent void where his Prognosticator had once stood chilled him to the marrow. It would happen one day, but he was relieved that it was not *this* day.

His duties in the chapel complete, Arrun had retired to his personal arming chamber where he had sat in deep contemplation, seeking to quench the thirst for battle that flowed through his blood. Things were constantly shifting around him and it was unsettling. He was no psyker and had never laid claim to any psychic ability, but over the course of the past few months, even *he* had sensed the winds of change blowing through the Chapter. Private conversations with his fellow captains and with Brand had accentuated the anxieties of the diminishing levels of experience and the rise of the impetuous. It was a shift in dynamic that did not sit well with the veteran captain.

Now, he felt a moment's guilt at the thoughts. 'Forgive me, distant Father,' he murmured quietly. 'I think poorly of my own brothers and such behaviour has no place in the mind of an Adeptus Astartes.' The Emperor had offered no word of reply, but it didn't matter. He felt sure that his words were listened to and that was good enough for him.

He closed his eyes and called to mind the soothing peace

of the chapel. Perhaps he should have lingered awhile. Its grandeur and familiarity had always offered a modicum of calm and he would often spend long periods of time in there, his eyes raking around the many and varied trophies of his company. The thought of those trophies now served to fuel his pride and obstinacy once again. Look at what his battle-brothers had achieved. Look at Volker. Look at everything the future held. All its opportunity. All of this glory. Thinking of this cast him back to a prior conversation with his advisor.

'The future,' Brand had said to him, barely days before the arrival of the Red Corsairs had accelerated the Resurgent Project, 'is a series of blank pages. These ambitious young warriors are waiting to fill them with their deeds and even as we watch, they act. It does us ill to dwell on uncertainty and regret. It is and always has been our duty to mould and guide them as best we can. We are moving towards a new episode in the history of the Silver Skulls, Daerys. Neither you nor I can prevent the passage of time. It is an inevitability, as certain as the tides of the Mare Argentium lap at the shores of Varsavia.'

They had been fine, eloquent words. Yet even now, they had done little to quell the doubts in the captain's heart. He almost reluctantly abandoned his meditations, rising to his feet and marching briskly from his arming chambers to take his rightful place on the bridge of his ship.

FOURTEEN
RED AND SILVER

A PALE LIGHT was creeping slowly above the horizon as the drop-pods carrying the warriors of the Silver Skulls Chapter screamed into sight. Watched by the Red Corsairs already deployed to defend the refinery, they were heralds of the battle to come. Both sides hungered for this fight. Both sides were ready.

Thunder rolled around the mountains, providing an ominous accompaniment to the proceedings. Added into the noise was the roar of the retro-thrusters on the drop-pods as they slowed to minimise impact. Together, the sounds were deafening.

As it hammered solidly into the ferrocrete of the landing port, the pod carrying Matteus and his squad stood proud; the steel-grey symbol of a Chapter's tenacity. It remained stable and unmoving for a moment or two, then charges detonated, blowing open the doors. Immediately, they folded out like the waking petals of a flower greeting the rosy fingers of the Gildar Secundus dawn.

Around them, other drop-pods were similarly reaching their destination. Hairline cracks spidered beneath his feet and ruptured the ground as more descended, landing with quite considerable force. Matteus, his mind and focus on the matter at hand, nonetheless allowed himself the pride and pleasure of gazing upwards. There was an unmistakable, simple thrill in watching the streaking comets still many kilometres above them, carrying the promise of more of his comrades in arms. The calm before the breaking of the storm was a moment that he never grew tired of and to see the deployment of his battle-brothers was an honour beyond measure.

Like all Adeptus Astartes in service to the Imperium, Matteus had nigh-on unshakeable faith in the Emperor and in the right to deliver His will and word to those who did not – or would not – heed it.

During the descent, he had received word from Captain Arrun that one of Porteus's squad was in the mountains and his eyes moved with inhuman celerity to the vox-rune on the retinal feed of his helmet. He blinked, setting a repeating signal sounding on a secure channel. Curis would no doubt be waiting for contact from his brethren and once he homed in on the transmission, then the lost warrior could rejoin the battle.

Matteus put a hand to his bolter and let his fingers close around the parchment that fluttered from the fresh purity seal. He silently gave thanks to its machine spirit, asking for its cooperation in the battle to come. Others around him acted in a similar vein, soothing their weapons and checking ammunition. The sergeant turned to the west. The vast, labyrinthine tangle of towers and pipework wreathing the refinery were clearly visible and on an almost direct route from their current position. The plans and strategies as decided by the two company captains had been communicated to all of the Silver Skulls taking the field and all objectives were clear.

More of the company's drop-pods had made landfall by now and almost the entirety of Fourth Company was accounted for. The two Dreadnoughts were still to arrive and Matteus felt again that stirring of pride at having two such honourable warriors under his command.

'Fourth Company,' he said across the vox, 'take your positions. Prepare yourselves.'

The command was almost redundant. The Silver Skulls were a finely honed war machine, well-oiled and compliant to the last warrior. They had, whether consciously or not, already arranged themselves in marching formation, ready to take the fight to the Red Corsairs.

AND THEY SHALL know no fear.

Porteus had never known fear during his service to the Silver Skulls. If he had known it as a child, it was a memory that was best forgotten. Fear was nothing more than a word. It was something used to give cohesive shape and form to things that were unknown. Know your enemy; face your worst nightmares and there was nothing to be afraid of.

It wasn't fear he felt now. What he felt now was rage that ran so deep that it went beyond human comprehension. It was white hot, an incandescent thing and restrained as he was, he could not act upon his base instincts. Instead, he was held here, helpless and unable to exact the justice these treacherous dogs deserved.

He could see the creeping dawn as it made its presence known in a sliver of light beneath the doorway that barred him from the outside world, but it made little difference to the stifling windowless room where he lay.

The sergeant shifted position slightly and the heavy restraints that bound him clanked dully. He had bitterly given up any further attempts to release himself from his bonds. It was an exercise in futility. The cuffs, chains and collar had been designed to hold Space Marines and were proof against even the greatest strength. There would be no way out of this for him now. Not unless his captors chose to release him. They were highly unlikely to do that. He was raging.

But he was not afraid.

The pulsing throb of hot fury in his veins helped him to retain his focus. It served as an anchor for his drifting thoughts; a physical reminder of his purpose and a wild ocean of untapped fortitude. It was an entirely good thing. It helped remind him that he lived.

He breathed slowly, 'cooling his heels' as one of his brothers described it. Outwardly, he calmed himself, allowing his training to take over and sought out an equilibrium. It wasn't a perfect result, not by any means, but it was the closest he could come given his current circumstances. Deep within his breast the darkness continued to seethe.

He turned his attentions reluctantly to the dull ache of his body. The supply of analgesics and combat narcotics that his power armour would have fed him to counter the burning, ceaseless pounding of his injuries had been denied to him and despite his post-human strength, he felt pain now. He knew that the pain was transitory and he knew that his body would mend in time, but those cold facts didn't stop it from boring deep into his nerve endings and settling into his bones.

Porteus had never imagined that he would become so deeply intimate with suffering. As a warrior he expected injuries, incapacitation and even more likely, a violent death, but as a battle-brother of the Silver Skulls Chapter, he had never once let his thoughts linger on the possibility of capture. The first was something that could be fought, denied or accepted; but the second was something else entirely.

Words rose without conscious thought to his lips. A passage he remembered from the books he had spent so long absorbing in his earliest days as a novitiate. Just like his brothers, he had devoured the litanies and prayers until he could recite them verbatim. In the darkened room, his voice boomed with surety.

'The meaning of victory is not to defeat your enemy but to destroy him, to eradicate him from living memory, to leave no remnant of his endeavours, to crush utterly his every achievement and remove from all record his every trace of existence. From that defeat, no enemy can recover. That is the meaning of victory.'

That was the meaning of victory. That was what he would do to the Red Corsairs the very second fate saw fit to grant him the opportunity.

They were words that loaned strength to his soul and he clung to them with zealous fervour. Occasionally, he could hear voices. Sometimes he thought, just for a fleeting moment, that he recognised the voice of one of his battle-brothers. But when the voices turned into screams of terrible agony which in turn ended in an abrupt silence, Porteus took back the hope ardently. Nobody, least of all his brothers, should ever have to give voice to such anguish.

He did not know why his captors had not killed him. Perhaps his tenacity amused them. The Corpsemaster had stolen his birthright, taking his gene-seed. Porteus's training and personal beliefs now led him to believe that he was nothing more than an abomination. Even his own battle-brothers would consider him as such. Should they find him, had they not already assumed him to be dead, they would do their best to end his pathetic existence. Were his own Chapter to grant him continued life, the cleansing process would be considerable. He was tainted. No better than a thing.

Stranger still… the fact that the Corpsemaster had even *healed* him. He felt violated by this transgression. There was no gratitude towards his saviour. He had been restored to health in order to suffer further torment. He knew that; he was no fool.

Better to be dead, fighting in the Emperor's service than this uncertainty. Far better.

The lack of knowledge regarding the fates of his men ate at him constantly, gnawing away at him. It added further fuel to his already quite considerable boiling pot of fury.

This was unacceptable. He would not lose himself to his temper. It would addle his ability to retain control. Calm, he told himself. Calm, Porteus. Remember your training.

He breathed slowly. In, and out. The dank air of the room and the lingering scent of decay that hung around the Corpsemaster wherever he passed filled his lungs and nostrils, offending his sensibilities.

Murmuring the words of the litany aloud once again Porteus added a private oath at the end. When – not if – he devised some way out of his current predicament, he would visit his wrath upon the whoresons of the Red Corsairs without mercy. He would no doubt die in the process, but retribution would be exacted. Oh, it would be glorious.

These were the things he had now. Divested of his tools of war, these thoughts and feelings were the only weapons he had at his disposal, and he would wield them well when the time came. His training and his creed would drive him to his ultimate demise gladly. He was not unprepared. He was clad in the armour of righteousness and faith and he was armed with the weapons of rage, anger and hate.

But he did not know fear.

He would *never* know fear.

'His mutterings are worthless.'

Beyond the door that was the only thing standing between the Silver Skulls sergeant and his much-desired vengeance, Huron Blackheart and the Corpsemaster were locked in a conversation of their own. The Master of the Red Corsairs scowled blackly and folded his arms across his chest. The movement dislodged the invisible presence and he felt its ethereal claws bite through his armour and dig for purchase.

'Everything he says is worthless. I despise the way he bleats the words of the Corpse-God. He has no value to us now, Garreon. He is no witch-kin. He is not even a proper commander. A sergeant? That is the best we can do? He is a rank and file warrior, no more.'

Blackheart uncrossed his arms and waved his hand dismissively. 'We do not need converts like that, especially ones so deeply rooted in false doctrine. We have taken what we need from him. I see no reason to keep him here any longer.'

'You know I do not like to disagree with your wisdom, my lord, but I have to say that you are wrong in this. I may have his gene-seed, that is true. But there is much, much more that our "guest" can give to us. Perhaps not now, but in time. His DNA is a valuable prize, most certainly; but whilst it will grant me precious access to his genetic legacy, it will never yield the secrets of his home world. I am sure that I can persuade him to part with them if you will allow me to bring him with us.'

'We have one of their Apothecaries on board the *Wolf of Fenris*. Can you not indulge your desires for torture with him?'

'Indeed I could, my lord, but the warrior within the room there is expendable. We need more Apothecaries. Did you not say so yourself?'

Curiously, the roles had reversed. Before, Blackheart had made his petulant demands and the Corpsemaster had obligingly catered to his whims. Now it was the Apothecary's turn to insert just the right level of wheedling into his voice to communicate his desires. Blackheart's scowl grew darker still and he glowered at his Apothecary. The two warriors met each other's stares without any sign that one would concede defeat to the other.

Blackheart tired of the battle of wills far sooner than the other. Garreon's presumption had always irritated him, but the Apothecary's value had saved him from execution on more than one occasion. There were very few who could remain defiant in the face of Blackheart's cold fury, but Garreon knew his worth. He knew the debt Blackheart owed to the Apothecaries and Techmarines who had rebuilt him following his critical wounding at the hands of the Star Phantoms – and he ensured he extorted as much leeway as he could muster from it.

Blackheart turned away and nodded curtly. 'Very well. I will... consider it. There is a long road ahead of us before it becomes a real issue, however. Now stop squabbling over your toys and make preparations for battle, Garreon.'

With those words, he stormed from the room, effectively dismissing the matter. The Corpsemaster lowered his head graciously, a triumphant smirk on his face.

'As my lord commands.'

* * *

THE PRIMARY DEFENCE turrets of the promethium refinery had roared into life, belching near-continuous lethal streams of flak and las-fire into the air. The two Thunderhawks carrying the Silver Skulls assault squads were well out of range of the warning shots but continued to keep their distance. Let the enemy see their approach.

The two gunships were keeping pace, flying side by side but as they closed on the facility they split, peeling off to the north and south flanks of the refinery. The teams manning the turrets redirected their fire accordingly, but the Thunderhawks held course and remained tantalisingly out of range. There was not a lot of ideal landing ground amidst the craggy peaks, but equipped with their jump packs the Assault Marines would not require their transports to make landfall. The mountain range provided enough cover for the Silver Skulls as they descended from the heavens on pillars of fire. Their rapid transit was stalled at the last minute by powerful bursts from their packs that kicked plumes of dust into the air and vitrified what remained into shimmering basins. With a crunch of breaking glass twenty Space Marines arrived within striking distance of their targets and began to advance in leaps and bounds.

Their objective was the anti-aircraft guns. Once they were disabled, then the Silver Skulls ground forces would be able to call in air support. With that on their side, reinforcements could be deployed directly into the heart of the enemy force.

Victory would follow soon afterwards.

'IT HAS BEGUN.'

Matteus lifted his head to the morning sky. The retinal display on his helmet scanned and zoomed in on the movement obvious in the far distance. The incoming roar of the gunships was unmistakable and the answering retort of the refinery's guns was every bit as loud in its shattering of the morning. From silence to uproar in seconds.

The initial drop of the two companies was all but complete now and the Thunderhawks that brought the heavy vehicle support were unloading. Most of Daviks's Devastator squads were already in place inside the Rhino carriers, with more versatile battle-brothers mounted on bikes. Matteus's troops would be making the approach to the refinery on foot, but they were not foolish enough to attack without serious heavy support.

Their approach was going to be made behind the three Vindicators that stood next to one another on the ferrocrete highway. The road was more or less a straight line towards the Primus-Phi facility and barely wide enough for the three tanks. The siege cannons they sported were a deterrent, no more. They could not be fired inside the compound of a highly volatile promethium refinery, but they could certainly provide great help in reducing the perimeter to rubble. In addition, their thick hulls and armoured dozer blades would provide superb cover for the ground force.

Their assault drop completed, the Thunderhawks boomed overhead as they repositioned themselves behind the assembled Silver Skulls. Everywhere noise and smoke belched from the engines of the vehicles, permeating the air with a chemical fog and clouds of ruddy dust. In less than an hour the shuttle terminal had gone from deserted to being a staging area for war. Yet, the Silver Skulls themselves remained remarkably silent but for muttered prayers and words to the machine spirits residing within their weapons. There was no pre-battle banter between brothers, only terse nods and clipped responses to direct questions and orders.

The hunger for this fight was very real. Every one of the Silver Skulls warriors present on the planet was ready, willing and eager to fight. Their minds were engaged with the finer points of battle strategy. There was no time for idle conversation.

'Squads Onyx and Garnet, are you in position?' Matteus opened a channel on the company vox to the assault sergeants.

Emareas's voice confirmed Onyx's position and a few scant seconds later, Dyami chorused his readiness.

'We have located Curis,' the sergeant of Squad Garnet added. 'He will scout ahead and join our effort as ground support when we acquire the target.' Matteus, who was leading the marching troops, nodded firmly. Directly behind him, the two massive bodies of the Ninth Company's Dreadnoughts stood almost motionless awaiting the word to advance.

Matteus flicked his vox-channel to contact the *Dread Argent*. His report was brief and Arrun's reply equally so.

'All is in readiness, captain.'

'Then proceed, brother-sergeant.'

The sergeant sought out the rune that would transmit a pict-feed from his helmet to the *Dread Argent*. Once it was running steadily, he blink-clicked it until it reduced to a tiny window in the bottom right of his display. He nodded and changed vox-channel once again.

'You all know your objectives, my brothers,' he said. 'Preserve the refinery. Purge the traitors.'

In the distance, the Primus-Phi facility continued to disgorge its endless clouds of smoke and steam into the air, casting a pall of gloom over the coming conflict. It continued to function despite its occupation, the unfathomable machinery at its heart grinding eternally onward heedless of the tread of traitors and mute testament to the skills of the Adeptus Mechanicus. The tech-priests would need to reconsecrate the site once the battle was won but, like the Imperium, it would endure.

Matteus smiled darkly beneath his helmet, then stooped to the ground. He ran his fingers through the packed red dust whilst a host of internal sensors calculated its density and consistency. Once battle was joined it would fill the air in a choking cloud but would do little to impede the senses of the Adeptus Astartes. Should the combat be prolonged, however, it would clog joints, jam weapons and score visors.

It was best then, to complete the operation with all alacrity. Matteus wiped his fingers dismissively along his armoured thigh, leaving two red streaks in their wake.

'Brothers! We fight for Gildar Secundus. End these traitors.'

The army advanced, dust swirling around them like a boiling storm cloud and heralding their arrival.

THE BRIDGE OF the *Dread Argent* seemed uncannily quiet following the intense pandemonium of the earlier battle. Despite the extent of damage and the death of many of the crew, things had returned to as normal as could be expected under the circumstances. Enginseers and servitors were already working on the ships internal repairs. The traces of Brand and Taemar's mighty battle had been removed completely but for the odd gemstone that could be seen glistening beneath a console.

Still clad in his battle plate, Arrun was seated in the command throne, casting a practiced eye over the data-slates containing the initial reports from the repair teams. It was truly incredible that the *Dread Argent* had not sustained more serious damage and he said a quiet word of thanks to the Throne of Terra that they had come this far with comparatively minimal losses.

He had yet to receive any further reports from the ground forces deployed to Gildar Secundus, but a transmission had been received from Sinopa who had taken the *Manifest Destiny* further into the heart of the system. The extent of the traitors' infiltration was starting to make itself known. On all of the inhabited worlds of the system, small battles were unfolding, invariably led by Red Corsairs sympathisers and bands of cultists. As of yet, there had been minimal need for Sinopa to deploy backup to the beleaguered militia. The very presence of the Silver Skulls battle-barge in orbit had been enough to cause one group of rebels to turn their weapons on themselves rather than face the wrath of an Adeptus Astartes battle force.

'Your orders, Master of the Fleet?' Sinopa's query had cut across Arrun's distracted thoughts. He had given the question a moment's consideration before replying.

'Continue to sweep for activity elsewhere in the Rift,' he replied, noting the *Manifest Destiny's* location around Gildar Quintus. 'Send down Scout forces to those inhabited worlds that have reported disturbances. Once they are cleared, we can concentrate on the rest of the planets in the system. They have undoubtedly deployed to those worlds as well. They will not last long, however. I will not stand for Red Corsairs infecting this system longer than necessary.'

'Orders received and understood.'

That last contact had been well over an hour ago. The only communication thus received from Gildar Secundus had been a clipped notification from Matteus confirming that all the deployed drop-pods were accounted for and that they were ready to attack. Within the next few minutes, the Silver Skulls would swarm onto the Red Corsairs and all this foolery would be over. They would take the skulls of their enemy and they would return to their home world triumphant. Victory was a certainty. None of the Silver Skulls believed anything else.

Impatience and frustration gnawed at Arrun. He had stood before the bank of pict screens until they spat into life with the images transmitted from Matteus's helmet. He stood and gazed intently at it.

'Argentius and the ancestors go with you, my brothers,' he murmured, making the sign of the aquila.

THE TRIO OF Vindicators formed a superb rolling barrier and their effectiveness was soon put to the test when the first shots from the refinery gate turrets were fired. More than capable of holding up to the task, the massive tanks held their return fire. Once they were within range, Daviks and his Devastators would deploy from the Rhinos and take care of the guns. The tanks would use their shorter range weaponry to flatten the walls.

The highway leading to the gates of the refinery was well used and as straight as a die affording the advancing company an unobstructed view of what lay ahead. The gates were closed and barred, but such things were not designed to repel Space Marines. Given the size of the approaching force the gates were akin to holding up a hand to stop a bolt shell.

As the vehicles moved, the ground beneath them shook, small pebbles flying and rebounding off the armour of the Silver Skulls beneath them with dull *thud* noises. The cloud of red dust that cocooned them was so thick it would have been choking without the filters of their helmets. Apart from the rumble of the Vindicators and the Rhino transports which followed them, combined with the sound of the Space Marine's boots snapping against the rock, there was no other noise. There was no out-of-place squeaking or groaning of overstressed metal from the vehicles. The Silver Skulls' attention to the repairs and maintenance of their vehicular support was every bit as minute as the care they gave their weapons and armour. Behind the well-armoured transports the company bikes cruised, their engines purring at a low ebb.

The two immense Dreadnoughts who marched with them did so without comment, hissing hydraulics and mechanical clanking accompanying their movements. The casing of the venerable warriors was etched in beautiful filigree work that depicted the honour tattoos they had worn in life. Each deeply worked groove had been crafted with care by the Chapter's artisans.

Occasionally, a sliver of steel-grey armour could be glimpsed through the red cloud.

High calibre shells spewing from the gate turrets began tearing up the road ahead, gouging out fist-sized chunks of plascrete and occasionally thumping harmlessly from the heavy armoured exteriors of the siege tanks. The fire was wildly misplaced, sporadic and inaccurate, but without the protective cover of the vehicles would otherwise have presented a serious threat to the Space Marines on foot.

At a hand signal, several warriors fanned out from the marching group, increasing their pace as they traversed the rocky outcrop either side of the road. No longer approaching in a column, the Silver Skulls began to form a v-shape attack squad.

'Garnet, Onyx, report.' Matteus sought for an update from the two assault squads who were even now making their way down the mountains either side of the refinery. Once the anti-aircraft weaponry was disabled, then the Thunder-hawks could make their first pass and clear the gates and the front of the compound.

'Target sighted. Estimate ten minutes to contact.' Emar-eas's voice was curt and clipped through the vox. Dyami suggested eight minutes. Emareas countered with seven. It seemed that the two squads were descending in relatively perfect symmetry. Matteus knew both sergeants well and didn't doubt for a moment that they were engaged in what they referred to as 'friendly' competition as to who would succeed in their objective first. It was a moment of harmless frivolity that promoted enthusiasm.

'Maintain contact,' said Matteus. 'Deploy together, who-ever gets there first.' He knew that they would, but it did not hurt to remind them.

The winding column of Silver Skulls advancing deter-minedly towards the gate had closed to within a few hundred metres of the structure, coordinating their approach with that of the flanking squads. Daviks's plan called for the assault to be simultaneous on all fronts and that goal was within moments of being achieved. Closeted within the bil-lowing plumes of dust and shielded by their tanks, the Silver Skulls presented difficult targets for the traitors manning the turrets. Such an incidental detail did not stop them pouring fire on their attackers.

Thunder rumbled once again in the mountains.

THE PICT-FEED WAS hazy and flickering; the interference caused by all the rubbish and debris in the heart of the Gildar Rift causing its usual problems. But it was adequate. From his vantage point far above the surface of the planet, Captain Daerys Arrun's hands unconsciously closed into fists.

'Purge them,' he said in a voice so soft it could barely be heard. But it was perfectly pitched for the vox-net. Almost two hundred Silver Skulls warriors heard the words and they moved to contact.

* * *

WHEN THAT CONTACT came, it was hard and it was relentless.

The three attacking forces struck as a single unit. Inside the compound, several mortar teams had gone to work launching shells over the wall to shriek down onto the besieging Silver Skulls. The Vindicators continued to soak the worst of the damage, but their armour was showing pitting and scoring in dozens of places where solid rounds had chewed away at them. The shots were most assuredly no longer off target, but every shell that rang from the blocky vehicles spared the warriors behind. Direct hit after direct hit pounded the three tanks that shielded them. It was a potentially costly gamble, but the more the Vindicators drew enemy fire, the faster the enemy's ammunition would deplete. Thus far at least, the strategy was proving itself.

The previous silence of the company vox-net became a churning mass of orders, commands and updates. There was never any sense of hurry or sense of confused disorganisation. The Silver Skulls were created to be perfectly honed machines of war. They knew their objectives and they knew the plan. There was no need to question anything.

During a momentary lull in the attack from the gate guns whilst the teams operating them reloaded, three of Daviks's Devastators stepped down from the lead Rhino with calm assurance. Two were armed with heavy bolters which they trained on the gates and began to pound at them relentlessly with a steady stream of explosive shells. The third warrior was carrying a rocket launcher with practiced ease and at a single command from Daviks, aimed and fired at the nearest tower.

The missile raced to its target on a plume of smoke, the warhead piercing the weapon mounting and bursting it apart with a thunderous explosion. Seconds later the ammunition hoppers detonated, consuming the turret in a ravening fire-storm. Screaming figures haloed with flame cascaded from the gate and fell to the hard earth far below whilst burning shrapnel from the destruction rained down on those both sides of the gates. It had been a direct hit, but then these were Space Marines heavily trained in siege warfare. The other gate turret had already begun firing again, this time turning away from the main force and directing its attentions specifically at the three Devastators.

One of them took a shot to the shoulder. The armour soaked up the worst of the damage, but sent him staggering backwards, the heavy bolter in his hands which had been trained on the gate firing uselessly into the air.

Sudden activity on either side of the compound caused a momentary distraction as aided by their jump packs the two assault squads hurdled the walls and began the job of relieving the other guns of their crews. From where he stood, Matteus could see the thruster-glow of the Assault Marines as they worked.

'Take those gates down,' Daviks ordered.

The centre-most of the three Vindicators, designation *Judicious Requital*, growled and began to advance towards the fortifications. Any of the enemy who suddenly found themselves in the unfortunate place of being right behind the gates were swiftly crushed beneath the weight of the heavily armoured vehicle as it tore right through the plasteel barriers of the promethium refinery. The flimsy portal was wrenched from its hinges without any real resistance. They had never been designed to withstand such an assault and gave way like tearing paper.

'Advance!' Matteus gave the command and the Silver Skulls poured in through the broken gates in a mercurial stream of gleaming silver. Weapons primed and ready, they began firing on the Red Corsairs who returned the attack with equal enthusiasm.

This was no epic, sweeping field of battle. This was up close and very, very personal. The Silver Skulls merged with the mass of seething bodies and began to unleash hell upon them. Chainswords clashed in earnest, their motors screaming furiously. The teeth of the weapons ground together until they were worn to nothing, or the hilts began to pour with smoke. When that happened, the warriors moved to fighting with other weapons or even engaged in hand-to-hand combat.

Any slaves caught up in the multitude of Space Marines were quickly dispatched; whether at the end of a blade, from a bolter shell or simply by being crushed in the mob. A number tried to defend themselves with what would have been commendable valour, but their status as traitors of the Imperium meant that there would be no memorial and never any commendation.

Vox traffic finally began to become more frequent as the battling intensified and Matteus caught the pertinent points. Dyami and Emareas had successfully disabled the anti-aircraft guns and were even now engaged in their own fighting along the perimeter of the facility. The walls were already beginning to crumble, falling to dust under the combined firepower of the Vindicators. The frequent burst of flame from the assault squad jump packs marked their bounding passage through the enemy.

With the artillery disabled, the Thunderhawks would be able to deploy and offer air support at any time. The Devastators were reaping a bloody harvest of the enemy cultists, swathing through them and felling them with consummate ease. The majority of souls on the receiving end of the attack were killed outright; others lay wounded and dying across the compound.

'Something's not right,' Matteus voxed. 'There are less of them than I would have anti–'

'Death to the False Emperor!'

Matteus spun at the unholy shriek and faced an oncoming Red Corsair whose dented and pitted armour bore the original colours of the Astral Claws. A white-hot bolter muzzle was practically level with Matteus's face and he ducked and spun, lashing out with his foot to catch his would-be attacker behind the knees, bringing him crashing down. He squeezed the trigger of his own bolter and the explosive shells slammed into his enemy's chest, shattering the breastplate and sternum beneath. The Traitor Space Marine's body convulsed in response to the impact and pitched forward. The corpse shuddered once and then stilled forever. There was no time for Matteus to rest on the laurels of satisfaction as he was jostled into the next fight. Everything was a blur.

'Repeat last transmission, sergeant.' Daviks was the epitome of calmness. Matteus, granted a brief moment of respite, lowered his bolter briefly and looked around the compound.

'Their numbers are thinning exponentially. Much faster than we anticipated,' he reported. 'There is no way that this can possibly represent their full force if reports of Huron Blackheart's activities are to be believed. There are perhaps...' He cast his gaze around, letting the sensors in his helmet do their job. 'Twenty? Maybe thirty of them. The rest are cultists and slaves. There is something deeply suspicious going on here.'

'Break into fire teams. Search the buildings. My men will clear and hold the compound.'

'Yes, Captain Daviks.'

'LOADING IS ALMOST complete, my lord.'

Huron Blackheart grinned. A string of drool ran from his metallic mouth down his chin and hung there for a moment before puddling on the floor. He flexed his hands, the power claw chinking ominously.

The facility had been stripped almost bare of anything that the Red Corsairs could use. Medical supplies, tools... even a short coffle of slaves had been bundled off.

'What of the subject?' The Corpsemaster nodded towards the room where his Silver Skulls captive lay. Blackheart's grin twisted into a scowl. The Corpsemaster opened his mouth as though he would remind Blackheart of his promise, but the leader of the Red Corsairs spoke first.

'He is singularly unimportant. Leave him there. Let his "brothers"...' The single word was loaded with venomous contempt. '...find him. You said yourself that there is dissension in their ranks, did you not? Let him go back to them and ensure it eats at them from within. He may unwittingly be of far more use to us if we let him go than if we drag him with us.'

No words passed between servant and master, but they locked wills silently for a few seconds.

'It is a terrible waste of a subject,' the Corpsemaster said, eventually. 'But as my lord commands.' There was a hint of spite in his voice, which delighted Blackheart.

'Prepare to depart, Garreon. I am going to personally remind the Silver Skulls of our martial prowess and then I will join you.'

'A foolish indulgence.' The Corpsemaster's scowl was almost as twisted as Blackheart's own. It earned him a backhand from Huron Blackheart that sent him spinning. He careened into the wall which was the only thing that stopped him falling and from being completely humiliated.

'A foolish indulgence perhaps. But a worthy one. Now go and carry out your orders as I have charged.' With that casual dismissal, Huron Blackheart exited into the main compound, power already charging his claw to deliver killing blows.

The Corpsemaster watched him go with fascination in his face, even as he raised his hand to rub at his jaw.

IT WAS MATTEUS who saw him first, but Daerys Arrun, watching events on the pict-screen was a very close second. Almost simultaneously, both of the Silver Skulls murmured his name, a peculiar mixture of hatred and disgust colouring their tones. Spinning from the sight, Arrun snatched up his helmet, worked into the half-skull of a Silver Skulls captain. He had already ensured that another wave of drop-pods be put on standby should they be required. This, he was certain, was such an eventuality.

He gathered a small retinue to travel with him and they made their way to the staging area. Arrun was so incensed, so furious, that he gave no thought to consulting his wounded Prognosticator laying in the apothecarion. His mind was focused on one thing and one thing only.

Huron Blackheart had not left aboard the *Spectre of Ruin*. He was still on the world below. If Daerys Arrun had his way, then the planet would become his grave and he would be the one to drop the traitor into it.

* * *

'THRONE OF TERRA,' breathed Matteus into the vox before he could give the command to search and clear. 'The Tyrant of Badab. He is here!'

He was huge; the bulk of his armour and the size of the power claw that dominated his appearance causing Huron Blackheart to loom menacingly wherever he went. His twisted, scarred, half-metal face was a rictus grin of self-indulgent amusement. Eyes, one mechanical and one inhuman beyond recognition, locked with those of the Silver Skulls sergeant and Matteus felt the acid taste of loathing in his mouth. It took every ounce of self-control he possessed not to simply launch himself at the foul traitor across the compound.

He had no need to. Blackheart was bringing the fight to him. In an easy lope, curiously graceful given his bulk, the Master of the Red Corsairs was heading directly for Matteus.

Decades of service and hours of endless training overrode the moment of intense revulsion and Matteus brought his bolter up, smoke still curling from its barrel. He could feel the shaking rage as he aimed the weapon. Every fibre of his being twisted in acrimony at Blackheart's existence. To have turned his back on the Emperor's light and the truth of the Imperium... it was a concept so alien to Matteus that it was completely incomprehensible.

He fired the weapon, launching several shots at the approaching warrior, but the monster seemingly had the fortune of a daemon and the fortitude to match. Despite Matteus's shot being perfectly on target, the first shell careened wildly to the side as though cast aside, tearing a chunk from the compound wall, while the second blew apart a cultist who stumbled fatally into its path. The third blasted a crater at Blackheart's feet, but he didn't even break his stride.

'Impossible,' breathed Matteus. He had seen Prognosticators defend themselves on the field of battle in such a way, but Blackheart was no psyker. The sergeant breathed, balanced himself mentally and physically and fired again. This time he scored a direct hit to Blackheart's right shoulder, but it rebounded with a metallic *chink*, the prosthetics and augmetics turning the shell aside before it detonated.

The traitor *laughed*. The sight and sound of that misplaced humour set Matteus's blood to boiling and he snatched his combat blade from its place on his waist, the bolter transferring with comparative ease to his left hand.

'Engaging the enemy,' he voxed and his voice was more of a growl than words. A deep-rooted feral fury, the Varsavian birthright, was churning in his soul and the urge to kill and take a trophy was rising. The rushing tide of his blind anger lapped against a wall of steady calm. Keep level-headed, he told himself. For the Emperor, for Argentius and for the good of the Imperium, this will be done. Huron Blackheart must die.

Blackheart was almost on top of him now, his power claw sweeping backwards ready for the strike. With a practiced flick of his thumb, Matteus switched the bolter to full automatic and exerted pressure on the trigger.

THE DROP-POD CARRYING Arrun and his retinue plummeted through the atmosphere, coming to a juddering stop just short of the other opened landing craft. There were a few of Daviks's company remaining on alert at the shuttle terminal and they nodded their respects to the captain as he emerged.

He had prepared his lightning claws on the way to the planet's surface. They had ever been his personal close assault weapon of choice and he wielded them with deadly grace. More than once, when training with his peers, he had caused more than mild injuries, much to Ryarus's rebuking consternation. He moved quickly and his skill as a strategist more than carried over into his ability as a combatant.

Now out of the stifling confines of the drop-pod and making his way with grim determination across the rocky terrain towards Primus-Phi, he felt the old familiar rush of adrenaline and combat hunger that he felt had been so long missing from his existence. He would never have refused the honour of his position when Lord Argentius had bestowed it upon him; but it had meant that opportunities to engage in field combat had been noticeably curtailed.

As he jogged lightly down the dusty highway, he voxed to alert the kill squads to his presence.

'This is Captain Arrun. I am en route to the battle.'

'Shouldn't you be minding ships or something?' Daviks's grumble was oddly welcoming. 'Good to have you alongside us, old friend.'

The stacks and pipework of the refinery loomed larger in Arrun's vision as he approached. Any attempts to raise a response from Matteus had been met with nothing but bursts of static in response. If the sergeant was still engaged in battle with Blackheart...

'Situation report,' he demanded as he reached the shattered gates of the refinery. The fighting had all but died out in the immediate area, but for a few pockets of fierce resistance that were stubbornly holding their ground. The captain cast his eyes around the compound, seeking his quarry. 'Where is he? Where is Lugft Huron?'

'I am right here, Daerys Arrun.'

The chirp in his ear from the vox-bead heralded a voice that was most certainly not one that belonged to any of his battle-brothers. It was a voice he had heard barely hours before and it did not bode well for Matteus's fate.

'You are far too late,' continued Blackheart, vicious gloating in his voice. 'But do not be too concerned. Your sergeant has no further need for his helmet now that he lacks a head for it to protect. Perhaps I should keep it as a trophy at the foot of my throne? What do you think?'

The transmission was filled with a grinding, wheezing sound which Arrun realised with creeping loathing was laughter. 'I will however extend my offer a second time, in case you have decided to come to your senses. Join your men with mine and the Silver Skulls will live to soar to new heights of mastery at my side.'

'You are nothing but a warp-tainted monster with delusions of grandeur and your "offer" is nothing but an insult,' Arrun responded through gritted teeth, the twin blades of grief and incandescent rage piercing him to the quick.

'Then you will die just like him. I will grant you this much, Silver Skull. Your pawn died bravely. Foolishly of course; thinking that he could best me. But bravely, nonetheless. The blood of the Silver Skulls burns strongly. One last chance. Give yourselves to me in service and you could be great once again.'

Arrun was shaking in cold anger at the mockery in Black-heart's tone as he announced the death of Matteus. 'Death is eminently preferable.'

'You have but to ask, Daerys Arrun, and you shall receive.'

The harsh, grating laughter was sickening and Arrun cut the transmission dead. The whoreson had one of their vox-beads. He had full access to their communications and he would be able to preempt any battle strategies they may put forward from this point onward. Time for another change of tactics.

'Your orders, sir?' One of Matteus's squad, pained at the loss of his leader, had naturally stepped up to fill the void. Having realised the death of their sergeant but being ren-dered effectively useless to stop it, they had swiftly reformed their unit, ready to avenge him. Arrun nodded. He looked around at the gathered warriors, *his* warriors, and he spoke in a voice that was laden with grim certainty. He also switched to one of the many tribal dialects from Varsavia. It was a guttural sound: harsh and sounding to the untrained ear as little more than a verbal assault of aggressive vowels. Every one of his battle-brothers was familiar with all of their planet's native dialects. For this particular situation, Arrun had chosen the language of the cannibalistic, violent natives who called themselves the xiz. It seemed somehow appropriate.

'We end this. We end this now.' Arrun gestured to the refin-ery. 'We strip this place bare if we have to. We search every metre and we scour every kilometre until we rid this planet of the Red Corsairs. And then, my brothers, when we have done that, we will hunt them down across the sector. We will make them regret ever bringing their worthless carcasses out of hiding.'

A resounding roar of approval met with his words and he held one of his clawed hands to the sky as though shaking defiance at the universe itself.

'It ends,' he repeated.

FIFTEEN
LOST AND FOUND

'WHERE IS HE?'

'My lord, with the very greatest of respect, Apothecary Naryn left me with very strict instructions and you should allow a little more time to–'

'Get out of my way.' Usually courteous, Brand's voice held a razor-edge of menace.

The female crew member who served as the doctor for the non-Space Marine crew didn't even attempt to reinforce her initial attempts to keep the Prognosticator in the confines of the room. She put her hands up almost in surrender and turned her back. Scowling, Brand very slowly and with some considerable discomfort levered himself from the table on which he lay. The doctor had worked alongside Space Marines for twenty years and she knew that tone of voice far better than to even attempt any kind of reasonable discourse.

Ignoring the Prognosticator as he made his way painfully towards the door, she turned her attentions back to dealing with the wounded crew. She had delivered the Apothecary's order and as far as she was concerned, that was her duty discharged. Humans and Space Marines may have worked together on the ship, but their co-existence was not always harmonious.

Brand had not known such intense pain in many long years. Every step he took jarred his ribs agonisingly against his bruised and battered body. His internal organs had already begun the process of healing and whilst he was by no means anywhere near fully fit, he knew his own physiology well enough to accept that he was on the mend. Even broken and bruised was preferable to dead. He gave silent thanks to the Emperor. He reached the control panel in the apothecarion and pressed a finger down on the vox.

'This is Prognosticator Brand to Captain Arrun. State your current position.' Even his voice sounded weaker to his own ears. He had always spoken in a soft whisper, but now there was no strength behind it. He knew that he was lucky to still draw breath after the injuries he had sustained in his fight with Taemar, but at this moment, his irritation was acting as an effective anaesthetic, dulling the pain and giving him something far more unpleasant to dwell upon.

Captain Daerys Arrun is not aboard the Dread Argent, *Prognosticator Brand.*

It was the voice of Volker Straub, oozing from the very walls and flowing around his psychic senses. Every hair on his body stood on end at the inhumanity of its tone and he felt a deep pang of regret. Volker had shown such great promise. Brand remembered well the long debates within the Prognosticatum as to his fate.

'Then where exactly is he?'

Captain Daerys Arrun deployed to the surface of Gildar Secundus exactly four minutes and thirty-one seconds ago, Prognosticator Brand.

He should have known that Arrun would be unable to stop himself. Should have known that the captain's tendency to act first and think later would have ended in this foolish action. He should have put measures in place to ensure that the impetuous fool had remained where he was. Should have, should have, should have. But he had been incapacitated, caught in the grip of healing stasis. Regrets had no place here.

He found himself lost for words again, only this time it wasn't through injury. It was through a mix of outrage and horrific foreboding.

'Get me an off-world vox-channel,' he said in a low, menacing voice. 'I want to speak to him... personally.'

FINDING PORTEUS, CHAINED and held in restraints within the peeling walls of the mess hall was a mixed blessing for the Silver Skulls.

True, the recovery of a battle-brother who until that moment had been considered killed in action was a cause for much celebration. But finding him and discovering what had been taken from him was something else entirely.

'Give me a chainsword,' he said, his voice cracked and strained. 'Give me a bolter, give me a bolt pistol – give me a combat knife. I will find that bastard and I will cut out his heart.' He stood there, a picture of defiance. He stood proud, wearing only the shredded bodyglove, his face as black as the thunderous sky outside. He was bloodied, filthy and furious. 'And then, when I have cut out his heart, I will slice it. Piece by bloody piece and I will force it down his thr–'

'Peace, brother,' Dasan said, keeping his voice calm and level. It had been his dubious pleasure to have found his fellow sergeant and release him from his restraints. Now Dasan's own sense of infuriation at Porteus's capture had been stoked. 'You are well. You still draw breath and you are unbroken. Let that be enough for now.'

Porteus could sense the uncertainty in Dasan's tone. He could *feel* his battle-brother's hesitation. The sense of tentativeness he felt emitting from one to whom he had always been so close was agony. But by far and away the most terrible thing was the *pity*.

He was a pariah. Bereft of his gene-seed, his heritage had been stolen from him. Despite having been found, he was lost to the Silver Skulls; perhaps forever. A moment of temerity took him and he snarled his reaction.

'By the grace of the ancestors, I am capable still. I cannot let the mere fact that I live "be enough", brother' he replied, rubbing at his wrists where the shackles had bound him. 'I will rejoin the fight. I will exact my justifiable vengeance on these traitors. Better I die in battle here and now. Far better than to perish in shame and ignominy locked within a cell, condemned by those who once called me kin.' His despondency and bitterness was unbecoming and he knew it. Something akin to sympathy flickered in Dasan's eyes, but he was interrupted before he could respond.

'Sergeant Dasan, you will select one of your squad to accompany Porteus back to the dropsite,' came Arrun's rumbling tones from the doorway. The captain had removed his helm and his tattooed face was unreadable as he cast his eyes over the battered Porteus.

'Sir, I...'

Arrun held up a hand to forestall comment and Porteus snapped his mouth closed. He was in no position to argue – especially not with the company captain – and he knew it well. Arrun scanned him again, his eyebrows feathering together as he tried to do what he could to soften the blow. It was not easy. He had delivered these words before and despite knowing that he was simply discharging his duty, it never failed to be painful for both him and the recipient. Daerys Arrun had never been particularly compassionate. That had always been Brand's role.

There he was, thinking once again about the Prognosticator he had left without consulting. That thought hardened his heart again. His expression grew grim and he addressed Porteus in a tight, clipped tone.

'Brother-Sergeant Porteus. You will do as you are ordered and you will be kept in seclusion aboard the *Dread Argent* until we return to Varsavia. You will speak only with Prognosticator Brand, myself or any of our elected representatives of what has transpired during your captivity here. Is this clearly understood?'

Porteus gave a brusque nod and Arrun found it within himself to add something that he hoped would be more encouraging. The Emperor knew that Porteus had not gone to the Red Corsairs willingly and all the evidence proved that he had prosecuted his own war effort to the best of his abilities. But for the unfortunate sergeant of Squad Carnelian, the battle of the Gildar Rift must end here and now.

He shot Porteus a smile so brief that it may never truly have been there at all. 'It pleases my heart and gladdens my soul to see you living, brother, but I cannot permit you to return to battle. I have no proof at this time that you have not been compromised by the enemy. You know the rules. It is the way things must be. I cannot afford to care how focused you may be. The fact remains that you have been in the hands of the Red Corsairs. Much as it pains me to say it, I cannot trust my life in your hands.'

The tone brokered no argument whatsoever and Porteus acknowledged the order with another sharp nod of his head, unable to properly find the words to express his feelings. He got carefully to his feet and felt his knees buckle slightly beneath him. It hurt him still further when from the corner of his eye he saw Dasan step forward, then stop as though not sure whether helping him or not would be frowned upon. Pride surged and gave him the strength to hold himself tall.

'As my captain commands,' he said. Arrun caught his arm.

'I said I cannot trust you with my life,' he said. 'I meant to add the word "yet".'

Relief showed behind Porteus's wounded expression and Arrun nodded. 'We will speak more later, brother.' Arrun glanced across at Dasan. 'Sergeant, I leave this matter in your hands.' The vox-bead in his ear chirped and he hesitated before responding. The strangest of premonitions told him exactly who it would be before the voice crackled through.

'This is Captain Arrun. Go ahead.'

'I am informed that you left the ship over fifteen minutes ago, captain. Why was I not notified?' Brand's cold fury carried through in every carefully spoken syllable. Every cadence in the brief message was designed to strike right at Arrun's guilt. Every barb hooked its target. Not for the first time in their association, Arrun found himself resentful at having to justify his every move to a psyker. Switching back to the tribal dialect, he continued.

'Prognosticator. I would explain myself to you, but I fear our communications are compromised. We will discuss this matter shortly. Stand by for further orders.' He cut the vox-link dead and pulled his helm back on. Outside, within the compound, the sounds of fighting had all but died away.

The Primus-Phi facility was enormous, fully four kilometres from end to end and it would take some time to search every hall and every building. But Arrun had already made it abundantly clear that the Silver Skulls were to leave no stone unturned in the search for any of the renegade Adeptus Astartes.

'No mercy,' had been his standing order. 'For any of them. There will never be second chances for traitors.'

Arrun studied the room that had been Porteus's prison. He didn't envy the sergeant's ordeal when they returned to Varsavia. He would be thoroughly questioned and interrogated. There would be endless genetic and blood tests. He didn't doubt, at heart, that Porteus remained true to the Silver Skulls, but there were precedents. Much as he needed the extra warriors right now, he could not afford to take the chance that they harboured a traitor – willing or not – in their midst.

Exiting the building, he emerged into the compound. Red dust was still flying, stirred up by the battle, but rain had started to fall now; a persistent drizzle that would soon turn the choking clouds to cloying mud. Far to the east, thunder rumbled once again in the mountains. It was, even to the captain's untrained senses, portentous and doom-laden. It nudged his sense of shame at abandoning Brand back aboard the *Dread Argent*.

'Find me Prognosticator Inteus,' Arrun said to the closest Silver Skulls warrior. 'I need to consult with him before we take this battle any further.'

* * *

BRAND HAD RAGED ceaselessly for the better part of half an hour, although he was far too disciplined to let it show externally as more than curt responses and carefully studied silences. Arrun's spontaneity was an insult to both the structure of the Chapter and to him personally. He accepted that he had been incapacitated at the time, but there were other Prognosticators on board. Arrun's actions were little short of rebellious.

His exasperation had heightened still further at the relayed news that Sergeant Porteus had been found. He had overseen the interrogation of captured battle-brothers before and he did not relish the thought of what was to come.

The Prognosticator had eventually brought himself to his own quarters where he had sat quietly in a meditative pose and allowed himself to cool down. The pain in his ribs had lessened considerably and he knew that he needed to regain his composure if the Emperor's gifts were to properly commence their healing work.

He turned, as he always did in these circumstances, to his tarot. It was not only the tool of his trade; there was great peace and solace to be found in the simple tactile process of handling the psychic wafers. It was a familiarity that bred an unmistakable sense of calm.

As he passed his hands across their honeycombed surfaces, their images flickered. His power was strong, but he had expended a lot of psychic energy whilst fighting Taemar. He tried to put the thought of the traitor from his mind but the darkness he had felt enveloping the Red Corsair's mind had left him reeling that one of his own, a brother psyker, could have come so far from his path.

Concentrate, he told himself sternly. He closed his eyes once again and felt the rhythm of his own breathing. He shut out all the ambient sounds of the *Dread Argent* until its constant thrumming was nothing more than a backdrop on which he could paint his predictions.

'Aid me now, great Emperor,' he murmured. 'Show me the skeins of Fate. Guide my hand so that I pull the right one, so that my brothers will not tangle or unravel.' His eyes opened and studied the arrangement of the tarot before him.

He rested a hand over one of the wafers and the image hidden in its depths flickered briefly. His power was largely spent, but his latent abilities were still strong enough to do this.

Brand despised feeling so weakened. It left him feeling impotent and useless. He took several deep, calming breaths and coaxed himself gently through it. His breathing slowed imperceptibly until he could clearly hear the dual rhythms of his hearts. The one, strong and awake, churning the noble blood of his Chapter around his body, the other sluggish and dormant. He forced all thoughts from his mind, allowing himself to present a blank canvas to the stroke of the Emperor's will. Let the Father of Mankind reach across the empyrean, past the lurking evils and horrors and shape the future.

Once he was in a suitable state of deep meditation, he began to exert his psychic ability. Compared to the empyrean-piercing brightness of the Emperor, his own light was dull and minuscule in comparison. But it was the belief of the Prognosticators that the Emperor would be drawn to a beacon of his psychic offspring, no matter how inconsequential it may seem. Across the infinite wastes of space, every pinprick of psychic light shone.

He felt, rather than saw, the image appear on the wafer and allowed himself to become distracted by it. The Emperor, inverted. He looked at it and he felt the acid taste of bile in his mouth. It was the second time in a short period that he had drawn that card.

Every school of thought within the Prognosticatum took the signs from the Emperor in slightly different ways, even those who read the tarot. The gift was, after all, unique to each psyker and whilst they could be schooled in how to handle the powers of the warp, invariably that power would manifest in a very different way. Prognosticator Bast, for example, had an affinity with the elements that was unsurpassed. Vashiro and, if rumour were to be believed, young Bhehan of Eighth Company, both possessed remarkable foresight.

His own skills, even dampened as they were right now, were more than adequate. The death of Taemar was a testament to that. But his ability to see the unfolding of the future had always been limited.

Passing a hand over the wafer, the image blurred and vanished. Once again, Brand let himself reach out to feel the engulfing warmth of the Emperor's light. He laid his hand over the surface of the first card and, allowing the power of the empyrean to flow through him and expel through the tips of his fingers, watched intently as the image began to form.

THE STORM WAS closing in now. Rain was falling harder, and the red clay-like mud clung and stuck to the bright armour of the Silver Skulls warriors like congealing gore. It dribbled slowly down their leg guards and pauldrons in sticky rivulets that were almost the same colour as the blood that had broken up the uniformity of their chosen livery.

Following the initial attack on the compound, the majority of the Red Corsairs holding force had been beaten down or were engaged in a fighting retreat that was still raging within the grounds of the refinery. Everywhere the eye fell, mangled, dismembered bodies of cultists littered the ground, sinking slowly into the quagmire, trodden further in by the passage of the Silver Skulls.

Inteus had attended Arrun at the captain's request, his own power armour blood-streaked and pitted. His force sword was worn in a scabbard across his back and his face was almost serenely calm. He had chosen to take the field without a helmet and the crystalline frame of his psychic hood arched from his gorget, the fine wires sinking into his skull in what looked like the most uncomfortable way. The two spoke privately for a few moments in low voices.

'I already told you, Captain Arrun,' Inteus said, his expression not changing at all. 'When we talked earlier, I told you the answer to this question. You must not fight this battle with thoughts of vengeance. Do your duty. That is all that is required of you.'

Arrun shook his head. 'It is not an answer, Prognosticator. I need something more solid before I commit my forces further.' He took a step closer to Inteus, his greater height advantage meaning that the psyker had to look up at him. Arrun's voice lowered to a hiss.

'I cannot join this fight without thinking of the brothers I have already lost this day. Does this mean I should call a retreat? Because I cannot do that, Inteus, whether it is the Emperor's will or not. I have embarked on a course of action that I cannot easily change. The tide, once in motion, cannot be turned. We must see this battle through to its outcome. And its outcome must be the eradication of the Red Corsairs in the Gildar Rift.'

'Your decision seems made, captain.' The sandy-haired psyker's tone was mild.

'I still need you to give me an answer.'

'If it were that easy, then I would provide you with that which you seek.' Inteus waved a hand expansively. 'The portents, the vision I had, did not relate to the entire Chapter.' Inteus's young face became serious and he unsheathed his power sword, holding it briefly in front of him and allowing a crackle of energy to run down its length. He considered it carefully, keeping his eyes from Arrun. 'They were specifically regarding *you*.'

'I need your blessing on this matter, Prognosticator.' Arrun's tattooed face was dark with anger. 'Do I proceed or do I not? You know as well as I that without your confirmation, we cannot, in all good conscience, make our move. And every minute you deliberate is another minute Lugft Huron gets further away from us.'

'I have noticed that you never refer to him as Huron Blackheart,' observed Inteus, curiosity in his voice. 'Why is that, captain?'

'Do not try to stall for time. An answer, Prognosticator. Now.'

A pregnant pause was finally punctuated by a sharp nod from Inteus. 'Proceed,' he said and his tone was bland, giving away nothing. 'Do not proceed. Either way, the Silver

Skulls will prevail. On this occasion, brother-captain, the choice needs to be yours.'

Inteus's cryptic reply infuriated the captain and their wills locked in a clash of baleful stares. Despite his training, Inteus looked away from the steel he saw in his superior's soul. He knew what Arrun's choice would be. He did not know the captain as well as he knew Daviks, but in the short time he had been in Arrun's sphere of influence, he had formed what was showing itself to be a remarkably accurate opinion.

'Then by your grace, Prognosticator, we will proceed,' Arrun said, ramming his helm back on his head until his voice was once again expressionless and distorted by the vox-grille. 'We clear this place.'

Inteus bowed his head graciously and sheathing his power sword again fell back to rejoin his own squad.

They pressed forwards through the compound, awash now with bodies and severed limbs, grisly remains of the enemy force. Taking up position at the front of the advancing line, Arrun's lightning claws flickered with blue energy.

With piercing shrieks of suicidal frenzy, a pack of cultists swarmed around a corner and broke against the line of silver. They were armed seemingly with whatever they had been able to pick up; in this instance, mostly tools, shovels and lengths of pipe and the speed with which they were dispatched to the depths of hell was almost pathetic. More than one of the traitors died on the end of Arrun's claws as he pierced and shredded them with the crackling, energised blades. The massive forms of the Adeptus Astartes made the cultists seem like ragged toys and even more so when their broken bodies were hanging limply from an extended claw, blood pooling on the ground below.

With an indifferent flick of his hand, Arrun rid himself of his prey. The dying cultist slithered from the blades and gurgled loudly and messily into oblivion. Arrun stepped forward, crushing the pitiful traitor's skull beneath his boot. Grey matter mingled with the rain and blood and the captain didn't even spare his victim so much as a glance before he pushed forwards.

Most of his company had fought at his side during one incursion or another, but it never failed to engender great pride in them to see their venerated captain carving through the enemy as though reaping their souls for the Imperium. He was inspirational and unshakeable. There was little glory in this slaughter however, and the Silver Skulls advanced through the refinery like the relentless machine that they were, grinding the traitors beneath their tread and leaving nothing but the dead behind them.

Behind the front line, the two Dreadnoughts followed, stooping to pick up fleeing cultists to crush in their mighty grip or simply riddling them with controlled bursts of fire from their assault cannons. Although both were heavily armed, their orders to minimise damage to the refinery stood. Just the sight of the massive machines in their ornately engraved armour was enough to stop some of the slaves in their tracks, sending them screaming like the cowards they were. Onwards the Dreadnoughts trod, the mud beneath their feet marking their passage in craters. As the fleeing cultists ran, the rest of the company discharged careful bursts of bolter fire and put a swift end to their escape.

Not a word was shared between them. Whilst they could issue orders in the tongue of the xiz, many of the Silver Skulls found the barbaric language almost revolting. Silence was preferable in this instance. As such, vox chatter was reduced to a minimum, the commanders giving messages by hand signals. It mattered little. The well-oiled cogs of Fourth Company spun freely and easily as they worked in perfect harmony with one another. Those warriors from Daviks's company who had joined with them slotted perfectly into their strategy.

Well out of the main compound now, they were being slowly forced to narrow their advancing line as the buildings grew more densely plentiful. What had been an expansive plaza was funnelling the Silver Skulls into a labyrinth of corridors and byways. All around them and overhead a maze of pipework and tubing groaned, throbbed and leaked clouds of thick vapour. They could make their way through, but the potential likelihood for ambush amidst the sprawling guts of the facility grew with each passing moment.

Arrun turned and gestured to the bike squad who were slowly riding through the compound behind them. They made no effort whatsoever to avoid the dead and dying, merely rode over bodies where they lay.

'Scout ahead,' he ordered the leader when he was within speaking distance. The sergeant nodded and with a roar of their engines, the squad of bikes pulled ahead of the rest of the Silver Skulls. Arrun moved back amongst the company, searching for Correlan. The Techmarine was carrying out emergency field repairs on the armour of his battle-brothers, cursing freely all the while. It was a vulgar trait, most likely a lingering byproduct of his childhood on the streets of Varsavia's one main city.

'Techmarine. Fall back immediately and lend your assistance to Captain Daviks. He is attempting to link in with the refinery cogitators. Your assistance will be essential in ensuring he achieves this task.'

'But...' Correlan indicated the damaged armour of the warrior he was working on. Arrun simply glowered at him.

'I am sick and tired of you questioning my every order, Correlan. Do as I say. Report to Daviks now.'

Without another word, not even an acknowledgement of the order, the Techmarine made his way back across the compound. Within minutes, the network had resumed its steady exchange of voices. The majority of the Silver Skulls themselves remained remarkably quiet however, as tended to be their way during battle.

The enemy numbers continued to dwindle as they made their way through the claustrophobic pipes of the Primus-Phi facility. The Dreadnoughts, far too large to manoeuvre through the superstructure without causing untold damage, remained at the edges of the compound. The fighting there continued to be reasonably intense. More cultists and a small number of Red Corsairs had taken up positions in and around the disabled turrets.

A steady rain of dismembered bodies fell from the walls as the assault squads pushed into the pockets of resistance, and the arrival of the two venerable brothers further added to the mayhem. One bunker disintegrated under a sustained burst from Brother Pallaton, spilling ragged bodies to the ground below. Squad Onyx advanced over the rubble, slaughtering the survivors with cool, dispassionate strokes of their chainblades.

'Arrun, this is Daviks.' The taciturn Ninth Company captain's voice across the vox-channel sounded irritable, which given his normally phlegmatic nature meant he was expressing unusually high levels of anger.

'Go ahead.'

'Correlan has got us access into the system and I suggest that you deviate from your present course. You should take your men immediately to the coordinates I'm transmitting you.'

Runes and digits flickered across Arrun's visor feed and the compass swung to indicate the direction he should take. The captain raised a hand and pointed in that direction, expertly guiding the Silver Skulls. Whatever it was that Daviks had found sounded important enough for him to investigate without immediate question.

'Course altered. Would you care to elaborate, brother?'

'I've compared the plans I acquired before we landed to those held internally here in the refinery. Regretfully, my strategy was based on plans that are some five years out of date. There has been a vital addition to the transport infrastructure on Gild–'

'Spare me the infernal details and get to the point, Daviks. What is it that I am supposed to be looking for?' Arrun's impatience was biting.

'They have installed a maglev system, Arrun. I would lay down any price that the Red Corsairs are planning to take the transport out of the refinery – if they haven't already done so.'

'How far?'

'No more than a couple of kilometres from your current position. The maglev serves the refinery and several of the hab-zones on the planet, well clear of the shuttle terminal. It carries personnel and cargo – and probably also prome-thium tankers to supply their generators. I have taken the liberty of assessing the other plans and details held here. There are several areas that have recently been blasted for fresh mineheads. There is no reason at all why the Red Corsairs may not have planned to set down their transports there.'

'Then we must make all haste.' Unconsciously, Arrun had picked up the pace, their steady trudge through the mud turning into a light jog. But even that plan was thwarted immediately with Daviks's next words.

'The system runs mostly underground, through the moun-tains.' Arrun clicked his tongue in exasperation.

'For some reason, brother, that news does not surprise me. Not one bit. Very well. Continue to assess the situation.' His mind worked rapidly as he considered the various options open to him and his men. He glanced around and consid-ered his resources before he finally addressed the entire unit.

'Brothers of Fourth and Ninth Companies, heed my words. Thunderhawk pilots, Captain Daviks and Techma-rine Correlan will shortly be sending you coordinates of potential engagement points. All mounted squads, head to the maglev terminal as fast as you can. All Silver Skulls – finish your skirmishes as quickly as you can then disengage and converge on my position. We need to stop them before they leave and their headstart is already considerable.'

A distant whine of engines, some from the attack bikes on the ground, the others from the Thunderhawks was his response. Seconds later, both of the gunships streaked overhead, heading for the coordinates that had been trans-mitted. The riders gunned the throttles of their bikes and tore from their scouting path towards the south-eastern corner of the compound.

As the Space Marines ran towards their new destination,

Arrun worked on controlling his absolute fury. It irked him beyond words that at every turn in this conflict, the Tyrant of Badab had outmanoeuvred him. There was never going to be any danger of Arrun respecting another brilliant strategic mind, particular not when it belonged to an animal of Chaos – but despite this, he grudgingly had to acknowledge that Blackheart was presenting him with a challenge. He suspected, without any proof of the feeling, that the whole thing was little more than a game to the traitor.

But that game was now reaching its climax. They had been circling one another for long enough, each sizing up the other's strengths and weaknesses and the time was rapidly approaching for them to make their final play and close on the enemy. Were he to employ clinical objectivity, Arrun would have acknowledged that Blackheart had been baiting him into this confrontation all along.

He was being propelled forwards by the tides of fate that so dictated his Chapter's every action. The pride and honour that was instilled in him, knowing that he carried his Chapter into this action, was great. Victory and vengeance were close at hand. He would hunt the Tyrant of Badab and run him to ground like the wild beast that he was. Then he and his brothers would erase the legacy of the Red Corsairs and purge the stain of their existence from Imperial memory. Blackheart was nothing more than a serpent and Arrun intended to snap its neck beneath his boot, just as he would have done with the snakes back home on Varsavia.

The words of Vashiro, the Chapter's Head Prognosticator, came into his mind. When every battle-brother of the Silver Skulls ascended into the full ranks of the Chapter, they were granted a personal audience in his presence. For each battle-brother, a private seer's blessing was given. No brother ever spoke of those deeply personal words or portents in front of any other. Their future was spelled out in that meeting and it was understood that it was improper to speak of such things openly. Of course, that future was often presented as a riddle or an old parable of some kind and rarely made sense.

Arrun hadn't thought of those words for a long time. Strange then, that they should come back to him now. Stranger still that words that had once seemed ethereal and wise could now suddenly be so very appropriate.

There is no sound as eloquent as the vashka snake's tail when it sounds before a strike.

Blackheart's words hadn't moved him at all, except to anger. There had been no eloquence in his attack. It had been pure brutality right from the start. The traitor's hatred for the Imperium would never colour Arrun's loyalty.

'WE HAVE A new problem.'

Daviks looked up at Correlan. The Techmarine had spent the past few minutes with the glazed look of one at the heart of the system. The mechadendrites that snaked out from the harness on his back were plugged into the refinery's cogitators and he had been running diagnostic tests and security sweeps.

'Something worse than the fact there are still Red Corsairs out there?'

'Potentially, yes.' Correlan blinked a few times and carefully detached himself from one terminal, turning to connect himself to another.

'Would you care to expand on this new and problematic discovery, brother?'

'A moment. I am running a secondary sweep.'

Daviks growled softly and folded his arms across his chest. He was a straight-talking soul and such prevarication was an irritant to him. It was only a few seconds, however, before Correlan whirled around and stared at the Siege Captain, horror in his eyes.

'Auspex analysis confirms my suspicions. There are demolition charges wired to the main reactor. I cannot tell if they are armed or counting down, but I will begin heading over there now and do my best to neutralise them.' The Techmarine began the laborious job of unplugging himself from the cogitator banks.

Daviks felt his anger fizzle away and he acted immediately,

picking up where the Techmarine had left off and instantly voxing through to Arrun.

'I HEARD YOU.'

Arrun answered Daviks's urgent words. 'I heard you, brother and I acknowledge. Squads Onyx and Garnet, break off your assault and begin sweeping the complex for any other surprises the Red Corsairs may have left for us. Daviks, begin arranging the extraction of as many of our forces as you can manage. Withdraw the companies to the staging area but be ready to redeploy if necessary. This may be a false alarm, but I will not risk the destruction of our men in a moment of complacency.'

'I agree,' responded the Siege Captain. 'I have already begun plotting the most efficient extraction strategy. Brother Correlan is making his way to the reactor. I trust in his skill and ability to neutralise the threat – but it is far better for us to err on the side of caution.'

'I also have faith in Correlan's skill,' replied Arrun. 'Let us hope that our mutual respect for him does not prove unfounded. Let us further hope that those charges have not yet been set to countdown. I don't believe that even Lugft Huron would be insane enough to destroy the refinery without retreating to a safe distance.' The words came easily enough but there was a hint of doubt in them. 'I will divert some of the bike squad in that direction as well. Should it be necessary, Correlan can talk them through the process.'

'That would be a most unacceptable state of affairs, brother-captain.' Correlan's voice across the vox was punctuated with the thuds of his running feet. 'There are litanies to be observed, they do not have the necessary knowledge or Mechanicus training–'

'Do as you are ordered, brother.' Arrun clicked off the connection with Correlan and gave the order to the bike squad to send support. Two of the riders immediately peeled off from the pack that was up ahead and raced away into the complex.

The nearby barking of bolter fire drew Arrun's attention

and he doubled his pace, covering the distance with long, powerful strides. He emerged from the warren of buildings into a plaza tiled with ferrocrete slabs and littered with tumbled plastek cargo containers. The squad of bikes had drawn up in the cover of one of the fallen stacks and with the support of some of Daviks's Devastators were engaged in a furious firefight with a defensive line of Red Corsairs. Behind the traitors, the panelled walls of several maglev cargo pods could be seen, though the bulk of the train remained out of sight.

Above the roar of battle, Arrun could hear a rising thrum that peaked just above the subsonic and caused particles of debris to jump and dance. It was the sound of a gravitic engine spooling up, the sound of Blackheart making his escape. Arrun growled, a deep predatory sound in the back of his throat and jogged through the whickering shells to where the Devastator sergeant crouched.

'Break that line,' the captain commanded. 'If that train leaves, we lose our best chance to keep the enemy contained.' He scanned the plaza quickly, drawing a hail of desultory fire from the Red Corsairs and then gestured to the largest mass of crates. 'Concentrate your efforts there,' he ordered and then turned to the bikers. 'Malachite, follow me in.'

The Devastators drew their weapons together as one, twin streams of bolter shells stitching ragged holes in the fallen crates and blasting several Corsairs from their feet. Barely a moment later, the barricade disintegrated in a white-hot flare of searing fire, leaving nothing but molten ruin in its wake. The Silver Skull with the plasma cannon lowered the smouldering weapon and Arrun surged past him, a feral cry roaring from his lips.

Bolts ripped through the air around him, gouging fist-sized chunks from the fallen crates, peppering him with debris and shrapnel. He was half way across the plaza when a well-placed shot blasted a crater in his pauldron, almost sending him spinning from his feet. Raw tenacity and determination pushed him forward. Then the bikers of Malachite surrounded him like a vanguard and the wave of Silver Skulls stormed into the breach.

Smoke and vapour still filled the hollow created by the plasma cannon and Arrun put his trust unreservedly in the senses of his armour as he waded into the enemy position. He felt one of the bikes speed past behind him, the displaced air pulling the smoke into lazy coils. A Red Corsair lunged forward out of the fog and Arrun parried with his claws, tearing the traitor's weapon into useless ribbons of metal before gutting him with the energised blades. The chatter of bolter fire drew his attention to the left and he hurried out of the obfuscating cloud into the open.

The Red Corsairs were in retreat, falling back in groups of five and using the available cover to mask their movements. Several had already mounted bikes of their own and Arrun recognised the modified insignia of the Iron Hunters, the swift raiders of the Astral Claws. His own warriors were weaving in and out of the stacked crates, harassing the traitors with bursts of fire from their weapons. He took all of this in at a glance. Then the bass throb of the gravitic engines vanished with an almost audible pop and the maglev accelerated away from the plaza.

SIXTEEN
PURSUIT

HIS LIGHTNING CLAWS retracted into the gauntlet with smooth, well-oiled precision. Like all of the Silver Skulls, Arrun spent a great deal of time scrupulously maintaining his wargear. There were, of course, serfs and artificers indentured to the Chapter who performed much of the work, but as captain, he had always taken particular pride in doing the job himself. The slightest fault in their performance could spell the difference between life and death.

The gauntlets themselves were beautiful weapons, relics fashioned for the Chapter armoury in a time so long before that none were living who could recall whose they had originally been. Handed down from captain to protégé over the centuries, they had come into Arrun's possession a hundred years previously. Opulent and intricately designed skulls decorated the back of them, the cabling of the power field generators snaking through the insignia. He had fought with them since his elevation to captain and whilst not every engagement called for their singularly brutal style, they were always his preferred method of dispatching the enemy. Like most Varsavian-born Silver Skulls, Daerys Arrun had a core ferocity and fearlessness that made him a terrifying foe in close combat.

He flexed his hands briefly and twisted the throttle of the armoured bike that he had commandeered. The maglev train had quickly picked up speed, but the captain was confident that he could easily catch up to it. What he did once he got there, of course, was an entirely different matter. He would consider those options when the moment demanded it.

He had ordered one of the bike squad to hand over his vehicle and had made the spontaneous decision to lead the pursuit into the tunnel. With the loss of his best Apothecary and the countless deaths of so many good Space Marines, Arrun's desire to end the traitors once and for all was a nigh-unstoppable force to be reckoned with. It had been many years since he had ridden such a vehicle into battle and he revelled, for the briefest of moments, in the speed and power it granted him.

There was something strangely exhilarating about living life in the moment and not having to be beholden to a Prognosticator's will. He had allowed himself, for the first time in many years, to simply react to a situation. Inteus had been part of the detachment corralling troops back for extraction. Arrun's absence would doubtless be questioned shortly, but for now at least, he was engaged in pursuit. That was where he should be. Leading from the front.

The bike growled easily under his control and with his head down against the buffeting wind, he led the pursuit squad into the tunnel directly after the train. It was only once they were swallowed by the subterranean darkness and were making their way across the undulating, rocky surface of the tunnel's floor, that the dangers of the manoeuvre were revealed.

The passage snaked its way through the interior of the mountains that covered much of the planet's surface and had very evidently been carved out with industrial-grade meltas. The floor and walls were smooth and rippled, vitrified by nuclear heat. The tunnel was only a couple of metres wider than the train itself and obstructed throughout by supporting pylons running down its centre. The Space

Marines were skilled enough to weave their way between them but it severely limited their manoeuvrability.

It required consummate skill to negotiate the hazards the tunnel presented and the Silver Skulls had plenty of that. Not only was there the uneven ground to cope with, but the speed of their pursuit was such that the smallest error in judgement or lapse of concentration could easily prove catastrophic, even to the heightened reactions of a Space Marine.

The bikes tore down the passage behind the train, powerful engines roaring like bestial predators. The maglev itself was a massive thing with no fewer than thirty or forty cars, all of which were no doubt filled with promethium and other assets that the Red Corsairs had stripped from the facility. Somewhere inside – most likely at the fore section – was Blackheart. The urge to reach him, the need to end his tenure once and for all was desperate and Arrun urged the bike forward.

'As soon as the opportunity presents itself then we begin boarding and eliminate any remaining traitors,' Arrun said across the vox when they reached a section of the tunnel that didn't require quite so much of his concentration. 'We need to advance to the control car and shut it down; stop this vehicle travelling any further than is necessary. That is our priority. That – and providing covering fire, of course.'

His voice crackled and distorted across the channel, interference from the maglev tracks and from the fact that they were deep within the belly of the mountains. Vague voices hissed in his ear, not one of them completely clear. He had to hope that the message had gotten through. None of the bike squad asked Arrun what his own priority was. They already knew.

The captain raised a gauntleted hand and pointed ahead. There were at least the same number of Red Corsairs bikers travelling beneath the train in much the same way that they were. The two groups would converge imminently and any fighting that took place would be swift and brutal.

Nodding in understanding, the Silver Skulls gunned their

engines harder and picked up speed as they approached the enemy.

'ENEMY IN PURSUIT,' came the vox report, just as broken and distorted as Arrun's had been to his men. Huron Blackheart laughed in sheer exuberant delight. Drool slavered down his chin and he made no effort to wipe it clear. The Corpsemaster, who stood beside him in the front car of the train, watched dispassionately. There were times when he had difficulty reconciling the former might and glory of the Tyrant of Badab with the insanity that had all but swallowed him. His service to Blackheart was eternally loyal, of course; that was never in question. But there were times when he ached to take Blackheart apart physically just to find out what made him who he was. The Tyrant's behaviour could easily be attributed to the trials he had undergone, of course, but that didn't quell the Corpsemaster's curiosity.

What secrets lurked in the darkest corners of Huron Blackheart's brain?

'Slaughter them,' Blackheart retorted. 'I want to drag their worthless carcasses behind this train like banners. If they will not join with us, then they will not live to regret it.'

The Corpsemaster considered him for a moment, then spoke. He had never hesitated to speak his mind before and yet he felt a certain reluctance at uttering his next words. He could anticipate, without any of the foresight that was so prevalent in the Silver Skulls, exactly what Blackheart's response would be. His instincts did not fail him this time.

'You should perhaps consider uncoupling the cargo, my lord,' he said in his soft whisper. 'We will make better haste without its weight holding us back. The Silver Skulls are fierce, tenacious and they will not stop until they have eliminated us. We have made our impact here. Why should we ling–'

He never finished the sentence and had no time to regret his poorly chosen advice. In a swift movement, Blackheart's power claw had closed around his body and thrust the Apothecary up against the interior of the train. The steel wall groaned and buckled under the pressure and a nearby armaplas window burst, filling the space with roaring wind. Bigger and more powerful by far than the Corpsemaster, the latter was wise enough not to attempt resistance. Mad eyes – one biological, the other mechanical – stared ferociously at the Apothecary. Saliva flew from Blackheart's misshapen mouth as he screamed his fury over the howling gale.

'Never, ever suggest to me that an enemy stands a hope of defeating us. If we believed that every time we engaged, we would have been wiped out decades past. I have never given up a prize willingly, Apothecary.' His fist closed more tightly around the Corpsemaster and his armour creaked alarmingly. Hairline cracks appeared in the breastplate under the stress of the grip. 'I have *never* given up a prize and you can rest assured that I will not be starting today. Is that clear? I propose that you refrain from giving me advice that is not asked for.'

The Corpsemaster nodded, a spare movement that was all that Blackheart's constrictive grip allowed him to make. Sneering, Blackheart released him and turned away, his anger gone as quickly as it had come. 'When we have finished our work on this forsaken rock, we will look to deal this Chapter a fatal blow. We will look to strike at their heart. Not immediately of course, but some time in the future when they think that everything is under control and that their ridiculous Corpse-God once again favours them.'

'You plan to attack Varsavia?'

'Exactly, Garreon.' A smile of infinite cruelty played around Blackheart's lipless mouth. 'But not only Varsavia. We will speak with our Silver Skulls guests and we will have them reveal the locations of their other recruiting worlds. Once we have that information, we will plunder them. We will take their able-bodied and make them our own. From what we know, their numbers are dwindling. Imagine how much further towards our embrace they will run when they realise who it is that has stolen their future from beneath their blinkered gaze.' A gurgling laugh emitted from his ruined throat. 'They may search the whole length of the Imperium for us, but we can easily hide. By the time they track us down, their recruits will be ours.'

The presence that always lingered around his master like a fusty scent stirred at the passion in Blackheart's words and the leader of the Red Corsairs listened to encouraging, secret whispers that only he could hear. The Corpsemaster could scent the faintest hint of ozone in the air, as though a psyker were using their powers. He felt discomfited.

'An excellent plan, my lord,' he affirmed eventually, his voice slightly strained whilst his vocal cords untangled themselves. 'And one in which I can see no truly obvious flaws. There must be no continued existence for those who will not see the truth. We will take their futures from them.' It was a regurgitation of words that Blackheart had spoken many times before and they were spoken almost as a matter of rote.

'I am glad we at least agree on that, Garreon.' Blackheart stooped to pick up the massive axe that he favoured as his support weapon. He ran one of the crooked fingers of his power claw down its length with a lingering, metallic screech that would set even the teeth of other Space Marines on edge.

The Corpsemaster turned from Blackheart, feigning great interest in the darkness of the tunnel ahead. To look at his master's face was to stare into the very maw of madness and despite his own arguable levels of borderline insanity, the Corpsemaster had never been able to manage it for more than a few seconds.

DROPPING BACK FROM the main escort, two Red Corsair bikers slid their vehicles sideways in the narrow confines of the tunnel before turning to face the oncoming Silver Skulls. The engines screamed in protest at the abrupt nature of the manoeuvre and then changed their direction. Now the traitors were racing headlong towards the Silver Skulls, their bolters roaring.

It was not much of a diversion or even that much of a delaying tactic and Arrun wondered what it was that they were trying to achieve. The lead Silver Skulls bikers returned fire with the twin-linked bolters on the armoured fairings of their vehicles. The tunnel was briefly filled with blistering crossfire as the rapidly approaching bikers sought to unseat their enemies. Shells chewed the passage walls and burst against the thickly plated vehicles but fortune and numbers were on the side of the Silver Skulls.

One of the two Red Corsair bikes blew apart in a cloud of greasy smoke and debris, its rider thrown clear and crashing heavily against the rock side of the tunnel. Blue sparks marked his passage as he scraped along the stone surface. It did little to impede the speed of his transit and he finally came to a halt some six or seven metres behind the Silver Skulls. He lay still and unmoving, whether injured or stunned it was impossible to tell. There was no time to consider whether or not he remained a threat.

The other enemy biker skidded briefly as his companion was unseated, but maintained his balance as he continued to ride towards them. His face could not be seen behind the helm he wore, but Arrun fancied there was a look of grim determination. Were that the case, then it was a look that would not last very long. A further exchange of fire shredded the front wheel of his vehicle and burst his skull in a welter of gore. The headless corpse maintained its grip on the bike for a few seconds before it slackened, then the bike and rider toppled and fell, sliding and screeching along the floor of the tunnel.

Hopelessly out of control, it careened into the Silver Skulls, causing three of them to overbalance and come off their own bikes. The others swerved as much as they possibly could to avoid the situation, but there was very little manoeuvring space.

What had seemed a pointless waste of life on the part of the Red Corsairs had proven to be a surprisingly canny move; blocking the passage until they were able to recover their vehicles. As for moving the corpse of the enemy out of the way, there was no need. The heavy bikes were perfectly able to grind over the armoured body with the minimum of difficulty.

For good measure, one of the riders at the back turned to the unmoving body of the first biker and fired on him with the meltagun he carried. The battered ceramite armour explosively vaporised under the weapon's fury and within scant seconds, all that remained of the rider were his melted gauntlets and a few other scraps of armour. He would most assuredly present no threat now.

Following this moment of cold – but necessary – brutality, the Silver Skulls resumed their pursuit, but the maglev had pulled further away from them during the brief altercation.

Gunning the throttle, pulling it round as far as the mechanism would let him, Arrun's front wheel briefly left the ground. He inched his bike ahead of the others, taking the lead. He was not going to let the traitors get away if he could do anything at all to prevent it. As they rounded a bend in the tunnel, several figures could barely be made out in silhouette as they mounted the top of the train.

Seconds later, the pursuing Silver Skulls were being subjected to covering fire. They increased their speed, tucking in as close as possible to the underside of the maglev rail and making themselves difficult targets. They wove masterfully in and out of the slender struts, describing strangely graceful figures of eight. Their control over the bikes was consummate and despite the hail of fire, they dodged and avoided without any seeming difficulty. The Red Corsairs, robbed of their moving targets, began firing instead at the tunnel walls. Rock and shell shrapnel ricocheted off the Silver Skulls, peppering them with tiny, razor-sharp projectiles and filling the tunnel with choking dust.

They pressed onward, passing several carriages and promethium hoppers, coaxing more speed from the bikes until they were more than halfway up the length of the maglev. Riding beneath the rail proved to be a good tactic, but it forced the Silver Skulls into a slower pace that Arrun found unacceptable. Every part of his being burned with the need to reach Huron Blackheart and these delaying techniques on the part of the Red Corsairs were unnecessary obstacles in his way. Enough, he determined. It was time to make his move.

With a bellowing roar of fury that resounded around the tunnel, the enraged captain made a gesture to his closest companion. The warrior whose meltagun had put paid to any threat from the fallen Red Corsair nodded his understanding and levelled the weapon at the train as he pulled forward alongside it.

The first blast of the weapon ate through the thin exterior of the train with ease, leaving a gaping wound in its side. The second eliminated the three Red Corsairs who appeared in the gap before they could return fire.

With a further twist of the bike's throttle, Arrun turned his body and pulled himself level with the maglev. With perfect timing, he gripped onto the sides of the aperture that the melta blast had opened up. He hauled himself up until he was standing. The gap wasn't quite large enough to accommodate him, but with his strength and bulk, it was a problem that was swiftly resolved.

His abandoned bike hurtled onwards, remaining remarkably stable until it finally fell and clattered noisily along the side of the tunnel.

'Silver Skulls, on me!' Arrun bellowed into the vox, not knowing whether his companions would even hear the command. He trusted them to follow his lead, however, and he righted himself inside the carriage. Slowly, he unfolded himself from his stoop to his full height, the silver half-skull of his helmet lending a macabre aspect to his profile.

His lightning claws extended themselves with a crackling whisper and he stood with his arms outstretched as far as the confining space of the train car would allow, like a hawk ready to swoop down on its prey.

The interior of this car was devoid of any further Red Corsairs. The three who had been in that particular section had been destroyed by the meltagun. For the first time since the pursuit had commenced, Arrun felt that something had actually gone in his favour. He prowled forward, down the length of the carriage. This one was completely empty; containing not a single passenger and no evidence of pilfered resources or anything that could have been taken from the refinery as a spoil of war.

Three more of the assault bike squad had followed his example and appeared through the hole blasted in the train and torn larger by the captain's ingress. Now all in the same proximity, their vox communications worked perfectly once again.

'Your orders, captain?' Merchus, the sergeant of Squad Malachite addressed him. He had barely been promoted to the position and not for the first time, Arrun's regret at the number of losses the company had suffered in recent times was strong. Merchus was proving every bit as solidly reliable as his forebears, however.

Outside the train, the sounds of gunfire continued to permeate everything and Arrun glanced upwards at the sound of heavy footfalls. The train had never been designed to carry the weight of a Space Marine and the metal was bending and buckling under the load. It would be bare moments, Arrun suspected, before those Red Corsairs presently fighting from the train's roof simply crashed through the metal as though it were paper and literally landed in their laps.

Let them come, he thought with a soft growl. He would be ready for them. A ripple of blue lightning ran down the length of his claws.

'We need to make our way forward through the train,' he said. 'Blackheart has to be here and we need to reach him before this train reaches its destination. So...' He pointed with the claws of his right hand. 'We move onward and we deal with each threat as it presents itself.'

Above them, the stressed metal creaked ominously. Arrun forced back the urge to tear through the ceiling with his claws and expose the Red Corsairs to the hungry weapons of his squad. There was no time for such indulgence, however.

Merchus nodded. During the brief exchange, two more of the bike squad had ditched their bikes and were climbing into the train as well. Outside, the last of the Silver Skulls had done the best they could to maintain distraction fire and had held their ground for as long as they were able. They had fired indiscriminately at the Red Corsairs bikers and, from the change in pitch and timbre of the shots, occasionally firing at those on the roof of the train. The silence that ensued now told of their unfortunate but anticipated demise.

The void was filled in due course by the sound of other bikes; the other enemy riders whose vehicles had pulled ahead had dropped back and would very soon present extra problems of their own. The time to act was now.

Arrun moved forward swiftly and punched his fist through the end of the train carriage. The lightning claws tore through easily, shredding the metal and shattering the armaplas window. He did the same with the rear end of the next car, providing them with an easy route through to the next car. The comprehensive destruction of the door complete, the remains of the squad moved onward.

HE COULD HEAR them. They were perhaps six or seven cars behind their current position. There was a lingering contingent of Red Corsairs and a few of the remaining cultists left who would act as a reasonably effective buffer. But Huron Blackheart could hear the Silver Skulls as they tore the train apart. It was music to his ears. Closer. Closer.

He laughed and swung his axe lightly in his hands. His own estimates put their exit from the tunnel at a good five to ten minutes more and he had absolutely no doubt that the arrogant Captain Arrun would be upon them well before that. His determination and tenacity was nothing if not commendable.

He had long devolved past owning a sense of anything that could pass for disappointment, but there was some core part of his shrivelled soul that felt the faintest pang of what he could only equate to regret. Regret that his offer for the Silver Skulls to become part of his own collective had been thrown back in his face. Regret that this delightful exchange of strategies and ideas with Daerys Arrun would soon come to its obvious conclusion.

Arrun's staunch refusal to bend to his will had irked him but had left Blackheart with no choice now other than face him down and bring him to an end. The Silver Skulls captain would undoubtedly fall under the power of the Blood Reaver and his death would mark the passage of a great strategic mind; perhaps even the first one in a long while that had actually genuinely presented a challenge for Blackheart. It was a waste.

A waste, perhaps – but their confrontation was inevitable now. If he couldn't engage Daerys Arrun's mind, then he would exact the necessary toll on the Silver Skull's body.

Blackheart swung the axe again, its finely honed blade cleaving the air with an electric snarl. Impatience gripped him and he fought down the urge to tear his own passage through the maglev train to meet his enemy head on. The mechanisms in his claw hissed and creaked angrily and liquid fire dripped from the nozzle discreetly designed to protrude from its palm.

He could, if he so desired, simply give the order for his Red Corsairs to obliterate Arrun long before he got anywhere close to the front of the train. But the Silver Skull had outwitted him once already. At this time, he had no way of knowing just how many of them were in pursuit and to pull his forces away from other areas of the train right now could prove to be an error of judgement that he was unprepared to make.

INEVITABILITY PROVED INFALLIBLE when the ceiling of the carriage finally gave way under the combined weight of the Red Corsairs above. Four of them, wearing the old Astral Claws livery, heavily scarred and defaced, dropped like stones into one of the cars. It was currently occupied by two of the Silver Skulls who had yet to make their way through to join Arrun and they spun around, ready to fight.

The altercation that ensued was brief and savage; the exchange of bolter shells on both sides ultimately resulting in the bloody, violent deaths of all four of the Red Corsairs and one of the Silver Skulls. The remaining battle-brother paid a price for the brief victory, too. His armour was pitted with craters and smoke curled from the muzzle of his bolter where it lay, still held by the bloody ruin of his hand. There was no real pain, merely a faint sense of annoyance at the inconvenience the temporary loss of the appendage would cause. A mangled scrap of flesh and ceramite was all that remained at the end of his arm. With cool, clinical detachment, the young warrior drew his chainblade and completed the job.

The Larraman cells in his bloodstream had already formed a rapidly-closing seal over the wound, and he simply switched to his bolt pistol before joining his brothers in the next car.

Heavy footsteps continued to sound above them. A moment's pause allowed Arrun to gauge the number of enemy still above them and he put the number at no more than five or six. So far, their passage through the train had gone largely unimpeded, but the sounds of angered shouting from the next car suggested that this would shortly cease to be the case.

Blue ripples of energy sparked from Arrun's lightning claws and he felt the old, familiar sense of hunger that always came right before engaging in close quarters combat. He had grown to young manhood in one of the more civilised tribes on Varsavia, but like so many others, he had fought for his survival from an early age. Hand-to-hand combat gave him an adrenaline rush and sense of exhilaration like no other form of fighting he had ever known.

Thus, when the melta weapon blew through the next carriage and the cultists tore towards them, he engaged in the fight with ferocious delight. His claws flashed like shards of silver as he skewered one cultist up against the wall whilst simultaneously slicing through another's abdomen with a well-placed low strike.

The carriage, already filled with the cultists' battle cries shifted in pitch until death groans and the sounds of war were the only things to be heard. The coppery stink of their lives being snuffed out was strong and the floor of the train quickly became a slippery mess of blood and viscera.

Arrun inhaled the stench of death through his helm's mouth grille. It fired his own blood, fed the feral side of his rational, logical personality and drove him onwards. He stormed towards the end of the carriage only to be blown backwards as the Red Corsairs on the other side duplicated what his own warriors had been doing. Arrun flew back and landed amidst the rest of the Silver Skulls.

Within seconds, the carriage was a seething mass of power armour clad bodies bearing down on each other with grim determination. The weight of so many post-humans in one confined space took its toll on the maglev, however, pressing its undercarriage so far down that it scraped along the rail with a squeal of protest. The speed of the train dropped sharply. A few short metres ahead, the white glare of impending daylight could finally be seen. It was tantalising and Arrun's adrenaline pumped harder still.

'Press forward,' he bellowed.

'HOW MUCH LONGER will it take before we can detonate the charges?' Blackheart snapped at the Corpsemaster, whose calm demeanour seemed to have taken something of a shaking in the sudden deceleration of the train. He gathered his wits to him, not wishing to demonstrate another moment of weakness in front of Blackheart. He tapped a long, thin finger on one of the many dials on the front of the maglev.

'According to the instruments, still another few minutes remain until we are out of the mountain pass. I cannot say for certain. I am no tech-priest or enginseer, my lord. But look ahead. Perhaps that will better answer your question.'

He pointed to where the chink of daylight shone through the darkness. Blackheart nodded.

'I do not doubt for one moment that the Silver Skulls will be out there waiting for us. I place you in charge of ensuring our cargo gets loaded. I will take care of whatever remains of them.' Blackheart swung his axe once again, this time with enough force to split the carriage door. He wrenched it from the shattered portal with ease and took a few steps forward. 'We will need to move quickly. The moment we are into wider vox-range, alert the others.'

The Corpsemaster nodded his assent and watched the bulk of Huron Blackheart as it made its way out of the front of the train.

Somewhere in his long, forgotten past, Lugft Huron had always been a master of strategy. His ascendency to the coveted position of Chapter Master had been testament to his skill and ability. Now, so many years after the end of the Badab War, his mental acuity was impaired only by his own unpredictability. He would change the direction of his plans with alarming, sometimes incomprehensible speed.

What had once been a mind that could produce plans to serve the Imperium now merely turned inwards and became truly self-serving. Blackheart did very little for his Red Corsairs other than provide them with a staging area for war. He never praised them or rewarded them but none of them questioned it; least of all the staunchly loyal Astral Claws. He expected them to die willingly at his whim, and they did. If they survived a campaign or a raid, so much the better; he could utilise their muscle again. Nobody ever spoke out against it and Blackheart never changed the ground rules. It was a perfect arrangement.

Objectively it could be argued that he gave his victims every chance to survive. More often than not, he laid out one-sided terms of surrender. When it came to Imperial lapdogs, however, they more often than not figuratively and literally spat them back in his face. The Silver Skulls had done that. Huron Blackheart was merely answering them in kind.

ARRUN PUSHED THROUGH the fourth cluttered carriage in as many minutes, but it was becoming increasingly difficult. The further up the train they went, the more littered and crammed with tools and supplies the train was becoming. They had travelled half of the length of the vehicle before boarding it so had no way of knowing what the rear cars may have contained. Bitter irony suggested that it may well have been the Red Corsairs battle force.

Here, towards the front, the Red Corsairs had clearly thrown anything that they felt they could use. Arrun was vaguely aware that such items fetched a good price on various black markets around the sector, but it was more likely that the traitors were gathering equipment for their own purposes.

Boxes were stacked haphazardly on top of each other, but most of the equipment had quite simply been thrown in, almost as an afterthought. There was no care or order to their storage. He pushed his way through the mountain of boxes, the sounds of battling behind him.

Then Arrun froze. Between him and the next car the armaplas window gave him a clear and unobstructed view. Unobstructed, that is, apart from the bulk in blood-red armour that stood there.

Arrun had never seen Huron Blackheart in the flesh. The one-time Space Marine was intimidating; almost as huge in his regular suit of power armour as First Captain Kerelan when he was clad in his Terminator wargear. A momentary flash of what Blackheart must have been like in his heyday, clad from head to foot in his own Terminator regalia gave Arrun a moment's hesitation. Now, the Tyrant's armour was a twisted amalgamation, built to accommodate the many enhancements and mechanical replacements that had saved the Tyrant's life. The declaration of his allegiance to the forces of Chaos was emblazoned on his chest and the motif repeated in other, smaller ways elsewhere.

All the sounds around him, everything else simply melted away in the moment of first contact with this hated enemy. Arrun's visor focused totally and utterly on Huron Blackheart. Red cross-hairs targeted him and a hunger rose in his stomach. As the Silver Skulls captain turned his head this way and that, he absorbed as much information as he possibly could about his impending foe. He was looking for any sign of weakness or stress in the armour, anything that he could use to his advantage in the fight to come. Because there was going to be a fight. There was such an inevitability about it that it was ludicrous.

He found no obvious weakness other than the usual armour joints and likely stress points. It surprised Arrun that Blackheart was alone. He had almost anticipated the retinue of Terminators that the Lord of the Red Corsairs was rumoured to take everywhere with him.

But he was alone.

And that was how he would die.

The moment drew out for an endless stretch until finally, Huron Blackheart's inhuman, half-mechanical face twisted in an expression of lustful hunger. He mouthed two words through the window. He could not be heard, but Arrun sensed the mocking tone even without hearing it.

Daerys Arrun.

Lugft Huron. Blood Reaver, Lord of the Maelstrom. All these were names that Arrun knew the self-styled Tyrant of Badab had borne in his time. He had never acknowledged the other's choice of 'Blackheart', always having referred to him as Lugft Huron and it was that name which fell from his lips as he faced him now.

With a warped smirk of unbearable arrogance, the Tyrant of Badab raised his power claw in a mock salute. The gesture infuriated Arrun and with a flick of movement, he ignited his own claws.

This was the moment. This was what this entire campaign had been leading up to. There would be a reckoning and it would happen now.

In a moment of perfect, unrehearsed synchronisation, the two warriors raged towards one another, all that impeded their contact being the door of a maglev train car.

WARNING SIRENS STARTED sounding throughout the train, their ceaseless shriek loud and vicious on the ears. Almost immediately, the vehicle, which had already slowed down immeasurably due to the sheer weight it was carrying in a single car, began to slow to a halt.

The maglev had emerged from the side of the mountain like a mechanical white snake wending its way through the red rocks. Thunder still sounded, rolling around the peaks and lightning flared periodically. The sky was grey and ominous, but the rain at least had ceased.

The maglev had barely cleared the tunnel when the reason for its sudden halt became blinding obvious. A kilometre or so further up the track, a Silver Skulls Thunderhawk hovered like a predatory bird, its cannon still smoking from where it had opened fire on the maglev track. All the automated systems built into the train and its tracks had come into play and an emergency halt had been initiated. It was a sudden enough motion that the half-dozen or so Red Corsairs still on the roof were flung off in several directions.

The maglev train was going no further. The Silver Skulls had delivered a potentially killing stroke to the Red Corsairs master plan. But as had been the case constantly since this had begun, Blackheart and his followers proved that they remained one step ahead of the game.

Rising up from a natural hollow in the mountains, a small curved valley that had not featured on Daviks's topographical map, several Corsairs gunships emerged. Six of them had been patiently hidden there, waiting for the moment they were summoned to the defence of their master.

Unable to stand up to such a sudden assault, the Silver Skulls gunship opened fire, its crew knowing it was doing nothing more than biding its time. The rear ramp ground open and several Assault Marines from Daviks's company dropped from it. The loss of the Thunderhawk was inevitable, but the warriors would live to continue the fight.

A second or two later, two of the Red Corsair Thunderhawks retorted by opening their own gunports. The Silver Skulls ship was blown apart in an instant, engulfed in white-hot flame. The Assault Marines were flung far off course by the blast, only their jump packs giving them any sort of control over where they landed. A few, whose proximity to the unfortunate Thunderhawk had been too close, were incinerated along with the vessel but the majority had managed to exit the craft before it was destroyed. It was a small mercy.

The area immediately outside the tunnel was swarming

now with Thunderhawks. The Red Corsairs who had been thrown clear of the train had landed heavily, but all of them were picking themselves up and climbing the rocks so that they could reach their Chapter's ships.

Even as they opened fire on the car that contained the remainder of the squad who had accompanied Arrun, there was a groan of over-stressed metal. A bulge appeared in the side of the maglev, distorting its shape until it ripped apart as though it were nothing more than old parchment. Two massive figures, one dressed in the gun-metal grey of the Silver Skulls, the other the unmistakable form of Huron Blackheart, tore through the train's side and tumbled together down into the valley, locked in a struggle to the death.

SEVENTEEN
SUM QUOD ERIS

AFTER THE CONFINES of the maglev, it felt strangely curious to have enough room to extend his arms fully. That was exactly what Daerys Arrun did the moment he rose once more to his feet. Standing on the side of the mountain with his arms outstretched and a growl in his throat, he cut an imposing figure. Arcs of lightning power crackled from his claws, a strange counterpart to the storm that still flickered on and off in the sullen sky. Despite the silver and hard-edged inhumanity of the skull-helm, the anger was evident in his stance, in the way he held himself.

Once the pair of them had stopped rolling, he had disentangled himself from the other warrior and leaped backwards. Warning runes flashed urgently at him, their low, stubborn insistence informing him via his retinal display that his armour was seriously compromised in several locations. Fluid was leaking from two of the servos which gave him slightly limited movement in one shoulder but it was nothing he could not work around. There was an unpleasant taste of blood in his mouth, but he swallowed it down with a grimace.

Behind him, his fusion pack hummed softly, occasionally changing pitch when he channelled extra power into his claws. He looked down at the Master of the Red Corsairs from his vantage point. Blackheart was even more hideously deformed than he had ever considered. More machine than man in many ways, he seemed to be less an Adeptus Astartes in power armour than a suit of armour with a man grafted permanently into it. It was a simplistic description, yet oddly accurate. He was offensive to Arrun's sight, an abomination that should not be. A creature corrupted by the forces of Chaos.

'Daerys Arrun.' The monstrosity spoke in a harsh, grating voice. 'This meeting has been a long time coming.'

Blackheart unfolded himself to his full height. He was standing a little further down the rugged mountainside than Arrun, giving the Silver Skull the temporary advantage of the terrain. Despite the hatred he felt, Arrun couldn't help but be briefly stunned at the full impact of the Tyrant's appearance.

The red ceramite of his armour was fractured in places, ragged at its edges. Any Imperial devices it had sported in its time had long been torn from its surface and replaced with the eight-pointed star denoting where Blackheart's true loyalties now lay. What little skin remained on the Tyrant's face was a sickly, grey shade. He looked for all the world like nothing so much as a corpse. An augmetic eye, red and malevolent, glared up at him. Its fellow, the remaining organic orb, was so milky white that Blackheart could be blind for all he knew. Yet in its depths was an eternity of mind-numbing madness.

'No more words,' said Arrun, his voice growling from the mouth-grille of his helm and sounding every bit as artificial as Blackheart's did without the aid of armour. 'No more words. There is nothing you have to say that I could possibly care to hear.'

'As you wish, captain.' There was a wet, grating rumble, a vile sounding thing and Arrun realised with creeping disgust that Blackheart was laughing. The noise tore at his self-control, begged him to release his pent-up fury.

He *hated* this traitor. He hated everything that he was, everything that he represented. He hated all that Blackheart had cost him during this incursion and most of all he hated the fact that the Tyrant of Badab had the temerity to have even lived.

The warning that he had received from Inteus, what felt like several lifetimes ago, went unheeded and he allowed his rage and fury to resolve into a steely and undeniable need for vengeance for all the appalling wrongs this animal had committed.

With a battle-cry that echoed around the mountains, Arrun screamed his company's motto with every breath in his lungs and flung himself bodily at the Tyrant, his claws ready to tear and flay the rest of the whoreson's face from his bones.

CORRELAN HAD PROBLEMS of his own. His mad scramble for the charges that had been set around the refinery had been hindered by a sudden onslaught of cultists. It had not taken much effort on his part to detach them from existence, severing their threads to mortality with a sweep of his combat blade. But even though he had made a remarkable pace, by the time he had crossed the refinery, he had been greatly delayed.

The two bikers from Squad Malachite were already there and, having heeded his hastily-blurted out instructions via the vox had, with the additional assistance of the assault squads, isolated the charges. There were no fewer than twelve of them, each one wired to a silo or tank and would create an explosion powerful enough to level the refinery completely. They were connected as a chain, but it would take a few more minutes for Correlan to identify the primary charge. If he could diffuse that device, then the trap would be rendered useless.

It didn't help the ill-tempered Techmarine that he was constantly being bombarded by questions from Daviks on the vox. In the end, he tore his helm off and switched off his vox so that he could better concentrate on the matter at hand. He ran a hand over his close crop of hair and stared at the bomb, desperately trying to fathom the illicit modifications that had been made to its sacred design.

Screams and the rattle of gunfire from the doorway announced a fresh wave of cultists and Correlan's battle-brothers were forced into a defensive position, kneeling at the entrance and laying down a curtain of fire. The slaves were only human and they didn't stand a chance against the controlled bursts of deadly bolter shells that systematically picked them apart. They died in their droves, leaving a grisly pile of broken and dying bodies on the ground before the generarium building.

Cool, clinical detachment took hold of the Techmarine as he concentrated on the blessed machine. He mentally filtered out the sounds of combat and the dying cries of the cultists outside. His mind focused, Correlan swiftly assessed the situation. The charges had not yet been armed. As far as he could tell it was the only thing working in their favour at this time.

'If whoever did this for the Red Corsairs has any skill at all, then simply wrenching them off the walls won't be good enough. They will almost certainly have fail-safe triggers built into them.' He spoke more to himself than to the two warriors currently defending their position in the doorway. Correlan withdrew an omni-tool from the forearm of his battle gear and two of the smaller mechadendrites on his harness snaked their way forward. The Techmarine's precision control over the devices only began to hint at the sheer degree of concentration that he was employing. The metallic tendrils moved with as much purpose as his fingers as he carefully manipulated the arming plate.

'I am going to connect to this one,' said Correlan quietly to the two Space Marines kneeling behind him. 'There is a small possibility that I will inadvertently activate it. I have no idea as to the detonation time. It could be several minutes, or it could be several seconds. You will know at the moment we are all welcomed by our ancestors to take our place alongside the Throne.'

Sensing, rather than seeing their reaction to these words, Correlan turned his head to look at them and for the first time in a very long time, he smirked. 'I am joking,' he said. 'I am familiar with these kind of charges. I have every confidence that they will be easy to disarm.'

'Your attempt at levity is at best misplaced and at worst, inappropriate, Techmarine.' Aviaq's tone was less than amused.

'Maybe. But it helped to focus my thoughts for a moment. And for that, you should be eternally grateful.' Correlan shrugged and turned his attention back to his work.

One of the snaking tendrils made a connection with a small aperture beneath the object's front panel. There was a *click*. Correlan let out the breath that he hadn't even realised he had been holding and fixed his eyes firmly on the runic display at the front of the bomb cluster. Nothing had changed, which was initially a good sign.

'Commencing deactivation now,' he said, providing a running commentary whether his companions wanted one or not. With meticulous care, he turned the inner workings of the device barely a centimetre to the right. Despite himself, he felt a creeping anxiety. Arrun's words came back to him about the miracle he had wrought in the shape of Volker Straub and the anxiety faded immediately to be replaced by confidence.

There was another *click*. It was followed by another release of breath and the smile on the Techmarine's face broadened. His assessment had been right. He knew the device, knew how it worked and to deactivate it would take him only minutes. A sense of relief flooded through him and he reactivated the vox-bead in his ear.

'Captain Daviks, situation is under control.' If Daviks was angry at his lack of contact, he had the grace not to let it show. Instead, he responded in his usual mild tone.

'Excellent. How long until you can safely evacuate?'

Correlan considered the question. 'I would suggest

perhaps fifteen minutes.' His eyes were drawn briefly by a sudden flicker on the front of the device. A red rune had burned into abrupt, angry life. It winked ominously at him and he put a gauntleted finger to it. Every last drop of good humour drained out of him like someone had pulled a plug. He swallowed. 'And counting.'

THERE WERE NO words spoken between the warring Adeptus Astartes as they pounded relentlessly into one another. Daerys Arrun's sheer, unadulterated rage made him far harder to dispatch than Blackheart had estimated. The Master of the Red Corsairs had already been taken unawares by the fighting tactics of his opponent. Despite the anger that clearly drove him, Arrun was well in control of himself and that by itself made him unpredictable.

Blue lightning spat at the traitor from Arrun's claws and was matched by the roar of super-heated flame that belched from the Tyrant's palm. The razor-edged talons of Arrun's twin gauntlets frequently locked with Blackheart's own power claw and the sound of the metal ringing out was clearly audible around the hillside.

Using his left hand, Huron swung a wide arc with his battle axe. It crunched into Arrun's armour-plated shoulder and whilst the bigger warrior was engaged with the necessary motion required to wrench the blade free, Arrun spun around, his claws flashing towards the Tyrant's face. The tips of the four claws of his right fist connected with the flesh of Blackheart's temple and he dragged them downwards, gouging savage track marks down his opponent's face. Had he managed to strike deeper, Blackheart's face would have been torn clean away from his skull.

Blood flowed freely, only to clot seconds later. The deep, rich red of his Adeptus Astartes vitae contrasted sharply with the greyish hue of his corpse-like skin. The sight reminded Arrun of what he was fighting; reminded him that the Tyrant had once been a great warrior who had served the Imperium. It was good to be reminded. The thought of such betrayal drove him onwards and gave him purpose.

With a bellow of laughter, Blackheart drew his head back and spat expansively at Arrun. The Silver Skull twisted as much as he could, given that Blackheart's axe was still buried in his shoulder. The milky fluid hit the Imperial aquila proudly adorning his breast plate and the acid that had been introduced from the Betcher's gland almost instantly began eating into it. It would take time to melt through the plasteel and ceramite composite, but if he didn't get it cleansed soon, it would be time enough to more than compromise his wargear.

The fact that his armour might be damaged was nothing compared to the insult directed at the Imperium and Arrun's anger rose to near-unmanageable levels. A low growl came from the vox-grille of his helm.

'What's the matter, Silver Skull?' Blackheart's voice was taunting and even amused. 'Do my manners offend you?' He had pulled his axe clear now and was swinging it easily in his hand. He pulled his head back again, his voice sounding thick with saliva and another gobbet of acid struck Arrun, this time plastering the side of his helm. As he spun away, lightning claws sparking, the Tyrant opened out the digits of his claw. A huge gout of liquid fire spat from the nozzle in his palm, directed at his opponent.

'It is not your manners,' retorted the captain as he leaped to the side to avoid the rapacious flame. 'It is *you*. It is everything you stand for.'

Raucous laughter followed this pronouncement and Blackheart struck down again with his axe. 'I was expecting more from you, Daerys Arrun. You disappoint me. Although you have provided me with substantial amusement.' He turned the ravening tongue of flame towards his opponent's head, but Arrun had already ducked away. The rock of the mountainside where the captain had stood barely moments before heated up quickly and then exploded under the shattering impact of the Tyrant's battle axe.

'Are you... *running away?*' Blackheart spun about to see Arrun scrambling with comparative ease up the side of the nearest rockface. It was not a clear cut route; he needed to gauge his leaps from rock to rock carefully, but every jump he made took him higher than the raging Tyrant. Roaring in fury as he sensed his prey escaping, Blackheart spat billowing streamers of flame after him. But Arrun, who had grown to adulthood and received his earliest training in the mountains of Varsavia was as sure-footed as any of the cloven-hooved animals that roamed there. This was his terrain. He knew how to work it to his advantage.

'STATUS UPDATE, CORRELAN.'

'Busy. Can't talk. Sorry, Captain Daviks.'

'Damn you to the darkest depths of the warp, Techmarine, I need a situation report and I need one now.'

'Situation report? Very well. A situation report.' Correlan took a deep breath. 'The current situation is that this demolition timer is counting down to the destruction of the Primus-Phi promethium refinery. There are presently two battle-brothers here with me preventing cultists from storming the generarium.' Correlan cast a brief glance at them. 'From the sounds they are producing outside of this facility, I would hazard a guess that they seem to be coping perfectly well. My own *personal* situation is that I would do a lot better at disarming it if I was allowed to work uninterrupted.'

There was a pause.

'Sir.'

'Very well. I will continue with the extraction. You are remarkably insubordinate, Correlan.'

'Yes, Captain Daviks. I am aware of that. I assure you that if I survive this current predicament I will answer for my poorly chosen words later. Should I fail, then I will consider my certain death penance enough.'

There was a responding grunt and the vox-bead in his ear went dead. Smiling grimly, he resumed the task of attempting to disarm the bombs. It should have been a simple thing to isolate the detonation mechanism, but whoever had designed this particular device had clearly strayed far from the teachings of the Adeptus Mechanicus. His lips pursed at the thought of such heresy.

Not for the first time since he had left the training halls of the Adeptus Mechanicus on Mars, Correlan pushed all of his knowledge to one side. He ignored the litanies and the rituals, although he promised himself he would be duly penitent for such blatant disregard later. Instead, he allowed his considerable mind to think around the problem instead of thinking at it.

He had less than ten minutes remaining.

A CLATTERING SHOWER of scree tumbled down towards Huron Blackheart as he scrambled his way up after his prey. Above the lip of the ravine into which they had tumbled, the sounds of a blistering gun battle could be heard. The assault squads who had leaped from the Thunderhawk before its destruction were doing everything in their power to stop the Red Corsairs from loading the goods from the maglev onto their own transports.

'You hear that, Daerys Arrun?' Blackheart screamed the words so that he was clearly heard. 'That is the sound of my victory on this world. It is a sound that will be heard all the way to Varsavia and your pathetic, weakling Chapter will shudder to know that its doom is imminent!'

Words. Histrionic, puerile, pointless words. Such a waste of precious breath and time. Arrun kicked another load of loose rocks down towards the Tyrant and continued his ascent. The flurry of stone rained down on the Traitor Space Marine, drumming off his armour. It was necessary for him to briefly concentrate more on averting his face to avoid the tumbling red projectiles than it was to keep a good pace on his pursuit and it was ensured that Arrun maintained his slight, but essential, lead on the traitor.

He was not running away; far from it. Daerys Arrun had not survived over two centuries as a Silver Skulls warrior, nearly a hundred of those as a captain, without utilising every skill and every last scrap of knowledge to his advantage. He had read and scanned the landscape on which he now fought as a matter of course; understood not only its obvious perils and limitations, but also certain geological indications that could be useful. It had been one such tell-tale sign that had sent him clambering with such agility up the rockface. He moved with adroit ease from ledge to ledge, the incensed roaring behind him indicating that Blackheart was close in pursuit.

No, he was not fleeing. He was leading Blackheart into nature's own trap. A series of warning runes lit up on his helm display, flashing dully and intermittently. A quick system check indicated that damage was now registering within the optic sensors of his helm where Blackheart's acid attack was ravaging the complex systems. Within a very few minutes, he would lose the enhanced helm vision in his right eye.

With a series of blinks, Arrun transferred his core displays to the left eye and allowed his vision to re-adjust to the now monocular readout. He concentrated on another expanse of semi-clear valley up ahead and vaulted onwards. The limited capability of his damaged visor, however, made his target less easy to spot. It was going to come down to timing and his own recall.

Blackheart discharged another gout of flame that seared the back of the captain's armour. The Tyrant's size belied a significant turn of speed. But the fact that he had resumed using the in-built flamer as his means of attacking Arrun was, if the Silver Skull's plan came to fruition, the best thing he could be doing.

He scanned rapidly as he made his way across the narrow ledge that was barely broad enough to take the width of his armoured foot. Then the working sensors in his helm picked it up again. It was there. Right there. The undeniable chemical haze of raw promethium that was bubbling close enough to the surface to be seen. All that was needed now was to drop down, wait for Blackheart to ignite it and then rejoin his brothers at the base of the mountain.

All that was needed.

It sounded so ludicrously simple when he put it in those terms; but Arrun knew better. He was a Silver Skull. He knew well that the odds were not stacked in his favour. He knew that he would more than likely be incinerated along with Blackheart. He had known – or at least had suspected – from the beginning of this situation that the price for ridding the Imperium of this traitor once and for all could well be his life. He had known it; Inteus had confirmed it and now here he was, facing it.

It was, he rationalised, a small fee. Like all those of his kind, Arrun did not fear death. It was an inevitability that he had long ago been taught to accept, even to embrace. It would be a glorious and spectacular end, worthy of any battle-brother of the Silver Skulls Chapter. But there was always a hope, no matter how slim and inconceivable, that he may yet get out alive.

His grand scheme was scuppered scant moments later when he became aware of a baleful shadow passing across him. The huge power claw that dominated Blackheart's right arm swept upwards, then jabbed sharply down. One of its finely-crafted, lethal talons pierced through the flexible joint at the back of Arrun's right leg, breaking through flesh, sinew, muscle and bone. The ceramite at his knee shattered as did his patella and he bit back a cry of pain as the Tyrant closed his massive fist around the Silver Skull's leg. The cruciate ligament snapped under the pressure and the captain's weight dropped to his foreleg.

'Not so fast now, are you?' Blackheart's sneering voice grated more than the pain of his wounds and anger fired his blood to pounding. He heard it flow into his ears with a deafening roar. Then his entire world shifted perspective as Blackheart threw him bodily down the cliff face. The slither of the talon leaving the wound at the back of his leg was sickening but Arrun had no time to linger on it. He tumbled downwards, crashing heavily against the rocks as he went. His armour absorbed much of the impact as he fell, but its resilience had limits. Power armour was a great gift to the Adeptus Astartes, but it was not indestructible.

Loping after him in long, superhuman strides, Blackheart utilised the speed of his descent to ensure that the moment Arrun crashed to a halt, face up to the darkening sky, he descended on him like a raptor snaring a rodent. The Tyrant's booted, armour-shod foot crunched down on what remained of Arrun's knee. This time, he couldn't hold back the yell of agony.

The spectrum of warning runes flashing before his eye were winking more angrily now, their pace steady and telling him what his battered and bruising body already knew. The damage to his armour was extensive and the core systems were failing rapidly. A steady hiss of gases escaped from the cracked fusion pack on his back. Summoning every ounce of his energy and that which remained in his armour, he flung his lightning claws out wide. Coruscating lightning arced from talon to talon, forcing the Tyrant back.

This close, he could see every detail in Blackheart's hideously deformed and reconstructed face. The grey skin was all but dead where it covered the many metal plates and augmetics that held him together. Where he had caught Blackheart in the face close to his jaw, he had torn strips of flesh from it and the cadaver-like expression that was leering down at him was the nightmarish vision of a daemon.

Dazed and injured, Arrun nonetheless gathered his strength and wits about him, dragging himself backward. He felt his tibia shatter under Blackheart's weight and pulled himself up as much as he could until he could pull himself into a sitting position. He stared up at his enemy through his damaged helm visor.

A thin trickle of spittle, still tainted with acid, dribbled from the Tyrant's mouth down his chin. It was evidently something that happened frequently; his teeth and lower jaw having long been replaced with augmetics. They were constructed from a metal that seemed at least strong enough to cope with his murderous salivation.

The captain was broken, but he was not beaten. A burst of chemicals flowed through his body; the pain inhibitor injectors had somehow survived the fall. The sudden release from the agony gave Arrun the impetus to bring his right claw round in a swing. But dazed as he was, his ability to judge the distance had become impaired and the attempted strike barely grazed against the cracked and pitted red ceramite. It was as though he barely patted the other warrior gently against the cheek.

'You disappoint me at the last, Daerys Arrun,' said Blackheart. 'Until now, you have proved yourself if not my equal, then at least a worthy opponent. Your Corpse-God would surely be proud to know how his servant has failed him.'

'I do not need your empty words of meaningless heresy, traitor.' Arrun went for another strike, but his energy was draining from him rapidly. His injuries could no longer keep him upright and he slumped back against the rock, arms outstretched with no strength to move them.

The Tyrant stared down at him dispassionately. There was no emotion in his mad face at all. His visage held no hate, no disgust, no pity... nothing. Not even triumph was evident in his expression. He was devoid of anything that could have marked him as remotely connected to sense. The one remaining eye rolled insanely in the half-metal skull and the power claw clenched hungrily, flame dripping from the nozzle in the palm. Lowering his axe so it rested against the Silver Skull's forearm, Blackheart's face slowly cracked into a cruel smile.

'Do you see clearly now, Daerys Arrun? So it must always end for slaves to the False Emperor. I will deliver you from the true horror of his so-called truth. This is my mercy.'

He raised the claw, ready to deliver the killing blow and then stopped abruptly as the whine of a jump pack caught his attention.

HE WAS CALM.

It wasn't really all that strange. He was used to dealing with tense situations and so over the years had developed a mental partitioning process, discarding those thoughts and distractions that threatened his focus. By the accurate and careful calculations of his own internal cogitators, Correlan estimated that he had three point two minutes before the bomb in front of him detonated. Even if they evacuated the building now, the chances of them surviving the blast were so tiny it was barely worth the calculation. So he didn't calculate it. There was no point.

Instead, the Techmarine did something he had not done since his earliest days in the workshops of Mars. All of the carefully recited litanies and knowledge that he had thrown at the current problem had not helped. So it was time to resort to the most basic of measures.

He guessed.

THEY WERE NOT loading goods from the maglev into the Thunderhawks. They were uncoupling the cars from one another. The reasons for this became obvious when one of the ships swooped in low enough for several Corsairs to scramble aboard. Cargo claws unfolded from the ship's belly and mag-locked into place around the cars. Big enough to take two apiece, three of the transports were airbound again swiftly.

As they rose into the low, swirling grey clouds of the stormy sky, Daviks espied them from his vantage point at the landing site. His brow furrowed as he stared up at them. They were transport vessels, certainly not going to be capable of any sort of warp travel. That meant that they had to be headed for another location, perhaps elsewhere on the planet or...

'*Dread Argent*, this is Captain Daviks.'

'Go ahead, captain.'

'Perform another series of sweeps within the Gildar Rift.' He raised his eyes to the rapidly disappearing Thunderhawks. 'There may just still be something out there.'

THE ASSAULT MARINE roared towards Huron Blackheart with such alarming velocity that when the impact came, it sent the Tyrant flying. Brother Nakos's chainsword roared a throaty promise of bloody dismemberment. The jump pack flared with a surge of power and Nakos hit the ground running before surging upwards again ready to dive upon his enemy.

Freed of the Tyrant's not inconsiderable weight on his leg,

Arrun was able to get himself shakily to his feet. He was gravely wounded and barely able to stand, but barely able meant that he still had strength left in him. 'Mostly dead is still slightly alive,' he had been told once.

Moving was a near impossibility because of the extent of his wounds; although it didn't stop him trying. He limped several steps down the mountainside and, gritting his teeth, urged a fresh surge of power through his claws.

By some providence, they still worked. 'Nakos...' Arrun attempted to vox to his battle-brother, but the transmitter in his helmet had been damaged along with nearly every other system as he had fallen. His own life support indicators kept fuzzing in and out of visibility.

He turned with agonising slowness towards Huron Black-heart as Nakos struck out with his chainsword. With an inhuman roar, Blackheart met the attack with charac-teristic resilience. The tungsten teeth of the weapon bit determinedly into his armour and ceramite chips flew in all directions. Blackheart threw the Assault Marine off as though he was little more than an irritating insect.

The Silver Skull stumbled backwards and in the fleet-ing second it took him to regain his footing on the rocky ground, Huron Blackheart had closed the gap between them. Fire flaring from his palm, he unleashed a gout of hellfire that was hot enough to melt the joints of Nakos's wargear as though they were nothing. A cry, muffled through the helm came from the unfortunate warrior and Blackheart completed his response by spearing Nakos through the chest with his monstrous claw.

'I do not like to be interrupted, worm,' the Tyrant said, his voice a breathy rasp. 'Time to pay the price for your inso-lence.' The warrior died slowly, struggling to free himself until the moment he drew his last breath. Arrun saw and noted Nakos's bravery; but more, he saw the body of one of his battle-brothers impaled on the hand of a traitor.

Every last shred of self-control left him at that point. To see yet another of his Chapter brought to ruin at the hands of Huron Blackheart drove him to levels of self-determination and super-human capability to which only a Space Marine could ever truly hope to aspire.

Above them, one of the Thunderhawk transports rose into the sky, two cars of the maglev clutched beneath it. Its movement only briefly distracted Arrun's focus, but he was rewarded moments later by a concussive blast of pressure as it exploded, a shot from one of the Devastator's rocket launchers ending its escape run. The sullen, angry sky blossomed into light, debris raining down on the ground below. The sound of the Thunderhawk's demise drew Blackheart's attention and he turned his head, a scowl on his face.

Ignoring his limp, ignoring the fact he was effectively blind in one eye, Daerys Arrun let out a savage roar of his own and bodily flung himself at the Red Corsair. Three more of Nakos's squad were rapidly descending into the crater, having picked up Nakos's urgent call across the vox. They saw the two Space Marines engaged in a furious fight, their respective claws locked together as each struggled to gain the upper hand.

The two warriors were almost a match for each other, even with Arrun as terribly injured as he was, but it was this in the end which gave Blackheart the opportunity to deliver a mighty backhand strike with his power claw. The impact ripped Arrun's skull-helm from his face and it bounced to a halt several feet from where they fought.

Stunned from the sheer force of his opponent's blow, it was easy for Blackheart to twist his opponent down to his good knee at the same moment as his power axe arced downwards with uncanny speed towards the captain's injured leg.

The crackling crescent blade sliced through the damaged ceramite, severing Arrun's leg at the knee joint. With his failing strength, Arrun swung one last time with his own claws but to no avail.

'Your Prognosticators did not foresee this, did they?' The taunt was cruel and barbed and had completely the wrong effect on his victim. With a half-smile that took every ounce of effort and will he could muster, Arrun raised his eyes to meet those of his killer.

'You could not be more wrong, Lugft Huron. They foresaw this with great clarity.' His voice was fading with the last of his strength, but he found it within him to speak again. He did not know if what he said was true, but he fought back at the last with the only weapon he had left to him. The words dripped from his lips, each one weaker than the last.

'And they have seen your end.'

The effect of those six words on Blackheart were devastating. For a fleeting second the madness fled and left nothing in its wake but cold, unadulterated evil. The Tyrant leaned closer; so close that Arrun smelled the acid-stink of his breath.

'Chaos knows no end,' he said in a whisper. 'I will take everything your pitiful, dying Chapter throws at me and I will crush it all.' He wrenched his axe viciously from the rock and without speaking another word, raised the weapon above his head, ready for the final blow that would cleave Arrun's final, tattered thread of life.

Blackheart struck downwards, the axe glinting in the refracted blue light still sparking uselessly from Arrun's lightning claws. The captain's eyes were transfixed on the razor edge as it fell towards his chest. He felt the first two blows as they struck: the blade biting deep furrows in his battered armour. Even to the last, his hallowed power armour stubbornly tried to shield him. The third blow shattered the breastplate completely, shards of ceramite and plasteel pattering from the Tyrant's own wargear and driving deep into the captain's crippled body.

Blackheart laughed, a cruel, unforgiving sound. Vashiro's words from so long ago blazed across Arrun's memory.

There is no sound as eloquent as the vashka snake's tail when it sounds before a strike.

Finally, at the last, Daerys Arrun understood.

The Tyrant's axe fell for a fourth time, crushing the fused ribcage, cleaving right through Arrun's torso and burying itself in the armoured backplate. The Silver Skull's body thrashed once or twice in reflexive spasm and then was eternally stilled.

Blackheart twisted the axe viciously, tearing the flesh of his victim still further. He yanked the weapon back out of the corpse and it was only with supreme control that he didn't fall to repeatedly smashing into Arrun's body until nothing remained but pulp. The smell of blood as it oozed slowly from the Silver Skull's body was maddening. The vitae coated his axe blade, dripping from its end.

Dropping to a crouch, Blackheart thrust his hand into the gaping wound his axe had made. Once, many years ago, the task of recovering the progenoids of dead battle-brothers had fallen to him when there had been no Apothecary to carry out the task.

The fates, it seemed, had chosen to favour Daerys Arrun more in death than they had done in life. Blackheart's blow had rent the captain's body apart, but the implant remained carefully cocooned behind a remaining chunk of bone. Without a reductor or further smashing of Arrun's chest, the prize would remain elusive; or his attempts to claim it would result in its ruination.

Hurling curses, Blackheart got back to his feet. He had no more time to spend concerning himself with the conceit; the Space Marines who had witnessed the death of their captain had regained control of their senses and were headed towards him. With a twisted smile, Blackheart reached up with his hand and turned his flamer in their direction.

'WE MUST LEAVE. We need to withdraw our forces from this planet now, my lord.'

The Corpsemaster's whisper came into the Tyrant's ear, even as he coolly watched the two Assault Marines burn. He made no response, concentrating as he was on the matter at hand.

'Lord Huron!' Again, the Corpsemaster's voice, only this time with much more urgent insistence. Blackheart's incinerating flame died out and the Tyrant hissed his response into the vox.

'Why "must" we, Garreon?'

'We are beaten here, Lord Huron. Even as I waste time supplying you with specific details, the Silver Skulls will no doubt begin deploying reinforcements. Without more of our warriors present in this place, we cannot hope to hold against their full force.' It was spoken very plainly and matter-of-factly, but it did not stop the inevitable reaction. Spittle flying from the corners of his mouth, Blackheart screamed his fury at the news. The two Assault Marines, both of whom had long since stopped thrashing in agony and succumbed to unconsciousness, would never realise how close they came to decapitation as the Tyrant swung his axe in a rage.

This was the life of a Red Corsair. Beaten into near annihilation by the hammer and forge of the Imperium, the Chapter's livelihood depended on hit and run tactics. They struck at their targets with deadly accuracy, took what they needed and retreated. No more for Huron Blackheart the satisfaction of making an entire world his own. Old hatred welled up in his gut. But he knew the Corpsemaster's words, however infuriating, were right. They may experience success and even domination within the heart of the Maelstrom. But true victory, true glory would elude him for eternity.

'I will speak with you back on board the *Spectre of Ruin*,' Blackheart finally said when the tantrum had subsided. 'There is a matter we must discuss.' He cast a glance over at Arrun's corpse. 'A... prophecy.'

'As my lord commands.'

'Take what you can from this pathetic rock. We will not leave this place empty handed. Leave the slaves if you have to.' For a warrior whose numbers ebbed and flowed constantly, losing cultists was never a hardship. Wherever mankind roamed amongst the stars, Chaos spread its taint easily enough. Cultists were interchangeable as far as the Red Corsairs were concerned. Fodder. A means to an end.

One of the gunships dropped to the lip of the crater and with comparative ease, Blackheart made his way back up to the top. He hauled himself on board and the ship powered its thrusters and banked steeply before ascending to the skies in a rush. Time was vital now.

He still had one final card to play. Daerys Arrun had been constantly one step ahead of him throughout this entire engagement. With the Silver Skulls captain now very assuredly deceased there would be no way that he could counter the detonation of the bombs that had been planted around the promethium refinery. The last victory in this battle would be his. He would find out too late that fate was no friend to him this day.

'CHARGES ARE DEACTIVATED, Captain Arrun. All explosives neutralised.'

There was no small air of smug satisfaction in Correlan's voice as he switched his vox back on. The response he received was not what he had been expecting at all.

One point two minutes ago, Captain Daerys Arrun's biometric read was fatally interrupted, Techmarine Correlan. There was a heartbeat's silence. *Had you not deactivated your communications, you would be aware of this fact.* There was more than a hint of reproach.

'Volker?' The realisation that the heart of the strike cruiser was actively speaking to him on the vox-net was both disorienting and curiously impressive. The boy had worked out how to manipulate the external communications array far quicker than he had estimated. Pride seeped in to join Correlan's present state of smugness.

It took a good second before his cognitive functions absorbed what he had just been told. Shock widened his eyes, the inappropriate emotions flushed away by the impact of what he had just heard.

'Captain Daviks, this is Correlan... I... the bombs...' In one single sentence, Volker Straub had reduced the Techmarine to a state of inarticulate horror; something that would have astounded Daerys Arrun, had he still lived.

'Good work on the explosives, Correlan.' Daviks's voice was terse; a blend of pent-up rage and grief that Correlan suspected every member of the two companies present on the planet was currently experiencing. He poked uncertainly at the wound, desperate to find some measure of a lie in Volker's words but knowing that he would not.

'Captain Daviks, did you receive the transmission from Volker just then?'

The briefest of brief pauses and Correlan knew the answer would be in the affirmative before Daviks spoke.

'I heard. As such, I am assuming command of this offensive. Entire company deployment under way. Full armoured support.'

'Prognosticator Inteus...'

'Prognosticator Inteus concurs with Captain Daviks's plan.' The psyker's voice was smooth and cold as ice. 'Do what you must, brother.'

'All Silver Skulls, this is Captain Daviks. We are throwing everything we've got at these renegade bastards. Do your duty. Fight with honour and should you die, do so in glory. For Varsavia! For the Emperor!'

The echoing cries in response to Daviks's words resounded for long minutes. Correlan retracted his mechadendrites. He moved towards the corner of the room where he had flung his helm and picked it up. His clear gaze took in the two battle-brothers still holding position in the doorway. They looked back at him and he realised that they were actually looking to him for orders.

He jammed the helm back on and let its systems come to life. The servo arm attached behind him seemed to react instinctively to his mood of quietly controlled anger. With a hiss, it turned and twisted, clamping itself around the thunder hammer that was mag-locked to his backpack.

Correlan could not remember the last time he had really stopped to consider that despite his genius and his work, he was an instrument of the Emperor. He was an instrument of war. The haft of the weapon felt good in his grip and he let his hands curl around it, an easy familiarity falling into his stride.

A glance through the mangled doorway and a quick estimation showed that the majority of the cultists were dead;

a veritable ocean of bodies cluttering the plaza beyond the generarium. Those who had still retained enough sense to hold back had found whatever cover they could and were returning fire.

'Enough is enough, I believe, my brothers,' said the Techmarine gravely, confidently hefting the weight of the weapon. 'I grow weary of this planet and its lack of colour.'

With a nod of agreement from the others at these words, Correlan strode purposefully from the refinery's core. Gunfire immediately crackled around him and solid rounds sparked from his armour and backpack noisily. His two companions followed close behind him, laying down a carpet of supporting fire as he made his way towards the enemy. His hammer swung, easily felling the first of the cultists in a single blow. The hammer crushed the woman's entire body in an explosive blast of red mist that sprayed across her fellows. As one of them tried to scramble clear, the servo arm swooped down in a movement that seemed far too balletic for something so bulky and gripped tightly. The body snapped in half and tumbled to the ground in two gore-sodden and misshapen lumps.

Enough, Correlan had said. And he meant it. He hacked his way without remorse or compassion through the onslaught of cultists, exacting vengeance for the captain who had taken his ideas and given him the free rein to develop something extraordinary. The catharsis of the slaughter dulled the ache of loss.

By the time he reached the rest of his battle-brothers, a line of dead and dying marked his passage. Daviks nodded gravely.

'Well met, my brother.'

'Captain.' Correlan shouldered his thunder hammer and inclined his head respectfully. 'I am sorry I am late.'

Daviks looked beyond Correlan's shoulder at the mass of corpses. 'It is no matter, brother. I see you met with some resistance along the way.'

'Nothing I couldn't handle.'

A deep, humourless chuckle sounded from Daviks's helm.

He put a hand on Correlan's shoulder. 'Arrun would have been proud of you.'

'Aye,' replied Correlan, feeling the sting of his captain's death once again. 'Aye, I know.'

EIGHTEEN
BAPTISM BY FIRE

BRAND'S EYES SNAPPED wide open, the faintest flare of psychic energy sparking from them. Since the relay of the news surrounding Arrun's unfortunate and untimely demise, the Prognosticator had been meditating quietly in his cell. It was the best way he knew to keep the temper contained. Now, though, he came to full alertness as an aetheric realisation came to him; a snatch of lucidity through the miasma of psychic noise. He drew in a shuddering breath as though he were breathing the thin, cold air of his home world.

'They have not left,' he said to the empty room and, reaching for his staff, used it to help him walk from his cell to the bridge. His pace was urgent. By the time he was even half way towards his destination, what the Prognosticator had sensed had become common knowledge to everyone on board the entire ship. Everything that unfolded from that point happened with such alarming pace that even his psyker's abilities couldn't hope to keep the Silver Skulls strike cruiser one step ahead of the game.

As happenstance would have it, there was something faster even than that on their side.

* * *

SARAH CAWKWELL

THE NEW SERVITOR slaved to the cogitators on the bridge of the *Dread Argent* had been female in a former existence. It was a strange thing to hear words he was used to hearing being spoken with a very slight but still discernible feminine cadence. It was a tiny thing in the great scale of all that had taken place, but served as a very strong reminder of the losses of the battle.

'Augur returns are negative. Residual life signs and energy signatures of the recently perished negligible.'

It was said with such calm indifference that it stung to be reminded. It was not the servitor's fault; she, as it had once been, had been programmed to feel nothing of the pain that the rest of the ship's crew knew. He had never once thought he would envy the lobotomised state of a terminal servitor, but for a fleeting moment, he did.

Yanus scratched irritably at his scalp. Captain Daviks had seemed quite sure that there had to be something out there, somewhere in the Rift. But despite their best efforts to find it, several sensor sweeps had revealed nothing at all. Much as Yanus was loathe to acknowledge the creeping thought, there was a possibility that Daviks had overreacted. He would never have dared to suggest such a thing to the Siege Captain and the rebellious thought was quashed before it truly had time to develop. So instead, he did the only thing he knew to do. He obeyed.

'Run another series of scans again anyway,' he said, doubt in his voice. 'Captain Daviks won't accept anything less and neither will I.' He had to physically check himself to speak the other captain's name out loud. News of Arrun's death had already travelled around the ship with alarming haste and those on board who had been in any way close to the Master of the Fleet were feeling his loss keenly.

'Compliance.' The female servitor returned its attentions once again to the banks of cogitators before it. Yanus leaned back in the command throne and stared out through the fore viewport of the vessel. His mind was as cluttered with thoughts as the scene which lay before him.

Outside the ship, the Gildar Rift was just as it had ever

been only now amplified; a vast debris field that was now significantly increased in its volume of broken ships and slowly turning corpses thanks to the recent conflict between the Silver Skulls and the Red Corsairs. Void servitors whose primary function was working on the exterior of the vessel swarmed across the surface of the *Dread Argent* like ants, working on repairing the worst of the damage caused to the strike cruiser during the raid. In addition to this duty, Yanus had charged them with a further task. Whenever the body of a Space Marine or a serf wearing the colours of the Silver Skulls drifted past, they were ordered to recover the dead.

Presently, the number of salvaged corpses in the cargo hold was minimal. Finding them in such difficult conditions was a slim chance, but one of great importance to the Chapter. For that reason alone, Yanus was prepared to try his hardest. They had saved the lives of his crew and his own on many occasions. Showing respect in death was the best he could ever hope to offer in return. The bodies that had been pulled in from the void were rimed with frost and some were so badly burned and scarred that had it not been for the Chapter's colours and markings, they were all but unrecognisable. Kept respectfully shrouded, they all awaited transport to the same destination.

The Silver Skulls funeral world was one of the three small moons that orbited their home world of Varsavia. In accordance with the Chapter's deeply rooted superstitions, they believed categorically that the spirits of the dead and the souls of the ancestors looked down on them from the moon, watching over them and guiding them forwards. It was an extraordinary place, with mausoleums and memorials that had been lovingly hand-crafted and engraved by the brothers of the Custodes Cruor meandering across its surface. The entirety of the moon was maintained with pride by a veritable army of Chapter serfs.

So many memorials and monuments were especially unusual particularly given that the Chapter's choice of burial was cremation. Whenever possible, the ashes of the honoured dead were placed in an urn that was ornately carved and fashioned from the skull of the enemy who had taken their life. If this was not a feasible option, then the Custodes Cruor fashioned a passable substitute from the finest materials. If opinion concerning the contradictory nature of cremating and yet honouring their dead with memorials bothered the Silver Skulls, they never acknowledged it.

It was a place where the last divide between the Adeptus Astartes and the non-ascended loyal and faithful who served alongside them was rubbed away. Here, artificers were buried alongside their masters. All those who swore fealty to the battle-brothers of Varsavia were, in death, ultimately treated as the equals they could never have been in life. It was a devoutly spiritual place, and one which frequently drew young warriors to its calming presence. Every battle-brother of the Chapter sought their own manner of quelling the furious Varsavian fires that raged in their bellies at the time of their ascension. This sense of peace could often be found amongst the walkways and corridors of the dead. This, along with the sacred, hallowed monument to the first Argentius had given the moon its name.

Pax Argentius was also where the battle-brothers who trained as Chaplains went to study the texts and tomes of their calling. There, amidst the spirits of the fallen, the belief was that they could truly feel and understand the lessons of the past. Like their more numerous psychic Prognosticators, the Chapter's Chaplains were deeply superstitious and fanatical in the discharge of their duties.

'Augur returns are negative. Residual life signs and energy...' The servitor's repeated statement broke Yanus's reverie. Sighing inwardly, he moved to activate the vox on his forearm. Before he could speak, Daviks's voice crackled over the network. His words were abrupt and to the point, underscored by the visceral background sounds of the battle going on down on the planet's surface.

'*Dread Argent*. Prepare for incoming. Thunderhawk transports are travelling up from the surface. I can give you no clue as to their bearing or heading.'

'Aye, my lord.'

His back straightening, Yanus began issuing commands. The *Dread Argent* had remained at high alert throughout the ground deployment so it would not take a great deal to return it to battle readiness. There was one major issue, however, that gave Yanus call for concern and he addressed that one straight away.

'What is the current status of the shields?' Of all their key systems, it would be the shields which would take the longest to restore. Rerouting power from other, non-essential areas was never a speedy process and when systems were off-line to start with, even more problems would be encountered.

'If we fire the shield generators now, we should be able to obtain approximately sixty per cent.'

According to our cogitations we believe that it will be possible for us to increase that to eighty-six point five four.

The second voice interjected smoothly, issuing from the very walls. It did not, of course; Volker communicated with the crew through the standard vox-channels. But there was something about the pitch and timbre of his semi-mechanical voice that created the illusion his frequent words came leached through the ship itself. Despite his best efforts, Yanus shuddered. He had not had much time to get used to a ship that essentially thought for itself. Even now, several hours after its inauguration, he didn't know how to speak to it. He shook his mind free of the unpleasant thoughts that cluttered it. He was, although he felt guilty admitting it, not entirely convinced that Arrun's radical experiment of blending the human Volker Straub with the *Dread Argent* was a good thing. But it had happened and there was nothing that he could do about it.

Bizarre though he found it, the Adeptus Astartes seemed to be deeply respectful of… it? Him? Volker Straub or the *Dread Argent*? The creation was neither human nor was it a machine. It was a taxing puzzle that Yanus had no time to discern an answer for.

'Very well, uh…' Yanus hesitated, his uncertainty as to the correct form of addressing the voice coming to the fore.

Volker. There was the faintest suggestion of amusement in the gentle response and Yanus felt more at his ease than he had thought possible.

'Of course. Volker. Do whatever it is that you must.'

Compliance, Eduar Yanus.

And the voice, the presence... whatever it was... vanished. Yanus briefly made an ancient sign of protection across himself. He could not help it. The brothers of the Silver Skulls might marvel at the 'wonder' they had wrought. Volker might indeed be a miracle of engineering and dedicated research. But his presence, his very existence, continued to unsettle Yanus. He dallied with the word 'abomination' and then he knew guilt.

'Five returns on auguries. Signatures concurrent with atmospheric or local support vessels. Breaking planetary exosphere.'

'Where are they going?' Yanus thought the question out loud and turned to his vox-officer. 'Those are Thunderhawk transports. They can't traverse long distance, they can't possibly escape into the warp...' His thought process was external and eventually, aware of expectant eyes upon him waiting for orders, he nodded. 'Something has to be coming for them. Alert any ships still patrolling the system perimeter. Tell them to monitor the stable warp jump points. Prepare for interception of one or possible more Red Corsair vessels.'

'Aye, sir.'

Yanus stepped down from the command dais, making his way through the still damaged bridge to the weapons bank.

'Short-range systems...'

'Have already been brought on-line.' The officer looked up at him. 'Volker, sir. He's already begun the subroutines and processes necessary to ensure that our weapons will be available as soon as we need them.'

'He has?' Yanus hadn't even given the order for this.

Affirmative, Eduar Yanus. We took the liberty of pre-empting our best defence strategy. Presently calculating optimum trajectories and extrapolating probable outcomes of further incursion.

'Oh. Oh, well... excellent. Let me know when you've finished your cogit...'

Chance of Dread Argent *eliminating the five ships approaching with weapons at full charge is approximately ninety-three point four seven per cent. Our apologies for the delay in this calculation.*

A brief, fleeting smile tickled at his lips. Speaking to Volker was like speaking to Brother Correlan, the Techmarine. Yanus wondered how much of that might be deliberate. 'It's no matter, Volker. Your cogitations are more than adequate.' He switched to a ship-wide channel. 'All gunnery crews and outfliers prepare to scramble on my word.' The last came with no small amount of trepidation. They had lost a good many pilots already this day. Further engagement would, without any doubt, take an even higher toll.

'Sir...' The voice came from one of the deck officers standing before the hololithic display. It had taken a severe beating with the weight of two fully armoured psykers falling on it, but a veritable flock of enginseers and tech-priests had succeeded in getting the damaged device working again. The visual output was nowhere near as clear as it had been, but it was serviceable enough and would suffice under the circumstances. The tone of urgency in the officer's voice drew Yanus's attention and he crossed the bridge swiftly.

The recreation of the debris field before him was far more cluttered than he had remembered from before and he felt a moment's sadness that the battle here had contributed to it more. His eyes followed the direction in which the officer's finger pointed.

'What exactly is it that I am supposed to be looking at?' Yanus's tone was testy, but the officer explained as succinctly as possible.

'We have been reading a broad spectrum of energy and radiation throughout the Gildar Rift since our arrival. It is an output that is totally anticipated from so many dead and dying ships. But there is a spot right... here... where those readings are starting to edge slowly upwards.'

'What the...?' Yanus moved closer and stared at the

hololith in suspicious disbelief. 'That's virtually on top of us!'

'Sir.' The officer had raised his head and was now looking out of the viewport. 'Sir, you should look at this.' Yanus did as he was instructed without thinking, a cold chill running down his spine.

'Systems are registering a power spike!'

The whole time. It must have been there the entire time. Sitting there with its engines dead and blanking any signs of life. All through the battle, it had never registered any activity. Yanus cursed loudly.

The ship peeled itself slowly and lazily away from the asteroid to which it had been anchored, righting itself and very evidently moving into position. So many times the sensor arrays had swept over it; nothing more than flotsam and jetsam space wreckage. It had most likely been in the system for weeks. This entire time it had just been sitting there like a predator. Just waiting patiently.

Rumour was that Huron Blackheart commanded Chaos sorcerers of extraordinary strength and ability. They would no doubt have been behind the problems they had experienced with sending astropathic messages and now this.

'Enemy vessel is powering up its forward lance batteries.'

All his hesitation and distrust regarding the human heart of the ship melted away in the face of duty and he barked a command. 'Volker. Bring those shields on-line as fast as you can.' Yanus activated the ship vox again, transmitting the report straight down to the surface. It was of little use given that the Adeptus Astartes were on the planet whilst they were in orbit facing this new threat, but protocols must be obeyed.

'Captain Daviks, enemy sighted. There are five Thunderhawk transports heading straight for a ship that's been right here all the time.'

There was a crackle of static, then Daviks spoke. 'I will no doubt get the full story of this peculiarity from you later, Yanus. I must ask you to trust to your instincts and deal with the situation as you see fit. We have our own...' The sound of bolter fire drowned out the rest of Daviks's statement, but it didn't take much of a leap to deduce the remainder of the sentence and to realise what was happening on the surface. For the second time since all of this had started, Yanus felt the weight of command drag him down.

Powering shield generators. Sixty per cent functional. Working to increase power...

'Enemy ship has opened fire.'

'Evasive manoeuvres.'

'Doing what we can, sir.'

Combined with the minimal amount of movement a vessel the size of a strike cruiser could muster in such a short time was the fact that the enemy had fired off a badly judged shot. Badly judged, maybe; but it was enough to glance across the hull of the largely unshielded *Dread Argent*. As it burned its way across the hull, it abruptly ended the existence of the servitors who had been set to work there. The shot scored a ragged line across the weakened ship, shorting out systems and collapsing bulkheads, but not enough to fully penetrate its armoured skin.

The impact groaned through the decks, knocking people from their feet. But something far worse brought the crew to a momentary standstill. An agonised, terrible scream of pain resounded from every part of the *Dread Argent*. The scream eventually resolved into a babbling voice, a very human voice that was perhaps even more unsettling than the mechanical alternative.

It hurts! Throne of Terra! System damage is creating a feedback loop and my systems are translating it into pain! It is like I actually feel the ship's pain! The void... it's so cold! I feel its touch on my very skin... Omnissiah, hear me! Give me the strength to bear this pain...

Volker's words drifted into gabbled prayers and words that ran into each other in their haste to receive some sort of blessing or some sort of reassurance. His voice became interspersed with a strange, high-pitched squealing that caused several of the crew to clamp their hands across their ears. The bridge's tech-priests responded in kind; bursts of machine code, Yanus supposed. He wondered, wildly, just what they were saying to him.

Yanus listened to the words spoken to him by the strange creature that now had such close control over his ship and he felt the empathy one would feel for a child. Volker had spoken about himself in the singular. He had said 'I'. Not 'we'. That somehow made the situation even more disquieting.

Volker's shock had been replaced by loud static that continued to sound through the vox and Yanus spoke loudly but with as much genuine feeling as he could muster. His tone was stern, but gentle. Strange creature though Volker was, he was effectively under Yanus's command and he had a duty to discharge. He could not speak machine code and he had no idea if he was speaking to Volker or the machine, but he did the only thing he could do. He reassured.

'Volker. Listen to me. You need to reroute more power to the shields or we will all be feeling the cold, the pain.'

There was a pause. It was barely a heartbeat, but when the voice returned, all trace of that moment of humanity was gone. The voice was once again so clinical that Yanus wondered if he had merely imagined the moment.

Yes, of course, Eduar Yanus. We apologise. There are many... there are many things that are unfamiliar to us at this time. Shields coming back on-line. Power being diverted from auxiliary decks and service areas Alpha through Delta. All unprotected personnel must withdraw immediately to their designated safe areas. Void banks one through seven now charging to full capacity. Eighty-three... eighty-four...

Yanus shuddered again. The shriek of pain had been earsplitting, but far worse had been the chink in the inhuman machine that had exposed its very human core.

BREAKING CONTACT WITH the ship, Daviks turned his focus back to the brief scuffle that had broken out. A few Red Corsairs had been left behind and their presence demanded immediate attention. The traitors had been put down swiftly enough, but the new broadcast from orbit had left him with newer, deeper concerns.

'Your orders, Captain Daviks?' The request was subdued. Every one of the Silver Skulls was devastated at the loss of Daerys Arrun. Arrogance may have characterised him and he had occasionally displayed tendencies to hot-headed behaviour. But that was neither more nor less than any of the other Silver Skulls. Arrun's leadership skills and excellence in his role as Master of the Fleet had been second to none. His passing would leave a huge gap in the officer's ranks that would be difficult to fill. It was up to Daviks to pick up command of Fourth Company as well as his own for now.

It occurred to him that perhaps at the heart of it, the challenge Arrun had faced in reconciling his duties as Master of the Fleet with those of the warrior he had always been may have finally proven the push that had sent him careening so violently away from the path of the Prognosticators.

Pushing the uncomfortable thoughts from his mind, he considered the sergeant who had spoken. 'Search every last centimetre of this refinery. Kill anything that does not belong here. Gather any of our fallen brothers so that the Apothecaries may recover their legacies.' He glanced around the immediate vicinity and looked up at the dull skies ahead. Streaks of fire burned across its expanse; the full deployment he had called was making its way to the surface. There was a chance that they would encounter little further resistance, but the cautious and methodical Siege Captain had not been prepared to take any chances. Now doubt plagued him. It was a brief moment though and he nodded assertively, squaring his shoulders.

'Prosecute my orders with all due haste, brother-sergeant. I do not know about you, but I have no desire to linger in this place longer than is necessary.' A breath of air exhaled through the vent of his helm, closely approximating a sigh. 'I will personally attend to Captain Arrun's body.'

* * *

THE TRANSPORT SHIPS screamed into the waiting frigate, dumping their prizes unceremoniously. The promethium tankers that had been recovered were lowered with considerably more care, but for the most part the maglev cars that had been stacked high with spoils from the refinery were just dropped to the deck.

Emerging from one of the transports, Huron Blackheart looked around at his Corsairs as they gathered. Already they were busying themselves with the task of emptying out the spoils taken from the planet. Everywhere, fights were breaking out. A smirk on his face, he left them to it and made his way towards the bridge of the ship, his slightly limping stride eating up the distance swiftly. The two Terminator elite who had accompanied him to the planet's surface were at his shoulder, their wordless presence a given. Not too far behind the trio came the Corpsemaster, eager to tend to his master's injuries as soon as he was told to.

The unnamed escort ship had formerly been part of an Imperial convoy. Due to a warp miscalculation, it had suffered the misfortune of straying into the Red Corsairs territory several weeks previously. It had then spent the best part of that time employed as a fail-safe backup to Huron Blackheart's plans. It had lain silent, posing as a hulk in the Gildar Rift. It had been easy enough to read and predict the Silver Skulls patrol pattern and to insert the vessel into the Rift. Everything had been shut down. Crewed entirely by Space Marines, there had been no need for life support systems and Valthex, Blackheart's trusted Master of the Forge, had designed a device that had kept the ship effectively dispersing its own energy signature, giving it the impression of nothing more than background noise.

It had also been Valthex who had designed the bombs that had entirely failed to detonate. Were it not for the fact that Blackheart thought so very highly of his long-serving Techmarine; were it not that Valthex's efforts and genius had been core to his very survival following the battle at the Palace of Thorns, he would have paid the price for his failure. Like the Corpsemaster, Valthex was largely exempt from

Blackheart's full fury. The Tyrant's hand strayed absently to the ornately worked green vial at his waist.

'Status,' he ordered as he walked onto the bridge. Dried blood caked his largely fleshless face, a remnant of the fight with Daerys Arrun and the subsequent efforts at locating the Silver Skull's gene-seed. Apart from the superficial damage to his face caused by Arrun's claws, the Tyrant showed no other obvious signs of injury. In the emergency red-hued half-lighting currently being employed in the ship, the leader of the Red Corsairs seemed even more drained of colour than before.

'All of our systems are back on-line, Lord Huron. The *Dread Argent* is bringing her prow weapons to bear. She will no doubt attempt to cripple us as we leave.' The Forgemaster himself had taken command of this stealthiest of missions. In the face of his success, Blackheart's anger at the non-detonation of Valthex's bombs subsided.

'Then get us out of here, Valthex.' A deep chuckle sounded from the Tyrant's throat and he turned his head to the Corpsemaster. 'The Forgemaster's little toys do not always work, Garreon, but when they do...' He brought his hands together in a thunderous clap, the gauntlet crashing against the power claw in a snap of sound. 'When they do work, they work superbly. Get us out of here,' he repeated. 'We have left several of our number behind. Those who are resourceful enough will find their way back to us. Those who are not will be culled. Either way is satisfactory. But we leave. Right now.'

'As you command, Lord Huron.'

'ALL UNIDENTIFIED THUNDERHAWKS have now boarded the escort vessel. Sub-routine Epsilon Gamma Six-Two engaged. Recalibrating the *Dread Argent's* guns to track escort ship.' The servitor's monotonous commentary went almost unheard.

'What are they doing?' Yanus moved closer to the viewport and stared out at the frigate. 'They're surely not planning to enter the warp at this proximity, are they?'

With mounting horror, the officer realised that this was

precisely what the Red Corsairs had in mind. Years of service and training took over.

'All hands brace for impact! Get me power to the shields!' He bellowed the commands rapidly. 'Volker, do whatever you can to protect us. The moment that ship enters the warp, we're going to get caught in the wake.'

Compliance.

IT WAS A gamble, a masterstroke: a parting shot and manoeuvre that could potentially cause as much damage to his own ship as to the one that they would leave behind in the Gildar Rift. But it was painfully clear to the crew aboard the *Dread Argent* that Huron Blackheart did not care one bit. It was without question both dangerous and foolhardy to open a gateway to the warp this close to a planet. Furthermore, so close to another ship and with all the debris that littered the Rift, opening a warp gate was going to be a risky move. Huron Blackheart had not survived as long as he had without being prepared to take risks.

This was certainly a bold tactic and evidently designed more as a means to add grave insult to serious injury. The Silver Skulls may have ultimately driven the Red Corsairs from the system, but it had cost them dearly to do so. As space itself began to buckle and bend, it was evident that it may yet cost them even more.

'In the name of the Emperor,' said Yanus, his voice little more than a hoarse whisper. 'The wreckage of the Rift will rip us apart.' He ran a shaking hand across his jaw and swallowed. Then the muscles in his neck tensed, his back straightened and he began to act with the calm efficiency that had made him such an invaluable officer for so many years. 'We need to begin an evacuation.'

'But the ship...'

'The cost of losing the ship will be great,' Yanus acknowledged. 'If we evacuate now, we stand a fighting chance. Disaster cannot be avoided. Not now.'

Your words are incorrect, Eduar Yanus. Give over full control of navigational systems to us. We are approximately two hundred per

*cent more efficient than your human crew and we can provide you
with a far greater chance of survival. We were created for situations like this. We are blessed beyond measure. Our mind is pure
and at one with the heart of the machine. Trust in our skill, Eduar
Yanus. Trust in the gift of the Omnissiah. Trust in the Emperor.*

More softly, the voice added three more words.

Trust in me.

Granted that second view into the heart of Volker Straub,
Yanus could no longer afford to let his discomfort rule his
thoughts. He nodded, although he knew that there was no
feasible way that Volker could see the gesture. 'Yes,' he said.
'Yes. All hands – switch controls to fail-safe.' He did this in
the knowledge that the overrides were directly wired into
Volker's chamber. He was essentially giving over complete
control of the *Dread Argent* to an inhuman child.

'Sir?'

'I didn't ask for a discussion on the matter. Do it. Transfer
full control of the ship to Volker. Now.'

THE WHOLE SHIP was effectively his.

Every system that mattered, everything that was needed for
the safe navigation and control of the entire strike cruiser
was his. In a state of panic, the bridge officers had even
transferred full communications across to him. It presented
him with a freedom and a swathe of knowledge that he had
never, in his wildest dreams, ever imagined could possibly
belong to him.

Part of him baulked at the sheer volume of information
that was flooding into his mind. The human brain, even
one enhanced with the gift of Adeptus Astartes genetics, was
not designed to withstand such a rush of data. He could feel
himself drowning beneath the pressure of it all. It was too
much. He could not cope. He was losing everything that he
was. His mind was fracturing, breaking apart. Eventually, his
mind would literally melt away, floating free from his body
and there would be nothing left but a husk, floating in the
tank.

The knowledge that his death was imminent brought a

strange sense of calm to him. Better death than this terrible feeling of failure.

Failure. I am no failure. We will not fail in this.

The very word was complete anathema to Volker. He had always been the brightest, always been the best and now, here he was. Ready to give up. His considerable pride and unshakeable loyalty bubbled to the surface and new-found purpose burgeoned within his heart.

No.

No. We will not fail.

The whole inner conflict had taken no more than three seconds. With a renewed sense of purpose, Volker turned his attentions to the situation at hand. In his previous existence, he had never piloted a vessel in a live exercise, although he had flown in many ships and had learned the controls. He had absorbed texts and manuals with an eager appetite. Everything that he learned flowed through the enhanced synapses of his brain and within seconds so brief as to be unmeasurable, he became the ship itself. He had no time to fully assimilate the vast reality of that fact, however, and he reluctantly forced the wide-eyed, Volker Straub part of himself to remain dormant, bringing the augmetics and inherent knowledge of the ship to the fore.

So much knowledge. So much power. The memory of the terrible moment of pain when the Red Corsairs had fired upon the *Dread Argent* rose to the front of his thoughts and Volker channelled the anger and hurt of that memory into a whispered promise. The message was broadcast through the void. It slid through the myriad frequencies of vox-transport and it broke through to the bridge of the Red Corsairs ship.

'INCOMING TRANSMISSION, LORD Huron.'

'Then let us receive it.' Huron Blackheart's metal teeth ground together in barely contained delight as the vox-channel opened. He was expecting a full surrender.

Words oozed through the vox, permeating the bridge of the stolen vessel like a whispered threat of extermination.

We are the Dread Argent. *Despite your best efforts, we are unbroken and we will one day be your doom. We will not be eliminated so easily, traitor of the Imperium.*

FOR HUNDREDS OF years, Huron Blackheart had travelled through the warp and even now, even twisted as he was, he retained a healthy respect for it. As the rent in space broadened and his ship nudged closer to it, as the words whispered into the augmetic aural sensors that served him now, he stared into its swirling depths.

'Therein lies the way of the insane,' a former sergeant had said to him in a life he had long mostly forgotten. The Tyrant had walked the brink of that insanity every time he had entered the warp. Many of those who had studied his behavioural patterns over the years had never been able to fathom the exact point at which he had fallen.

They never would. The Tyrant of Badab, Lugft Huron had not fallen from grace. He had not fallen into madness. He had willingly jumped.

He had seen into the heart of Chaos and he had survived. He had fought for his own survival against countless enemies and he had always emerged, even if he had not always been victorious. He had contended with terrible agony for countless years and yet he endured. He was bold and he was fearless.

But those whispered words that leaked through the walls of his ship, coming as they had so close after Arrun's final words, chilled the very marrow in his bones. The voice was almost as coldly detached, as uncaring and emotionless as he was. It was something that he had not known the Silver Skulls were in full possession of. In all the years he had devoted himself to his life of treachery he had never once met his emotional match. It chilled him and fired his imagination at the same time; a unique experience. Right there and then, the Tyrant decided that whatever it was the Silver Skulls had been hiding would be his. But the discovery had come too late. Time had run out. Hell's Iris awaited them.

'Translation to the warp in three... two...'

As the ship was sucked into the malevolent depths of the

empyrean, a huge shock wave radiated out from the point of entry, its trajectory wild and unpredictable. It stirred up the debris field and turned it from a perilous series of obstacles into a relentless onslaught of wanton destruction. All souls aboard the *Dread Argent* were fully braced for impact, but the moment the shock wave struck, they were flung in all directions.

Halfway to the bridge, Prognosticator Brand stumbled, but he did not fall. His mind was filled with the murmured thoughts of the youth who had once been Volker Straub as he struggled to cope with the situation. The thoughts touched his own as a jumble of binary commands laced with human thought. There was a sense of urgency, of determination and even of fear. Pushing outwards with his own mind, despite his exhaustion at his earlier exertions, Brand offered whatever emotional support he could lend. He was rewarded with a bloom of sudden confidence.

Diverting non-essential power to shields. Incoming projectiles.

All the ship lights dimmed to emergency levels as Volker rerouted all superfluous systems and infused the shield generators with enough power to take them to maximum efficiency. The ship juddered and shook as it rode out the initial bow wave of the Red Corsairs' departure, but the worst was still to come.

Once the initial shock had broken over the strike cruiser, a relentless and punishing barrage hurtled towards it. The *Dread Argent* was huge and unwieldy and was unlikely to be able to dodge much of the onslaught. Yet to Yanus's amazement, Volker rose to the challenge in a way he could never have imagined.

Demonstrating the reactions and response time of a machine, the heart of the *Dread Argent* shifted power relays with effortless ease, channelling and decreasing power to the shields and thrusters as required.

Despite the success of Volker's tireless work, the ship was in no way invulnerable or invincible and the vessel took direct hits from a number of broken hulks and asteroids. When it was over, when the ship had taken its last battering, the *Dread Argent's* thrusters stilled, the engines dropped several octaves to a low, throbbing ebb and the lights winked out for a few seconds.

'Is that it?' Yanus could hardly dare to believe that they had somehow survived the bombardment. Had the control of the ship been left in the hands of the crew, they would almost certainly have been torn apart.

There are small fragments, came Volker's *voice. But the main threat has passed. He sounded weary. We will work to restore all the systems to full compliance. Even now we are recanting the appropriate litanies. The machine spirits are restless, but with the aid of the tech-priests and enginseers, they will soon be soothed. We hope to establish basic systems shortly. Running damage reports. We may have to linger in this system a while longer.*

'But we will be alive to carry out the repairs.' Yanus's voice had a hint of incredulous wonder in it. 'Thank you, Volker. You may just have saved us all.'

It is our purpose, Eduar Yanus. Nonetheless... you are welcome.

'He truly is a wonder,' mused the officer to nobody in particular. He was rewarded with the soft, rumbling bass of the Prognosticator.

'Aye, that he is.' Brand had reached the bridge. He had felt every moment of Volker's determination, the fear that had coursed through him as much as the machine code and binary. He had lived through the horror of surviving the death trap of the Gildar Rift with the same intensity as Volker had and, like the ship's heart, he felt the same dogged weariness.

THE THREAT IN orbit now no longer an issue, another wave of drop-pods ripped to the surface of Gildar Secundus. Several of them had experienced rough landings; the planet's meteorology having been upset by the Red Corsair's proximal warp jump. As providence would have it, several were damaged on their way down, but none were destroyed. It was a small mercy, but it was a mercy nonetheless.

Most of the Chapter's warriors were deployed close to the refinery to support the troops already working their way systematically through the dregs of the Red Corsair strike force, but others were landing closer to the other inhabited areas of the planet. All across the industrial world, the drop-pods bearing the stylised skull of the Chapter descended to the surface ready to neutralise any remaining threat.

The final cleansing of the promethium refinery took less than an hour. The majority of the cultists the Red Corsairs had used as a distraction already lay dead, their bodies strewn throughout the compound and its buildings. The Silver Skulls made no effort to remove the corpses. They had retaken the refinery for the Imperium and for the humans of this forsaken world. *Let the humans perform their part* was the unspoken consensus of opinion. A deputation was sent to Talonport, the global Administratum hub, to speak with the Governor there and to dispatch local law enforcement to deal with the clean-up.

This in itself unearthed another situation that was dealt with swiftly and with the clinical detachment that only the Adeptus Astartes could demonstrate. Angered and made somewhat ornery at the loss of the Master of the Fleet, the Silver Skulls were in no mood for the trivial matters that had transpired and had no patience to deal with anything in a diplomatic fashion.

Opportunistic, would-be rebels against the Imperium's regime had taken their chance to strike at the time the refinery had initially fallen into the hands of the Red Corsairs. Their pathetic attempts at rebelling against the Planetary Governor were quashed with barely a dozen shots from bolters. The death of their disorganised leaders had terrified the others. They had turned themselves over to the local militia without hesitation, deciding in some misguided way that this was surely the better option. The Governor's residence was liberated. The would-be rebellion was quelled.

The people had rejoiced at the arrival of the Emperor's Angels, but that joy had not permeated the wave of silver fury that had swept through the hab-zones, cleansing every last scrap of filth that could be routed.

The planet's Governor, a sweaty, unpleasant man with terrible halitosis, had nervously expressed the people's thanks to the Adeptus Astartes, but he may as well have saved his words. The Silver Skulls chose a taciturn response *choosing* to demonstrate a very visible reminder of their silent strength. Gathered together, they were solid, implacable and truly terrifying. Most of the people of this world had only ever heard of the Emperor's Angels. To stand in such proximity to so many of them was unsettling – and their continued silence was more than a little unnerving.

'You have saved Gildar Secundus. The refineries will continue to produce for the Imperium thanks to you, noble warriors. You came to our aid and for that, you have our eternal gratitude.' The Governor's words were clumsy and did not flow easily. Aviaq, who had led the deputation to Talonport, had turned a helmed head on the man. His eyes, hidden behind the helm, gave away nothing.

'We do what we must because we must.' The low rumble of his voice seemed to reverberate in the ceramite sheath of his chest. 'We do not rid this planet of the Red Corsairs purely for the benefit of you and your people, Governor. We rid this planet of a cancer that would otherwise grow and contaminate everything in the system. All those who would oppose the Imperium will learn from this object lesson.' He had turned his head towards the armed enforcers. 'Your own protectorate would do well to learn from their mistakes as well. Laxity leads to heresy. And heresy leads to retribution.'

With those words, the warriors had marched away, moving onwards.

DAERYS ARRUN'S BODY had been desecrated by the Tyrant's repeated attacks. The damage to the Master of Fleet was extensive and unpleasant, but in death, there was a peace in his eyes that had never been there in life.

Daviks had knelt beside the dead warrior and had spoken the Varsavian Catechism of Peace Eternal. By the Emperor's grace, the captain's progenoid gland had not been removed. The shell of Daerys Arrun may have been forever destroyed, but the essence of who he had been *in life* would live on in the next generation. It would be a favoured son indeed who would be chosen to receive Arrun's Quintessence Sacred.

Reaching to close his friend's eyes respectfully, Daviks had shouldered the body with as much grace as the situation allowed him and had climbed with him to the top of the crater that had been his place of death.

'Return the captain to the *Dread Argent*,' he ordered one of the waiting Thunderhawk pilots. 'Afford him as much respect now as you would have done had he lived.'

'Aye, my lord.'

The gunship rose from the planet's surface and lifted into the darkening clouds. The battle for the refinery had lasted less than a day. Dusk had not yet even fallen. Daviks allowed himself to marvel at the fact. It had felt much longer, probably, to them all. Night would come soon, but they would not leave until they were absolutely certain that everything had been restored; that every trace of rebellion and heresy was obliterated.

There were other worlds in the Gildar system that would need to feel the judgement of the Silver Skulls yet; but on Gildar Secundus at least, they had experienced a victory.

No matter how hollow it may have been.

NINETEEN
WHAT PRICE VICTORY?

The Gildar Rift
In geostationary orbit above Gildar Secundus
++ Four days later ++

'ON YOUR FEET, Porteus.'

Lifting his eyes briefly and with reluctance to the door of the cell that held him, Porteus rose to a standing position. Protocol demanded that he not look directly at the Prognosticator who stood there, but truth told, protocol didn't need to be called to mind. The sergeant's sense of displacement and shame at his situation was too great. He hadn't met the direct gaze of any of his battle-brothers in the time he had been back aboard the *Dread Argent*.

Brand moved into the room, still with a noticeable limp in his step. His eyes raked over the bruised and battered Space Marine. Most of his injuries had faded to barely visible now, but there were two new scars on his face that had not marked his visage before. Had Porteus been looking, he would have seen the sympathy that flitted onto Brand's face.

'I have read the preliminary reports from Apothecary

Naryn,' the Prognosticator said in an officious, stern tone. 'In Captain Arrun's... absence... it falls to me to formally speak with you concerning the situation.'

Four days had passed since the events on Gildar Secundus and in that time, Porteus had largely been left to his own devices. Following a cursory examination in the apothecarion, he had been confined to his quarters. There had been no need to restrain him. He had been so dejected and stricken down with his own misery that he had barely moved. He had paced, at first. Then he had lost the will to do even that and eventually had spent the majority of his time indulging in seemingly endless meditations and recital of litanies. His devotion had not gone unnoticed. As Brand studied him now, he noted the younger Silver Skull's stance. He may be defeated in spirit, but Porteus still held himself like a warrior.

'It is true, then.' It was a statement rather than a question and he did not meet Brand's eyes as he made it. Porteus's voice, once so rich and commanding, sounded flat and emotionless. It pained the psyker to hear how far the sergeant had fallen on an emotional level. 'I had heard talk that the captain had fallen in battle. Nobody would confirm it for me, though.'

Brand sighed softly and nodded. There was little point in keeping the truth from Porteus. Without that shred of knowledge, the warrior would simply brood more.

'Aye, brother, much as it brings pain to both of us, I can confirm that it is true. But at the least, take heart that the battle is over. The Red Corsairs are purged and the Gildar system is freed from their influence.' He noted the look of infinite pain that flashed across Porteus's face and continued. 'For what it may be worth, I would lay down good odds that they will not dare venture from their pit too swiftly.'

'And what of Huron Blackheart?' The name fell from Porteus's lips tainted with venom. 'What has become of him?'

'Regretfully, Porteus, the Tyrant of Badab roams free.' Brand put out a hand to rest on Porteus's shoulder. 'I understand that this news must cause you grief and pain. Your hatred runs so deep that even the non-psychic aboard this ship sense it. But brother, you should not trouble yourself further with matters that are – for now, at least – out of your concern.' The Prognosticator folded his arms across his chest and leaned back against the wall. It was partly meant as a comfortable, friendly gesture but also in part to take the weight off his healing bones. The damage he had caused to himself during the fight with Taemar had been quite extensive and although he was rapidly returning to full fitness, there was still a way to go before he would take the field of battle again.

'I mean no transgression, Prognosticator. I merely ask out of respect for my captain and for my battle-brothers.' At last, a fiery spark of the old Porteus shone through and the former sergeant raised his head. He still made a point of not meeting Brand's direct gaze, despite the fact that the Prognosticator's eyes were mostly hidden behind the voluminous hood he wore. He kept his focus very firmly fixed on a point somewhere over Brand's left shoulder when he spoke. The older warrior quietly admired his perspicacity, not to mention his observance of protocol. Even when he had been ordered to give up his rank, Porteus had not objected. He understood fully and had been compliant from the moment he had been returned to the *Dread Argent*. It was such behaviour that would be noted when he reached Pax Argentius.

Temporarily stripping Porteus of his rank had not been done with any cruel intent, but had been a necessity. The rules were there to protect Porteus every bit as much as his brothers. He had not been in the hands of the enemy for long, but by his own admission, he had been tainted. He saw the removal of his progenoid gland as the ultimate shame and violation of his position. From the whispers Brand had heard and the surface thoughts he had skimmed, he was not the only one who felt that way.

He would be returned to Varsavia, taken to the Chaplains on Pax Argentius and would be subjected to a battery of interrogations and physical tests. On the basis that he emerged from these without any major issues presenting themselves, then he would with very little doubt be granted his command back once again. Moreover, the lack of experienced officers in the Chapter meant that he would be *needed*.

This was what Brand had told Porteus in those early hours since his return. It was not the complete truth. Yes, he would undergo the interrogations and the tests. But his future was as unclear as anything Brand had ever known. He could not bring himself to give Porteus the full story, not given the sergeant's mental state. The warrior's depression was a very real thing; a black shadow staining his otherwise pure soul. Brand could almost taste his misery as a bitter tang in his psychic aura.

Physically, Naryn had noted that Porteus was in reasonable shape considering the trauma of close-range damage to his internal organs. Psychologically, however, the loss of his progenoid gland had left him bereft and with a tendency towards moping on his situation. Self-pity at its very worst. Whilst it was to be expected, could not be indulged any longer.

It was the loss of that progenoid gland that had flummoxed Naryn. 'I cannot say,' he admitted when Brand had asked him what would happen to Porteus in the long term without the Quintessence Sacred. 'Perhaps nothing, but from research that I have been able to find...'

Naryn had swallowed hard before continuing. 'He will most likely begin the process of shutting down. Without the Quintessence Sacred, without the gift of our forefathers and our ultimate progenitor, he is just a man. Large and strong, but just a man. He will fall prey to the ravages of time and he will eventually die.'

'We all die, Apothecary.' The thought of growing old was so alien a concept to Space Marines that it had shocked Brand far more than he had admitted.

'Yes, Prognosticator. Of course, it may not happen.'

It had not been optimistically spoken. As such, Brand had made the decision to keep the full extent of the truth from Porteus for now. If the Red Corsairs had left him with a lingering death sentence, better by far to honour his deeds. The truth would come in time.

'Look at me, brother.' Brand's voice was soft but held the edge of command. Porteus raised his head again. The Prognosticator pushed out gently and felt the shape of Porteus's feelings. What he felt could best be described as a tangle of emotions that were coloured a dank shade of dark, moody blood-red. Pushing aside his sense of empathy, Brand allowed his superior rank and wisdom to take control.

'What has happened to you is gravely unfortunate,' the Prognosticator said. 'Understand, Porteus that I have great sympathy for how you are feeling. But you are no child to be indulged. You are a Silver Skulls warrior. You are one of the chosen of Varsavia. One of the Sons in Silver Bound. Have faith in yourself and in the Emperor's light and you will get through this ordeal intact.'

'I will never be "intact" again,' came the unexpectedly bitter retort. Porteus's words were hurled at the Prognosticator and were so edged with feeling that Brand was temporarily taken aback. 'Without the Quintessence Sacred, what am I, Prognosticator? It was my birthright. It was the mark of all that I have strived to be. I am now no more than… than… a genetic abomination. You would be better to kill me. Better that they had killed me on the surface than this shame.'

His words touched too close to one of the choices that had been discussed about Porteus's future. Brand had fought for the warrior's continued existence and to hear the sergeant speak so dismissively about his own life angered him. Porteus had gone too far this time and brand was no longer prepared to cater to his self-pity. The Prognosticator's stance stiffened. 'Silence, Porteus.' Brand pushed the order out not only with his voice, but with his mind as well. Despite his display of defiance, Porteus found himself compelled to sit down on the end of the hard cot bed that was the only furnishing in the cell.

Pushing back his hood, Brand thoughtfully studied the younger warrior. 'You have been tainted by the enemy, so much is true. But this was not your fault. You are capable of functioning well enough without the implant – and in time, there may be another that can be given to you. You know as well as I the value of the progenoids. We cannot spare them. Not given our situation. We do not even know if you would survive the process of a second implantation. Such a thing has never happened in our Chapter's long history. You must allow time.'

'I know.' It was the sullen response of a teenage child and Brand felt a twinge of exasperation. He pushed himself forward from the wall and pointed an accusing finger at Porteus.

'Enough of this. Stop this childishness. Stop this pitiful and tiresome display, brother. Focus instead on the trials ahead. There are *none* aboard this ship who would speak a word against you. This ordeal will be difficult enough and you will be your own worst enemy if you insist on this attitude. If death is what awaits you, then face it as a Silver Skull. Not as a grizzling coward.' The words were cruel perhaps, but served their purpose well enough. Some of the darkness around Porteus began to recede.

'I know.' This time, the words were not so much sullen as grudgingly accepting the situation.

'You have time before we reach Varsavia to cleanse your spirit and your soul, brother. Do not ever think that I have not noted your devotion to your recitations since your return.' These words evidently surprised Porteus, but the darkness around him brightened just a little. Brand continued.

'I suggest that you continue to pay due obeisance to the Emperor and to your teachings. My own duties, which have increased since the captain joined the ancestors, mean that I cannot spare much time to spend with you. The other Prognosticators will attend you in due course, but you will have to spend much of the journey home alone. To that end, I have brought you something that may be of comfort.' The Prognosticator reached into the inner depths of his robe and withdrew a book. Leather-bound with ornately worked silver clasps, it was a thing of beauty. 'I considered long and hard whether to loan you this. But despite your current situation, none of us deny your actions in taking a stand.' He proffered the tome.

'Is this...' The warrior inhaled sharply and his eyes widened. 'Your Orthodoxy?' Porteus's moment of sulkiness was forgotten as his eyes were captivated by its rich, deep blue surface. Unconsciously, he reached out a hand to touch it. He had expected it to be as cool as the midnight colour it bore, but instead it was warm to his hand. Sincere reverence shone in his eyes.

'Aye, brother. My Orthodoxy. The book of the Prognosticator's creed. Specifically, this represents my own modest contribution to the whole. When we return to the home world, its collected works will be added to the Librarium.' Brand lay his hand on it fondly. 'As you know, the Great Librarium houses many of these books. This is just mine, and this volume covers just the past five years. Its pages are almost filled. Imagine, Porteus, the collected wisdom and prophecies of the Prognosticators cannot be forever held only in the minds of my psychic brethren. Through the Orthodoxy, we bind that knowledge. We capture our dreams and vision and although it is the lesser medium, we contained them for eternity within the pages of a book. In this way, we ensure the knowledge and foresight of the ages is passed down to all the Silver Skulls.'

Brand smiled, more to himself than to Porteus. When he spoke again, it was with an unmistakable air of reminiscence. 'The Orthodoxy holds predictions and words of lore that may not even come to fruition for many centuries. Within these pages are many of my own dreams, recollections and unexplained dreams. Those I have been unable to read and decipher, those that have not come to pass... those will be considered by the Prognosticatum and judged for their veracity as prophecy. Should the Prognosticatum decree them suitable, they will be added to the Great Orthodoxy.'

'I spent many long hours in the Great Librarium, Prognosticator. But we were forbidden to enter the central chamber.

Our instructors would read from the pages rather than let
us fetch them.'

'Indeed. Vashiro would never want the grubby hands of
novitiates all over the books.' Brand smiled again, warmer
this time and continued. 'The Orthodoxy consists of far
more than just books. It is a living, breathing thing. Some
Prognosticators believe that it is symbolic of our Chapter's
belief that we can only ever be as great as the sum of our
parts. The fate and destiny of one battle-brother can impact
on the Chapter in a variety of ways. Sometimes small, sometimes far more vast. Arrun's death, for example, will ripple
through our ranks and cause any number of aftershocks.
But we will weather the storm and we will be greater for
it. Actions and consequences, Porteus. The simple cycle of
cause and effect.'

Porteus was studying the decorative engraving on the
book's clasp, a number of stylised skulls. He ran his finger
over their embossed surface. He looked up at the Prognosticator and Brand knew the question before it was even asked.

'You warned him, didn't you? Captain Arrun, I mean.'

'I did not. Prognosticator Inteus, however... did.'

'And yet, he chose to go against your warning.'

'It is in the nature of man to be independent, Porteus. As
Adeptus Astartes, we are able to deny that urge more than
most. Where Prognosticators are concerned, our ability and
skill to divine the future is sometimes difficult to express
in words. It can be hard to turn to your captain and forbid
him from doing something. Understand this, Porteus, for it
is important.'

Brand moved to look through the tiny porthole of
Porteus's cell. 'The brothers of the Prognosticatum are
frequently called upon to lend their advice. For the most
part, our opinion is heeded and our decisions adhered
to. At other times, a son of Varsavia will act on his own
initiative. This too is always for a purpose. Unlike visions
and prophecies, however, we cannot divine this purpose
until afterwards. I will be spending long hours meditating
on Arrun's choices. I will be asking the question "Could I

have changed what happened", even as you do now.'

Turning back to Porteus, Brand smiled bitterly. 'Let me save you a lot of personal anguish, brother. The answer to that question is always "no". Do not linger on what you could have done differently. Instead, focus on what you can do to prevent it happening again. It is the best any of us can hope for. Choice is always ultimately down to the individual. The repercussions will happen one way or the other. But the choice taken determines the outcome.'

A thoughtful silence settled over the cell. Eventually, Brand tapped the leather-bound book. 'Take this for me, brother. Look after it until our arrival. I want you to read it and I want you to consider its contents.'

'Prognosticator... the honour! I am not worthy of this. Even taking my circumstances out of the equation.'

'I am more qualified to make that decision than you, Porteus.' The older Space Marine reached out and gripped the other's shoulder in his hand. 'You have borne much, but you have also more than proved your mettle. Read it. Absorb it. Learn what you can and later, when you once more wear the sergeant's colours as I am confident you will... preach it. Remember, brother. Those who are most worthy are those who consider themselves least so.'

THERE WERE MANY rituals and rites that were necessary to observe in the wake of a commanding officer's death and the loss of Daerys Arrun had been no exception. Once he had been brought back aboard the *Dread Argent*, a self-volunteered funeral escort had taken him to the apothecarion. They had carefully stripped whatever could be salvaged from his power armour – painfully little in this instance – and had then given him into the care of the Apothecaries.

Naryn had diligently stitched closed the gaping wound in the dead warrior's chest where Blackheart's claw had all but torn out his primary heart. There had been small pleasure to be found in the fact that the Apothecary had successfully reclaimed the captain's progenoid gland. It had been placed into cryogenic storage along with as many others that they had been able to reclaim from the fallen.

It was a pitifully tiny number.

The toll on Fourth Company had been a heavy price to pay for the liberation of the Gildar system from the influence of the Red Corsairs and despite the knowledge that duty came before anything else, there were still whispers; secret, forbidden whispers amongst the survivors that the decisions taken had been rash. That the Prognosticators divinations had been read poorly. They were words of course that were never spoken within earshot of the Prognosticators themselves. The Silver Skulls were brave but they were not foolish.

From a company that had been ninety-five warriors strong, they had been reduced to barely seventy. It was a devastating loss to a Chapter whose numbers were already dwindling. When news of their efforts and the outcome reached Varsavia, it would likely not be well received. An empty, hollow victory from which little could be taken as positive.

A certain state of equilibrium resumed aboard the *Dread Argent*. Repairs that could be effected commenced and once the situation on the surface had stabilised, the brothers of Fourth Company returned to their usual routine of daily training and prayers. But with the loss of their captain, there was an air of subdued dissatisfaction and grief in the air that was almost palpable.

The Chapter serfs and bridge crew, the human workers and servitors resumed their duties, keeping themselves as far out of contact with the Adeptus Astartes as they could manage. Given that the Space Marines generally chose to keep themselves to their own decks, keeping out of their way did not prove that difficult.

Only Brand spent any time on the bridge. He had reluctantly inherited the mantle of senior officer and maintained good relationships with the bridge crew. He had personally written a commendation for Yanus. The officer's actions during the incursion had been worthy of any battle-brother of the Silver Skulls Chapter. They were words that had not been given lightly but which had been received with great pride.

For most of the crew and warriors aboard the *Dread Argent*, things began to return to normal. For others, their worlds were shattered and would never be the same again.

We are pleased to see you again, Jeremiah.

'You are?' The Navigator's surprise was gently amusing and Correlan suppressed a smile. Ever since Volker had drawn Jeremiah out of his shell, the scruffy little man had been a regular in the chamber that was now the heart of the *Dread Argent*. Correlan had come in several times to find Jeremiah seated, cross-legged on the floor in front of Volker's tank engaged in what had largely been a one-sided debate. He almost invariably left food cartons wherever he went.

Indeed we are. If our instruments are reading accurately, we will have need of your services very soon. The Dread Argent *will once again sail the tides of the empyrean. It will be most exciting to work with you at that time. Are we not correct, Brother-Techmarine Correlan?*

Correlan inclined his head in acknowledgement of the stated fact. Repairs were progressing well. Without a Master of the Fleet in place, Daviks and Sinopa, as soon as he had returned from dealing with the various situations on the system's rim, had drawn up a temporary roster for patrols within the Gildar Rift. The *Dread Argent* had not been included in that by mutual consent.

'She is more than just a patrol vessel,' had been Daviks's words. 'Indeed, she is more than just a strike cruiser. She is something unique. A testament to Daerys Arrun's memory. As such, I will not allow her to waste away in this forsaken sector.'

Other conversations had taken place, too. There was a school of thought that believed Arrun's work with the *Dread Argent* was tantamount to blasphemy and heresy of epic proportions. Wiring neural networks into servitors was not unheard of, but to take a fully functioning, non-lobotomised mind and connect it to something as valuable as a strike cruiser could be frowned upon and censure would be grave.

Ultimately, although the words were not spoken aloud, the decision was simple. What other Chapters did not know could not give rise for concern. It was a little unsatisfactory, but for now at least, Volker's existence needed to remain as secretive as possible.

The Silver Skulls had no way of knowing that Huron Blackheart had been given a momentary glimpse of what it was that they would now be hiding.

Stowing away the dark thoughts of the Chapter's necessary concealment, Correlan concentrated on his work. Behind him, Jeremiah jabbered away happily to Volker, not interested in the slightest whether or not the Resurgent responded. Every once in a while, Volker would make an encouraging noise or ask a pertinent question. It was more than enough to keep the Navigator happy. Volker's tone was invariably clinical and detached. It was a shared general opinion now amongst all those who knew him that whatever shred of humanity remained of Volker Straub had been so deeply absorbed into the *Dread Argent* that it was not even a spark. Yanus had shared with Correlan that horrible moment he had seen through to Volker's human soul, but it had not happened since. That moment of fleeting humanity was long gone.

Yet these little moments that Volker shared with Jeremiah were touchingly poignant in their own way. It was almost as though the little Navigator offered Volker the last refuge of humanity that he could find nowhere else.

After the sacrifice the youth had made, Correlan didn't feel that he could deny him anything.

THE LIGHT IN this room was lower than the cell in which they had kept him and it took a moment or two for his eyes to adjust to the gloom. As he moved forward, the shackles around his legs and wrists clanked ridiculously loudly. The chain that threaded through the manacles and attached them to another loop on the collar he wore hindered his movement drastically.

'Why are you showing me this?' He asked the question of

the figure behind him. 'I have already told you that I will not serve you or your foul master.'

'I am showing you this because you need to understand, brother.' The softly spoken words were earnest and drew nothing but a scowl from the chained warrior.

'Never call me that. I am not like you. I will *never* be like you. I am Apothecary Ryarus of the Silver Skulls Fourth Company. I am no traitor.'

'Perhaps you are all those things,' said the Corpsemaster, sliding from the shadows behind Ryarus and moving into the dim half-light of his most secret laboratory. 'But above all else, you are an Apothecary. Look around this place. Tell me what you see.'

Despite himself, Ryarus moved forward a few shuffling steps and leaned in to the closest vessel. Throughout the chamber, tanks of fluid bubbled and hummed softly with the power that was diverted to them. Low, violet lights uplit the room casting bizarre shadows and generally giving it an otherworldly, horrific caste.

The vessel into which Ryarus now peered was small, barely wider around than his own thigh and within the milky contents floated something disturbingly familiar.

'Do you know what that is, Ryarus?' The Corpsemaster was breathless, as though the presence of all these objects excited him. Revulsion turned Ryarus's stomach.

'Yes,' he acknowledged reluctantly. 'It is a biscopea. What my people call the Warrior's Vigour.' He looked around. In various tanks, other implants were being stored. Harvested or grown, he could not tell.

'This particular organ was harvested from a Blood Angels warrior who fell many decades ago. A Devastator if memory serves. That one there is from a White Consul. This here...' Garreon pointed to another tank. It was clear that he was deeply enjoying this personal tour of his grisly hoard. 'This secondary heart was taken less than a year ago from the body of one of your own battle-brothers. A Silver Skulls Assault Marine.' Delighted at the look of outrage on Ryarus's face, the Corpsemaster dug the knife deeper.

'I also have a store of progenoids from every Chapter you could name. And soon, we will no longer be dependent on receiving those who have seen the corpse-Emperor's lies for what they are.'

'What do you mean?'

'Our numbers swell from time to time when the disillusioned turn to the light of my master's truth. But we need the ability to create our own warriors.'

Ryarus was disgusted. 'They would be mongrels. Made from disparate body parts that you harvest on the battlefield? There would be no telling what abomination you would forge. You would need the talents of the greatest Apothe...' His voice tailed off and he bit back the rest of his sentence. But the Corpsemaster simply nodded.

'You see at last, brother, why it is that we have kept you alive. Your skills and your knowledge are worth far more to us than any of the goods we stole from the planets in the Gildar system. My previous apprentice...' The ugly face darkened. 'Is no longer with me. He chose another path.'

'I will not help you in this heresy. I would die first.'

The Corpsemaster shrugged, indicating his indifference to Ryarus's needs or desires. 'Help me willingly or not. If you choose not to, you will simply be used as a vessel to mature progenoids. I will keep you here for as long as it takes to build up our stock. Who knows? In several generations' time, the bloodline and pedigree of the Silver Skulls could course through every servant of Lord Huron.'

The Corpsemaster's taunts cut Ryarus's soul into shreds and he felt physically nauseous at the implications of what was being suggested.

'I would die first,' he repeated, raising his head high.

'Ah, cousin,' said the Corpsemaster, his cold eyes taking in the shackled Apothecary. 'You and I both know full well the truth of being an Adeptus Astartes. Being functionally immortal outside of a battlefield...' He moved in and Ryarus's head jerked back involuntarily at his rancid breath.

'It merely means that you will have a very long time

to consider your options.' He waved a hand dismissively. 'Return him to his cell. I have work to do.'

The Gildar Rift
In geostationary orbit above Gildar Secundus
++ Six weeks later ++

THE RADIANT LIGHT of the Gildar star bled through the stained windows of the *Dread Argent's* chapel. It fell on the floor in a myriad glorious colours, catching in the motes of swirling incense smoke that had burned continuously since the battle of the Gildar Rift. It was held briefly in the silvered trophies, the macabre skulls of the Chapter's enemies gleaming in shades of green, red and blue.

Barely an hour before, the chapel had been filled with the remainder of Fourth Company and others, too. Many from Daviks and Sinopa's companies had travelled across to pay their respects. So many Silver Skulls gathered together in the *Dread Argent's* chapel had been an inspirational sight in itself, raising the spirits of Fourth Company.

Brand and Inteus had shared the duties of reciting the battle honours of the fallen, giving special recognition for the heroic efforts of Porteus's team. Although the former sergeant was not present to receive the praise due to him, Brand ensured that both he, and Curis, the only other survivor of that mission, had their names entered in the Book of Honour, standing resplendent on its plinth at the front of the chapel. Had it not been for Porteus and his squad's tenacity in securing the communications tower, things may well have been far worse.

Acknowledging the efforts of a shamed battle-brother caused a wave of scandalised murmurs to ripple through the chapel, but at a look from Brand, the noise had stilled. The service for the fallen had ended on a positive note as the announcement that the *Dread Argent* would return to the home world in order to bring back the bodies of the dead raised levels of morale. Fourth Company and their honoured guests had filed out. Daviks and Sinopa had lingered a while, soaking in the ambience of this most sacred of places but in due course, they too had returned to their duties. Inteus and Brand had not spoken to one another. Not in words, anyway. The psychic interchange between the two, however, had been enlightening and Brand had much to consider.

Then they had all gone, leaving Brand alone once more in the vast chamber.

Kneeling before the altar, his head bowed low, the Prognosticator murmured his own personal prayers and litanies of remembrance for all those who had fallen over the course of the battle. So many heavy losses had hit Fourth Company hard and for days since the last world had been cleansed, the remaining warriors of Captain Daerys Arrun's command had spent countless hours in prayers for the departed. This service marked the end of that observance. Now, perhaps, they could regroup and rebuild themselves to the supreme fighting force that Arrun had commanded.

In the end, it had taken a number of weeks to fully cleanse the Gildar system of the filth that had infiltrated it. The *Manifest Destiny* had sent a series of astropathic messages back to Varsavia giving updates on the situation but they had yet to hear back from their home world. The decision was taken to send the *Dread Argent* back, as Brand had known it must be. Despite its triumph and uniqueness, it was a ship in crisis.

The astropathic choir remained in tatters. The number of psyker casualties, their brains broken by the strain of communication, had been huge. There had been no satisfactory explanation as to how Huron Blackheart had instigated such a powerful psychic block and there was little point in pondering the matter now beyond the whispered rumours of his vanguard of Chaos sorcerers. There had often been talk that he commanded his own warp entity as well. There was perhaps truth in that.

The choir was now, at best, broken and at worst useless. Although he was Adeptus Astartes, although he considered himself genetically superior in every way, Brand still felt a keening loss at the deaths. The psychic song of the astro-paths was one of those background emanations that until it was shattered had never even really been noticed. Every one of them had perished in service to the Golden Throne and every one of them had given their all. The waste of life sat heavily.

The Head Astropath himself had been a ruined man; his grief absolute. He had gone to see Apothecary Naryn barely hours before the service for the dead and had begged pitifully for the Emperor's Peace. Every shred of his former arrogance had melted away and all that remained was a terrified shell of a man. He carried the weight of his choir's losses on his own shoulders and he had been unable to cope with the pressure.

Much as it had pained him to see one of their own so deeply scarred and damaged, much as he pitied the human's terrible pain, Naryn had refused to give him what he had asked for.

Scant hours later, his body had been found hanging from a girder. The magnitude of his actions had rippled through the ship causing unrest and disquiet in both human and Adeptus Astartes camps. All of them knew the real truth of the matter. All of them knew why the Head Astropath had taken this terminal step. Far better death than a slow, horrific and potentially lethal descent into the madness of the warp.

Thus, even as he remembered his deceased battle-brothers, Brand murmured prayers for the human casualties, too.

On their return to Varsavia, there would be further rites and rituals held in accordance with the full Orthodoxy to honour the dead. Then there would be the ritualistic crema-tions, but for now, the best the Prognosticator could do was to remember them.

We are sorry to disturb you at this time, Prognosticator Brand.

The voice was Volker's. It had become so much a part of daily life aboard the *Dread Argent* that Brand no longer mar-velled at it. The eyes of the ship were everywhere. There was nowhere on board where privacy could be assured. Volker was always there, listening and monitoring.

'Speak, Volker.' Slowly, Brand got to his feet, making the sign of the aquila before the statue.

There are matters on the bridge that demand your attention. Deck Officer Eduar Yanus has asked us to let you know that they need your abilities prior to leaving the system.

'Inform Yanus that I will be there imminently.'

Yes, Prognosticator Brand.

'Volker?'

Yes, Prognosticator Brand?

'I need something from you. Just for a few minutes. Would you... turn your sensors away from the chapel? I need a moment to gather my wits about me and with the very greatest of respect, I wish to be alone.'

Protocol Epsilon-Gamma four nine two...

'Protocol override. Listen to me. Really *listen* to me. I beseech the human part of you that remains. Volker, leave me in peace for a while. Please.'

Perhaps it was the simple plea at the end but whatever the reason, there was a fleeting hesitation, and then there was nothing. Despite no words of confirmation, Brand knew that Volker was gone.

For several more minutes, Brand allowed himself to let go of the tight hold on the grief he felt for his fallen brothers. Sadness and anger mixed with feelings of deep regret and shame that his abilities to read the omens had not prevented such heavy losses. The years of being taught to keep his emotions in check aided him in levelling out his rage and finally, with a final litany of sworn vengeance, he nodded firmly. He turned to face down the length of the chapel.

'They are with the ancestors now and they will never be forgotten,' he said. His voice was low and yet the acoustics of the vast chamber carried his voice far. It echoed from the walls and buried itself in the niches bearing the skulls of the Chapter's many enemies. 'And on the witness of the Emperor and here, on the skulls of the fallen, we continue the battle in their name. For Varsavia. For the Emperor.'

Brand stood in contemplation for a moment longer, then in a single fluid motion, pulled his hood back up and over his eyes. He strode with purpose from the chapel, the richly embroidered robes of ritual sweeping the floor. The time for mourning was at an end. It was time to move onwards and continue what it was they had been created for.

As he strode down the length of the chapel, the Prognosticator's robes flared behind him, creating a gust of shifting air. Dust was stirred and in the wake of his passage, glittered briefly in the candlelight. A row of candles had been lit in memory of the dead and had burned steadily throughout the two-week mourning period. Now though, as Brand passed by, the flames flared once, guttered and then died.

ABOUT THE AUTHOR

Sarah Cawkwell is a north-east England based freelance writer. Old enough to know better, she's still young enough not to care. Married, with a son (who is the grown up in the house) and two intellectually challenged cats, she's been a determined and prolific writer for many years.

When not slaving away over a hot keyboard, Sarah's hobbies include reading everything and anything, running around in fields with swords screaming incomprehensibly and having her soul slowly sucked dry by online games.

Also by Sarah Cawkwell

An extract from *Bitter End*

a short story featured in

HAMMER & BOLTER
Issue 12

THE SORCERER LOOKED. And he saw.

'I confess, my lord, that I did not believe the rumours to be true,' he said. He had considered the tale of the familiar to be nothing more than a figment of the mad Tyrant's overwrought imagination. Yet his witchsight gave him a unique view. 'I have never seen its like before. Is this what they call the hamadrya?'

'Indeed it is. And you would do well not to concern yourself further with its origins or its purpose. Consider instead the question my agent put to you.' Always quick to the point, Huron Blackheart did not care to linger on matters past.

'Yes, Lord Huron.' Dengesha bowed from the waist. 'I consider it a great honour that you seek my assistance in this matter. I understand that your... blessing loses power, that it becomes weaker the further from the heart of the Maelstrom you travel. In conjunction with your own cabal...' There was unmistakable superiority in Dengesha's tone as he said the word. 'I have determined what you need to overcome this limitation.'

'The hamadrya is a thing of the warp,' Huron said. He drummed his fingers idly against his armour-plated thigh. The noise reverberated through the cavernous chamber, the acoustics oddly distorted. 'It draws its strength from the powers therein. And the further from its source I travel...' He broke off and raised his head to study Dengesha. 'My cabal have told me what I need. A potent soul, shackled by arcane powers. The hamadrya can feed from its torment for all eternity. But my sorcerers, strong as they are... cannot do this one thing.'

Huron's red, artificial eye whirred softly as it focused. 'Give me my solution, Dengesha and we will share the spoils of war.'

'You need a potent soul.'

'I have found such a thing. Sister Brigitta of the Order of the Iron Rose.'

'I have heard of this Order and of this woman. The self-proclaimed saviour of her people. She who bears the sins of a generation on her shoulders.'

'Aye. One of the faithful. A powerful symbol.'

'You need a suitable vessel. Such a thing will not be easy to locate, my lord. It could take many long months of searching...'

'You underestimate my resources, Dengesha.' Huron's twisted face distorted in a smile again and he twisted a loop on his belt bringing an object slowly into view.

The bottle was exquisite. Deep, emerald green in colour, it was a fusion of bottle and vial with a wide lip tapering to a long, slim neck that fed into a small oval bowl. It was encased within beautiful fretwork, wrought from copper or brass or some other burnished metal that snaked around its delicate surface.

'My cabal attached this vessel to my belt,' said Huron. 'They told me that only another sorcerer could remove it, that if I were to touch it myself, the power would be tainted.' He shifted his hip slightly so that it was facing Dengesha who snapped open the belt loop, taking the bottle in his hands. He could feel its imbued power, a thrum of psychic energy that made his hands vibrate gently as he held it. Huron studied him.

'On the understanding that you will give me what I ask for, I make a gift of this vessel to you so that you may work whatever fell deeds necessary. Do you accept?'

'Gladly, my lord. Such an arcane item… such a relic must have cost you dearly. Where did you locate it?'

'My sources are many and varied. Do not bother yourself with detail. Is it adequate for its purpose?'

'More than adequate.' Dengesha studied the bottle in admiration for a while, then with a series of hand movements, caused it to disappear. It was little more than cheap theatrics and it did nothing to change the expression on Huron Blackheart's artificial face. 'This Sister Brigitta of yours will be heavily guarded, of course. I will need absolutely no distractions whilst I perform the binding.'

'Leave that side of the bargain to me, master sorcerer. My Red Corsairs will distract whatever pitiful forces guard her and you will take your coterie and perform your rituals. You will present me with what I want and, in return, I give the Heterodox the world in her charge for your chapels and its people for…' he gave a creaking shrug, 'whatever you see fit.' His augmetic eye darkened briefly as though he blinked; a slow, thoughtful thing that was somehow unsettling. 'Do we have an agreement?'

'A world and its subjects? My lord, that is… very generous of you.'

Huron shrugged. 'My Corsairs will still take what spoils we desire, but it is not beyond me to show gratitude and generosity. Now tell me, Dengesha of the Heterodox, do we have an agreement?'

'We do.'

There were many who boldly sealed their agreements in blood. Dengesha of the Heterodox was one such individual.

Sometimes, Huron Blackheart even kept his word.